Agave Blues

a novel

RUTHIE MARLENÉE

Relax. Read. Repeat.

AGAVE BLUES
By Ruthie Marlenée
Published by TouchPoint Press
Brookland, Arkansas
www.touchpointpress.com

Softcover ISBN: 978-1-956851-36-6

Cover Design: Michelle Thorne
Cover Image: Mexican landscape with agave and agave plantation,
watercolor illustration by Ollga P (Adobe Stock); Agave plant scene separator
(iStock)

Visit the author's website at www.ruthiemarlenee.com

First Edition

Printed In The United States of America

Para Mi Familia. Que Dios los bendiga a todos.

Praise for *Agave Blues*

"Marlenée wraps a touching mother-daughter reconciliation in a freewheeling road trip narrative."

—*Publishers Weekly*

"Agave Blues... is as illuminating as it is memorable, and its core themes — self-discovery and following your dreams — are timely for curious souls longing for newfound hope and purpose during existential times."

—Greg Archer, *The Desert Sun*

"The book is a gripping family saga, poetry, and lesson in transformation."

– Lillian Ann Slugocki, *Angels Flight . Literary West*

"Marlenée probes the undeniable bonds of family, the powerful rootedness in the land and the transformative essence of love...Set largely in Mexico where the magic of agave and the generational roots of the land bring its heroine home and into her true self."

—Suzanne M. Lang, *NPR's A Novel Idea*

"An ode to magic realism and the storytelling that permeates Latin American culture, Agave Blues tackles complicated themes wrapped up family, faith, and healing."

—A.E. Santana, *Kelp Journal*

"In the footsteps and spirit of Latin American magic realism masters, Ruthie Marlenée's *Agave Blues* transports readers on a journey of self-discovery. It's an exceptionally well-written tale of love, loss, family and following dreams. What a phenomenal book!"

—Rob Samborn, author of *The Prisoner of Paradise*

"Ruthie Marlenée's *Agave Blues* is distilled in secrets, ghosts and magic, a beautiful testament to the power of family, place and Tequila."

—Mary Camarillo, Author of *The Lockhart Women*

"A tale of Tequila and misplaced fathers, *Agave Blues* offers potent sips of magic and soars with memories of a half-forgotten childhood in Mexico. A charming read."

—Stephanie Barbé Hammer, Author of *The Puppet Turners of Narrow Interior*, and *Pretend Plumber*

"Fighting tooth and nail at work, in her love life, and in US culture, Maya is having a rough time. Despite her success as an attorney, she feels like an outsider, ashamed of her Mexican heritage. Called back to Mexico due to her father's death, Maya rekindles her joy and revels in the deep well of mystery and magic in her culture, past, and history. She grapples with what has haunted and hindered her and heals parts of herself she didn't know needed healing. By the end of this rich, evocative novel, you will come full-circle with Maya as she finds 'home' in all ways possible. A wonderful read."

—Jessica Barksdale Inclán, author of 15 novels including *The Play's the Thing, The Burning Hour, Her Daughter's Eyes, The Matter of Grace*, and *When You Believe*

"Marlenée's rhythmic writing creates ancestral notes between the past and the present ultimately rewriting the future."

—Vanessa Chica Ferriera, Editor of *What They Leave Behind: A Latinx Anthology*

Every human is an artist. The dream of your life is to make beautiful art.

—Don Miguel Ruiz

Feet, what do I need you for when I have wings to fly?

—Frida Kahlo

A garden is evidence of faith. It links us with the misty figures of the past who also planted and were nourished by the fruits of their planting.

—Gladys Taber

Chapter One

La Sangre Atrae: The Blood Calls You Back

BESIDES BURNING IN HELL OR SPENDING time in the Los Angeles County jail, a Mexican morgue was the last place I ever wanted to visit. And I'd already been to the jail to post bail three nights ago, so burning in hell loomed next on the horizon.

On an unseasonably warm October 2007 afternoon, within the bowels of a mortuary in the middle of the pueblo of Sagrada Familia, Mexico, I trailed behind a young mortician sporting a *Chivas* ball cap.

I wasn't supposed to be there. Hadn't we gone north to the City of Angels in search of a better life? A life full of promises, hopes and—some of us dared to dream—el príncipe encantador. *Prince Charming—yeah, right.* I couldn't shake the image of my ex-fiancé Zane.

TWO NIGHTS AGO, back in Los Angeles, he'd stood in my ripped little black dress on the threshold of the front door, eyes wide, pupils dilated. I tossed him a suitcase filled with his stuff.

"I promise," Zane had said, his promises flimsier than a negligee. "It's not what it looks like. It's because I miss you, Maya." He reached to pick up his baggage, hugged it to his chest. "I miss us."

Who's more pathetic? I couldn't bear to look at him anymore and slammed the door, screaming until no sound came out, until my larynx was good and bruised, until I tasted blood, and then I slumped to the floor. *Damn you. You've ruined my life.*

A moment later, I heard a quiet knock on the door.

"Maya?" Zane pleaded.

I opened up as I had too many times before, but this time I threw out my engagement ring, once and for all. "And don't ever call me again. You'll need to find a new attorney for the next time it's not your fault."

Behind the door, my stomach growled like some sort of she-wolf within. I tried to ignore it, but the rumbling grew more intense as bile rose to the back of my throat, burning along the way. I bolted to the bathroom and lifted the toilet seat just in time to throw up.

Staring into the bowl, I wondered how my mind had exiled so many symptoms to the underworld of my body. I got up, rinsed and then wiped my face with a clean hand towel and refolded it before slumping back down to rest my cheek on the cool tiles. Through the floorboards, I could hear the plumbing gurgling a duet with my own tortured boilermaker of a stomach. The pipes clanged louder, and the sound of church bells gonged in the bell of my chest. Another jolt shot through me, scrambling the last of any sanity and then time stopped, crashing in on itself, too heavy for me to handle.

I opened my eyes and through an early morning blue fog, I saw the bell tower in the old rustic village of Sagrada Familia, the place from where my family came.

My side ached, but it wasn't my body. I held up a liver spotted, wrinkly hand. I was an old man and I'd fallen onto a weakened hip. A rooster crowed and I lifted my head to curse. ¡Que la chingada! A gust of wind sent my hat floating along down the street.

On my back, I beheld the starry night. I rolled over and took a deep breath of the red soil. The iron smell of earth seemed to comfort me, like some sort of metallic medicine. The wind whistled and howled as I tumbled like Alice in Wonderland down a well. I reached the bottom where the old man sat slumped over singing, *soy hijo de Pancho Villa.*

I'm not his son. The church bell gonged again and this time I bolted up in the dark, completely disoriented.

I'd crashed into sleep so deep I hadn't heard the house phone ringing in the distance. I'd turned off my cell. By the next ring, I ripped off my sleep mask, blood rushing to my head. The telephone rang again. *It's probably Zane. Maybe, I'll give him one more chance?* I bumped into the bathroom sink before stepping out to stumble down the hall toward the kitchen. By now, a message recorded on the answering machine. "Mom, are you there?" She sobbed. "Mom, pick up!"

Her desperation detonated every cell in my body. With one shaky hand, I clutched at my blouse over my heart and with the other, I grabbed the receiver, holding it tightly to my ear. "Lily? Are you okay?" I asked my eighteen-year-old daughter who'd been sequestered away—a forced semester abroad at the University of Guadalajara. Every time she called, my heart stopped.

"No. It's Abuelo. They found him," she said quickly, sucking in a breath. "He's dead."

When you give this sort of news, aren't you supposed to say something like you'd better sit down for this? The news knocked the wind out of my sails. I imagined myself collapsing inside, my body numb and empty, hanging limply in stagnant air. My father had been missing this time for more than a year and to hear he was dead, and that Lily had been the one to break the news, made me shudder.

"Your cousin Angela called me. She couldn't get a hold of you," Lily said.

I slumped onto a bar stool at the kitchen counter and rested my elbow on the tabletop. "Papá?" Cradling my head, I closed my eyes, squeezing my temples to hold in the many questions swirling inside my brain. But the question of how he'd died wasn't as pressing as the question of why he'd been the way he was—how his life had come to this. His name hadn't been uttered for so long nor had I heard anything from or about him—as if he were already dead. In a way he'd been dead to me a long time.

"Mom, I don't know what to do. You need to come down to take care this."

My tiny boat of a body started taking on water. Sinking, I opened my eyes and gasped. The room had filled with a blue fog—I was definitely drowning in a sea of pain and confusion. But through it all, I stared at the horizon of the kitchen counter—curiously, at a Tequila bottle that had been left on the counter, out of place. And then, with a deafening pop, the cork blew off. Screaming, I clapped my hands to my mouth as a vapor escaped the bottle. The azure light continued to flood the room, blinding me, choking me.

It was back—twice this week, already.

Papá is dead. I tried to catch my breath and felt a prick in my hand. I looked down to find myself absentmindedly twirling a little gold angel pin piercing my index finger, a droplet of red staining the white Corian countertop. When the pin first arrived in the mail a couple of days ago, I'd dismissed it as simply part of some solicitation from the church. I'd been too busy to ponder anything further about it.

"Mom, did you hear me?" Lily asked. "You need to come down here!"

Oh God, no. Another bead of blood trickled down my wrist as I continued to hold onto the pin. And then through the ringing in my ears, I thought I heard a voice, deep like—like my father's. "You wanted me dead!"

"No," I shouted, smacking my hand to my mouth. *I must be hallucinating.* Shaking, I closed my eyes as if I could blink it all away—will it all away. But when I licked my lips, I tasted blood. I laughed out loud. *I must be going crazy!* And then, as if warding off some sort of vampire, I held up the little pin.

Yeah, like this can really happen. I'd been under so much stress lately. This was all just my wild imagination—*el patio del diablo*, Mamá used to call it. Indeed, the voice cackled like a demonic hyena running wild through a child's playground.

"Mom!" Lily sounded so far away. "Mom! Are you there? Answer me!"

"Give me a minute." I kneaded my brow, trying to clear my head. "I—I have a new trial starting next week." Squeezing my eyes shut, I hoped the image would disappear. "I know this isn't your concern." I blinked one eye open, but still it remained. "I'll see if I can send my brother."

"Mom, no," Lily yelled. "You have to do it and you need to call Abuela." The specter came closer, and I slapped at it. "Back off!"

"What?" Lily sounded incredulous.

"Oh Lily, I wasn't talking to you," I said, raising a clenched fist at the apparition. But it didn't budge. And then as if it were a normal reaction, as if these sorts of phantasmagorias appeared every day, I reached for a cigarette and clamped it between my lips. Shrugging the phone, ear to shoulder, I ignited the lighter. A small flame leapt to the ceiling, and I jumped—the Marlboro flying from my lips before I roared

4

with idiotic laughter, jutting out my arm toward the annoying genie. *Take that!*

"Mom!"

"Lily, don't worry, I'll take care of it." I watched the thing vanish. "I'll call you in the morning. I've got to go now."

Still trembling, I hung up, staring down the shrinking genie. When it finally disappeared, I got up, corked the bottle and threw it into the stainless-steel trashcan under the sink, covering the lid with a giant frying pan as if that would keep it restrained. I slammed the cabinet door shut. Whether it kept trying to hurt me or just mess with me now, I'd never understood why it made its appearances. Either way, it distressed me beyond compare.

Shaking so badly, my face flushed with fear and anger. *Since when does Lily get to tell me what I need to do?* And for her to have such a strong reaction about her grandfather, made my heart sink. *Had she met him? Had she seen him?* To imagine the two together troubled me even more and caused my stomach to lurch. *Was Lily okay? And what was up with the blue pest this time? ¡Ay Papá!*

My head sped out of control on a precipitous emotional rollercoaster. And when I thought more about the blue genie, my world dropped out beneath me. I'd dismissed it as simply a side effect of my medication—a medication for an illness I'd been pretty good at managing, including the pain and any flare-ups. I was practiced at downplaying the fact that I suffered from Crohn's—a moderate case—I liked to fool myself. I'd even named my disease, 'Pepita.'

"Settle down, Pepita," I whispered now, clutching my stomach.

I felt an abrupt iron heaviness behind my eyes and a tightness between them as my eyebrows slammed together like prison doors. I stared at the trashcan, massaging the sides of my head, worrying about the blue manifestation. Sensible enough, I knew I'd obviously dredged something up from my past. Papá had been the one to tell me about the *genio azul* when I was just a girl, but then again, I always thought it was only after he'd had too much Tequila.

I'd also read about cases where people saw and heard things that weren't really there. I'd even represented a mother during a custody battle who'd been sleep-deprived. Her husband and his attorney had alleged that she was schizophrenic, and thereby unable to care for their children. The judge found the husband to be sadistically abusive, waking her at all hours, and then he awarded the mother one hundred percent physical and legal custody. I also remembered that sleep deprivation could actually cause other symptoms that mimic mental illness, such as disorientation and paranoid thoughts. But I also recalled that in contrast, people with schizophrenia often have auditory hallucinations, hearing things that are not there. *A little crazy, but I'm not schizophrenic.*

And that night as I brushed my teeth, I opened the medicine cabinet to see all of my pills lined up like little soldiers on the front line. I removed one of the bottles, noticing the warning on the label and then recalled having read about certain side effects, including agitation—I was agitated, that was for damn sure—neuropathies—this I needed more research on—and hallucinations. I laughed. I didn't know whether this made it all better or not, but at least there were answers. Maybe the time had come for me to go out and find some more.

Oh my God, please, I can't do this.

But there was no getting out of this latest responsibility. My brother Rudy wanted even less to do with our mother, much less our father who'd abandoned him. In turn, Rudy abandoned the Catholic Church. He then converted when he married a Mormon girl and moved across the Rockies to Utah. He was never coming back. Besides, he'd fathered half a dozen kids by now, so he wasn't going anywhere. And Mamá—well, that would be like moving the Rocky Mountains.

In addition to my fair skin, I'd also inherited Mamá's tough skin—stubbornness was probably the better term. So, I already knew she'd refuse to make the trip to identify the body of el cabrón. I could already hear her say, like she had so many times before, *"Juré nunca volver."*

While he was still alive, she'd sworn never to go back and now that he was dead, why would she? She'd only been his wife, not blood like me and as soon as that thought skipped across the forefront of my brain, the tiny hairs on my arms shot up like antennae and my insides burned. *La sangre atrae,* the voice in my head said. The blood calls you back. I sucked on my finger. *And so, this must be what hell tastes like.*

Chapter Two
Hell

I WATCHED THE FIDEO-THIN, BALL-CAPPED MORTICIAN descend deeper into the mortuary and couldn't help thinking about my work. Instead of treading down this dark corridor, I should have been marching down the halls of the Los Angeles Superior Court to represent my client during a pretrial hearing for a wrongful death lawsuit. I had a responsibility—a virtue I prided myself in—I'd let him down. And now here I stood in the bowels of this godforsaken place for the first person of many in my life who'd let me down.

On the outside, I tried to appear unflappable—nice suit, albeit wrinkled, hair in place, shoes shined—but on the inside, my gut twisted like the labyrinth of the dank, poorly lit hallway. My stomach hadn't stopped growling, so I popped another Tums. I straightened my linen skirt—good for trials and for absorbing the heat, but hopelessly crumpled after the long plane trip. Lifting my chin, I took a step toward the door.

I can do this. Death was a business—even if this wasn't a client—so as soon as I handled this matter, I'd get back to my own affairs at the Los Angeles law firm where I was up for partnership. I'd worked so hard, long hours, weekends—not an unusual drill if you wanted to get ahead in this world. (Especially as a woman, most especially as a Latina.) I'd asked for a short continuance, promising to be back in time for the trial, figuring that anyone at the firm could handle the pretrial. The only reason I found myself here now was because no one else in my family could handle— would handle—the funeral arrangements.

Except for Lily studying at the University of Guadalajara, there'd been, and would be, nothing to hold me in Mexico anymore. My family—at least my mother, brother and I—had immigrated to el norte when I was just a ten-year old kid, and the City of Angels had become my home, my refuge until the call to come back.

INSIDE THE MORGUE, the harsh smell of formaldehyde shocked my lungs, nearly knocking me off my feet when I stepped into the next room. I pulled my jacket up to my nose but started to sway. My silk shirt pasted to me with sweat and I felt as if I were falling down a deep, dark hole. Wanting to throw up would have been nothing unusual for me lately. "It's going to be okay, Pepita," I whispered, tenderly clutching my bloated stomach.

The technician rushed over, took my elbow and directed me to a wooden bench. "Quieres agua?" he asked, handing me a bottle of water.

"Gracias," I said, looking up at the kind young man. "Ulcers." That's what I'd told Lily, too. I brought the water to my lips.

"Too much stress," the tech said.

"Sí, it's kind of hard to avoid," I answered, unnecessarily adding, "I'm only here out of obligation and as soon as I take care of this matter, I'm on the next plane."

"¿Obligación? Pero, el señor es su papá, ¿no?"

"Yes, he's my father."

"La sangre atrae," the young man said, dipping his head reverently.

I stared at the young mortician wanting to explain this wasn't the first time I'd shown up for my father out of duty. I'd been doing it ever since I was a little girl—taking charge, taking on grown-up responsibilities. But I was good at it. One of the reasons I'd decided to go into law was because of my dealings with authority as a young girl. Mamá's English hadn't been so good—or so she claimed—so I'd stepped up to negotiate with the police when they came to the house. "No officer," I'd say, "there's nothing wrong here. No shots fired. No yelling. Not here." I'd accompanied Mamá on her doctor's visits, meetings with attorneys and to the jailhouse. And I'd loved doing it just not all the drama that came with it. Conferring with adults made me feel so important and needed—the family hero. And now, like an old dog, Papá had returned home to die. As if to spare his owner's grief, he'd come back to Sagrada Familia. I also remembered all of the times he never came home. But then, just like our family pet Chico, he'd eventually show up after a few days. I swore I could read the mischievous smile on Chico's furry face when he came through the door. But how could I read my father if I couldn't even look at him?

After a few nauseating moments, I raised my head and gazed around the morgue. Flush along the wall, looking more like oversized post office boxes, were half a dozen vaults. With the back of my hand, I wiped my brow, knitted together like a snag in silk, and stood ready for what came next.

I straightened my back, proud of the fact that I'd always been practical and cool-headed, mighty tools for an attorney. *I can handle this.* Stoic even, I wasn't one to be immobilized by death. After all, it was life that had numbed me. Lately though, I wished I could run away to find a new serene one. Death was simply the inevitable conclusion to life and now that it had happened to my own father, I would still be in control of my emotions. *I'll be damned if I shed a tear.*

It wouldn't be right. If I hadn't allowed Lily's troubles to collapse my world, or those of my *loco* ex-fiancé, I wasn't about to fall apart over my father's death. It would be too confusing to figure out who or what I mourned. It would be dishonest. I came here to be strong as always and to take care of the business of death.

But I didn't want to be here standing next to the tech as he pulled on a pair of green latex gloves.

The undertaker pulled back a frayed, dingy sheet. "Señora Hidalgo," he asked.

"Ms. Miller," I said, feeling a betrayal.

He nodded. "¿Puedes identificar este cuerpo?"

Of course I could recognize him, even after all the years. I turned to look and gagged, bringing my hands to my mouth, my caged heart swelling in my chest. My whole body trembled and as soon as I looked into the prune-shriveled face of my father, my legs buckled.

I hadn't seen him face-to-face for a long time. His lips clamped, I stared at his now smooth forehead, once deep with creases, and around his eyes where sadness had at long last gone to rest. Finally, he'd found peace. Perhaps, now I could, too, I thought, terrified of how I sounded more like Mamá every day. Well, anyway, now at least I could stop worrying about him, too.

What struck me now was, without his sombrero, just how neat his hair looked on a man whose life had been so disheveled; shiny as a dime, every strand knowing its place. I pressed back my own curly hair I'd been training for years; would it continue to behave even in death? I blinked repeatedly, in an effort to reign in any tears wanting to escape. I then closed my eyes and for a moment, I stopped breathing as if I could dam the memories from flooding forward—memories like the strange dreams too, about my father, always tinged in blue.

I felt a snag in my breath remembering the one where he would wander the earth looking for his mother and father. After a while, I'd be right there beside him looking through the heavens. And then there was the one where we were fishing. He'd started telling me a story about why and how the pueblo ended up drinking Tequila. The memory blurred in with the part mixed in about my abuelo, Pancho Villa. *Yeah, right*—my grandfather Pancho, the infamous old revolutionary general. *Ay Papá, tan loco.*

"Damn it, Papá," I whispered, squeezing my eyes to shut the door on the past—now was not the time to go down memory lane—more a trail of sorrows than a Sunday skip through the park. "I hope you've finally found them," I whispered, running a hand over his cool forehead. And then pierced through by an overwhelming sadness, I clutched my aching stomach, and turned to leave the room.

At the front desk, I signed the necessary documents, collected my father's belongings—all I'd inherit, beside the memories buried like dog bones—including the weathered leather wallet he bought years ago when we'd traveled to Puerto Vallarta and the old, soiled white sombrero; the hat he'd hung onto until his dying day—Pancho Villa's hat, he'd told me. *Yeah, right*. The family used to joke that he'd be buried with that damned, filthy thing.

I exited the funeral parlor and stood out on the narrow sidewalk, looking up to the sky for answers. And then I looked down at my wrinkled clothes and dusty Jimmy Choos. *Now I really know I'm in hell.*

Chapter Three

A Good Tabernero Listens

CANTINA, THE BLINKING NEON SIGN beckoned me. After identifying my father's body, I stood across the street from the morgue, blinded by the Mexican sunlight, contemplating the windowless tavern wedged in between two whitewashed casitas. Like a couple of strays, sadness and fear came licking at my heels. I scurried across the road, heels clicking over cobblestone and stumbled into the dank watering hole, instantly sucking in the familiar tang of sweat, cheap cigarettes, beer and Tequila. Sad mariachi music—music I'd learned to despise—blared out of the jukebox.

Undeterred, I approached the bar and took a seat on a three-legged rickety stool. I gasped when I saw my reflection through a smudged mercury glass mirror on the back wall, and quickly smoothed back my unruly hair. I noticed how my brow furrowed with stress-like tiny rows raked across a field of pain. My eyes feel gritty and, peering closer, I see my sclera red as the soil of the region, my irises still the color of agave. I looked around, surprised by what I didn't see. No young people. No young men. No women of any age. Everyone who'd been able had left Sagrada Familia to go north long ago like my mother, brother and I had. Tucked into a dark corner sat a man, ancient as Rico Van Winkle. Behind me, at a small, lacquered metal table with *Cerveza* painted in black letters on top, were two more mature, scrawny, milky-eyed men hunched over their beers. The skeletal bartender, dusty as the bottles on the glass shelves, flashed a gold-framed toothy smile as he approached me.

11

"A shot of your best Tequila, por favor," I said, setting my father's belongings down onto the counter. I pulled out my cigarettes and only stared at them before stuffing them back into my purse.

The barkeeper rubbed his bony hands together, grinning mischievously as he backed away. He twisted around, creaking as he reached up for a bottle on the highest shelf. He dusted off the jug, pulled off the wax seal, uncorked it and brought the lip to his nose. Inhaling deeply, the cavernous wrinkles on his face smoothed out like a tumbled river stone and when he opened his cloudy eyes, I noticed they were amber, the color of the Tequila he poured into two small glasses. As soon as he opened the bottle, the mixed bouquet took me back, both the sweet scent of my childhood and the bitter odor of my father.

"We'll drink to Joaquin Hidalgo," said el barman.

"Wait, you knew my father?"

"Sí, he was a regular. Pero antes, we used to work out at the Tequila farm when we were younger," the bartender said, holding up the old bottle. "He gave this to me when I left to open this cantina. I promised I'd only open it when he came in to share it with me one day. Joaquin said it was only for a special occasion. I waited." The bartender then poured two glasses. "I'd say this was a special occasion. You are his blood. La sangre atrae." There's that saying again. Only two days ago in court—it already felt like a lifetime ago—a client had whispered the words. It's the first time I'd really paid attention to the saying: *La sangre atrae.*

"*Sí*, I suppose the blood has called me back." I began to understand.

He held up his glass. "Salud." He peered a little closer. "Tienes los mismos ojos de su papá—tapatíos."

So I have his eyes. Tell me something I don't know. Tell me I have nothing more in common with my father than the color of his eyes. I'd never be anything like him and I'd never been able to understand why he acted the way he did, why he'd done the things he'd done. Was I destined to end up like him, sharing a drink called loneliness with this strange bartender or worse yet, alone? Would I end up crazy? And then for one irrational moment, I wondered: *Do I have Pancho Villa's eyes, too?*

I felt the tears welling—every pore in my body swelling with gooey emotion. With a shaky hand, I lifted the glass. "Here's to you, Papá." *Hijo de puta*, I could imagine Mamá uttering so crudely. And I could hear Papá

12

yelling back, *I warned you never to call me son of a bitch!* Laying a hand on my stomach, I braced for the pain, bringing the glass to my lips. Expecting the warm liquid to burn a fire road down my rough throat, I swallowed—surprised when it didn't burn.

"Bueno?" the tabernero asked.

I nodded and as the next sip trickled down my throat, I thought again about the first time I'd heard the blood calling me back. I'm sure it had been summoning me for some time, but two days ago it hit me in the head like a ton of bloodied bricks. The bartender poured us each another shot.

"This is some good stuff." I toasted the timeworn man.

"It's from Los Olvidados."

The Forgotten Ones? "The Tequila farm?"

He nodded. "You should visit."

I entertained the thought for a painful second and then dismissed the idea, but by my next sip, I felt tiny butterflies flapping their golden wings gently along my throat, sliding down, and nesting in the pit of my stomach. But as the butterflies settled, I realized it could only be the Tequila, a soothing salve lifting the weight of the crushing grief lodged in the trenches of my stomach, an unguent that coated the lining of my insides. I eased into a smile and looked at the nodding bartender. My pain had become phantom-like, only a memory—olvidado—forgotten.

This is wonderful, if only I could hang on to this feeling forever. I stared at my father's old hat on the chair next to me and felt something stirring in the hollow of my gut. I pulled out his dried-up wallet and set it on the counter where it yawned open like it was ready for a drink. I chuckled. No money, of course—story of our lives. I felt my smile fade when I pulled out a tattered black and white photo. I blinked and, in an instant, my childhood came washing down my face, cracking my tough veneer. A single tear spilled onto the picture, distorting the image of the little girl running through the agave fields.

In the photo, the fields pulsated with azure light, the genio azul, my father used to talk about. And then, the picture seemed to glow, illuminating the space around me. I looked around the bar to see if anyone else noticed the flashing blue or my water works display. But the patrons couldn't afford to pay any mind. Examining the picture even closer, this time I remembered the whole story—recordé toda la historia—not just fragments from my dreams.

The tale was a family legend—more urban myth—I'd always thought. Besides, Papá was loco. He'd last told the story the week before Mamá had driven us to the states, leaving him behind.

I was ten years old when I sat along the riverbank on a red rock, dangling my bare feet into the icy, chocolate-rose-colored water, trickling down from the mountains of Los Altos. Next to me, hat crooked on his head, sat my papá gulping from his bottle of Tequila.

"Papá, why do you drink so much Tequila?" I dared to ask.

He burped and the words dribbled from his lips in his rich native tongue.

"Mija," he said, blue-green eyes glistening like dew on agave.

My heart raced like an anxious caged canary as I looked up at my father, already taking another sip.

He swiped his mouth with the back of his hand. "Once upon a time, years after the hacienda burned down, there was a handsome man with dark, rugged features and a strong jaw line. His name was Domingo because he was born on a Sunday. One morning, he staggered home along the cobble-stone road through the fog which, for many years, kept the valley fertile."

I calmed down once my papá removed his maroon dust-smudged sombrero. I settled into his story as he spread his arms wide open, as if cradling the whole world. I loved when he told his stories in an accent as rich as the Mexican actor, Pedro Infante; stories that made me feel special; our special bond. The tales seemed only to get more colorful the more he swigged from the bottle.

Tequila-soaked words flooded out of Papá's mouth. "In the distance, spiky fields of agave sprouted forth from a red soil as the fog dissolved with the rising of the sun," Papá said, pointing across the field. "Toward the north, loomed a dormant volcanic mountain that had not erupted since before La Revolución. Through a grey-blue mist, Domingo could hear the cooing of the palomas." Papá cupped his mouth. "*Coo coo roo coo coo.*"

Papá took another nip. "Like his ancestors," he said, combing his fingers through his dark hair. "Domingo was blessed with a luscious, thick mane, now gray and covered with the greasy sombrero he stole off a dead soldier during La Revolución."

I peered into Papá's pooling eyes. "The hat belonged to Pancho Villa," Papá said, hooking a thumb toward his chest. "My father."

14

"Your father?" I asked, tilting my head? "Wait, wasn't Domingo your papá?"

"Escúchame, Hija," he said, swaying now like a river weed.

"I am listening, Papá."

"So, in the Zócalo beyond, Domingo recognized the steeple on the church where he had been baptized and knew he was nearly home. He smiled, revealing a big toothless grin, as he forged ahead." My father took another swig and smiled as wide as el rio, wobbling too close to the water's edge.

"Domingo's smile was infectious before then, and with emerald jeweled eyes, not uncommon in these parts, he had been able to charm the women and most of the men of the village," Papá said with a sloppy wink.

"Suddenly, a gust of blue-tinged wind blew off his hat," Papá said, running in place now like a French mime.

I giggled but stopped suddenly when my father lost his footing. I quickly reached out to help him up and as he grasped my tiny hand, squeezing a little too hard, I held my breath, uttering nothing about the pain.

"And as he held his head with both gnarly hands—" Papá paused to steady himself. "The hat was already sailing down the street. The church bells tolled and the palomas scrambled out of the tower as the wind pushed Domingo forward, arms flapping wildly like a gallina."

I started laughing again, mimicking my papá as he flapped his arms like a chicken.

Papá took another nip before continuing the story. "He picked up the pace when he saw that the sombrero had come to a halt, but before stomping on it with his chancla, the wind picked it up and scooted it along down the road. He held up a fist, cursing the pinche viento. The sombrero came to a rest once more. Domingo reached down and grabbed it, falling onto his weakened hip. Laying there, clutching his hat, rubbing his side with his free hand. The bell gonged. 'You will not let me rest!' He raised his head long enough for another puff of wind to come along and snatch his sombrero right out of his hand, skipping it down the street. Face down, Domingo was drained. He took a deep breath through the gaps between the cobblestones, comforted by the smell of the earth, the smell of home. He rolled over and stared up at the sky, sprinkled lightly now with dimming stars and a waning moon."

I loved hearing the part about the stars and the moon. I'd been looking at the sky when Papá grabbed my arm. Squinting into his face, I sensed the fight or flight stress of a jaguar's prey. I never knew what to expect when Papá drank too much Tequila.

"Óigame." He'd raised his voice.

"I hear you, Papá," I replied.

"You see, Domingo wanted to rest, but he needed to make it home to his bed before sunlight woke his wife," Papá said, letting go of my arm, raising his to the sky. "Suddenly, a ray from the morning star pierced his being as if infusing him with energy," Papá said. "The church bell gonged once more."

I took a deep breath, massaging my arm, trying to rub in some understanding.

"Struggling to get up, he dusted himself off, and proceeded on his mission. And again, Domingo found the sombrero at his feet. The wind had nothing better to do at this time of the morning than to play games with him. 'Fine,' thought Domingo, 'I can play your silly games,' and he bent down to pick up his hat. Lightning cracked in the distance, waking all the dogs, wild and domestic, throughout the valley. A draft pushed the hat away from him. Poor Domingo hobbled behind as the wind howled, mocking him. He chased it until it came to rest on the lip of a well, the pueblo's only source of potable drinking water. The bright genio azul shot up from the well, calling him near. Domingo saw that his hat was now within his grasp and took a couple of steps toward it. Tired, frustrated and teetering like a top, he tripped on the step at the base of the well and fell to his knees, releasing the hat at the same time. Lost to him once more, the hat tumbled into the deep hole. Domingo raised himself up and peered into the well. 'Ay Dios!'"

Papá's tongue now sounded heavy as a heartbreak. I strained to listen. "The church bell gonged again as the hat landed on a ledge. The way he saw it, Domingo did not think it was too far out of his reach and stretched his arm to retrieve it. Just as he snatched the sombrero, he lost his footing. But, on the trip to the bottom of the abyss, he was able to put on his sombrero one last time only to meet up with old San Pedro at the Pearly Gates. San Pedro asked that Domingo remove his hat before passing over.

"The church bell gonged for the last time. The pueblo's Tequila sales spiked slightly that week for it was not a very good idea to drink the water."

Papá stared at me, captivating me. "Ves, Mija—" He chuckled before taking another sip, "por eso tomo Tequila."

I picked up my father's hat and handed it to him. "So that's why you drink, but what about Pancho Villa?" I asked. "Am I Pancho Villa's granddaughter or what?"

"Ay," Papá belched. "That is a story for another day."

But before he would ever have the chance to tell me about my relationship to the Mexican Revolutionary general, Mamá would pack our things to take us away, back to the states in the yellow Ford Falcon.

And our leaving had been all my fault, I'd always believed—because I hadn't been able to keep a secret. But that wasn't true. "¡Mamá, no le dije a nadie. I promise I didn't tell anyone!" Mamá wouldn't look at me the whole trip north, much less talk to me except when it had to do with helping my little brother.

Never mind what happened to me. Years later, Mamá would say, "Imagine how that made me feel."

Peering even closer now at the picture, my body felt as if it were on fire. I put my hand on my cheek and could still feel the sting. *How could you? Wasn't I good enough? Did you even love me, Papá?*

There's something about death you can't escape. But I didn't cry now over the death of my father. I cried over the death of my childhood; a childhood I'd never get back. And none of it had been my fault. I'd only been a kid. Just because my mother had taken us away, I had every right to be here. And as an adult, I could make my own choices. The bartender handed me a napkin. I swiped my eyes and blew my nose before sliding the photo back into my father's wallet.

And then as el barman examined me closely with his balmy, yellow eyes, I sensed something comforting about him; after all, any tabernero was only worth his weight in salt if he could comfort his patrons, be a good listener. Sitting across from this kind man now, I let myself bleed my story.

Chapter Four

Tengo un Cuento

TWO DAYS AGO IS AS GOOD A PLACE AS ANY TO START MY TALE.

The morning before the blood called me back, prior to the final breakup with my fiancé, the temperature in October had already soared to one hundred and two degrees. I'd rushed along the 101 Freeway just to get to court on time and by the time I'd arrived, dressed in a purple Ann Taylor suit, I felt like a wilted eggplant. I dashed through the stuffy, dimly lit halls but before pushing through the door of Department 12, I rushed into the ladies' room, straight to the toilet. Pepita had been acting up now for a couple of days. At the sink I splashed my face, noticing the dark puffy circles cradling my eyes like little purple aprons. I patted back my hair, tucking a stray back into my bun, and then I touched up my rum-raisin lipstick.

Before pushing through the doors into the department, I smoothed my skirt. I walked up the aisle to check in with the clerk, a plump middle-aged woman who looked like she'd rather be playing church Bingo than marking off the court calendar.

"Good morning, Ms. Miller," the clerk said without looking up. "You smell good. Coco Chanel?"

"Yes, thank you. I hope it's not too—"

"Take a seat," the bored woman said. The courtroom, clearly her jurisdiction.

I scanned the room for Mr. Montoya, my client whom I represented in an unlawful death lawsuit against Allstate Insurance. So far, there were only a couple of people seated in the gallery. One, a young woman wearing a bright pink scrunchy in her ratty-looking hair, sat on the carved-up bench checking her phone. She wore large, hooped silver earrings and a tight fluorescent lime-green tank top with her black bra straps hanging out like they were trying to escape the nineties. I thought about Lily, grateful she finally walked the right path. Another, a middle-aged businessman who looked like he had better things to do than to sit there and wait for clients or his attorney, checked the clock on a side wall as he adjusted his tie. And another, a spacey tatted-out dude stared dead straight ahead. Mr. Victor Montoya wasn't amongst them.

I took my seat for what was to be the final day of pre-trial and set down my leather briefcase, a gift from my fiancé—probably paid for with my own money. I placed my French manicured nails on my lap, splaying my left fingers as I gazed at the modest one-carat diamond engagement ring—probably paid for by—*oh stop,* but I couldn't stop thinking about Zane. I hadn't heard from him for a couple of days. At least thinking about him took the focus off Lily, and even though I'd lost sleep agonizing over Zane's whereabouts, at this moment, nothing mattered except to do my best representing my client.

I reached into my purse and like my own obsessive teenager, I checked my phone again for the hundredth time. Nothing. The waiting and wondering were slowly killing me.

And then seated to my left, I noticed a short, disheveled male with just a shroud of color-treated hair. To see Attorney Richard Hughes in court on time certainly surprised me. All week long, he'd been making his side snide comments, whether to rattle me or just because he was a slimy iguana. He leaned over and I could smell the combination of stale coffee and misogyny on his breath. "You know, you don't even look Mexican," he said.

Holding my breath, I looked askance at him, ready to claw out his beady eyes. "With your light complexion," he added, "you could pass for Italian."

I closed my eyes, shaking my head. I'd heard such remarks before and now that he said it, I was pissed off even more—as if Italians were really all that and a piece of pizza pie, or as if Mexicans weren't, but I kept silent. I'd climbed this far and wasn't ready to die on the mountain arguing with a moron.

Inhaling deeply, I turned to him, smiling. "I'm pretty sure you can't even pass for human."

He laughed. "Your English is flawless."

Like you would know. But it's true. I'd practiced very hard to soften my R's, to get rid of any trace of an accent, any trace of my past and it was because of people like him. This cute shy little Mexican girl, the object of boys' desires, could only be safe if she got rid of her Mexicanness. Once we got to the states, Mamá insisted I assimilate. I rarely spoke Spanish again, especially not in school were it was banned, and not even at home where Mamá forbade it. Sadly, Lily had to learn the language in high school from a teacher with roots in Milwaukee. There was no reason for it; no reason to stay connected to the shattered past. I'd erected a wall so high, but still the memories seeped through the cracks and fissures of my mind.

A kiss of cool air gushed in as the courtroom doors whooshed open. A faded old white hat came sailing up the aisle, preceding its owner, my client, an aged lanky Mexican man with closely cropped white hair. Mr. Montoya had run a family landscape business in Calabasas, and it was his son who'd tragically been electrocuted on the job. The old man bent down to retrieve his hat and, for the first time—never mind that I'd been working with him for months now—there suddenly seemed to be something familiar about the humble Victor Montoya, almost as if he were a relative. Those green eyes and thick, dark brows. How had I not seen it before? Simple. With all that had been going on in my life lately, I hadn't noticed the forest through the trees. *What part of Mexico did he say he was from?* Jalisco, but what part? It sat on the tip of my memory, but then I felt a vibration in my pocket and only one thing occupied my mind. Without hesitation, I pulled out my cell to see a text, and without a moment to spare. But it wasn't from Zane.

From a side door in the back, Judge Owens entered the room and took his seat. I loosened my collar and blew some air down onto my damp chest. A dapper man in his early sixties, he had a healthy tan and a head full of wavy hair like vanilla cake frosting (I suspected L'Oréal 9A because he thought he was worth it) only he wasn't as sweet, and I'd been warned not to piss him off. As the judge took his seat, I quickly took a moment to return the text.

And when the next text came in, I laughed out loud before noticing Richard approach the bench. Both he and the judge gaped at me.

Judge Owens pointed a spindly chastising finger, summoning me forward. But, still grinning, I didn't need an invitation. I had this in the bag. As I made my way up to the bench, practically skipping, I whispered to myself, "Merry Christmas and a Happy New Year."

"What's that Ms. Miller?" the judge asked.

"Oh nothing, Your Honor."

The judge put on his glasses, snapped open the case file and cleared his throat. "Mr. Hughes informs me you've reached a settlement?"

I held up my phone as if it were the missing Exhibit A and turned to Richard. "One million and we'll call it a day."

"Dollars?" Richard asked, chuckling nervously.

"Well, I don't mean pesos."

"Miss Miller is this some sort of joke?" the judge asked, peering over his bifocals.

"Oh, no. I'm not joking." I looked up at the judge. "Your Honor, when it comes to my clients, I'm dead serious. Had your nephew not been so hasty killing forests to bury us in discovery, perhaps he might have sought a recusal."

Richard's eyes widened and his jaw yawned open like a bottom-feeding flounder.

"What are you talking about?" Judge Owens pounded his fist and stood. "Both of you, in my chambers, now!"

Inside the judge's chambers—much cooler than the courtroom—Richard and I took a seat in front of a massive mahogany desk. So worked up, the rush of adrenaline had finally kicked in. It was the moment I'd been waiting for—that high you get when you're on top of the world, holding it by its scrawny neck; that fight or flight feeling you get when you're pinned to the ground and someone's breathing in your face. And then Pepita started a Mexican Hat Dance in my stomach. The hot wetness pooled now in between my breasts. I should have known better than to wear this blouse. *Whoever said silk breathes?* I wiped the palms of my damp hands on my skirt. Except for my earlier days when I clerked to pay my way through law school, I hadn't been inside many chambers, but Judge Owens' digs were certainly more elaborate than your average superior court judge's chambers. And then on the credenza behind his chair, I noticed a crystal trophy the size of a small child. The etched inscription read "Pacific Palisades Singles Champion."

I looked around as I eased into a leather club chair, trying not to focus on my pain. In this court, he might have been champion, but when it came to the sport, and not to brag, a tennis court was my venue. As an outlet, I'd taken up the sport in law school and played with friends in a local park—

Lily with a babysitter on the sidelines. I surprised myself at how quickly I'd learned. Boy, how I'd love to take the judge on now. I'd mix it up, first serving him wide with one of my "girly" serves hated by most opponents, male or otherwise, making him run off to the side of the court and drawing him into the net to return it. Then I'd lob him—another girly shot. After throwing him off, next, I'd power a slice down the "T" and watch him swing at it and miss. I could see the ropy veins in his red neck popping now and I started to laugh.

"Ms. Miller," the judge, still standing, shouted. "Not to get personal, but your behavior has been pretty bizarre this week. And now this maniacal laughing like some sort of hyena."

"I was simply reacting to something funny." This whole scene was pretty absurd. "And speaking of personal, Your Honor, you really should keep better track of your kin," I said, slinging a thumb toward Richard, before tossing up my first serve. "I thought it was funny to learn that Mr. Hughes here is your brother's son-in-law. I hate when people aren't truthful." *Fifteen/love.* I couldn't help but curl into myself a little, wrapping my arms around my middle.

Eyes popping. "Ex," the judge yelled. "Ms. Miller, ex son-in-law. Am I going to have to—"

I ignored the pain and stood, hands-on-hips. "What? Recuse yourself?" I said, really pumped now. "Or put me in time out?" I continued to hold my watery gaze on the judge, face now red as a blister. "I'm prepared to take this matter to trial at the end of which, should we lose—" I said, holding up an index finger, "which is highly unlikely—I will seek to have it declared a mistrial." *Thirty/love.*

With his snowy white-capped head and crimson face, the judge looked like Mt. Everest about to erupt. He inched toward me, but I didn't budge. "Ms. Miller, sit down."

I stood my ground, swiping my sweaty brow. "I suppose you forgot about the shares you hold in the defendant's company, Your Honor?" *Forty/love.* As subtly as I could, I'd been exercising some Lamaze breathing, but now Pepita had put her boots on and stomped around my stomach pretty lively.

Richard shot out of his seat, blinking and stuttering. "I do have authorization from my client to tender another fifty thousand toward—"

I forced back my shoulders and walked up to Richard, towering over him. I reached out to straighten his tie, tugging it noose-like around his neck. "Bite me, Richard. Add a couple of zeros and I don't take this joke to the Bar." *Game/set/match.*

My heart raced. While it might have been true what the judge said about my behavior—my illness and its treatments (a veritable cocktail of pharmaceuticals) really made me do silly things. But I thought I'd done a good job keeping my sanity and focus on the hearing, despite the worry over Lily and Zane and my health. Right now, all that mattered was the truth. For wasn't verity the answer to everything? Wasn't that why I'd gone into law? The law was all about presenting the facts and as long as you represented the truth everything would be okay. But right now, I didn't feel okay. I felt as if I were on a runaway train, out of control and unstoppable— little Pepita screaming as she ran up and down the aisles. I swiped my sweaty brow.

I looked up at the judge. "May I be dismissed? I really have to visit the ladies' room." Without waiting for permission, I shot out of the chamber room.

OUTSIDE, THE AUTUMN SUN BLAZED, and the Santa Ana winds did nothing to cool things down. As I exited the courthouse, out on the street, the people carried signs about the freedom to live, to be educated and to work in this country. I felt bad for them, but what could I do? I had my own problems.

"God, you were so caliente in there," Richard said, catching up to me. "A little hot Latina lawyer. Such passion in the courtroom. I can only imagine you in the bedroom."

I smiled wider than el Rio Grande, knowing better than to respond, but what I really wanted to do was cut off his comb-over flopping in the wind. I left him standing in the dust.

Walking to the edge of the steps, I heard shouting. I looked out to see a herd of protestors marching down the street yelling things like, "Sí se puede!" and "No more walls!"

And still others shouted: "Mexicans, go home!"

But I am home, I felt torn. The words stung, leaving me itching to do something. *We are home.* Things were a little different when my family and I had come to the United States. It had been slightly easier. During a season when her family picked fruit in Salinas, Mamá had been born right out in the field and I—well, I could pass. At times I acted more like a reluctant Mexican, standing up for the many causes, but today I didn't have the energy to join mis hermanos gritando, "Dignity! Respect! Amnesty!" This wasn't my battle for today. A personal war simmered back at my home in the valley, and I needed to return in order to either add more fuel to the fire or quell it, once and for all.

I noticed the sweat in the faces of the marchers and felt the perspiration dripping again from my armpits. I took off my jacket before descending the courthouse steps. As I checked my cell phone, it slipped out of my damp hands, and if not for the quick hands of Mr. Montoya, I would have stumbled pell-mell down the stairs, too. "Cuídate," he said, releasing my elbow.

"Gracias," I said, thinking how nice it would be to always have some sort of angel around to watch me—how nice it would feel to have someone like Mr. Montoya guarding over me.

"Lo siento," he said, handing me a slightly cracked phone.

"No, I'm sorry, Sr. Montoya," I said, speaking in Spanish, the language I'd all but abandoned. I noticed I was even thinking more in Spanish. I looked at the splintered glass on my phone. "Puedo comprar otro," I said, looking up. I tried to imagine my own father appearing for me day after day, much less my own mother who'd said I was so smart, I didn't need anyone's help taking up my cause. I felt like the broken phone, easily replaceable. "Your son was worth more than the settlement."

"Es lo que es."

"It's what it is?" I shook my head. One thing I'd come to learn about some of my humble people was that they didn't feel like they deserved anything, not even the air they breathed. "I wish I had your attitude, Sr. Montoya."

He bowed his head, and I was sorry I hadn't done more. I'd desperately wanted to get Mr. Montoya more money, but he'd said that no amount would ever bring his son back and so we'd settled. Here was a man who'd handled death with humility and dignity, traits from a time long ago, a world far away. Mr. Montoya seemed to be such a kind man, hardworking, too. I knew he had family somewhere in Mexico that he also supported. In a way, bittersweet, even the lower settlement would be a godsend. Mr. Montoya's family would be able to live like royalty down there.

"Miss Miller," he said, eyes gleaming. "Can you help me now with my immigration papers?"

But why? I wondered, hating the thought of telling him immigration wasn't something I handled. The truth was there'd never been any money in that area of law; I had a daughter to take care of, after all. But now that I looked into his eyes, something tugged at my heart. "Why don't you call my office and ask for my secretary Betsy. She might be able to refer you."

"Gracias," he said.

"De nada." I turned to leave.

"Señorita Hidalgo," Mr. Montoya said.

My skin tingled and I turned around to see his smiling face. "Wait. How did you know my name?" I couldn't recall ever sharing with him my maiden name and why would I? Even after the divorce, I'd kept my married name for the sake of Lily.

"Someday you should go back—get to know your family better. La sangre atrae."

"The blood calls you back?" *So, why are you still here?*

"I did go back not too long ago to visit my family," he said as if reading my mind. "But when I tried to return to the states, I was detained at the border for a couple of days. It was my son who drove down to help me." Mr. Montoya dabbed his nose and eyes with a white handkerchief. "I'm going to miss him so much."

I reached out to pat his arm. "I'm so sorry." Losing a child was horrible, no matter how old. I thought about Lily and her twin that didn't make it and a lump lodged at the top of my rib cage. I would just die if anything ever happened to my daughter, too.

Just then a gust of wind lifted his sombrero from his head, but this time Mr. Montoya's hands were ready, and he held on.

The police barked orders for the people to disperse. I hurried toward the parking garage, thinking about Lily now living in the place I once called home, the land of the Hidalgos. I hoped she was safe. *What good would it do for me to go back?* What I already knew of my family history was enough and I certainly wasn't interested in digging up the bones of my past. Besides, if I were never to go back to Sagrada Familia, it would be no skin off my nose, but was that fair to Lily who lately seemed to be having more questions about her heritage, a heritage for which I had so few answers? Hadn't I withheld the truth from Lily long enough? The rift between mother and daughter had grown greater than the Gulf of Mexico.

Chapter Five

Dream, But Not Too Big

INSIDE MY BRAND-NEW BMW 740I, I lit a cigarette, a no-no even for me in the car and especially for someone with my "condition." I left the window cracked about an inch as I maneuvered through a sea of immigration protestors, police barricades, and bullhorns. "Freedom is overrated, folks," I muttered, sorry for feeling so cranky and apathetic. I knew they were escaping poverty and crime and only wanted a better life—a life like my family had found in the north.

Since before I was born and until I was ten years old, my family had migrated back and forth between the two countries, working the fields on either side of the border. And then Mamá finally ripped us away before our roots could go any deeper. She tried to plant us in the states, but it was another world where I felt like an untethered planet drifting alone through the galaxy. I'd always felt like a foreigner in either country, like an outsider full of fear, but I'd become even more frightened when there was no longer any support for food or necessities coming from my father. I'd grown tired of hearing from Mamá how no man was ever going to take care of me, "So get used to it. Get over it." It had become painfully obvious that we could not depend on Papá. And from an early age, the misogynist attitudes, present in both cultures would make me tougher. Brick by brick, I'd put up my own wall.

Another thing I'd learned from my mother and for which I was grateful was there was no shame in working hard. "Mija, you can never depend on a man," she'd preach. "Don't trust him even when he makes promises. If you want anything in this world, you must work for it yourself." Sure, and at the same time, I'd been told to dream of a better life—there was that American dream out there, only available to everyone else. "Follow your dreams, but don't dream too big." So, by the age of twelve, I went into the rich neighborhoods to walk their dogs, clean their houses, sell them Avon and babysit their kids. When I was old enough, I waitressed while in school, earning enough tips to save for college. And, because of my dual citizenship, things were a little easier. "Mija, learn to type," Mamá told me, "so you will always have a good job for when your husband leaves you with all the mocosos."

But I had bigger goals than to become a single mother, with a dozen kids, bigger than being a secretary. Sadly, no matter my legal status, no matter that I'd worked hard to save, no amount of money would be able to see me through. The dream of becoming a rich lawyer died the day I found out I was pregnant.

I drove up the onramp and turned on the radio only to hear about another young singer back in rehab—no kidding. The homeless and the housing crisis. The Somalian refugee crisis. Another six dead soldiers in Iraq. I switched over to Sirius XM.

By the time the first car horn blared, I'd gone from zero patience to one hundred percent bitch and laid on my own horn. "Dammit." I rolled down the window and flicked out my cigarette that had done nothing to calm my nerves.

And then, as if I needed more torture, I picked up my cell phone and called just to hear his voice. The familiar dull ache grew like a hot seed in the pit of my stomach. It was his recording. "Hello, you've reached Maya and Zane. We're not home right now. Please leave a message." I hung up and tried the next number. "This is Zane. You know what to do. Just do it."

By now, the tiny seed of a tree had grown into a full-on forest fire. An alarm went off in my stomach, clanging as a bright blue tinge pulsated along my periphery. The aching was not unfamiliar—more of a nuisance I'd learned to control, but this time it seemed worse. I thought about pulling off to the side of the road to wait it out, but gripped the wheel tighter, to push through it, nails piercing my palms. I knew better. When had I ever been able to will this ache away? Finally, I reached into my briefcase for a Tums to try and douse the flames. I put on my melanin sunglasses to block out the bright Arctic glacier now sliding across my irises, so cold it burned. I'd known this pain for a while now, and I knew others had it worse, so I'd tried to stay quiet about it and not complain.

A logical person, I always pushed myself to be better than everyone around me. I took pride in getting up early, in seeing how many different things I could juggle successfully before even getting to the office, in seeing how busy I was at being busy. Hurry up and run, I was a hustler made for the rat race and foolish enough to believe I could beat it and win. I'd been diagnosed now for about three years; thinking at first, it was probably nothing more serious than an ulcer. After all, who goes through law school, especially as a single mom, without at least one ulcer? And while I understood that my disease was a disorder of certain etiology, these painful occurrences were also no doubt stress-related, job-related, relationship-related, and daughter-related. The stabbing pain was nature's way of telling my gut the time had come to make some changes, but sometimes I found myself right in the middle of the forest with the flames shooting up all around me and I could only manage to pop an antacid or two or three.

I turned up the radio when I heard Carlos Santana singing *I Ain't Got Nobody That I Can Depend On.* Well, if that isn't spot on the nose, I thought, singing along as I sat on the freeway in bumper-to-bumper traffic. *No tengo a nadie.* Ain't that the truth.

Chapter Six

Life at Home

THE BLUE GENIE WOULD BE WAITING FOR ME IN THE KITCHEN.

Dusk descended like a sheer grey curtain across the valley when I finally pulled into my driveway two hours after leaving the courthouse. I wanted to weep when I saw the plants on the porch drooping over the sides of their terracotta pots like dead ballerinas—another sign that Zane hadn't been home, not that he'd ever lifted a finger. Water might bring them back, but what could save my relationship from drowning. The mail spilled out of the box, crammed full of useless flyers mostly—more senseless tree killings—and some bills that couldn't be paid online. And, at the bottom of all the junk mail was a postcard. I flipped it over, but before I could read where it came from, something small and gold fell to my feet. I picked up a lapel pin of an angel—a little guardian angel—like the kind worn by the old ladies I saw in church when I used to go. I took off my sunglasses and peered closer. How did it get into my mailbox?

My heart pounded, my stomach somersaulted as I braced myself and slid the key into the door, calling out as if warning him I was home and giving him enough time to hide the dancing girls or whatever. I never knew what I might find. I shouldn't have been shocked, but when I opened the door and found everything just as it had been when I left earlier in the week—nothing out of place—I had to run for the bathroom down the hallway.

My feet carried me slowly out of the bathroom and then back down the hall into our bedroom. Our bed hadn't been slept in, the pillows still poofed. My heart hurt. There was still one more place to look as I wandered into the lonely-looking family room. I almost hoped to find him passed out—at least I'd know he was alive—but when I peeked over to the empty leather sofa, my heart hit the wall inside my chest, splattering all my blood throughout my body. He was gone. Drained, I felt hollow, a normal reaction for me. I pushed a loose strand of hair behind my ear and walked into the kitchen to shuffle through the mail like normal.

Even though it was pointless, and a waste of time since I'd already called home from the hotel and the car several times—like the obsessive-compulsive maniac I'd become—I checked the messages, anyway. Maybe, there was something wrong with the house phone or the answering machine. After all, I'd had the machine since college and it had served me well, but maybe it was broken—well, that wouldn't explain why he hadn't called my cell phone. I pressed the button on the old machine, holding my breath. My palms tingled, but so far, no surprises. There were a couple of hang-ups, but mostly messages from me sounding desperate. "Zane, are you there? Please pick up."

And then, like a voice from another dimension—oddly robotic and in control—I heard how my voice changed. "Okay, I guess you're not home. Trial should be finished tomorrow. I miss you. I love you." I sounded calm, yet pathetic. "Call me."

I sorted the mail into neat stacks—bills, flyers, junk mail, and then absentmindedly set down the little pin when I heard the next message from my doctor's office.

"Ms. Miller, this is Dr. Vaisman's office. We have your lab results and—" I felt the needle pricking sensation starting in my fingers as my heart whacked inside my ribs. Clicking off the machine, I squeezed my hands over my stomach. Again, during my last visit, Dr. Vaisman had told me to slow down, get some rest, eat better and stop smoking. I'd been able to manage with the medicines I took, even achieving remission for long periods of time—times when I could forget I had the disease. But then recently, I'd started having more flare-ups and so Dr. Vaisman had ordered more tests. I'd been waiting to get the results. And now, my stomach simply couldn't handle any more bad news.

I thought twice before lighting up. *Just two puffs.* I just needed to unwind. There were bills that needed to get paid without delay, and as I proceeded to sort through them, I noticed the postcard and froze.

In the palm of my hand, I held a sapphire sky, purple and yellow jacaranda, rich red soil and the fields of blue agave, a banner of heaven. As I carried the colorful card with me down the hall to my bedroom, I recognized the Mexican scenery. For once, the thought of Sagrada Familia warmed my heart. I closed my eyes and could almost feel the cool air as it tumbled down from the ancient mountains of Los Altos. Except for the electric buzz of insects, I could hear the golden silence. I practically smelled the rich soil after the rain and oh, the taste of the maguey, even sweeter when I'd snatched it straight from the ovens. Imagining all of this now, I realized my stomach had settled down.

But then, like a cloudy sunset, I felt my smile fade away when I looked into our empty bedroom. My head started to pound as I slipped the postcard into my pocket. I'd been so focused on negotiating a good settlement for Mr. Montoya that I hadn't eaten anything that day—hadn't eaten much at all during the pre-trial. I wandered back into the kitchen to scrounge through the cupboard. I found a box of Saltines and opened it up. Chewing on a dry cracker, I opened the refrigerator.

Except for the bottle of beer hidden behind the milk that had expired last Tuesday, there was nothing else. I grabbed the beer, walked to the cupboard for a glass and nearly choked when I opened the cupboard. There on the shelf boldly stood a near-empty bottle of Jose Cuervo.

"Cheapskate, Zane. At least buy the good stuff," I mumbled, angry now as I struggled to uncork the Tequila bottle so I could pour it down the drain. *This will show him.* But, as soon I opened the bottle, a liquid gold shot up to the ceiling, followed by a fiery-azure beam blasting into my face, nearly blinding me. The hairs on my arms stood at attention. Eyes blinking and burning, I managed to pour out the rest and watch it dribble down the drain. And then just as quickly, a bright blue light shot geyser-like up and out of the sink to the ceiling.

It wouldn't go away. Jumping back, I smashed my hip into the stove. "What the hell?" I screamed out loud, rubbing my eyes to make sure I wasn't just seeing things or that my mind wasn't playing tricks on me, but then the liquid splashed me again and the smell of Tequila permeated my skin. *This might be real.* I grabbed the cork to cap the bottle as the flame turned from red to blue to green, to yellow then red again, finally losing its power. As it slithered down the drain, I tiptoed toward the sink, giggling nervously. *This isn't real.* I reached for the spigot and blasted the sink with water before pumping some soap into my hands and rubbing them together furiously. *I'm hallucinating; I haven't slept in days.*

After a few moments, I managed to calm down. *I'm okay. I'm okay. The blue genie isn't real. Tú y tu imaginación,* I could imagine Mamá saying. But this time my mind had not been idle.

I stood in the kitchen, heart still hammering, looking around. The blue apparition was finally absent. Even though it wouldn't go away permanently, I would continue to deny its existence. Grabbing the beer, I took a seat at the kitchen counter, keeping an eye on the Tequila bottle. Zane was gone, too, but Pepita nudged me now to let me know I wasn't alone. My illness, my one constant and loyal companion.

Together with the stress of trial and the knowledge that Zane had disappeared once again, I wasn't sure of anything anymore. Indeed, it was during a moment of uncertainty and weakness, after Zane had come over one day to find me in the fetal position, that I'd even considered letting him move in. But it had been nice knowing someone had my back—and my stomach. And then later when he proposed, my gut had only sent up one more small burning red flag. I might have confused that with passion. But the initial heat of passion had died before reaching any thermal equilibrium. There seemed to be nothing left to keep our roots entwined.

I brought the beer bottle to my lips and took a sip, closing my eyes as the beer fizzled on my tongue, oozing toward the back of my throat. And then when it reached down to where it bubbled in my belly, a memory started to brew. Slowly a vision played out on the backside of my eyelids— the one where I'd been fishing with Papá when I was a little girl.

I'd caught a fish, no bigger than a minnow. He'd laughed, but then he got angry—roaring mad, the fiery blue flames like an aura surrounding him. I remembered running across the dusty maroon soil through the fields of blue agave, my cheek stinging, and a rash burning the insides of my thighs from the pee running down my legs.

Now, at the kitchen counter, I reached into my pocket for a cigarette, but instead pulled out Lily's postcard. Staring at the photo, *how could a place filled with so much pain be so pretty?* I pulled the cigarette from my pocket and when I clicked the igniter, a blue flame darted out of the lighter and I panicked but then chuckled as if having a psychotic episode was something to laugh about. *I have to get some sleep tonight.* In the meanwhile, I needed to find a way to put all of this out of my mind.

The phone rang and I gasped, nearly falling out of my chair, feeling both that Spidey-sense the mother of a teenager gets and that gut-wrenching pain you experience waiting up all night for your never-to-be husband. Exhaling, I picked up the phone, "Hello?"

"Hey, Mom."

Chapter Seven

My Lily

SHE SOUNDED GOOD. EVEN THOUGH LILY AND I had been butting heads lately, I was grateful to hear the sound of her sweet young voice—a soothing ointment for my chafed nerves. No matter the distance nor the obstacles, we had a sort of thermal equilibrium. No matter that she now studied in Mexico—another world—I'd always had a keen sense of where she was. Even when it wasn't in a good place, still we were always attached by an invisible thread of love.

"Hi sweetie. What's up?" I pressed a button to put the phone on speaker and then ran water into the sink again just to make sure the blue light couldn't make another appearance. I then proceeded to straighten up the kitchen, as if it needed straightening—obviously, no one had been home for a while. I folded a dishtowel.

"Why would something have to be up?" Lily asked. "You're the one that's acting strange, lately."

I chose to ignore the statement as I organized a spice rack, making sure the labels all faced forward. When I noticed that the cinnamon was lined up before the cayenne pepper, I switched the small containers.

"You're finally home. Let's Skype," Lily said and hung up.

I took a seat on a bar stool and before Lily could see my face on the screen, I stubbed out my cigarette in the ashtray she'd made for me in kindergarten. Poor kid was probably sorry she'd been such an enabler starting at a very young age. All the other kids had fashioned little animals out of clay or stamped their own tiny handprints. Fine example I'd been letting Lily see how much I smoked while reading through all of those boring books from law school.

Wild, curly hair like mine, except the color of butter crème, Lily's sweet luminescent face appeared on the screen. She also had my almond eye shape, but she had her father's liquid blue coloring, like a chip of sky. Lily was the love of my life. Before her, I was like a rudderless ship drifting through life without purpose. It was as if the gods had sent Lily as a moral and navigational compass, getting me back to my moorings. Once she was born, I made no decisions without considering my baby compass rose. Because of Lily, I'd ultimately made a decision to go to law school. Someone was going to have to support us after I divorced Elliot.

"So, how are you?" I asked, adjusting the screen on the computer.

"Well, I'm fine." Lily's voice had a joyful, tingly sound like a splash of dimes. "Except that I'm out of money."

"Lily, how the hell is that possible?" I asked, and then quickly sucked in my breath when I noticed a blue light pulsating inside the Tequila bottle on the counter behind the screen. My heart thumped, but I remained still, as if the light was a bear that would notice me if I moved.

"I'm going out to see the family again this weekend."

"The family?" And now I could really feel Pepita kicking up. "Again?" I asked, keeping my eyes on the bottle. I wondered what that meant. How had she connected with them?

"Yeah, and I could use some spending money. Finally gonna visit the infamous Tequila farm," Lily said with a lilt in her voice.

I fell silent just as the Tequila bottle flashed again like life had been breathed back into it.

"Mom, are you there?"

I nodded. "They're charging admission?" And then quickly, as if the life had gone out of it, the bottle stopped flashing.

"Funny," Lily said.

I blinked. "What?" Hand shaking, as discreetly as I could, I reached for the bottle and then dumped it into the trash under the sink and slammed the door.

"Never mind," Lily said, changing the subject, "So how are you feeling lately, Mom?" She sounded suspicious, almost as if she knew I didn't just have ulcers.

"I'm tired, of course. You know I was in trial this week, stayed at the Otani," I said, my foot sliding a chair in front of the cabinet under the sink.

"Yeah, I know. I called the house and Zane told me."

Pepita kicked me in the stomach when I heard his name. "I had my cell phone with me. You could have called me."

"You know I don't like to bother you at work," Lily said. "So, how's he doing?"

I could sense something even more caustic than usual in her voice. "Who Zane? Fine," I answered quickly, suspecting that she was trying to put the focus back onto him. It was no secret she didn't approve of the relationship. She'd told me time and again, that I could do better; that I deserved better. I wasn't so sure.

"He's probably working late," I said.

"So, he got a gig?"

"Lily, I don't know. Anyway, we settled, and I'm exhausted."

"You know, Mom, you really need to slow down. Come down to Mexico for a while."

Yeah, that's never going to happen. Who are you, my doctor all of a sudden? "This is my home, besides somebody's got to pay for college and those trips abroad."

"But this place is cheap."

"And that's why you're out of money again? Anyway, your college ain't cheap. And you will finish what you started, sooner or later."

Mustering a stern face, I peered through the screen so she could see I was dead serious.

"Yeah, yeah." Lily turned away in profile. It had always been hard for me to get mad at such a cute turned-up nose, but I'd had to learn to turn her down while practicing tough love.

More silence filled the space. I could play the game, too, and looked down from the screen to stare at my nails, in desperate need of a manicure.

We were both good at the quiet game, but since Lily was a little girl in preschool, her silence had been a concern. More than just a passive aggressive trick she'd learned early on, there was the fear she might suffer from ADHD and there was medication for that. But I'd refused to believe there was a problem, and there would be absolutely no medicating my daughter. For the most part, Lily, a curious child, always asked questions, to the point of annoyance. She liked doing things her way and her playmates adored her when they could keep up. Lily flitted around the schoolyard like a little hummingbird from one spot to the other, taking charge and organizing games. After testing, it was determined that Lily had a very high IQ, and she was put into a gifted program. But that didn't seem to make the problems go away. I recalled one of many times being called to the school because again Lily wasn't turning in her homework assignments. How could that be? I sat with her—practically on top of her—in the evenings and watched her do it. But there stuffed in Lily's school desk were weeks of homework papers not turned in. "But don't you ask them to turn the work in?" I'd asked the teacher. "Every morning, the children are to turn in their work without being told," the teacher replied, pointing to the homework tray on the counter. "It teaches them responsibility."

Responsibility? Beside myself, except for the fact that I'd never let Lily work and except for the most recent incident with her high school teacher, Lily was the most responsible kid I'd ever known. Perhaps, that wasn't such a good thing, I thought now. With responsibility came a great burden and a lot of stress. Or, perhaps, she wasn't burdened, at all. Her off the charts IQ also meant she was adept at manipulation, able to get away with a lot without putting much of an effort into anything. All she had to do was nothing—stop talking—remain silent and people would jump through hoops for her. Maybe it had been a mistake for me to always pick up the pieces for her.

She finally broke the ice. "So, I sent you a link for some stuff online at Urban Outfitters."

"I'll take a look in the morning. Right now, I can barely even keep my eyes open. Let me call you back tomorrow sometime, all right, sweetie? I love you."

"Okay." Lily's voice trailed off like a crimson-colored ribbon.

I hung up and reached over to pluck my cigarette out of the ashtray. I noticed all of the butts, like mummies piled inside Lily's piece of art. Had I already smoked that many since I got home? I picked up the ashtray, running my fingers along the sides of her creation. Had I shaped my daughter right? How was she possibly going to make it in this world? Had I been too overprotective? I'd only tried to give her everything that I hadn't grown up with; to be a better mother than the one I had; to make up for the fact that she didn't have a father. Hell, I didn't really know my own father, but you didn't see me running off with some older man, a married high school teacher, to boot. I grabbed the butt, relit it and then blasted the room with smoke. My stomach constricted when I thought of her teacher, Mr. Lloyd Parker.

Lily had barely turned seventeen when the news hit me.

"But he's getting a divorce. She's such a bitch," Lily had exclaimed. "And then he's marrying me."

I'd wanted to kill the man, and if the police hadn't arrived after I'd gone to pay him a visit, I just might have. And then I'd be stuck behind bars and Lily would become a ward of the court, or worse, an orphan should something horrible happen to me during my incarceration.

"You're just jealous," Lily had cried when I wouldn't let her out of the house anymore.

Jealous? That stung, but I knew not to take the remark personally. I hadn't been in a serious relationship since my divorce from her father. That was a choice I'd made. And I'd made it to protect her. If a little girl wasn't safe with her own father, then surely it could be worse with a stranger. Only after Lily had moved away had I allowed Zane to come into the picture.

"Mom, you're not being fair."

"The fair's in Pomona," I'd replied with a laugh.

In the end, Lily agreed that it would be best to lay low until the trial and until the news of the statutory rape had died down. That's when I suggested Lily consider studying abroad. Seniors had been given the option of either traveling to Spain, Ecuador, or Mexico. Much to my dismay, she'd chosen Mexico. But Mexico was a big country and what were the chances Lily would run into any family? Besides, at least she'd be closer to California.

Really feeling guilty now, I decided to check out Lily's email for Urban Outfitters to see what she needed—wanted. *Oh, what the hell?*

Cigarette clenched between my teeth, I carried my beer into my home office and then turned on the desktop. Drum-rolling my fingers on the desk, I startled myself looking at my reflection. My hair, like a rat's nest, I was too young to be sporting these skunk-like roots. I looked like a creature from *Day of the Dead* or *Zombieland,* gaunt, ashen with body bags under my eyes. Finally, the screen lit up. I tapped in my username and password and then scrolled through my email, choosing to ignore the message from my doctor—I couldn't stomach any more bad news. I set down my cigarette and took a swig of beer, continuing to scroll down and when I saw the alert flashing from my bank. *Fuck!* A shot of beer blasted out of my mouth, spraying all over the monitor. Neurons sparked throughout my body, sweat poured out of my armpits. I tried to steady my shaky fingers as I clicked on to check my account. *Shit!* Not only was I overdrawn, but there'd also been a huge withdrawal from my savings. Lily could be mischievous, but I knew she wouldn't have done this. I bit my cigarette in half, knocking my beer over onto the keys. "What the hell, Zane!" This wasn't the first time he'd taken money—why couldn't he just admit he stole it? But this was the first time he'd practically wiped out my entire bank account, leaving me barely enough of my hard-earned dollars to buy a cup of Starbucks much less some gas money to get to work. How had he gained access? I reached for the phone to call my bank, but then I hung up.

Thursday night at ten-twenty-one, I paced the room, scratching my head, searching for answers. Unless I filed a fraud report, there was nothing more I could do about my bank situation, and even less I could do about Zane. I needed time to figure this all out. I needed sleep. Maybe, it wasn't him? In the morning, I'd have answers. In the meanwhile, I hoped I was wrong about Zane.

The moon illuminated the room as I walked to the window to look out. Sunsets and full moons had been our thing, but it had been ages since Zane and I had been together to witness either one. Oh, what was I still doing with him? As much as I feared being by myself, I knew I'd be better off alone. Heck I was already lonelier than a left-handed glove. I brought my hands together and thought about praying, but to whom, to what, to the moon?

Sharp pains stabbed the inside of my stomach as if I'd chewed and swallowed glass for dinner. Doubled over, I gritted my teeth, balling my fists as I did my Lamaze-style breathing in and out slowly, waiting for the aching to pass. As I waited, I squeezed my eyes closed, trying to think only good thoughts about Zane, but it was like sucking on candy when you had a cavity.

I came away from the window, barely making it to my nightstand. I opened the drawer and popped a couple more antacids, chasing them down with a glass of water. I also took a sleeping pill. It had been a long, grueling week; I needed to sleep. Right now, I couldn't deal, besides and unfortunately, all of my problems would still be there in the morning waiting for me like a wide-eyed, bushytailed mongrel.

Two in the morning and I'd been tossing and turning like flotsam on an ocean of fire. Outside the window, the moon sat higher. Inside, the pit of my stomach burned like the inside of a volcano, my mind spun like an untethered satellite. I could feel the hot dampness of the sheets beneath my back, the sweat trickling down into my ears and onto my pillow. And then as I felt another wave of pain and sorrow rising, I heard the sound of glass breaking in the kitchen. And then a blast.

Huddled up flush against my headboard, eyes wide open, I screamed when I saw my bedroom door silhouetted by light. The cloying stench of Tequila made its way across the threshold first. Petrified, I watched as the fiery blue mist seeped in, filling the room like a swimming pool with sparkling azure light. I held my breath, preparing to go under, squeezing my eyes shut. I then reached over to my nightstand and felt for the bottle of antacids—and my sleeping pills. I popped some into my mouth and then pulled the covers over my head.

The last thing I remembered after flipping over was the white orb slipping into the ocean, its reflection a blanket on the surface, and the sense that I'd never again share the moon with Zane. I'd fallen asleep deep down on the ocean floor like a drowned child of La Llorona, so far away from the surface of life. And then in a dream world, I bobbed on water as if I were a little sailboat. Drifting farther away from land, a foghorn sounded. I took on water as the shrill ringtone from the phone startled me awake.

"Hello," I answered, sounding like a croaking frog.

"Maya?" He sounded like a hoarse toad.

"Oh my God." So relieved to hear his voice, for a moment I'd almost forgotten just how much hell he'd put me through, even in my dreams. "Zane? Are you—are you okay?"

"Please come get me."

Chapter Eight

Zane

ONLY ONCE HAD I EVER BAILED A CLIENT OUT of the Twin Towers Correctional Facility of the Los Angeles County Jail. And, in Santa Ana, when I was just a girl, I'd accompanied my mother to spring my father out of jail after an arrest for a DUI. But I'd never been to the Reseda police station to bail anyone out.

While seated in the Reseda police station lobby waiting, I picked at a petrified piece of gum stuck to the underside of the carved-up bench. Better to pick at the gum than my face or my eyebrows that were already thin and splotchy as skid marks. When this was all over, I'd treat myself to a facial and a massage—maybe even get my eyebrows tattooed back on. Already five in the morning and I'd been here since four. My whole body felt achy and bruised as if I'd gone nine rounds in a boxing match, and I was either going down for the count or I'd throw in the towel. My eyes burned trying to focus on a couple of officers who were joking around behind the counter.

"You're bad. I might have to arrest you," the young female officer said as she slapped the young male officer lightly on the shoulder.

"And I might have to report you for touching me inappropriately," the male officer responded with a mischievous grin and a gleam in his eye.

Was this a police station or the freakin' front desk at the YMCA? I wondered, rubbing my scratchy eyes. I couldn't believe I was here.

Finally, just before six a.m., Zane was escorted down the hall by a young Hispanic officer who was dwarfed by him. I swallowed, feeling my throat constrict as my pulse raced. Every nerve in my body prickled when I saw him. At six foot-four, he'd always been lanky, but now he looked skeletal. I'd

42

always envied his ability to eat and drink anything he wanted and still remain thin as a coat hanger. He'd order a double cheeseburger and cheesy fries while I ordered a salad with vinegar and oil on the side. Any weight he ever lost would find its way onto my gut, except for lately. Now his clothes hung like laundry flapping on a clothesline. His ashen hollow cheeks looked as if he sucked them in like I'd seen him do when he passed a window or a mirror. In just the week since I'd seen him last, his hair seemed like it had more salt than pepper. I stared at his wide, red-rimmed brown eyes—drug eyes—and wanted to cry but wouldn't give him the satisfaction. Satisfaction wasn't even the right word for it implied some sort of approval or contentment, and at that moment I couldn't look at him anymore.

Zane trailed behind me out the smudged twin double glass doors and into the parking lot where all at once a series of flashes detonated, as if we were at some Hollywood movie premiere or the frontlines of a battlefield.

"Zane, Zane. Is it true . . . ?" some chubby, shorthaired reporter asked.

This was a new low for TMZ. They must have been desperate for news if they were stalking Zane.

I pushed through the small group and ran for my car as Zane pulled his sweater over his head and dodged behind.

"I'm so sorry, Maya," he said as we pulled onto Reseda.

"Please shut the fuck up."

"You don't deserve this. I know you're going to leave me."

I gripped the wheel with both hands and stared into the rising sun. "God damn it, Zane! Isn't that what you want?"

"They wanted me to do a commercial for erectile dysfunction. That's what my career has come to. Just an old dysfunctional male."

"Oh for God's sake," I said, "I feel for you, Zane."

"There's that sarcasm. All you feel is pity. If only you'd—"

Pounding on the steering wheel, I slammed on the brakes. Zane's body snapped forward and, had he not been wearing the seatbelt, his head would have hit the dashboard. Had there been traffic, my brand new 740i would have been smashed down to the size of a 340i.

I turned, glaring at him. "Oh my god! What do you want me to say? If only I'd what? What do you want from me? God damn it! How dare you! Like I called your agent and told him to give you some more of those ringing-in-the-ear, shaky leg, gotta go, can't get-it-up AARP commercials!"

Zane sat in his seat looking like a bad dog getting punished for chewing on the leather sofa and then pissing on the Oriental rug. The truth was I did feel for him—too much. I'd let myself become only a minor gear around the cog of Zane. I let go of the wheel and clutched my stomach, on fire, sweat pouring from my forehead.

"Maya are you alright?" he asked. "Please don't die on me."

I felt the sparks fly out of my gritty eyes as I glowered at him, so helpless, so hopeless, so selfish. When we'd first learned I was sick, he'd been so attentive, so fixated on getting me better. I'd loved the attention—almost surrendering to him—but it didn't last. Zane lacked sustainability. I almost wished I'd die right here and now just to punish him.

I pulled myself together and burned rubber out onto the road.

As hard as I tried, I couldn't scrub my life away. I turned the shower up the hottest it could go until it felt as if my heart and soul were being burned away. *Let go, let God. Live and let live . . . God just grant me some freakin' serenity already.*

The remnants of my spirit slowly slipped and swirled down the drain. I got dressed, left Zane passed out in the guest room and then headed downtown.

MY SECRETARY Betsy, mid-forties in need of a root touch-up and more than five hours of sleep per night (addicted to QVC, I knew Betsy also spent a lot of time at work buying stuff online, but I let it slide), walked into the office around nine in the morning. Betsy had been like the mother I'd always wanted—concerned and caring with a sparkle in her smile to match the latest gems that glittered off her fingers when she hit the keyboard.

Betsy cleared her throat. "Good morning, Maya."

I lifted my chin to see her shocked face.

"Oh my God," she said, setting down my cup of coffee. "You don't look good. Why are you even here?"

"Beats me, Betsy. I don't know anything anymore." Overcome with a flurry of emotion, I felt like crying, but held it together. *Never let them see you cry.* I pinched my nose with my fingers.

Betsy peered even closer. "What happened to your eyebrows?"

I reached up to feel something missing and then reached into my purse for a mirror. "Oh shit. I didn't realize—"

"You should go home, Maya," Betsy said, wrapping a soft, saggy arm around my shoulders. "The trial is over. I can handle any paperwork."

"Thanks Betsy, but the new trial starts on Monday and—"

"And it won't do anybody any good if you're sick. Go home. Get some sleep. You look like hell."

"Thank you, Betsy. You do say the nicest things. Thanks for the coffee."

IN THE REARVIEW MIRROR, I checked out my eyebrows again. *For God's sake, this has got to be the final straw.* I reached up to touch what was missing. Before the disease had come a knockin', my identity had become rooted in my career. A career meant money. Money meant security. At some point after Lily went off to school, my job had completely taken over. I'd allowed it. Poor Zane, he never really had a chance. And then slowly, I started forgetting why I was doing anything, detaching myself from life. Most days, I woke up lethargic and drained, without the energy to even get up. I'd spend those mornings, deaf to the morning birds chirping, staring blindly out the window, and contemplating life. *Who am I? How did I get here? What was it I wanted?* I'd started thinking maybe being an attorney wasn't all it's cracked up to be. Maybe I had it all wrong. I was still young. I could let go of my ambitions and go into sales or teaching. And then I'd beat myself up for not appreciating what I had. And now with the disease, all I wanted was to be healthy. I wanted a stress-free life. I wanted my eyebrows back.

I got home where thank God, all was quiet. I tiptoed past the guestroom where Zane was still asleep—or so I thought—and went straight to bed.

Around seven that evening, I heard the television blaring. Maybe Zane could also use a hearing aid. I padded out of our bedroom. Still groggy when I entered the den, my eyes widening when I saw a bottle of Tequila on the coffee table. *Keep it together. Asshole isn't even trying to hide it.* I wouldn't allow myself to react. But then when I saw the white powder on the coffee table and—*are you freakin' kidding me?* Reclined on the sofa, high as the moon, he was wearing my little black dress, and a vacant stare. An invisible hand wrenched my gut until I could barely squeeze out a breath.

"What's going on?" I managed to yell, words spilling out all over the coffee table.

Startled, he turned toward me, smiling as if he had nothing to lose. "No more secrets, Maya."

Secrets? Scared shitless, I dropped to my knees to clean up the mess on the coffee table. Like this was normal. Like the time when I was little and dripped grape jelly, I'd torn a hole in the flimsy rug from scrubbing so much. I'd been able to drown out my parents' yelling, but there was no covering the hole.

"So, what—you've gone all RuPaul on me?"

"Now, that's funny," Zane said with a chuckle. "You're the one that should be in the business."

"Even Lily asks permission before she goes into my closet."

He laughed, but as he looked past my shoulder, his pupils dilated to the size of quarters. I turned and wheezed when I saw his mug shot on the big screen.

The chubby shorthaired Hollywood television reporter spoke into a mic and in the background, you could see Zane and me rushing out of the Reseda Police Station to the car.

"Nineties heart throb, and award-winning actor Zane Crowe was arrested this morning for sideswiping a parked vehicle," the reporter said, ". . . for driving under the influence, and possession of marijuana. When police searched the vehicle . . ."

The room spun. I reached out to hold onto the table. I looked away from the television and panned the room toward the hearth where the fire hadn't burned for ages. I looked for a focal point and, on the mantle sat the unfinished seascape Zane had started (never could complete a task) and a gold-framed picture of an exuberant Zane with his Golden Globe Award. I stood next to him in the picture, smiling ear-to-ear in the little black dress that he now stretched to the limit. *Oh the irony.*

My patience had also reached its limit and with the strength of Wonder Woman, I flipped over the coffee table. Roaring, I frightened Zane, looking at me like a naughty puppy, and myself. He backed away, his eyebrows raised as I walked toward him and then reached out to tear my dress from him. I then hauled off and slugged him in the stomach.

I didn't know who I was anymore or what kind of character I'd become in this crazy, sick drama. Standing in the middle of the room shaking, I held up my hand, gazing at it as if I'd grown a third one. I'd turned into a monster. Our story was over.

Hours later, Lily would call to tell me Papá had died. I'd need to return to Mexico immediately to claim his body.

Chapter Nine

Dolores

IMAGES OF ZANE DANCED IN front of me as I waited to board the plane just before daybreak. I wanted to either scratch out my eyes or dump my cup of coffee all over the nightmare. Prior to booking my flight, I did file a fraud claim with my bank but the investigation would take a few months to resolve, so pending a bank reversal of my stolen funds, I would continue to use my credit cards for purchases such as Starbucks. And then, there was the news about my father. I could have kicked myself now for taking on this responsibility of traveling back to Mexico to identify his body. What was worse, I couldn't put the call off to Mamá any longer. I set down my coffee and punched in her number.

A minute would be all I needed, but I'd waited for the right one; an instant before Mamá could start with the chisme about her *Guadalupana* church friends or pressing questions as to why I'd divorced and left the Catholic Church and was raising Lily without God and how God would never forgive me for living in sin. Yes, I'd waited until the last second to call her. Besides, there'd been no need to wake her any earlier. My mother had never cared for the man, anyway, and she made sure I knew it. Finally, Mamá picked up the phone.

"Mamá, I'm calling about Papá."

"You mean that no good borracho. I'll never forgive him for—"

I held the phone out as if my ear were on fire. It hadn't taken long this time for my blood to start to boil. I'd learned to just let Saint Dolores go on until she ran out of transgressions to complain about. This could take a while. I knew Mamá would get angry when Papá drank and they would fight when I was little, but that was a long time ago and she wasn't letting go. I tried to remember those moments when he wasn't drunk. Sadly, of the two malcontents, he'd been the fun parent.

Growing up Papá would call from Mexico ever so often, apologizing, begging Mamá to let him come back, to let him see his children. She'd refuse, slamming down the receiver. I felt worse for my little brother Rudy who would cry and beg—face red and wet. "Please, Mamá, let him come home," he bawled, swiping his runny nose with the back of his pajama sleeve. Ironically, Mamá not only alienated Papá from Rudy, but her refusal also led to my brother becoming alienated from her, too. A couple of times Papá had even made the trip north only to be turned away. Once, Mamá had even called the cops. I never could understand why they fought so much. It was one thing when he was drunk—which I learned later was the craziest time to try and reason with an inebriated person—but then when he actually acted normal (for him), Mamá would lay into him, reminding him of what he'd said or done while drunk. If only Mamá hadn't made him drink so much, I used to think. But now, I knew better. No one could make anyone drink.

I stared at the phone in my hand. I could still hear Mamá talking. "Maya, you know I've been thinking—"

"Mamá, stop. Listen to me. Papá is dead," I yelled over her into the phone, embarrassed now when I noticed a couple of travelers staring at me.

Silence. My tongue had frozen.

"God rest his soul. I can have some peace at last," Mamá said, and I instantly recalled my puppy she'd had gotten rid of because it ruined her peace. I'd come home from school to learn that Suzy was gone and wouldn't be coming back.

Peace? They'd been separated for over twenty years, but even if it wasn't part of the Ten Commandments, as the good Catholic that Mamá tried to be, she wouldn't get divorced.

"I don't suppose you'd want to fly down and offer an olive branch to the family so we can take care of things," I asked, knowing Mamá to be nothing like the peace-loving dove we'd heard about in all those sad Mexican songs when I was little. The paloma that cried *coo coo roo coo coo*. No, Mamá was more like the ferocious jaguar lurking along the perimeters waiting to pounce on her prey. *Roarrrrr!*

"I can't," Mamá said.

"That's what I thought."

Earlier, when I'd booked the flight to Guadalajara, I'd only purchased one ticket for one passenger—and near the toilet. I knew Mamá wouldn't want to travel back to Mexico. And asking Rudy was even more remote a possibility. He wanted nothing to do with either parent. Though I'd still given him the courtesy of letting him know Papá had died.

"But I promised I'd never go back. When—"

"Never mind. I'm at the airport now waiting to board."

"Ay dios mío, Maya, there's no way—"

"I know. I know. I'll talk to you later."

And then Mamá had gotten in the last word, again. "Besides, you're the smart attorney now. Make yourself useful."

I HADN'T BEEN BACK since childhood and as the jetliner soared into the heavens, I got sucked back into my seat. Through a slight marine layer, barely out over the dark navy Pacific, the plane veered left, hugging the California coast. I looked out my window straight into the rising sun, directly into a blinding past I was not prepared to deal with, but then who's ever prepared for death? So angry I had to be the one making the trip, I gripped the arms as the plane hit an air pocket and braced for more bumps to come. Only in an airplane could I turn over control. I had no choice.

Looking out the small window, a sadness overwhelmed me like the fog shrouding the marina below. And then I felt something black wrapping its tendons around my chest, squeezing my ribs together like they might crack. I panicked, pulling my jacket tighter, staring out the window to look for comfort in the clouds that weren't there. I squirmed in my seat and told myself that if only I could befriend the dark snake coiled around me, I might be okay. *Melancholy, I do feel you, now please let go of the grip around my heart.* Soon it stopped hissing in my ear and by time the jet flew over Long Beach, Melancholy had slithered away. I closed my eyes. The roar of the engines was almost better than the sleeping and anti-anxiety pills, drowning out the chatter in my head, lulling me into letting go of my apprehension, one finger at a time.

And then I felt a small, warm hand slide into mine and I was flying through the agave field, my red-ribboned braids flapping in the wind like a couple of kite tails. I turned to look into the face of the little boy beside me, my ten-year-old cousin Gabriel. He opened his mouth, and I could hear a horn honk and then Mamá's voice. "Maya, get in!" I wiped the fog from the inside of the window and saw Gabriel, a puzzled look on his face, standing on the side of the road. A smile trembled on my lips as I waved goodbye. "But for how long?" "We're not coming back," Mamá said.

Still in the middle of the dream, I woke up heart sore to the sound of the flight attendant over the speakers announcing our arrival into Miguel Hidalgo Airport. Funny, I thought, wiping the drool from my chin, I was sure there could be no relation, but still found it interesting that I shared the same name as the man the airport was named after. Now, if Papá had told me stories about being related to Don Miguel Hidalgo, "the father of Mexican independence" instead of Pancho Villa, "the Mexican revolutionary and guerilla leader," I might have wanted to believe him.

As the plane taxied, I swiped the inside of the fogged-up airplane window, trying to piece together the torn images of my dream, hoping perhaps to get a different outcome. Instead, I recalled the trip north many years ago from Sagrada Familia in the family's yellow Ford Falcon—sadly, not a dream, but a reality. Seated next to me had been my little brother, tears streaming down his face. I remembered rolling down the window and seeing an older boy standing next to my cousin—Antonio, my silly little girl crush. My heart hurt now as I reminisced. The car had pulled away, both boys growing smaller and smaller. I knew it would be forever. My eyes stung as the car filled with the familiar earthy, sweaty smell like the farmers from the field. I rubbed my eyes with the back of my hand and then turned to see the back of a man's head in the front passenger seat. But when the man took off his hat, it wasn't Papá. Mamá sped away. Papá wasn't with us and Mamá wasn't looking back.

I wiped my eyes before getting up out of my seat to grab my bags from the overhead bin. Smoothing the wrinkles out of my linen skirt—a futile effort—I put on my suit jacket before stepping onto the tarmac, instantly blindsided by the sun. Slipping on my sunglasses, I then followed the other passengers to claim my baggage.

Chapter Ten

Guadalajara! Guadalajara!

A LONELY SUITCASE ROTATED ON THE CONVEYER belt at least half an hour more as I waited for Lily. I looked down at my own two pieces of Louis Vuitton luggage, including the carry-on—*not very efficient*. From the moment I'd gotten home from trial, I'd never unpacked. Instead, I'd hastily filled a new suitcase with clean underwear and Lord only knew what else. I hadn't been thinking straight.

Cradling my elbow, cigarette in hand—dealing with death always calls for a smoke—I paced the floor in front of my luggage. Lily was probably still paying me back for all the times I'd kept her waiting after school, at a friend's house, the babysitter's, or daycare. Hey, but I'd been a single mom; I had to work. What choice did I have if we were to survive—if Lily was to have a decent life? Lily clung to her resentments like she was hanging onto a baby blanket, blaming others for her misery. Just like Mamá who would never forgive me for supposedly ruining her life when I got pregnant out of wedlock and then got a divorce. How would she ever be able to hold her head up at church? Why couldn't she just let go? Of course, it wasn't that easy. I knew that all too well. I also knew about blame. I could fill up a whole legal pad on the subject starting with my own name at the top of the list and because I understood so well, I took on the hurts and pain of my own daughter.

But sometimes my efforts weren't appreciated. I promised myself I'd try harder not to let Lily get to me. It would be tough, nothing I couldn't handle though. But like a teetering Humpty Dumpty, I was just about ready to crack. I took a drag, checking my watch again and then like most attentive mothers, I recognized the sound of my own child's distinctive cry.

"Mom!"

I exhaled quickly, hoping Lily hadn't noticed, and stubbed my cigarette out in a nearby ashtray.

Lily, in a colorful Mexican Baja hoodie and distressed jeans, waved as she walked toward me. Arms open wide, I reached out to embrace her, but she headed straight for my luggage.

Ouch! It felt like her hand had reached down my throat to squeeze my heart, but I wouldn't take it personally. Instead, I picked up my bag, straightened my shoulders and headed toward the exit where I noticed a Starbucks. "Oh my God. I'm going to survive this place, after all."

"Mom," Lily said, tugging on my bag. "You could probably feed a whole village in Oaxaca or buy a new pair of Jimmy Choo's with what you spend on that stuff."

"Not to mention Urban Outfitters."

"Touché," Lily said, letting go of the bag.

"Oh well, maybe while I'm here I can give up some bad habits." I rooted around in my jacket pocket, relieved when I felt the hidden pack of Marlboros. "Starting tomorrow," I said, heading toward the coffee shop. "But right now, I need a good cup of Joe."

Lily heaved a loud sigh, but not as loud as she would when she learned the truth. I knew it was finally time—I had to tell Lily the truth about my diagnosis.

In the distance loomed the metropolis of Guadalajara. The cab cruised along the highway passing large billboards advertising Coca-Cola and Fanta and the *Chivas* Soccer Team. Next to old, dilapidated shacks with corrugated steel sidings, I noticed bloated horses grazing on the side of the road.

"I see they haven't changed their zoning laws since the last time I was here."

Lily rolled her eyes.

Be careful or your eyes might get stuck I wanted to say, like I used to except that the smell of petrol, smog and garbage filled the cab, making me nauseous. I rolled up the window and before long, we'd entered the city of Guadalajara where more modern buildings were juxtaposed next to ancient architecture, including the Catholic Basilica with its mishmash of Gothic, Moorish, baroque, and neoclassical styles. I remembered visiting the church as a girl and looking up at the cathedral's spiral towers that seemed to puncture the clouds in the sky above the sprawling metropolis like fingers poking into the heavens. I envisioned my young self, stretching my arms to the sky.

By the time we pulled into the bus station, dizzy and soaking with sweat, I was ready to get out of the stuffy taxi.

And then, entering the bus depot, except for the 'No Smoking' sign, it felt as if I'd just stepped into sacred territory. Dozens of candles burned on a flower-covered altar as heavenly clay angels hovered over the Virgin Mary. A rush of emotion surged through me. Even though it was only a bus stop, it felt like I'd just stepped into church. I reached up to touch the little gold angel I'd pinned to my lapel.

Lily peered at me. "I see you got the pin."

"I found it in the mail," I responded a little disappointed. "I thought it was a sign."

"A sign? I knew you liked angels. I pinned it to the postcard."

"That was so sweet, Lily." I chuckled to myself. *Now there's a sign.* I hoped someday Lily and I would have a better relationship. I missed the bond we'd shared when she was little and would leave me things—like our cat Scratchy who used to leave me tiny critters and her toys.

So far, we hadn't been able to get onto the right foot, but even though I only traveled here to make arrangements for my father, I was determined to make the best of this trip. I'd missed Lily so much. If only I could go back and make things right; back to the time she'd been my little angel; back to the time before everything had changed—the time before Lily had to leave town to save herself from the humiliation. From the moment she came into this world, I was in awe witnessing the wonder of my little girl blossoming a little each day. As her own personality bloomed, Lily quickly mastered words and began to articulate how she felt. Except for when she chose silence, she was never shy about speaking up and I never tried to stifle her, but now I wondered if I might have created a monster.

Just outside the bus, I grew a little embarrassed when I noticed my fellow passengers climbing on with their assortment of carriers; plastic mesh sacks, and paper bags wrapped in twine. You couldn't miss my two pieces of brown and gold-toned monogrammed designer luggage, including the matching carry-on.

"Hey Lily, get my picture in front of the altar."

"Mom, no. We don't want to look like tourists."

"And you think taking a picture is going to give us away?" I smiled at my blonde, blue-eyed daughter.

"Come on. I think it's funny," I said, eyeing a sign for the baño. "Hurry, I have to go. I'll bet there's an altar in there, too."

"Mom, it's for the travelers."

"So, I'll probably find a statue of St. Christopher in there," I said.

Lily narrowed her eyes. "Who?"

"The patron saint of travelers," I responded before disappearing into the bathroom. One good thing about going to parochial school is that you learn about all the saints—and the sinners. Poor Lily had missed out by going to public school; she'd have to learn the hard way.

In the bathroom, careful not to swallow any water, I splashed my face; more modern times or not, I couldn't take the chance. The last thing I needed was Montezuma's Revenge. I looked in the mirror, shocked to see the pale-looking person staring back at me. The whites of my eyes were pink and bags, heavier than my carry-on, hung under my lids. I reapplied my rum-raisin lipstick, pushed a loose strand of lusterless brown hair behind my ear, and walked out.

There were two empty seats together at the front of the bus. I scooted over to the window seat, leaving the aisle seat for Lily. Lining the dashboard of the bus stood another statue of the Virgin, a crucifix, a statue of St. Francis of Assisi and, one of St. Christopher, of course—enough saints to start a holy order.

Once outside the city, with my head resting on the seatback, I turned to watch the picturesque countryside go by. I recognized the crimson soil, the yellow and lavender jacaranda, the scrubby mesquite, and the puffy clouds like woolly lambs bouncing through sapphire skies. *I'll be fine, we'll be fine,* I told myself in time to the rhythm of the wheels, screeching in time with the tempo of my heart.

After a while, the passengers thinned out—apparently, no one had been traveling as far as we were. Lily snatched the empty seat across the aisle. We sat now what seemed like an ocean apart again and I was left alone to drown in my wounded thoughts. *I'll be fine, we'll be fine.*

Not that Zane hadn't been sloshing back and forth across my mind constantly, but when I noticed Lily texting, the urge to hear his voice again grew strong. I reached for my phone, but it was dead—probably, a good thing. I'd have to wait until I could charge it again.

Lily smiled as she set down her phone and then she turned to gaze wistfully out the window. I wanted to ask who it was she'd been texting, but unless I'd prepared myself for the look that could cut me down to the size of a two-year old, I wouldn't dare ask.

"Pretty landscape," I said.

Lily turned toward me, bobbing her head. "So, was there an altar in the bathroom?"

"A what?" I asked, and then smiled weakly. "No altar. Just a porcelain god."

"Mom, you're lame."

"Sadly, I already know that. No need to remind me."

"Just joking," Lily said, quickly bringing a hand to her mouth. She then ran her fingers through her hair and stretched her arms to the ceiling. "So has the news died down yet?"

I looked her in the eyes where a reflection of the landscape whirred past.

"News?" *He's not that famous. Oh my God. Did she already know about Zane?*

"I mean, is there anything about the trial yet or anything?" Lily asked.

"Oh, you mean—" I exhaled a sigh. She meant her teacher, Mr. Parker. "It's just all going to take time, sweetie. You should be fine."

"You know, at first, I didn't know he was married, but then—" Lily said, trailing off softly.

"How about that he was too old for you?" I responded, immediately sorry for the sarcasm. It didn't take a psychiatrist to know Lily had been looking for a father figure.

She puffed her lips out without looking up.

"At least no one knows you're here," I offered.

She glared at me and then checked her phone.

I wished I'd been able to share stuff with Lily about her father, but that wall had gone up years ago. She'd only been two-years old when I left Elliot. Family life came with grown-up responsibilities and at nineteen, who's prepared for parenthood? We were both so miserable, so young. But I'd been mature enough to know that someone needed to make some changes. I wouldn't wait around for my husband to leave me (it scared me to realize how much I was like Mamá), and even though I'd been the one to leave the marriage—the one to propose it, too—it was Elliot who'd thrown the baby out with the bath water. I'd carried the guilt around like a piece of beat-up luggage. *You think you know someone.* I'd believed that since he'd loved me as much as he said, he might have understood and simply let me go. *What was that saying? If you love something, let it go.*

After Elliot, I made sure never to bring a man around the house. Besides, I'd never found anyone worthy enough until Zane, but only after Lily had moved away had I allowed myself to fall under the spell of the smooth-talking actor. We'd had painting in common, after all. We connected on a spiritual level, too (or was that the pot talking?) and so, even though my stomach had sent up warnings in a myriad of flashing, vibrantly colored smoke signals, and only after Lily had gone, did I let him move in—another mistake and someone else to add to my long list of people, places, and things to blame. I was grateful now I'd spared Lily all of that drama.

God, I was dying for a smoke.

Chewing on a hangnail, my eyes trailed out the window as I cast my mind back to the morning Lily had come home unannounced.

"Why aren't you in school?" I'd asked.

She asked me to take a seat in the living room, a sparse place filled minimally with white furniture and lots of accent throw pillows and a painting of a calm seascape on the wall—a safe haven where no one was allowed to yell.

"Now, don't get all freaked out," she'd said, balling her fists as she stood rigid before me, as if bracing for the storm about to slam ashore. "I'm pregnant."

The wave broke hard, knocking the wind out of me. I felt a stabbing pain just below my rib cage. Between a gulp and a gasp, I tried to swallow. I wanted to spring from my seat and strangle her. But, behind Lily's mask of bravery, I caught a glimpse of fear in her eyes. All at once, she looked so vulnerable, so tiny, so David-like against her Goliath of a mother.

I couldn't help but recall the moment Mamá learned I was pregnant. How I wished I could have gone to my mother to be consoled. But instead, to save her from the shame, I'd eloped with Elliot. And then when I learned I was having twins, I really wanted my mother, and reached out to her. She seemed surprisingly supportive, until the day after the deliveries. Baby Michael died and the only words of comfort from Mamá were that it was God's will to take the boy—punishment for a life of sin—and thank God he'd spared Lily. At that moment, although I wanted my mother, I regretted ever calling her. In my moment of despair, her words pierced deeply, imprinting themselves, never to be forgotten. "And I guess you just couldn't keep your legs closed," Mamá would say later—a nail in the coffin. "Siempre fuiste tan promiscuo."

You were always so promiscuous. I would always wonder what she'd meant by that. I wouldn't be like my mother. All I'd ever wanted was to protect Lily from the world, and now was not the time to let her down, to shame and humiliate her. Now was not the time to strangle her. I took Lily into my arms, feeling her muscles loosen up as I held my baby again.

After a few moments, she pulled away and I returned to my seat where I clutched the arms of the side chair listening to her spill the rest of the story.

"The father—" she stuttered. "Mr. Parker is the father."

I came unhinged. "Are you freakin' kidding me! Your social studies teacher?" I sprang from my seat and charged toward the phone. I couldn't help myself. "I'm going to kill the motherfucker!"

"No, Mom," Lily screamed. "You'll just make everything worse." She then ran down the hall to her bedroom and slammed the door.

I thought twice before dialing the phone but left the house, instead, and called the police from the car. They arrived at the high school shortly after I did, but not before I'd given Parker a black eye. When asked what had happened to his face, Parker—probably hoping this would just all go away—told the police he'd run into the door. But that didn't stop me from having him arrested. I'd taken him down for hurting my baby, my innocent angel. And, within the next few days, we'd learned that it was only a false pregnancy—a blighted ovum—but by then, the cat climbed out of the bag and then after months of depositions, discovery and other motions, the *State vs. Lloyd Parker* trial had been set for the following year. Throughout the discovery process, the stress had gotten to me. I'd wished I could be more like my daughter who seemed unfazed by it all, until one day when Lily drove herself home drunk off her ass.

"Mom, I can't stand people staring at me like I'm some sort of a slut," Lily cried, mascara bleeding down her face. She'd obviously been crying for some time. She smeared mucus across her cheek with the back of her hand. "I just act like nothing bothers me but honestly it hurts." She hiccupped. "I didn't ask for him to come on to me. He wouldn't leave me alone. I didn't know what to do. I didn't think it would go that far. I thought I could handle it."

Often smarter than her own teachers, or so she might have thought, Lily challenged everyone, always questioning the textbook answers or calling out a teacher for being inconsistent or unfair. Never a teacher's pet, she was certainly smart enough to know just the right things to say and do, if she wanted. I failed to understand how Lily could have fallen for such a stupid jerk.

THE BUS HIT A pothole and we bounced out of our seats. We looked at each other and laughed. It felt good.

It had been quite a while since I'd had communication with anyone from the remote village of Sagrada Familia, three hours outside the big city of Guadalajara where my family originated. What had prompted Lily to go there? As much as I'd wanted to protect my daughter, I knew I couldn't stop her.

Lily had grown up an only child. Maybe it hadn't been fair for me to keep her away from them. My cousin Angela often wrote to ask about me and Lily, and to send her love. I'd always kept my responses to Angela short and simple. And then I remembered when I was little, Angela had been like a big sister to me. She might be perfect for Lily, maybe give her some guidance where I'd failed. And now that Lily had reconnected with the family, I could do nothing about it. I had to accept that Lily was old enough to make her own choices.

"I guess sending you down here wasn't a bad idea after all," I said, clutching the seat in front of me.

"The jury is still out on that verdict as far as I'm concerned," Lily answered, her smile quickly dissipating.

"You gave me no choice, Lily. You were only seventeen."

"Like it's up to you? It's still my body."

My jaw dropped to say something, but instead I sucked in the stale bus air and turned away. I knew she just wanted to debate with me but in her heart, she knew I was right.

"Well, just so you know, the sentence sucks," she said, her grin returning.

"Yeah, sometimes life isn't fair," I said, swiping away the dampness forming in the corner of my eye. "I don't want to be here either to deal with my father's mess. He never really gave a flying fu . . ." I said. "Shit, I should stop cursing while I'm on this trip."

"Why the fuck would you do that?"

"So that it doesn't rub off."

"Too late. Fuckity fuck, fuck." Lily giggled.

She'd laughed twice now.

"Well, I hope you picked up some of my good qualities, at least."

She turned toward me now, smiling almost devilishly. "So, what's up with Zane?"

Kapow! The fireworks went off in my stomach. The girl knew how to fling zingers and hit below the belt. *That's no doubt something she picked up from me. She'll make a good lawyer. (Because flinging zingers is such a good tool in the courtroom, right?)*

"It's over," I answered.

"So no wedding, just a funeral."

I reached for my purse and rummaged around for the container of Tums. I popped one into my mouth and then chased it down with my lukewarm coffee before pulling out a pack of smokes but stopped when I noticed Lily's disapproving mug.

"So, I hope they have running water," I said. "You know, when I was little, there was no plumbing, no bathrooms, no electricity."

"What about cars?"

I peered at Lily. "We rode in on donkeys, smart ass. And we had to go to the bathroom out in the hen house barefoot up a mountain and through the snow. We used newspapers to wipe ourselves."

"Seriously? That's disgusting."

"Yeah, but everyone appeared to be happy back then."

"So then, why did you abandon your roots and never come back, Mom?"

Before I could protest, a sharp pain jabbed me in the stomach just as the bus pulled into a small-town stop.

"Baño?" I asked the driver and he pointed to the restroom. Pepita could no longer wait.

I darted over and handed a tiny, old wrinkly attendant some coins in exchange for a couple strips of toilet paper. I lined the toilet seat with paper and then tried to only hover. *Why had I abandoned my roots?* I wondered as my thighs burned from squatting. My roots were even more tangled than my insides. Since I was a baby, the constant migration of my family between Mexico and the United States had instilled in me the sense of always straddling the two countries, but never belonging to either culture. I'd had to make my own way in the world. And now, even with my wild imagination, I couldn't envision how coming back would make things any better.

Afterward, I felt better, but needed a smoke. The weathered attendant smiled at me as I lit up and suddenly, I felt guilty. I thought about Dr. Vaisman and how as soon as I could get a connection, I'd call her. I stubbed out my cigarette before boarding the bus and when I got to my seat, it tickled me to see Lily with her head buried in a book this time and not her phone.

Not surprising, since preschool, Lily had always been a voracious reader with tons of interests ranging from everything in between and including aardvarks and zebras; reading books like *Corduroy, Are You There God? It's Me Margaret,* and *Diary of a Wimpy Kid* and then later books by King, Kingsolver and Kafka.

"Whatcha reading?" I asked, noticing the pretzel-posed woman on the cover.

"For my class."

"I'm paying your tuition for you to take Yoga?"

"You should try it," Lily said, handing me the book as another pain punched me in the gut; this time doubling me over.

"Mom, are you okay? You don't look so good and you're way too skinny, by the way."

"Well—" I said, correcting her. "You don't look so *well*." I grimaced. "You know what they say about that," I said, reaching into my purse for a tissue to wipe my damp forehead. "You can never be too thin, or too rich." I forced a giggle. "I think Papá's death is really getting to me."

Lily cocked her head slightly and then shook it as she peered at me.

"What?" I asked, looking back.

"You just smeared off your eyebrows."

I reached in for my mirror to examine myself and laughed out loud. "Oh my God." I pulled out an eyebrow pencil.

"How's the new medicine working?" Lily asked with a wry look.

Caught off guard, pencil in the air. "Fine so far," I responded, continuing to fill in my brows.

Lily's voice lowered an octave. "You think I don't know about your condition?"

I put down the pencil, snapped the mirror shut and looked up at Lily. "What are you talking about?"

Locking eyes with me, she wouldn't let me escape. This time it wasn't like the game we'd played when she was little, and we'd wait to see who blinked first. Now, Lily shook her head. "You're freakin' unbelievable. You think I'm stupid? Not only do you need some rest, but you should also leave your face alone. And, for fuck's sake, quit smoking!"

Chapter Eleven

Agave Azul

AS THE SEA OF BLUE AGAVE CAME INTO VIEW—rising wiry and pointy as spearheads—it felt more like butterflies tickling the inside of my stomach. I sensed how much closer I'd come to the place I once called home. Beyond the religious articles on the dashboard, mountains of chopped agave heads sat stacked beneath an arched veranda on the side of the road. And then, as the bus slowed, I noticed a well-dressed man, maybe in his late thirties, placing flowers on a roadside shrine. He turned in our direction. Under his hat, I recognized the piercing blue-green eyes so similar to my own and the people of the region. And then nearby, I noticed a second shrine on the road.

"This place is still so religious," I said to the bus driver. "Two shrines? What's up with that?"

"It's the spot where their ghosts left their body. Bad accident. Too much Tequila. Familia pobre."

"Yes, poor family."

IT WAS ALMOST NOON when the bus rolled into the dusty little town of Sagrada Familia. I put on my wide-rimmed sunglasses and pulled a white floppy hat out of my bag—I'd packed it when I went to court, optimistically thinking I'd have a minute to relax by the hotel pool—and then took a seat on the bigger piece of Louis Vuitton.

"What? Are you trying to look like a movie star?" Lily said.

"Yeah, that's it. Joan Crawford in *Mommy Dearest*."

Lily rolled her eyes. "Leonardo should be here—"

A gust of wind blew my hat off my head, sending it sailing down the street. I could hear Lily bust out laughing as I got up to chase it.

"Geeze, Mom, just buy a new one, already."

"But—" I stopped and turned around just as Lily removed her hoodie. She wore a flower-patterned halter-top and when she pulled her blonde hair up into a ponytail, I could see a new tattoo inked across her shoulders.

"For goodness' sake, Lily. When did you get that one? What is it, anyway?"

"They're wings. Like on an angel," she said, slipping her shirt off her waggling shoulders. "It's not like a tramp stamp. Those are nasty."

"Yeah, the ones on the shoulder blades are so much classier. Any other surprises?"

"Hmm, let's see. I'm pregnant?"

"Lily, that's not even funny," I said, narrowing my eyes, my heart suddenly hammering. "You're not, right?"

She snorted, shaking her head, as a rust-colored station wagon approached. "Hey, wait 'til you get a load of Leonardo."

"Lily, he's your cousin. Put your jacket back on."

"Ten-times removed. Besides, everyone around here's a kissin' cousin, anyway."

My heart still pounding. *She's trying to kill me.* "Well, we're not the monarchy," I said as the sedan pulled up.

"And here's our pumpkin now."

A lofty young man, handsome as a Disney prince, stepped out of the car and hurried around the hood to greet us. He wore a starched white long-sleeved shirt tucked into his crease-pressed jeans. His turquoise-colored eyes were set deep in a kind face framed with caramel-colored hair.

Leonardo hugged Lily before reaching out to shake my hand. "Soy Leonardo," he said with a straight-toothed smile. "Mucho gusto."

"Soy Maya Miller."

"I know. I've heard all about you."

Like what? I wondered, and how long has Lily been visiting family?

"All good things," Leonardo added with a grin.

It had been more than thirty years since I'd been here, but my visit to see the rest of the family would have to wait until after I took care of business. "Leonardo, please take me to the morgue."

LATER IN THE CANTINA, AFTER MY VISIT TO THE MORGUE, the bartender held up the bottle of Tequila and offered me another shot. I put my hand over the glass to show him I was finished.

"So, after identifying Papá, I walked into this bar," I said, gathering my things. "That's my story for now. All she wrote. Thank you for listening."

"De nada," the bartender said.

I laughed. "It must have been the Tequila talking," I responded, numb to the shame—a little sin vergüenza.

"Que encuentres tu final feliz."

Happy endings are only in children's fairy tales. "Muchas gracias." I donned my sunglasses and exited the cantina.

OUT ON THE COBBLED street, one hand clutching my purse to my stomach, warm now from the Tequila, and the other holding my father's hat. Unsure which direction to go, I crossed to the other side where I stood in the strange day, staring back and forth between the cantina, a place like purgatory, and the morgue.

As I walked down the road, out of the corner of my eye, I saw something dark orange coming my way. After a moment, I recognized the station wagon—Leonardo at the wheel and Lily in the passenger seat.

Out the rolled-down window, Lily yelled. "Mom, where are you going? Angela lives that way," she said, hooking her thumb behind her.

I climbed into the backseat. "Leonardo, I want to visit Los Olvidados."

He turned his head. "Sure, we can go tomorrow or—"

"Now."

Still, the family reunion would have to wait.

Chapter Twelve
Los Olvidados – The Forgotten Ones

THROUGH A REARVIEW MIRROR DRAPED IN rosary beads, the church steeple and the bucolic village grew smaller. Blue-green agave sprouted in rows, fanning into the distance like tiny aqua stitches on a red poncho and meandering endlessly on either side of the road leading to the distillery. When the old station wagon turned right through a tall rusted-over gate that read Los Olvidados, gravel pinged as it spit out behind the tires. I looked around at the expansive campos and the vibrant crimson soil, rich with magnesium and iron that spewed years ago out of the distant carcass of a volcano, dormant now and looming, haunting the villagers for generations. Rouge-colored dust powder puffed up and hovered above the road, creating a trail of cloudy memories. My body remembered.

The setting was the same scene from when I was only ten—back when Mamá sat behind the wheel heading in the opposite direction, leaving the farm in the dust trailing us. My cousins had stood on the edge of the field, shrinking in size as Mamá raced down the dusty road back to the Estados Unidos. I recalled the pain in my tummy as I realized I might not ever play with my cousins again; I might not ever see this place or Papá again.

Lily, Leonardo, and I now crunched up to the gate to where a windowless phone-booth-sized guardhouse stood. Inside the small building, on a stool sat a gray-haired man whose chin rested on his chest, rising up and down like a bellow. Old Rico Van Winkle came to life, springing to his feet, when I knocked.

On stork-like legs, he hobbled out to greet his new visitors. He stretched up is arms. "Te espera Don Pio," the guard said, yawning so huge, I could see his tonsils.

How could he be expecting me, I wondered.

"Thank you," I said, turning to look at Lily, shrugging my shoulders. "How did he know?"

Lily shrugged her shoulders, too.

"Leonardo," I said. "I don't want you to keep Angela waiting. You two go back. I'll call a cab or something."

"Just don't start walking." Leonardo laughed. "Call me. No hay problema."

I raised my phone to remind him I had no signal. Leonardo hooked a finger at the old hacienda. "Use the house phone."

While I waited, the guard allowed me to go inside the gate where I walked to the fringe of the field, a border divided by agave plants. Without thinking about it, I pulled out a smoke, but only stared at it, realizing I wasn't having any cravings. Only out of habit had I pulled it out. *How pathetic.*

STANDING AT THE border, breathing in the field, I suddenly missed this place, like I'd missed a favorite cousin. And then when a small dove landed on the tip of an agave plant, I stepped a little closer, but the bird took off deeper into the field. Dwarfed by agave on either side, I chased the dove, remembering how I would run through here as a child with my cousin, Gabriel.

When I came to a slight peak in the meadow, I stopped. Hands on my knees, I lifted my head, gulping in more air. The sounds of children squealing pierced the wind but when I looked all around, I was alone. As I took in the view across to the north, like a valley of death, I felt my eyes go wide, goose bumps erupting on my arms. What used to be rows of thriving agave were now just shriveled plants in dirt choked by weeds. Beyond the edge of the field, scrubby mesquites and ancient oak trees dotted the landscape. Further out, I could see a dried-up riverbed where a couple of emaciated-looking cows grazed. I rubbed my arms and then reached into my pocket to pull out the picture from Papá's wallet. I held it out in front of me. *The river used to be full.* I felt a twinge in my stomach, steeling myself for the pain to follow. But, incredibly, nothing ached.

Stretched before me was the exact panoramic view where my father had taken my picture as a girl. I could almost see myself running toward the camera, legs thin as churros caked in red cinnamon powder, twin braids flying in the wind.

"Papá," I whispered now and then cleared my throat as I continued to wander back through the rows of agave.

The ancient sky above this part of the field seemed to sparkle with more sapphire and certainly bluer than any sky I'd ever seen in Los Angeles. The dew on the tips of agave glistened like liquid sugar drops. The heart of the field pulsed with life. Insects appeared larger—butterflies more vibrant. Bees buzzed boisterously. The belly of the field was sweet and incandescent, like a child's birthday cake topped with a generous arrangement of candles.

An orchestra of sound vibrated through me, infusing me with a warmth penetrating my being, dulling my pain—like a good Tequila. I twirled slowly, so enthralled by my surroundings. Another dove joined the first one, and I followed them both deeper into the field until, out of nowhere, I came up behind a man seated in front of a short easel and a canvas.

I stopped in my tracks, taking a moment to watch him paint. With his back to me, I strained to peek over his shoulder. He sat barefoot and cross-legged and I could see that he had a reedy frame draped with a loose, gauzy linen-colored tunic and drawstring pants. His head full of obsidian-colored hair gleamed halo-like in the sun. Staring at the canvas, I sucked in a quiet breath when I noticed no brush gliding across the painting—no hands involved in the creation bleeding onto the work. Shaking my head, I squeezed my eyes shut, but quickly re-opened them. And then before I could try to make sense of what unfolded before my very eyes, and as if sensing my presence, without turning around, the man said, "Come closer, Maya."

Mind scrambled now like a kaleidoscope of vividly colored emotions, I stammered. "I'm so sorry. I just—hey—how did you know my—that it was me?"

The young man remained seated, turning his head slowly. Seemingly, ageless, genderless, he beamed as radiantly as Buddha, himself. And as he tilted his head back to look up at me, I peered at him, mesmerized, almost able to see his soul. I saw the field weaving through his blue-green eyes and at once I could see myself as a child running through that field hand-in-hand with my cousin, giggling like raindrops.

"Oh my God. Gabriel you're all grown up," I said, quickly distracted by the sound of a child laughing. I looked all around and then turned back toward him.

"Do you still paint?" my cousin asked me in a voice so delicate I feared he might crack if I answered too loudly.

I heard the child again and cocked my head slightly. "Not anymore. I've lost the touch—don't you hear that?"

"Yes, I hear her." He paused and returned to his work. "It's all in the brushes."

I walked over and picked up one of his brushes, examined it, then put it to my ear. "The brushes?"

"The touch, the strokes," Gabriel said quietly, dabbing on some paint from his pallet this time using a brush.

As I looked closer, I kept seeing things, like a hidden picture quality where you see something, then look again, and then you don't see it. There was an underpainting in turquoise, giving it a glowing backlit feeling. He'd layered so much paint, very thin, like washes, so fine and translucent that I could see the layer underneath. I noticed the intricacies of the agave plant he painted—small insects crawling across the points, clouds floating lazily across the sky. And then as the clouds overhead drifted by, the painting took on a different look in the different light. In one moment, the dominant color glowed a teal green, luminous, as if being lit from behind. And then in the next moment, the red tones came to the fore, glowing garnet. Peering closer at the agave plant, I gasped. In the gathering dew, I saw a distorted reflection of my own face and held my breath. This painting was alive.

"Oh my God! Is this one of those magic fields like in *Field of Dreams* or something?"

"This is a field of reality," he answered, matter-of-factly.

I opened my mouth to ask another question, but the sound of a braying burro sidetracked me.

"You heard that, right?" I asked, craning my head.

"Of course," Gabriel, responded never lifting his head. "Chuey and Don Pio."

Chapter Thirteen

Don Pio

IN THE DISTANCE, THE SUN ANGLING JUST SO, I could only see the silhouette of a man. I couldn't make out the details of his face yet, but already I had a sense about the person approaching on the back of a donkey. The anticipation now of seeing my tio again was like waiting for Christmas and as he got closer, his face swam into view. It wasn't hard to recognize my uncle, the man everyone—even his family—addressed as Don Pio. A nut-colored old man, he had wrinkles now as deep as the cracks traversing the parched dark soil, yet seemingly quite fit. He had to be in his eighties by now.

He strode up wearing a broad white, weathered Mexican hat and threadbare leather sandals. Leaning out of the saddle, he extended his hand. "Maya," he said in a raspy, yet soothing voice.

"Don Pio?" I welled with even more sentiment. Without understanding how or why, I knew, whether or not I wanted it, this man was my connection back to my roots. I remembered observing him as a child, wanting to be a Tequila farmer just like him when I grew up. I'd watched him working the field, treating it kindly; the same way he'd regarded his wife, caressing the plants the way he caressed her cheeks. I remembered my aunt and how I'd dreamed that someday I'd have a marriage like my tía Arisel and my tío Don Pio—a union where two loving people were always passionate about whatever they were doing as long as it was side-by-side, where discord did not exist. In the end, after Tia Arisel died, he'd been the one to keep this field alive, and I would come to learn why.

"Han pasado tantos años," he said, dismounting Chuey.

"Yes, way too many years," I said as the sound of giggling startled me.

70

I turned my head to search for the child and then searched Don Pio for an answer, but he now regarded Gabriel who merely nodded.

"I see you remember Gabriel," Don Pio said.

"Of course I do," I replied, eyes darting around, looking for the laughing child.

"Well, when you're all caught up here, I can show you the fabrica."

"Sure. I'd love to see the factory again." I turned toward Gabriel and patted his shoulder. "So nice to see you again." He seemed so content and lost in his work. "Please don't get up," I said, realizing at that exact moment, that even if he'd wanted to stand, he would be unable to. Propped beside the easel, I took notice of the crutches.

CHUEY, A KIND-EYED beast of burden with a white snout and underbelly, swished at a fly with his long floppy ears as he trailed behind Don Pio.

I caught up to stroll alongside my uncle. "What happened to Gabriel?" my uncle peered at me as if he was surprised I didn't already know. "I'm sorry I haven't stayed in touch. My life's sort of been in upheaval."

"Automobile accident. Un borracho," he said.

"A drunk driver? Will Gabriel be okay?"

"He's in acceptance."

I stopped in my tracks. *Acceptance?* "I'm so sorry."

"And I am so sorry about your Papá," Don Pio said.

"Another victim of too much Tequila," I replied.

"I've witnessed the ugly side. It gives Tequila a bad name. The heart of the agave is pure." The pleasant pitch of his voice sounded just as genuine and suddenly I realized what I'd missed all these years.

I felt bad I hadn't stayed in touch with the family and was glad that neither Gabriel nor Don Pio had asked me any questions about my life since I left years ago, almost as if they'd always known the reasons. With them, there'd never been any need to really explain myself, after all when you're little, what's there to justify.

I heard a whistle like a catcall and cringed. If I were more like Lily, I'd turn around and flip someone off. "Too bad the heart of a man isn't pure," I said.

"I think they were whistling at me," Don Pio said with a grin, and I noticed a couple of workers stopping to wipe the sweat from their brows. I looked closer and could see that they were young women. One even had a baby strapped to her back. They smiled at me now as I walked past.

"So now the girls are working the field?"

Don Pio nodded as we headed toward a small hill. Once we climbed to the top, I took a moment to look around, remembering how I'd once asked my father why the field was called blue agave when the plants really looked green. "It is because when the moon is full, the agave shines blue," he'd told me, and indeed during the next full moon, I'd seen the truth of what he'd said.

Now, toward the northeast part of the field, and across the valley, I could see a small house perched on a knoll. I laughed, remembering that as a kid, Gabriel and I thought it looked like a boob. "Isn't that where Gabriel and—"

"Just Antonio," my uncle said and kept walking without looking back.

My heart picked up the pace. *Antonio? Hadn't he gone north with the other men?*

AT THE FRINGE of the field stood the old distillery like a border patrol station that processed the Tequila. Huge hearts of unsuspecting agave were lined up and stacked, waiting to be put into the adobe ovens.

"These are the hornos where maguey is baked for hours," Don Pio said. "We've tried to keep to the old way by roasting the piñas in the brick ovens."

He motioned with his head for me to follow him around to the other side of the ovens. "It comes out here—"

"The cactus?" I asked.

"Ay dios mio. No, not cactus. Agave is actually related to the lily family."

I smiled and while I could remember a lot, I was embarrassed at how many things I'd forgotten—or put out of my mind. "I named my daughter Lily."

Don Pio smiled, nodding.

On the other side of the oven, a yoked burro pulled a mulcher, a big volcanic stone shaped into a wheel, around a circle. The older men paused what they were doing and removed their hats to welcome me.

A man about my uncle's age with a weather-beaten face stepped up and reached out to shake my hand.

"This is Flaco," Don Pio said. "He's our jimador."

I tilted my head slightly and peered at Don Pio. "A jimador is the harvester, right?"

"*Sí*, the one that says when the agave is ripe enough, usually between eight to twelve years. If it is not ready, it is no good."

"So, I don't remember. Is there a regular harvest season?"

"Not really. Harvesting is done year-round because the plants mature at different stages in the fields. It depends on when the agave was planted."

The men returned to their work and Don Pio leaned over to pick up some baked agave from inside the mulcher. He handed me some of the fleshy, fibrous pulp.

I chewed on it and as the sugary juice exploded in my mouth, I exclaimed. "Wow! It's like candy."

Licking my lips, I looked around the property and munched some more, realizing that the distillery smelled exactly like the juice tasted. And then as I swallowed the nectar, like a sweet memory, it all came back.

Gabriel and I had been around eight or nine years old when we'd come in from the field, leading burros, ladened with piñas—the heart of the agave, Don Pio had told me—to the distillery where a yoked burro pulled the mulcher around the circle. A worker reached into the pit and handed Gabriel some baked agave to share with me. We chewed, juice dripping down our chins, and giggled before running back into fields without a care.

Don Pio now winked at me now as I wiped my mouth with the back of my hand and continued to chew. "A secret family ingredient," he said.

I FOLLOWED MY uncle into the distillery where the Tequila fermented in large stainless-steel vats. Across from the vats were five operating pot stills—three wash stills called destrozadores and two copper spirit stills. The entire production was all snuggly fit under one roof. A worker approached and handed me a sample of the product directly from one of the stills.

I sipped it slowly and turned to my uncle. "Ay, qué bueno." Simply divine. I took another sip, so warm and mellifluous; it tasted like liquid sunlight going down. "May I have another sample?"

"Por supuesto. Get your glass up there under the spigot and fill it up."

I laughed, holding my glass up to the spout. "It's a good thing I'm not driving."

"It is very difficult to get drunk on our Tequila. It is so pure," Don Pio said, "but yes, it is true. There are crazy drivers. That is why we still keep guest rooms."

"And burros?" I said and took another sip.

We entered through another room where I wandered between hundreds of Jack Daniel's oak barrels stacked to the rafters. Crossing through the threshold of a hangar-sized factory, I noticed a row of boxes lined up to the ceiling and then snaking through the middle of the room, a conveyer belt moved empty bottles down the line. On either side of the belt, young girls in hair nets and masks bumped hips to the beat of a radio blasting hip-hop.

"Today, they bottle the reposado," Don Pio said, flourishing an arm.

"Remind me again. What is reposado?"

"It is our Tequila that has been taking a siesta for nearly three months. It is a bit more mellow and more refined than the blanco."

"And which bottle gets the worm?" I asked with a chuckle, noticing Don Pio lift an eyebrow. I poked his arm gently with my elbow. "Just kidding," I said, knowing that worms in the bottle were only a myth.

He laughed. "That would be mezcal."

"So what's the difference between mezcal and Tequila?"

"Only Tequila can be called Tequila if it's from this region and it must be at least fifty-one percent blue agave. Mezcal can be made from any variety of maguey succulents," Don Pio said. "As for the worm, around here, people are very superstitious because the larva buried itself in the heart of the agave, moving along like a cancer that ravished the plant."

"Híjole. That's interesting."

"But people took to the Tequila. Pretty soon there was a huge demand. The gringos brought in their expertise, and then the crops expanded too fast. All of sudden New Yorkers wanted to be farmers."

I squinted into the sunshine as we exited the factory. In the distance, I noticed the weed-infested field and a sadness sprouted deep inside.

Don Pio extended his arm and pointed to the north where little white flowers had shot up out of tops of the withered vines. "The blue agave has been suffering from an outbreak of many diseases ever since. Our north field is a good example."

"But those flowers seem to be thriving," I said.

Grimacing, Don Pio shook his head. "Quiotes. They suck up the sugar and attract the predators. They're like candy to children." He turned and headed toward the side of the distillery. "Antonio thinks we should plow the fields under and plant corn. Now the gringos want ethanol. It's driven up the price of corn."

I trailed behind him. "So, you'll compete with OPEC? That's not a bad idea." I thought about it for a moment. "But this is a Tequila farm, after all."

"And now the export tax is so high. Bruno thinks we should sell the business to the Japanese."

"Bruno? That's crazy," I said, searching my mind trying to recall anything about Bruno. Older than Gabriel and Antonio, I remembered him being off in the military for the most part when I was little.

"We need your help," Don Pio said before I could ask anything about Bruno.

"My help?" I asked, following my uncle through a doorway that opened up to a hallway. I noticed a sign that read "Baño" and excused myself. Out of habit, I charged in—never passing up the opportunity to go—but then, I just stood there realizing I didn't have to go.

Back in the hallway, I asked again. "My help? What can I do?"

"We'll talk," Don Pio said, and continued down the hallway. I followed him toward a small office off to the side. The door was open. Beyond a series of agave paintings like the one Gabriel had been painting, I could see the back side of a man seated at an ancient, boxy computer.

"Antonio," Don Pio said, and my heart thudded at the mention of his name. "Remember Maya?"

Antonio swerved around in his chair, standing, his head practically hitting the ceiling in the small office. His shoulders were hunched slightly the way some are when people are self-conscious about being too tall. He had to be in his late thirties by now. The floor seemed to shift beneath me like some sort of arroyo splitting the parched red earth. I thought I might get swallowed up and then when I looked up into those same familiar piercing ocean-colored eyes, I thought I'd drown. Antonio extended a chapped hand and smiled, the lines around his eyes like electric currents, zapping me to my very core. Flushed, I lowered my eyes, noticing his long legs stuffed into mud-caked boots—making him at least six-foot five. He was ruggedly—or was it devilishly—handsome.

"Mucho gusto. I see you're not as skinny as I remember."

My face burned. "I don't know if a thank you is in order," I said, touching my cheek. I looked up, thinking he was still so sarcastic, but instead, I said, "I see you're even taller."

I needed air and licked my dry lips. Reaching into my purse to find some lip-gloss, I looked around the office so as not to have to face my cousin who in the meanwhile, had sat back down at his desk. Along the ledge of the window, facing the field, a row of bottles was lined up like ragtag volunteer soldiers in various shapes and sizes, each with a different label. I recognized the artwork and examined closer.

"Cool. That's Gabriel's work," I said. "Why so many different—"

"We bottle for different companies," Antonio said, staring at something on his computer.

After an awkward moment of silence, Don Pio cleared his throat. "Maya, why don't I show you the hacienda," he said. "Magdalena has your room ready."

Antonio turned and fixed his questioning eyes on Don Pio.

"Oh, but I'm staying in town with Angela," I said, still shuffling through my purse.

Don Pio's face sagged. "But there is so much more I need to show you about the business."

Need to show me about the business? I looked up, noticing Antonio's narrowed eyes. "Maybe, I can come back some other time," I responded.

"Yes, maybe another time," Antonio said, knitting his fingers together on his desk, an indication he was finished with the visit.

"I'll let you know," I added.

"Very well," Don Pio said and guided me toward the door.

Outside, I leaned against the wall, took a breath, and started to reapply some lip-gloss when I heard Antonio call my name. "Maya." I felt my heart stop. "I am sorry about your father."

I returned to thank him, but he was already clicking away on the computer keys. His back toward me, his denim shirt stretched taut across his muscular shoulders, I grew weak in the knees. Heart racing, I swallowed and gave silent thanks that he hadn't caught me blushing—a heat that could have set the cigarettes in my purse on fire.

Chapter Fourteen

Mi Familia

A RESPECTFUL SILENCE FILLED THE CAR AS I RODE back into the village seated in the front seat of Leonardo's station wagon. The landscape swept away as the path carried me back along the rhythmic thumping over the gravel, and then the pavement, and then the cobblestones beneath the tires, all lulling me into moments where I was conscious of the quiet self-regard of grief. An overwhelming sadness washed over me, as if I'd left everything behind once more. My sorrow confused me.

We turned onto a narrow street where each little house rose up like a weed out of the cracks in the fastidiously swept cement sidewalk. We pulled up in front of one of many whitewashed stucco walls bordering the street. Next to a door painted bright purple, the silhouette of a heavy-set woman floated ghost-like behind a sheer-curtained window. A hand pulled back the curtain and then before I knew it, like an apparition in an apron, she knocked on the car window on my side. And then behind the woman, Lily came bounding out of the casita.

"Maya, finally. You've returned. Come in. Come in. Poor thing, we're so sorry about Joaquin," Angela said, reaching over to hug me. "How are you doing?"

Peace like a waterfall washed over me at once. My cousin, tall and sturdy, had always made me feel comfortable, like a safe port in a storm. "Just fine," I answered, knowing it was a satisfactory answer for my cousin whom I remembered to be so much like her father, Don Pio, and didn't pry. "I'm okay, really," I added. At least I was still recognizable to myself.

"Turn around. Let me look at you," Angela said with a gold-lined toothy smile. She placed her hands on my shoulders to spin me. "You look the same as that skinny güerita with the sunburned nose."

I was glad Angela had also recognized that skinny girl—a testament to my being just fine. "You look the same as I remember," I responded.

"Mentirosa."

"I'm not lying, Angela. You look good."

"I'm as old as dirt and as big as the Jalisco sky, but you—the States are good to its people," Angela said. "And you've raised a lovely daughter," she said, hooking an arm around Lily. "Muy chula."

My *cute* daughter rocked back on her heels, tiny roses blooming on her cheeks.

"Thank you," I said, mood lifting in the presence of my fifty-year-old cousin.

"What about your fiancé?" she asked, and my spirits plummeted faster than a river-tossed stone. I hadn't even thought about the anvil-around-my-neck Zane for at least a few moments.

"Lily tells us you're getting married."

I glanced at Lily, shrugging her shoulders. "I'm not getting married," I said.

As if she hadn't heard, Angela turned and proceeded into the house surrounded by guava-colored walls. I shrugged, too, and followed. Within a few moments, a young woman in blue jeans walked in with two young girls and a little boy in tow.

"This is my daughter, Sylvia, and my grandchildren," Angela said, beaming like the proud grandmother she was. "Mateo, Patricia and Cristina."

"Mucho gusto," I said, extending a hand.

Sylvia, holding a dish, handed it to her mother before hugging me.

"Bienvenidos," Sylvia said, and then we all followed the children into the kitchen.

I was impressed to see Leonardo already setting the kitchen table when the family walked in. I couldn't remember my brother or my father ever stepping in to do a dish, much less set a table.

"Please take a seat," Angela said as Leonardo pulled my chair out for me. He did the same for Lily.

"I'm so sorry," I said. "I didn't mean for you all to wait for me."

"No worries. I can afford to skip a meal," Angela said, patting her ample stomach, "or two."

"Or three," another young woman said, chuckling as she entered the kitchen. She wore jeans and a white-pressed shirt.

"Ay, Ofelia," Angela shouted, swirling a dishtowel and playfully snapping Ofelia's derriere.

The chair scraped as Lily sprung up to greet her. "Hola Prima," Lily said. "Mom, this is Ofelia. She's a schoolteacher. Well, not just a teacher, she's also working on her master's at the University. I've already learned so much from her about everything around here."

"Welcome, Primas. Yes, I'm Ofelia, the beautiful, unmarried one," she said.

"The town's old spinster," Sylvia added with a smirk.

Definitely feeling overdressed, I stood to be hugged by my tall, gregarious cousin. I wished I could change into my jeans, too.

Throughout the meal, Angela never sat down as she continually prepared and served everyone more food, shuffling back and forth to the stove to flip tortillas. During our short stay, Angela would prepare at least four home-cooked meals, featuring fresh corn sold out of the back of a pickup truck that honked out front when it was ready to deliver, bread from the local panadería, and pigs' feet from the local butcher—the latter a favored delicacy for her cousin-husband, Juan.

Lily constantly checked her phone on her lap while I picked at my food.

"¿Seguro que no podemos ayudar?" I asked.

"Yes, let us help," Lily added, looking up from her phone.

"No, gracias."

"So, where's Juan?" I asked.

"He's up north trying to secure visas for the family," Leonardo answered for his mother as she returned to the table carrying a stack of tortillas. "Mamá wants to go to *Disneylandia*."

Everyone laughed.

"It's been hard for Juan. He has to travel back and forth. Just a little more time, he tells me," Angela said, "And then it's off to the happiest place *en todo el mundo*." I could see the sadness in her eyes. "Maya, y tu mamá, cómo está?" Angela asked, setting down the tortillas.

"My mother is fine. She's waiting to hear any news about what happened to Papá."

"Yes—well, he called when he heard Lily was coming to visit. He thought you might be with her," she said, ladling me some more green nopales. Lily looked up and sat straight. Angela shook her head. "He started walking and never made it."

Before I could react, Lily dropped her loaded fork, her face flushing crimson and her eyes turning glossy. She fought to hold back her tears as I reached over to pat her hand.

But she pulled her hand away from me. "I wish I could have talked to him again."

"Again?" I was stunned.

She turned to me, accusingly. "Why did you keep him away from me?"

"Lily, when did you talk to him?"

The sound of the chair scraping startled me as she pushed away from the table, leaving the question hanging in the air.

Embarrassed with the telenovela family drama, I turned to Angela and whispered, "Lo siento." And then I turned to catch Lily staring out the window. I couldn't imagine the conversations my daughter might have had with her crazy grandfather.

She stood next to the window, arms crossed over her chest, and my mind cast back to see a precious newborn—my perfect little angel. Near the window in our apartment, I'd been rocking my baby to sleep, breathing in that wonderful baby-like mix of talcum powder and sweet milk, when the doorbell rang. The mailman stood on the other side and handed me a postcard, every inch of which had been scrawled on in pencil like chicken scratch. Papá could barely read or write, much less have my address, but he knew where I lived. He'd drawn a map with arrows pointing to my place and landmarks, like the Lucky grocery store on one corner of Second Avenue and the Shell gas station on the other. "Felicitaciones, Mija," Papá had written, followed by a drawing of a puppy holding out a bouquet of lilies.

Wiping the corner of my eye, I tried to recall whether or not that was the time he'd been in jail.

Lily returned to Angela's kitchen table but wouldn't look at me.

"When did you talk to him?" I asked again feeling bereaved. "Please, you don't know everything."

"He was coming to meet me," she said with a huff, before crossing her arms over her chest. "Now, he'll never know how much I loved him."

Love him? But you didn't even know him.

Ofelia, who had also left the table, returned now with a box of tissues as Angela placed her hands on Lily's shoulders. "I'm sure he knows it."

She turned to face me, "Your father was quite a character," she said. "Everyone just loved him. He made everyone laugh."

I narrowed my eyes at Angela. "You're kidding, right?"

Lily twisted around in her seat to look up at Angela. "Grandpa was funny?"

"Funny, funny?" I asked. "Or, funny, *haha*?"

Angela and Lily stared at me as if I'd just grown a third eye.

"What kind of question is that, Mom? Obviously, he was appreciated down here by more than just family." Lily pushed away again from the table, this time walking out into the courtyard.

I followed her into a lush patio, a tropical jungle full of plants, potted red geraniums, fuchsia and plump succulents—crisscrossed with clotheslines and clothespins attached like music notes on a stanza.

Lily took a seat on the bench and picked up her phone to text.

"Who's—what's so important?" I asked in a singsong voice, hoping she wouldn't tear my head off.

She opened her mouth and let out a recalcitrant huff before clamping her mouth shut. Obviously, she didn't feel like sharing. And, I didn't feel like pressing, just yet. I took a seat next to her. The yard opened to the sky and as I gazed up, I got dizzy, unable to tell whether it was the clouds fleeting along like lost little lambs or whether it was just life itself swiftly passing me by. Any more time wasted, and I'd lose Lily forever.

Until the fiasco with the professor, I liked to think that I knew everything about my daughter. I knew about her first kiss in preschool; her first shoplifting foray at age five when she walked out of Lucky market with a tube of Necco candy. I'd marched her right back into the store, and because she had the courage to apologize to the manager, she would only miss one night of television. I liked to think we could share about anything and everything—well, except for family, and her father, Elliot—but the time was coming. It was all one-sided. Of course I could see the hypocrisy, the double standard I practiced with Lily. But, after all, I was the mother and wouldn't dare talk about my own mistakes, my bad choices; about Zane and his troubles, me and my "ulcer." I tried not to let my daughter know how fearful I was of just about everything and everyone. Becoming an attorney had only given me the tools to act tough, but my insides were just like a bowl of hot jelly, turning and burning.

Across the red-brick paved courtyard toward the far end, stretched a colorful floor-to-ceiling tiled-mosaic depicting either a saint or an angel. In the corner, hung two wrought iron birdcages where, nestled together in one were two little love birds; in the other, a small green parrot whose talons scraped the wooden perch as he paced back and forth. Above her, I heard scuffling and looked up to see a motley black-and white dappled dog running along the rooftop. The dog stopped occasionally to poke his nose over the edge. He barked at us.

"Chacho, our ferocious guard dog," Ofelia said with a chuckle as she entered the courtyard ahead of the others. "Chacho, *cállate!*" She yelled up toward the dog. "Don't tell anyone, but Chacho's only good at barking. He wouldn't come down even if a burglar was carrying out the television set and all of Mamá's fine silverware. He likes it up there where he can see everything that's going on."

"Lot of good he is," Sylvia said, looking up as she walked in.

"I just like knowing he's up there," Angela added as she stepped into the courtyard and took a seat across from me. "El mantiene alejados a los fantasmas," she said with a chuckle.

"Which ghosts does he keep away?" Lily asked, and my ears perked up.

Angela sobered a little. "When your abuelo would visit," she told Lily, "he'd climb up the ladder to give Chacho a treat. Chacho loved him."

"My dad was nice to everyone else, even the dogs," I remarked softly. "I remember when we lived here—"

"Wait," Lily said, setting her phone down at last. "You guys lived down here?"

"Lily, you knew that."

"No," she said, glaring at me. "Obviously, I did not. I thought you just visited."

"We lived in a little house in between here and the hacienda, close enough for my father to work out at the farm and for my mother to work in the shoe factory in town."

Lily scrunched her nose. "But I thought Grandma's family was from California."

"Now they are. But years before, Mamá's family migrated north to work the fields and then during that Great Depression, they were 'repatriated'—deported. Their services were no longer needed."

Lily chuckled. "So, Grandma is illegal?"

I shook my head. "My grandparents had nine children, and most were able to become citizens sometime later. Mamá used to tell us she was born right out in the field up in Salinas and her mother just picked her up, cleaned her off and swaddled her before strapping her to her back to continue picking strawberries."

Lily's eyes grew big as tortillas, her mouth wide enough to catch moscas.

"Mamá was one of the four who survived and was also the one selected to never leave or marry, so that she could take care of her parents and a sick little sister. Mamá was already twenty-eight when her father—who was much older than her mother who'd been a little indigenous bride at fourteen—died."

"What about the little sister?" Lily asked, shaking her head.

"She died, too."

"What was wrong?"

I simply shrugged my shoulders, but I knew the truth. I looked around into the faces of my cousins and wondered if they knew, too. Little Cecilia, a product of her father's sin—his syphilis—the disease that had eventually taken him out, took her first. Suddenly, I felt sorry for Mamá and then when I thought about her having to travel across the border into Tijuana to retrieve her father's body, the coincidence was not lost on me. Mamá's mother, my grandmother, hadn't waited for his body to get cold before she'd already hooked up with another man in the TB ward of the hospital. My mother would have a stepfather, before she'd ever get to be a wife. To say she was bitter would have been an understatement.

"Your grandfather Joaquin used to go north every season to pick fruit," I said. "That's where they met and then one day—"

"Instead of getting the *leche* for free, he bought the cow?" Lily laughed, leaning in to tap my thigh.

I smiled. "Your grandma would have a heart attack if she heard you accusing her of having sex out of wedlock. Anyway, according to her, she ran off and married my dad and came back down here."

So, whether it was a marriage based on love, desperation, or revenge, they settled in Sagrada Familia, but then it didn't take long for Mamá to notice a change. As she grew bigger, she also perceived a difference in Joaquin, or perhaps that's when she woke up.

"Wait a second." Lily's face scrunched up. "Are *you* even legal, Mom?" she chuckled, hoping to pin something on me, no doubt.

I gave a weak smile. "Only three months after getting married and already pregnant with me, Mamá went back north to stay with her mother and stepfather in Santa Ana, California, where I was born. So, yes, I'm *legal*. When she was well enough, she came back to Mexico with a new baby, me—Maya Refugio Hidalgo. After that, we used to travel, one place to the other, depending on the season—depending on Mamá's resolve.

"We were always coming back and forth, first on the *Tres Estrellas* bus. And then one day, we never returned to Mexico."

"Is that when you left him, my abuelo Joaquin?"

I could see that all eyes were now on me. *Oh my God, did they all know what had happened to me? Is that why no one has ever pressed me about coming back all these years?* I could sense Lily's disapproval but nodded anyway. "One day, my brother and I followed Mamá as she marched into the cantina. Papá didn't even recognize us." Or maybe it was because Mamá wore sunglasses to hide the black eye he'd given her the night before. "He thought we were some kids selling Chiclets. She told him we were leaving. Mamá was finally done with his drinking and swore never to come back."

But both Mamá and Papá were always making promises and breaking them. *I swear, I'm going to leave you,* or *I swear, I'm going to kill you,* or *I swear, I'll never touch you again.*

After that, my brother and I moved into a small house with Mamá on our grandmother's property in Santa Ana where I would live until the day I eloped.

"I guess that's why Grandma always wanted to keep out all illegal immigrants—to keep Grandpa out," Lily said, with a nervous chuckle.

"There are those who make it through a window and then want to shut the door on the others, even if it is family," Ofelia said.

"And put up a wall," Lily added.

I shrugged my shoulders, still caught up by the weight of my own memories.

"I've been reading this book from the University," Ofelia said, pulling a leaf off a ficus tree and rubbing it between her fingers. "It says that for years our families have been migrating back and forth in order to survive. Back in the twenties, Mexican border crossing was never restricted because our labor was so needed. We weren't considered immigrants, so there was no restriction. But because we're Mexican, we were discriminated against. And now, apparently, it's perfectly legal to deprive people of citizenship because of their race."

I envisioned a wall along the borders stacked to the heavens. I could picture Papá magically walking through it to get to the other side. I cast back to the day I thought I saw him standing in the shadows under the sycamore across the street from our home in Santa Ana.

"Mamá, I see Papá," I'd shouted, running for the door.

"Que dijiste?" she yelled.

Rudy had also come running to the window—barred to keep the bad guys out—but Mamá quickly bolted the door before I could exit. Even after what he'd done, I still worried about him. I wanted to see my papá again. And then Mamá shut the curtains.

"Estás loca," Mamá said.

"I am not crazy," I screamed, stomping my foot. How I hated when Mamá said that! I was adamant about what I'd seen and as detail oriented as the good lawyer I'd someday become. "I saw him standing there. He was wearing khaki pants, a whitish shirt with a pocket for his cigarettes and his white hat."

That night I heard strange noises coming from Mamá's bedroom. Papá would be staying this time and the iron bars on the windows would only keep the bad guy locked in. The next day, however, in a box outside our door, stood a puppy like Papá had promised—his apology, my guaranteed silence. Though, I wanted to see him, I would try my best never to be alone with Papá when he came to town, and would constantly be looking over my shoulder, until the day I escaped, until the day I eloped.

In the courtyard now, Lily stared at me, looking completely enthralled when Angela announced it was time for some dessert.

Inside, Angela served us a huge helping of egg custard.

"Yum. What is this?" Lily asked.

"Flan," Angela said, motioning, with her hand to mouth, for me to eat.

"Oh, no, thank you. I'm so full."

"Nonsense, Maya, you ate like a bird. You look like one of those puppets from Día De Los Muertos—only prettier."

"Thank you." I slid a spoonful of the creamy dessert into my mouth. Lily and I then turned to each other, simultaneously wide-eyed.

"Oh my God," Lily exclaimed. "This is better than an orgasm."

I peered at Lily with one of my motherly looks, but then nodded. "Multiple."

"We make it with agave sugar," Sylvia said.

I took another spoonful of heaven, thinking I'd died and gone there. Strange, but my stomach felt better, too. "This is divine."

"*GAS! GAS!*" The sound of the petrol truck awakened me as it rounded the corner outside making its deliveries. And then, I could hear the shuffling sounds of the workers' footsteps, mostly young, single women headed to the shoe factory down the street where my own mother used to work. The older women stayed behind to sweep their porches and get ready for the day and the passersby or perhaps the return of their men? Out in the courtyard, the parrot and the lovebirds were awake, too. I lay in bed in this little house, in the pueblo of Sagrada Familia, a place where the time zone was different in more ways than one. I remembered how every cinco de la madrugada, the church bells would sound *La Guadalupana*, followed by six noisy gongs, and then every hour on the hour—on Sundays, four times per hour. Here it was hard to forget you were católica.

The clock ticked rhythmically as the room grew more illuminated. I looked around the room, noticing now the treasures that filled it: a Spanish flag, a wedding photo of Angela and Juan, and the tiara Angela wore as a teenage beauty queen during the Fiesta de enero held every January to celebrate the return of family. Lily was still sleeping, her chest rising up and down like a calm sea, her eyes fluttering in the REM stage of sleep. I glanced at the clock. It was time to start my day. I pulled back my covers and Lily opened her eyes.

"Do you really have to go back, Mom?" It wrenched my heart to see the twisted look on her face.

"I might try to stay a couple more days."

"I really like it here," Lily said. "I never would have left."

"Yeah, there were some good times." There was a certain freedom kids nowadays don't enjoy—hours spent in the fields with my cousin and the other children of the workers. We'd chase each other or play *escondidas* until dusk. I never wanted to come inside—not where the biggest monster of all lurked.

"Even if you hated Grandpa so much, I can't understand why you stayed away from here."

"I didn't hate him," I answered. "You don't really hate someone unless you love them."

"Did you hate my father?" She looked at me expectantly. We hadn't talked about Elliot since she was a very little girl.

I smiled. "No, he was the first person to ever tell me that he loved me." Sadly, I didn't know how to say it back.

THE CHURCH BELL tolled again as the family walked up the cobblestone road after a hearty breakfast of huevos con chorizo. Wearing a pair of jeans, I'd also put on my face before venturing out—I didn't want to scare anyone. Angela, in too much pain to walk stayed behind; besides, she had all those meals to prepare. I looked up to see the bell tower poking out of above the rooftops like one giant candle on a cake covered in sprinkles.

Leonardo and Lily walked ahead.

"Are you enjoying the city?" I heard Leonardo ask Lily.

"Yes, thanks," she answered, pocketing her cell phone into the back pocket of her jeans.

I took a deep breath when I saw the wings tattooed across the back of Lily's shoulders—as if she were about to take flight.

"So, where can you get a good Margarita around here?" Lily asked, facing Cousin Sylvia.

Sylvia smiled and then whispered something to her son tagging along just as a couple of young men strolled by and whistled at Lily.

"Güerita, que guapa!"

Lily did that maddening thing with her eyes.

"Mexican men just like to flirt," Leonardo said with a smile. "You are definitely a pretty gringa."

She smiled, flipping her hair coyly, staring the boys down with a smile and then mock belligerence at being ogled. "Yeah, well, it's just so irritating."

I watched her, wondering where she'd learned how to be such a tease, such a little *Lolita*, but I shocked myself thinking that way, so wrong and unfair of me. I knew all too well, to say 'no' was to be seen as a tease. A smile was only a defense mechanism. The "flirting" wasn't just a Mexican thing, I'd learned. *Smile and play nice*. Lily had learned it from me, and I'd learned it from my mother.

Coming up and nestled between two little casitas—talk about zoning— I noticed the town had progressed enough to put in an internet café. Since there'd been no service at the house, at last, I'd be able to check my emails.

"So, what are you studying at the University? Going to be an attorney like your mom?" Leonardo asked Lily.

"Hell no! I don't like bleeding ulcers," she said loud enough for my ears. "You gonna be a Tequila farmer like your dad?"

"I am an attorney," Leonardo said.

Touché, I thought, grinning.

"I'm so sorry. I didn't . . . I didn't mean—" Lily stuttered.

Leonardo chuckled. "Don't worry," he said, making his way toward the café's entrance. "Excuse me, while I step in and check my messages."

"I didn't mean to be so rude," Lily said, turning to Ofelia. "I just don't want to be an attorney. I want to help people."

"Excuse me?" I said.

Ofelia grinned and reached out to embrace Lily. "You're a girl after my own heart, Primita."

"Yeah, and don't mind me," I added. "I never help anyone, especially not my college daughter with a laundry list of ways I need to assist."

Lily responded again with the skyward eyes, and this time I couldn't hold back. "I swear, someday, they're going to get stuck in your head and who ya gonna call?"

"Ghostbusters!" Ofelia laughed, obviously impressed with her command of the English language.

"I think I'll go in, too, just for a sec to check on my emails," I said, making my way toward the internet café. "You, know an attorney's work is never done." *And the bleeding ulcers don't go away either.*

INSIDE THE CAFÉ, the slow Mexican connection really perturbed me. I took a seat next to Leonardo, pulled out a cigarette and lit it. There was no hiding my habit now, besides, I felt some sort of camaraderie with another attorney, even if it was my newly found young cousin.

"Finally, a connection," I said, and Leonardo nodded.

I scanned through my emails, my heart sinking when I found nothing from Zane. And then, I opened an email from my office: "Maya, we need an answer on the Rothman Complaint."

"What pains in the ass," I whispered to myself. Leonardo turned to me, tilting his head.

I typed back: "Can't someone else handle it? There's been a death in the family, for God's sake. I'll be back next Friday. Adiós!"

I clicked open another e-mail, "Let us meet to discuss business. Sagave.Hidalgo@mextel.com." I peered at the message and then turned to tap Leonardo's shoulder. I pointed to the screen.

"Who is this?"

"Bruno, the uncle who is trying to steal the Tequila factory," Leonardo answered, returning to his computer.

"Steal it?" I laughed, recalling that old silent film where the villainous, mustached landlord shows up at the farmer's door. "How can he steal it?"

Leonardo stuck out the palm of his hand, rubbing his fingers together.

"So, what does he want with me?"

Leonardo shrugged his shoulders.

Lily walked in when I was in the middle of an email to my doctor. I clicked off, dropping my cigarette to the concrete floor and stubbing it out.

WE BLESSED ourselves as we entered the narrow church where mass was taking place. *In the name of the Father,* touch your forehead—so far, no lightning—*the Son,* touch your heart, the floor hadn't opened up to swallow me—*and the Holy Spirit,* touch each shoulder—all good. Looking up to the arched cathedral ceilings, I stepped deeper across the pink marbled floors inside the Templo de Sagrada Familia where gloom was slashed by shafts of light flooding in through high windows like portholes on a tall ship. Beneath the windows were the twelve Stations of the Cross. The smell of incense immediately took me back to my days in parochial school where I'd sit in church every morning before school started, staring at the stations that told the story about the cruelty of man as they nailed Jesus to the cross. Perhaps, that's why I went into law—to defend the helpless. But Jesus wasn't really helpless, I'd learned, and God helps those who help themselves.

All the way to the back of the church, mantilla-covered women, little old men and small children were on their knees facing the priest on the altar; his arms lifted in silent supplication. Through a gilded haze, I could see dust particles floating down like sediment upon the parishioner-filled pews. I could see my seven-year-old-self kneeling at the rail for my first communion. Resembling a little angel in my virginal mantilla like a halo over the Shirley Temple curls; I'd hated sleeping in Mamá's rollers the night before. My seven-year-old cousin Gabriel and I had paced in the foyer of la Sagrada Familia, me in my spotless white dress and Gabriel in his white shirt, black tie, and black slacks.

"It's time. Are you ready?" I'd whispered to Gabriel, his teal eyes wide. Then I let go of his hand.

At least twenty-five little Catholic school children lined up and clicked in their polished shoes (Mamá had bought me a new pair from the zapatería where she worked) over the cool marble up to the altar. Ahead, penny candles flickered from little crimson jars, the color of the blood that dripped from Jesus' palms up on the cross.

And there in the pew, sat Mamá, wearing her red lipstick and sporting a pair of sunglasses not because her future was so bright, but to shield eyes that weren't just brown, but black and blue. In Mamá's lap sat my little brother, Rudy.

"There she is!" Rudy shouted as I made my way up the aisle, my little, white-gloved hands held together in front of my nose in silent prayer.

Across the row, sat Don Pio, my tía, Arisel, and my prima, Angela. My heart fluttered when I saw my primo, Antonio, all cleaned up like a shiny moneda. There were other faces I could no longer remember, but there was one face obviously missing. I'd prayed to Jesus that Papá wouldn't be a no-show. Absent for my birth and my baptism, why would this sacrament be any different? And like traces of frankincense permeating the church, Papá would only be a hint of a memory.

Only the Friday night before, I'd accompanied Mamá to the cantina where Papá liked to listen to sad mariachi music on the jukebox and drink. "Go inside and get his wallet," Mamá told me.

Like a mini-Joan of Arc, the saint's name I'd use for my confirmation, I marched into the proverbial fire, immediately assaulted by the stink. The joint smelled like Papá—hand-rolled cigarettes, dirt, sweat and Tequila. I found him resting his eyes and head on crossed arms at the bar. His wallet peeked out of his back pocket and practically screamed, *Take me*. So I did and I charged out onto the street to hand Mamá his pay.

He didn't come home that night and continued drinking through the next day. Come Sunday, obviously he was too hung over to think about his wallet, much less come to his daughter's First Holy Communion ceremony.

I hadn't eaten the morning of my First Communion. By the time it was my row's turn to stand and make our way to the altar, my stomach growled like Papá with a hangover. The scent of the burning incense nauseated me. I teetered like a bowling pin when I stood and staggered up to the communion rail where I genuflected, looked up to the padre, and stuck out my tongue. I'd been so hungry that morning I thought the wafer tasted like a tortilla.

"In the name of the Father *touch your forehead*, and the Son *touch your heart*, and the Holy Spirit *touch each shoulder*." I returned to my pew and bowed my heavy pin-curled head.

That morning, I floated out of the church into a brighter world—Mamá with her sunglasses, hiding a lifetime's worth of tears—with all of God's newest little saints-in-the-making. In the span of an hour, I'd transformed into Saint Maya, patron saint of drunken fathers. I now had a mission, feeling an energy so powerful that I knew if only I prayed harder, Papá would stop his drinking. I stood in front of the church, beaming into the camera. I'd have something to show Papá after he sobered up.

After the ceremony, the family headed over to Farolito's Restaurant where a mariachi band was already in full swing. Had he known there were going to be mariachis, Papá might have made an effort.

Gazing at Lily now, I remembered her baptism, but that was it. There'd be no more sacraments for her. I wondered if I'd done her a disservice by not bringing her up in the church. It was just another thing to add to my list of screw-ups and another reason why we were all going to hell, according to my mother, Saint Dolores. Lily and I followed Ofelia up the aisle until she turned right into a little candle-lit alcove on the side of the church. Inside, above a mosaic-tiled floor, there were more statues and painted tiles depicting the suffering saints.

Ofelia pointed to a crypt just below a picture of the Last Supper and whispered to me, "There's a spot for Don Pio. The rest of us will end up in the north field."

"Unless Bruno and Antonio have their way," Sylvia added, making the sign of the cross.

"Antonio would rather run the place into the ground than let Bruno take over," Ofelia added.

Why would Antonio want to do that? I wondered, and just the mention of his name and my heart clanged like the little altar bell ringing at communion time.

OUT BEHIND THE church, colorfully painted wooden booths strung with vibrant streamers were set up for the vendors who were selling local food like roasted corn, watermelon, papaya ice cream, and shaved ice. Rap music blared in competition with the Mariachi music echoing from the Zócalo out front. As I approached a booth, I noticed an opening, a hole in the ground, near the back wall of the church. I remembered hearing the story about the tunnel.

"Isn't that where the people of the pueblo hid when Pancho Villa's rebels came through?" I asked, pointing to the hole in the ground.

"That's right," Sylvia said. "They say he came through here."

"On his way to join forces with Zapata," Ofelia said. "The Federales came through, too. But it was mostly the drunken Villistas who raided, drank our Tequila, and raped our women. They burned down the hacienda and killed Don Pio's mother. Later, the town came together and helped rebuild it. One thousand acres with a thousand workers, and a thousand cattle. It had been the livelihood of the people."

"They also raped Don Pio's sister," Lily said, and I gasped, narrowing my eyes at her.

"What?"

"Grandpa told me he was Pancho Villa's bastard," Lily said.

I stopped breathing; my world spun on its axis.

As if it were anything to be proud of, Lily smiled, tapping her chest with her thumb. "That would make me Pancho Villa's great granddaughter."

"Lily, when? When did he tell you that?"

"Mom, you act like it's true. Shouldn't you be telling me Grandpa was crazy on a cracker, like you always did?"

"He was crazy," I responded with emphasis. "Again, when did you talk to him?"

Lily cast her eyes down. "Sometimes we talked on the phone."

"What?"

"He was hard to understand, but the part about Pancho Villa—that was quite clear."

I wanted to know more, but now wasn't the time to get into details with Lily in front of everyone; I'd wait until we got back.

"His family wasn't even around during the revolution," I said. "They'd already fled north."

"Lots of people did," Ofelia added. "My mother hasn't seen some of her brothers since they were little."

"Poor Mamá," Sylvia said. "She waited all this time to go see Hollywood and now since los torres gemelos—"

"Twin towers?" Lily asked. "9/11?"

Ofelia nodded. "The only ride she'll get is the one in the back of the truck to Arandas."

Everyone laughed and then Ofelia added, "And if they're able to build a huge wall—"

"So sad," Sylvia said.

"Our Tequila will be taxed so heavily; it won't be worth exporting. How will this town ever survive?"

IN THE AFTERNOON, dappled shadows from the ficus trees danced across the Zócalo where the family had taken a seat on a park bench. In front of the church, the townspeople milled around. On the perimeter of the plaza were more vendors selling shaved ice, corn-on-the cob, and papaya-on-sticks. Except for the children running around or playing with simple handmade toys, life seemed way too slow for me. I noticed all of the young women wore jeans—so different than when I was a girl. Back then, girls never wore pants, much less came up to the plaza unchaperoned.

"So, this is how you pass the time?" I asked. "Where are all of the men?"

"A few work on the farms," Sylvia said. "But mostly all the others have gone to el norte. And now, it's too dangerous for them to return."

"At least seventy-five percent of the town's residents have left, at some point, to work in the States," Ofelia added. "Even Papá, a leading citizen who was once president of the municipality and who was the first to bring potable water to Sagrada Familia—even he has spent the last ten years in Los Angeles working in factories and car plants—all the while sending money back to us."

"We all miss him," Sylvia added. "Especially, Mamá."

"Only to keep her feet warm at night," Ofelia said with a mischievous laugh.

I laughed too while noticing all of the sandaled, cold-footed women. "And what kind of ambitions or dreams do these women have?"

Ofelia opened her mouth to speak just as the church bell gonged scattering the pigeons like pepper across the sky. Ofelia and her sister then raised their right hand to make the sign of the cross. I noticed everyone in the plaza doing the same.

"Innocent," Ofelia said, after the bells were finished. "She prays that God will bring her a man—a man to be in love with—to take care of her."

"Not too different from a lot of women," I added.

"Yeah, we see how far that got you, Mom," Lily said. "I'm never depending on a man—even to keep my feet warm."

I reached over to squeeze Lily's thigh, as if that would quiet her. "Lily, down here children have respect for their elders."

"Yeah, well—" Lily said, standing to take little Mateo's hand.

Wistfully, I watched as Lily was being chased now across the plaza by little Mateo and Patricia. I wished I could go back for another chance at raising her. Perhaps, if I'd stayed married—kept her father around . . ..

"Like the caged canaries," Sylvia said, "she imprisons herself—lets herself go. Upon his return—"

"If he returns," Ofelia added. "Sometimes, the men end up with other families up there or girlfriends or," she added with a whisper, "that güero disease, la sífilis."

Sylvia glared at her sister, bringing an index finger to her lips, "Hay los niños. ¡Cállate, Ofelia!"

Ofelia smiled mischievously. "She will give herself to him as many times as he wants, ashamed of her own nakedness and petrified another child will be on its way," Sylvia said, staring off. "But children are gifts from God."

"Caramba, Sylvia!" Ofelia said, hooking a thumb toward a toothless woman seated placidly across from us. She was surrounded by her raggedy, barefoot children. "This town has been blessed by God with so many gifts. Maybe he could bless Estella over there with more food to feed her little brood."

"Is her husband up north, too?" I asked, chuckling until I thought I recognized my hat, the one I'd lost earlier, sitting now like a crown on top of the shabby lady.

Ofelia pointed down, shaking her head. "South. Con el diablo. She killed him after the last beating."

"Seriously?" I asked.

Sylvia also shook her head. "Rumors. It could have been anyone. He wasn't well liked around here. Town drunk. Too much Tequila."

"You know how people like to gossip," Ofelia said. "Chisme is a whole other language around here. Very intimate. It makes them feel closer to each other." *Oh, is that why Mamá does it?* "Misery loves her company," Ofelia added. "Another rumor is that not all of her children are from the same father. Her older daughter, Teresa works out at the Tequila farm to help support the family."

I stared even harder now at the children just as Lily came running toward me from across the plaza, her young cousins chasing behind. Huffing. "Hey Mom, isn't that your hat?"

"Looks good on her, doesn't it?" I said.

Little Mateo ran up to ask his mom for some ice cream and Sylvia opened a coin purse, murmuring something to him as she pointed to Lily. She then handed him a coin.

"Let her keep it," I added, gazing at the old woman in my hat. I glanced back and forth at Sylvia and Ofelia. "It all sounds so damned sad—hopeless for the women around here."

"Some work in the Tequila distillery," Ofelia said. "But those are the younger ones filled with hope. But if Antonio gets his way—"

"My god, you make him sound like a monster," I said.

Giggling and out of breath, Sylvia's youngest daughter came to take a seat next to her mother to catch her breath. Sylvia smoothed back her daughter's hair. "He's not that bad, I suppose. I've been lucky, my husband's family owned a bakery and left it to us."

"Life here is slow to change. We like to keep things the same," Ofelia said. "Antonio, especially, has a difficult time with change. It's hard with the outside influence."

Sylvia nodded.

"We want to hang on to our traditions," Ofelia said, staring across the plaza. "Many have left but *la sangre atrae*."

"The blood calls you back?" I asked.

Ofelia smiled and nodded. "It's our job to keep things the same for their return."

"Kind of like tending the garden," I said.

Ofelia laughed out loud. "Sí! But sometimes the weeds are so tough."

"Tio Victor worked so hard," Sylvia added. "After his wife died, he left everything behind—I mean his family, the Tequila farm, which is not saying much since the agave was suffering so. He started a new family and finally opened his own landscaping business up in el norte, but then his son was electrocuted . . ."

I gasped. The plaza spun.

"Now he is either going to jail or is going to be deported," Sylvia said. Trembling now, I knew who they were talking about.

"Or both," Ofelia added. "He never fixed his papers."

"What's your uncle's name?" I asked, voice shaking.

"Victor. Victor Montoya, why?" Sylvia asked.

I sat frozen as shaved ice, mouth agape recalling the conversation with my client on the courthouse steps: *Someday you should go back for a visit. La sangre atrae.*

"The blood calls you back," I mumbled. This was no coincidence, I thought, turning to my cousins who looked at me rather curiously.

But before I could speak, Sylvia's little boy Mateo returned, ice cream dripping down his arms. He handed a cone to Lily.

"It tastes like a Margarita!" she said, licking her lips.

"Well, you asked where you could get a good one," Ofelia said with a chuckle. "Made from agave."

I cocked my head. "You know, Don Pio invited me to spend some time out at the farm. I think I need to go back to Los Olvidados to learn more about this agave plant."

Ofelia, almost too eager, smiled and nodded as she glanced at Sylvia. "I'll call my grandfather and let him know you are coming back."

Chapter Fifteen

Fiesta Time

WORN SALTILLO TILES PAVED THE WALKWAY along the portico of the Los Olvidados colonial. The walls were chipped with what used to be a bright yellow paint, faded now, but a reminder of more cheerful days. Fragrant lemon trees and rose bushes lined the perimeter and fuchsia hung from beams in colorful clay pots. Flower beds overflowed with red geraniums along the borders of the walkway and in the middle of a courtyard splashed a fountain as if there wasn't a drought. Workers were already carrying in chairs and rolling out tables for tonight's celebration.

Inside, Magdalena, wearing a crown of silver threaded braids, led Lily and me down a hallway where hanging from the white-washed plastered walls were pictures of relatives from long ago and photos of the olden days of production.

"This is your room," Magdalena said, opening a door and then walking across the old, tidy, sparsely furnished room to pull open the muslin curtains.

"Thank you," Lily and I answered in unison.

A clay vase full of flowers and a statute of the Virgin of Guadalupe adorned a little table. A crucifix hung on the wall just above and in between the twin beds covered in washed-out pink chenille. Opposite the door leading out into the hallway to the main house, another door opened up to the courtyard. Next to it was a writing desk near a window that looked out onto the porch where there was a rocker and a hammock.

Lily bounced on one of the beds.

"Well, it ain't the Hilton," I remarked, turning to see Lily jump off the bed and head toward a rifle mounted on the wall near the door. She reached up to take it down.

99

"Leave it there." I hated guns.

Ignoring me as usual, Lily pulled it down from the hook and then pointed it toward the window. "Take us to your presidential suite." She laughed.

Out the window and beyond the barrel of the rifle, were a couple of stray goats nibbling on the burgundy bougainvillea draped along the portico. Magdalena wasted no time, waving a dishrag as she chased them off. Tiny lights strung from dozens of olive trees, twinkled in the courtyard. It was twilight and already the three-quarter moon shown bright, but there were also thunderclouds knocking on the horizon like unwanted guests. They certainly weren't invited to tonight's celebration.

Fireflies darted above the fields in the distance. And beyond stood the lonely-looking house on the hill, a tiny mysterious box filled with secrets, a mystery to withdraw. I wondered about its occupancy.

FEELING ENERGIZED and yet nervous, I entered the courtyard wearing a colorful traditional Mexican dress I'd purchased in the plaza. I walked across, the dry grass crackling under my sandaled feet and reached for a cigarette. The dress without pockets was like some sort of bright transdermal patch a smoker wore to quit. And then when I saw Don Pio, as if a time-released force had seeped in through my skin, something pure took root. I no longer felt a craving.

I walked up to kiss my uncle on the cheek before taking a seat next to him. I looked around, hoping to find Gabriel, but instead, I spotted Antonio sitting near the fountain with a guitar on his knee. My nerves stretched thinner than a guitar string.

"Do you celebrate like this every night?" I asked Don Pio, noticing the girls from the factory swooning around their boss as he strummed his guitar.

"Not every night, but tonight, we celebrate Flaco's retirement."

"Oh, I didn't bring a gift," I said, lifting my empty hands.

"No worries."

And then I heard a familiar song—one I'd long since forgotten—and I turned my head. The young group gathered around Antonio sang, "*Cuando caliente el sol aquí en la playa . . .*"

A wave of nostalgia splashed over me as I remembered the time my family had caravanned to Puerto Vallarta—the first time I'd ever been to the ocean. I remembered Gabriel had tagged along. Papá had sung that song to Mamá on the shore, a song about the sun getting hot here on the beach. A fond memory, but faded by now, washed away like my tiny imprints in the sand.

In the background, over the gurgling of the fountain, I could barely hear the guitar and wondered if Antonio was any good or if he only used it as a tool to lure people to him—and then push them away later.

"*Cuando caliente el sol aquí en la playa . . . I feel your body tremble close to me,*" Don Pio sang now. "*Es tu palpitar, es tu cara, es tu pelo, son tus besos, me estremezco, oh, oh, oh.*"

I cleared my throat and then tried to sing along, the lyrics coming back to me as naturally as breathing. "*I feel your body tremble close to me. It's your heartbeat, it's your face, it's your hair; it's your kisses, I'm trembling, oh, oh, oh.*"

"He's pretty good," Don Pio said. "Do you remember the trip we all made to the playa?"

My eyes were glued to Antonio. "What?" I asked, turning to my uncle.

"Everyone except for Antonio. He stayed behind to work. He's never really liked to mix with people."

"Yeah, I don't remember him as being very sociable," I added.

"Now, he just prefers to stay in and do his reading," Don Pio said, looking in Antonio's direction.

For some reason, that surprised me. Antonio didn't come across as someone who'd ever cracked open a book, but then again, maybe he only read comic books. I smiled at the thought of him being into Batman or Wolverine.

"Yes, he's pretty good," Don Pio added, "but not as good as Victor."

"Victor?" I peered at my uncle, noticing the yellowing that happens both in old books and the eyes of the aged. "You know, it's such a small world. I represented Victor in Los Angeles. It had been so long that I never recognized him." I wondered now whether Victor had recognized me. *Was that how he knew my maiden name?* "I really only ever got a good look at the back of his head when we first drove north."

"I miss him," Don Pio said. "Flaco was good, but Victor was the best jimador in all the land and business sense—well, there is no other."

I looked around the courtyard. "Why isn't Angela here tonight?"

"Angela never comes out here anymore."

"What about my father? Did he come out here much?" I asked.

Don Pio shook his head, "Was your room to your liking?" he asked, obviously redirecting the conversation for some reason.

"Oh yes. So, what's with the rifle?" I giggled nervously. "Is Pancho Villa riding through again?"

Don Pio smiled, handing me a brandy-snifter shaped glass filled with a gold liquid. "Perhaps his ghost."

I felt my eyes go wide as I raised my glass to toast. "Salud."

"Salud," he said before taking his shot. He wiped his lips with the back of his hand. "You know, the history of Tequila's development mirrors the turbulent growth of Mexico herself. Do you believe in ghosts?"

"I'm scared of ghosts." I chuckled, turning to see Lily floating in wearing a white peasant dress. Under the moonlight and the twinkly lights strung across the courtyard, she looked radiant—almost angelic, even ghostlike. And then behind her, I saw Antonio staring, almost searing a hole into me, from across the courtyard. I felt dizzy and hot like a drunken firefly flitting around the inside of a mason jar.

"Don Pio, this is my daughter, Lily."

My uncle extended his hand. "Lily, part of the agave family. Welcome. Sit, sit."

"Mucho gusto," Lily said, taking a seat on the bench next to me.

"Let me know if there's anything you need," he said.

"Thank you, Don Pio," I said, looking around. "Where's Gabriel? I wanted Lily to meet him."

"Oh, one never knows about that one," my uncle said, reaching for a glass of water and looking away.

Workers chatted at the long tables, laughing as steaming plates of food were passed around. Lily handed me a plate and I felt a tap on my shoulder. I turned to see Antonio holding out a bottle of Tequila. He pulled up a chair and straddled it with his long legs.

"I see you've returned?" he said.

Thunder sounded in the distance like drumbeats in a deep, dark jungle, signaling trouble. Unable to match the intensity of his liquid blue-green eyes, I focused instead beyond his shoulders, out into the field where the wind whipped up little red dust devils. Above and beyond, a sheet of rain blocked the moon.

Lily leaned in. "Who's he?" she asked, suspiciously.

"Antonio is a distant cousin of ours," I answered without ever addressing him. I still reeled from our last encounter.

"Mucho gusto," Antonio said.

"Igualmente," Lily answered and whispered in my ear, "Remember Mom, we're not the monarchy."

I elbowed her gently. "Not to worry, sweetie."

"We'll start with the blanco," Antonio said, pouring a shot for Don Pio and me.

Even though I'd always said it was okay in moderation and at home where she was safe, relief washed over me when I saw Lily raising her hand to stop Antonio as soon as he started to pour her a shot.

But soon I could see it was because Lily was distracted by a gathering of younger people motioning for her to join them. "Excuse me," Lily said, and got up to walk over toward the group.

Antonio raised his glass to toast and then downed his shot. I sipped mine.

"Maya paints," Don Pio announced, after setting set down his glass.

Not one to accept compliments, and not like I thought I was any good, I could feel my face flush—the primary color of red, I imagined. "Oh, I simply dabble. You know, paint-by-the number, that sort of thing. Nothing like the masterpieces Gabriel—"

Antonio stared at me, nostrils flaring like a penned-up bull. Was he getting sick? What had I said to anger him?

"He says it's all in the brushes," I added. "Well, I've seen enough to know, it takes more than—"

Antonio slammed the bottle onto the table and turned to confront Don Pio. "What is she doing here? I see she still runs her mouth like that little skinny girl."

"Cálmate. She is our guest." My uncle looked at him like a little boy pleading to keep a puppy.

Antonio poured himself another shot and chugged it down as I leaned in to whisper to Don Pio. "He hasn't changed. Same temper."

After a few moments, Antonio held the bottle out like a peace offering but this time I put a hand over my glass.

"Driving somewhere?" he asked.

"No. My uncle invited me to stay, as a matter of—" Lightning cracked, and I jumped. The sky lit up illuminating Antonio's face—eyebrow arched now as he studied Don Pio.

"Maybe you'll have time to show her around the office tomorrow," Don Pio said.

"Oh, I wouldn't want to take you away from your work," I said. "Besides, I have to get back."

"What's the hurry?" Don Pio asked. "I wanted to show you the business."

"Well, really I—"

I shuddered as thunderclouds clapped. Beyond the mountain range, more clouds moved in swiftly. I turned back around to see Antonio marching off.

Don Pio called after him. "Ay Dios mio. Tonio, why do you act this way?"

And then I heard a beep as a text came through on my phone. Thinking it might be my office or worse, Zane, my heart pounded. But it was neither. It was a text from Dr. Vaisman's office. I lost the connection and pushed away from the table to ask to use the house phone.

"Just go and ask Magdalena," Don Pio said, looking concerned.

INSIDE THE HACIENDA, I held the phone to my ear, twisting the cord around my fingers. I'd planned to call as soon as I had a chance, I rehearsed. I've just been so busy. Deep down, I knew something was wrong and now I could no longer ignore the last message where I was to make an appointment to discuss my lab results.

Finally, the doctor herself came on the line and I gave my list of excuses. I was out of the country on a family emergency. I couldn't make an office visit.

"This isn't how I like to give my patience news," Dr. Vaisman said.

Nodding, I listened intently as Dr. Vaisman spoke, "Maya, I'm sorry. It's cancer."

That's all I would remember. After I heard the word "cancer," I lost my ability to hear anything else. I dropped to the floor like a mound of chewed up pulp.

Chapter Sixteen

Blue Gene Genie

ABOVE THE COURTYARD, STREAKS OF MOONLIGHT spilled like a bucket of silver paint across an inky sky. The storm seemed to have passed quickly over the farm, leaving a few shimmering puddles and a few stragglers remaining after the party. The workers needed to get up before sunrise. Stunned by the news from my doctor, I wandered back to the party in a daze. I panned the area looking for Lily, but assumed she'd turned in already. On the table, where I'd been seated, I noticed the open bottle of Tequila Antonio had slammed down earlier. *Idiot*. I picked up the bottle, still more than half full, the same as the moon as I stormed out into the night.

DEEP INSIDE THE field, I stood out of breath, my heart jackrabbiting inside my chest. The news terrified me. I balled my fists and screamed, feeling a catharsis like that therapy where you scream into a pillow or even punch it, only now there was no pillow as I shouted at the top of my lungs, punching the sky with one hand, still holding onto the bottle with the other.

Not one for pity parties, I'd definitely reached a breaking point and needed some sort of release. "Damn it! When am I going to catch a break! Where's anybody when I need them?" I asked the sky. "You were never there for me!" I screamed and took a swig from the bottle.

And then, as if a light switch flicked on at a surprise party, the sky lit up, casting a blue mist over everything. A dizzying azure radiance pulsated around the field. I was at the center of the surprise party, surrounded by the illumination.

Oh shit! How much have I had to drink? I hugged myself, clutching my stomach and then quickly thought about running away, but in which direction? Instead, I dropped the bottle and sank to my knees, curling into myself and squeezing shut my eyes, squashing out what obviously appeared to be some sort of psychotic episode.

"I didn't get to say goodbye," I cried. "I didn't even know where you were!" I buried my head into my hands and sobbed.

But the blue glare came streaming in through my laced fingers. I pulled my hands away, blinded by a fiery azure glow gushing out of the bottle like a geyser.

"I've always been here," the blue luminescence thundered, its eyes a fierce and lustful glaze of fire. "Every time you open this bottle, I am with you."

"What are you talking about?" I shouted, wiping the tears with the backs of my hands. In a flash, I remembered the fantastic stories my father had told me about the genio azul he'd come across in the field. "I don't believe you." I screamed now, pausing when I didn't recognize my own voice—squeaky now like a child— "Papá! Get out! I hate you! I wish you were dead!"—the very words I'd screamed as a child at my father, I recalled now, after he'd slapped me. He'd been drunk and full of Tequila. I hadn't meant to say those words back then. I'd only wished he'd stop drinking, because Tequila was the reason why he did those bad things, he'd told me. If only he'd stopped, then Mamá would be happy, and we could have stayed together as a family. Life wouldn't have gotten so hard. I might have made better choices for my life.

I picked up the bottle and hurled it across the rows of plants, but a flame shot back like a boomerang, unfurling toward me, punching me in the gut, slamming me backward onto the ground and knocking the air out of me. Motionless, I stared at the sky until I could catch a breath. Finally, I flipped over, scrambled to my feet and ran off.

"You wanted me dead," the blue genie roared, echoing across the field. I charged toward the north field, screaming. Through the rows of agave, the plants were growing into tall monsters, like an army of those inflatable air dancers seen advertising at car dealerships. I had to be hallucinating, but then the plants grew taller, blocking out the moon and I stumbled, falling face first into the dirt. Red soil up my nose, I could smell the cool sweet, yet metallic earth and then slowly, I pushed myself onto my knees and got back up on my feet. It was as if I'd inhaled iron courage from Mother Earth or rather, the fall had knocked some sense into me. I brushed off the dirt, and turned to face the light, back straight now. But I busted out laughing at the plants when I noticed they were casting eerie, yet comical, elongated shadows across the path.

I'm really sick, I thought, and now I'm going crazy, too. I covered my face, scrambling to think and then suddenly, filled with a sense of shocked euphoria, I wanted to laugh and cry. Hands-on-hips, I faced the blue mist and without raising my voice, I said, "You don't scare me."

The image swelled, but still I held my ground.

"Hey, Vegas called." I giggled now at my warped sense of humor. "They want their Blue Man back."

I then turned to walk away.

But the earth started to rumble. The vibrations began between my toes, shooting electric currents up through my body. My feet lifted off the ground as the brilliant blue light swallowed me. Now caught in the eye of the raging storm, everything swirled clockwise around me, but my stomach churned counterclockwise. Finally, the thing spit me out and threw me to the ground. I threw up and passed out.

TIME HAD PASSED when I woke to the sound of water splashing all around me. *Am I dead?* No. I was never more alive than when I was scared to death, and I was definitely scared to death. Afraid to move, I lay like stagnant water. And then, as raindrops danced on the backs of my legs, the warm water collecting around me, I wondered if I might liquefy straight into the earth; my skin slipping from my bones; my spirit joining the others who traversed the primordial sky. But I could hear myself breathe, feel my heart beating against the earth, and my body swelling like tiny ocean ripples. I inhaled a cleansing breath, swallowing purification and pluck and wondered if my backbone was strong enough to support my heavy head cresting now like a big wave. I rolled over to face the ancient sky sprinkled now with dimming stars and a waxing moon.

"Oh, please help me," I whispered to the brilliant constellations, recalling the story Papá had told me about the morning star that had pierced Domingo's being, infusing him with energy. And then, in the distance, I could hear the gong of the church bell. As it resounded in my heart, the plants started to shrink back to size, the blue glimmer dissolving into the once parched soil.

Sapped of any strength to stand, I crawled away.

I hadn't made it very far down the path when I came upon the hooves of a large animal. I lifted my head, startled to look into the big brown eyes of Chuey, the donkey. And when I noticed Gabriel assessing me from the back of the beast, relief spilled over me.

With a muddy hand, French-manicured fingernails now chipped, I wiped my tears. I didn't want Gabriel to see I'd been crying.

"Your face is full of mud," Gabriel said. "Did you lose something?"

I simply stared at him as he dismounted. With the support of his crutches, he hobbled over and knelt down, handing me his white kerchief. He wrapped his arms around me. "It's okay. You need to cry. Your father just died," Gabriel said in a voice purging me of any shame, a sound as soft as a baby's blanket, as soothing as a lullaby.

"I'm not crying over him! My knees are bleeding and I'm—I'm sick—and didn't you get a load of Aladdin's buddy out there?"

"Quit defending your illusions," Gabriel said, and I pushed him away. I could hear Mamá again, *Tú y tu imaginación.*

I stood, wiping my hands on my muddied dress. "Are you saying what I'm experiencing is not real?"

"Perception is a big part of our reality," Gabriel answered, moonlight bouncing off his smile.

"So, this is only my perception?" I squeezed my forehead. "It's not real?"

"Only love is real," Gabriel said.

I felt real pain shooting throughout my body. *So then why does love have to hurt?*

Chapter Seventeen

Stage One - Denial

THE NEXT MORNING, THE SOUND OF A ROOSTER woke me and my cancer up. What a horrible nightmare, I thought. Thank God it's not real. But then as I looked over at Lily, still asleep, the relief melted away, and there was no denying this reality. *How am I going to tell her?*

And then by the second time the rooster crowed, Lily opened her eyes. Already plunged into a depression, I tried my best to hide it from Lily who sat up staring at me, rubbing her eyes.

"Mom, what's wrong?"

I grabbed a tissue from the little nightstand. "Nothing, sweetie," I said, voice cracking before blowing my nose.

She pulled the sheet up around her neck.

"Don't worry, it's not contagious," I said. "I think it's allergies."

"But we were supposed to go with Ofelia to her school."

"You should go."

"Are you sure? Her class is decorating the altars for the big celebration."

"I'm sure. Have fun."

Once Lily had left, I went down the hall to use the house phone. I made sure no one was around as I punched in my doctor's number. I wanted to hear what I'd missed the day before. Maybe it was all a mistake. Wasn't denial the first stage of grief, or was that death? All I knew was I was a long way from that acceptance stage—stage five. Maybe I didn't have cancer after all. Or maybe I hadn't heard clearly. But this time when I called, it still sounded like I was calling from the bottom of the ocean.

The words, still muted and distorted, sunk down into my ear canal like a lead whisper, a heavy anchor that could only drag me down even further. "It's cancer," Dr. Vaisman said, confirming her previous proclamation.

The doctor hoped it hadn't spread through the walls of my intestine. She'd order an MRI and a PET Scan, to see if there were any more tumors. After surgery, I'd most likely need to start chemo. In the meanwhile, I was to keep taking my medication.

"Can it wait until next week?" I asked.

"Not any longer," Dr. Vaisman replied. "We can't risk letting it spread."

I hung up and wandered back to my room where I pulled out my computer but when I couldn't get a connection, I burst out crying. *Oh God, please help me!* And then slowly, miraculously, I had service -- *probably from the factory across the property.*

I spent some time researching my type of stomach cancer brought on most likely by my Crohn's disease. And then I worried about Lily. Was it hereditary? I remembered reading about the inheritance pattern of Crohn's and how it tended to cluster in families and that having an affected family member was a significant risk factor for the disease. But now what about this cancer? Would Lily also be at risk? Oh God! My head pounded and my stomach constricted when I read about the limited treatments, including chemo. I should have taken better care of myself. I should have quit smoking, especially knowing the Crohn's placed me at an increased risk for cancer. They weren't called cancer sticks for no reason. I slammed my computer shut and spent the rest of the day in bed, hoping no one could hear the blubbering from the bottom of the deep, dark ocean.

I'D EXHAUSTED myself crying and didn't wake up until the next morning with the same thought it was all just a bad dream. But then I looked over to see Lily had not slept in her bed, and suddenly I felt even more alone. I'd have to do this cancer thing by myself. And then as if all the crying had cleansed me of the toxins in my body, at that moment, I made the decision to take this beast on headfirst. By God, there had to be a cure! This was the

twenty-first century, after all. This was not a death sentence, just
something else I'd need to handle, and right away.

I shuffled down into the kitchen where everyone had already taken a
seat around a big rustic oak table.

"Buenos días," Don Pio said.

"Buenos días."

"Lily called last night, but she didn't want to wake you," Magdalena
said, pouring me a cup of coffee. "She stayed with Ofelia to help her with a
project. She said she'd see you at dinner."

Everything smelled wonderful. Remarkably, my appetite had returned
after my long-lost voyage, but I wasn't quite ready to dive into the huevos con
chorizo nor the bowl of birria de chivo, a peppery, goat stew that Magdalena
had set in front of me. She'd also set out some fresh cut fruit on the table.

"Oh, this looks—" I stared into the bowl of bloody-looking soup and
gracefully pushed it away. "I think I'm just going to enjoy my café first and
maybe some of that pan dulce." Sylvia had sent along some pastries from
her bakery.

I added some crema and as I added a spoonful of azúcar de agave into
my café, I remembered sneaking sips from Papá's mug. He would add at
least four teaspoons of azúcar. It tasted better than los dulces.

"You really should try Magdalena's birria." Don Pio said as I reached
for a slice of watermelon.

I smiled and nodded, pulling the bowl in front of me. I then tore off a
piece of corn tortilla, handmade just that morning by Magdalena, and
dunked it. I tore off another piece using it to grab a chunk of goat meat. I
slid it into my mouth. The tender meat fell apart on my tongue, waking up
senses I didn't even know I had. "Delicioso," I said. I practically licked the
bowl. Where had this hunger been hiding?

Pushing away from the table, I felt energized, pretty optimistic. The
cancer will only make me stronger, I thought and then remembered
another saying, *God won't give me more than I can handle*. I laughed to
myself. *As if he hasn't already given me too much.*

And then after another good night's rest, I felt pretty good, better than
I expected. I felt like I had superhuman powers. Whether it was
hopefulness or a last minute, panic-induced mania, like a fight or flight
response induced by the same natal response that causes all your blood

vessels to explode in a vain attempt to warm you moments before you die of hypothermia, I thought, *I'm going to fight this.*

After the hearty breakfast, I wandered over to the distillery. Adrenaline had kicked in, preparing me to take on the enemy, even if it was only my perception of an adversary. I was walking into the judge's chambers again when I crossed the threshold into Antonio's office. On the underside of the notebook I clutched to my chest, my heart tapped a message of warning. Anxious, but like most other challenges I faced, I welcomed what lay ahead of me. I was pumped.

He sat facing his computer. Behind him stood a girl no older than Lily looking over his shoulder, straw hat dangling by a piece of thin leather down her back. She seemed startled when she turned and saw me walk in.

"Buenos días," I said, and Antonio immediately swung his chair around. I gasped when I saw a baby in his arms.

Quickly, he handed the baby off to the girl, and then he swiveled back around to his computer. The girl hugged the baby close, staring at me, as she picked up a document from a desktop printer. Eyes lowered, she scooted past me on her way out the door.

There'd been no mention of Antonio being a father nor whether he was married or even seeing anyone. Not that it was any of my business and I wasn't jealous, but it was all very curious.

"Can I help you with something?" Antonio asked without turning to face me.

"No, just observing." I looked around the office for any sign of fatherhood. There were no photos on his desk like the ones I kept of Lily in my office—from kindergarten through high school—well, except for her senior year. No ceramic ashtrays or handprints. Except for a desk, a computer, and the shelf with an assortment of different bottles, his office was sparse.

"Is the baby yours?"

Antonio swiveled around, boots pounding down on bare cement. "Why are you not in the field painting, mujer?"

"Don Pio asked me to come. He thought I could help," I said, rolling up a sleeve as I leaned in a little closer to the desk, preparing for battle. "Is there a problem with my being a mujer?"

"I do not need your help. This fábrica has been running just fine without any woman's help. Much less help from el norte."

"Seriously?" I said. "That's why the factory is filled with young girls and a majority of your fields lay fallow." I stood up straight, a little more poised.

I jumped back when Antonio shot up from his chair, nearly punching his head through the ceiling. "And just what do you know, mujer?"

Reining myself back, my fingers trembled as I pushed a loose coil of hair around my ear, forcing an uneasy smile. "Maybe I'd like to know more about Tequila." I drew a breath. "The nature of the beast. Why it destroys families—"

"I say if you can't ride, then why mount the beast?" he said, cutting me off, staring me down.

I gnawed the inside of my lip, wondering how to proceed with this obstinate creature. In the courtroom, I'd come up against worse pigheaded opponents. I could handle Antonio. "My uncle thinks I should learn the business. I can't very well sell something I haven't researched."

"Our Tequila is selling just fine!"

"That's not what Don Pio—"

"¡Ay que la chingada! Your uncle is wrong, besides if a salesperson is any good, he or she should be able to sell anything."

He'd cut me off again. This time I sucked in a breath and then swallowed back the anger that crawled up my throat.

"I did do pretty well selling—"

"It also helps to have your youth."

Whoa! That did it. I bit my lip and tasted blood, the taste of rage, acidic on my tongue. "Do you get off on being an asshole?" I asked, hand on hip.

"'Get off'?"

"I'm trying my best here and I always give one hundred percent, and I don't need to take this crap!"

Antonio stared at me for a moment. "You were cute when you were angry," he said, dismissively, and then with a smirk, he added, "but now, not so much."

I felt my nostrils flare as I took a deep breath. *What a machismo thing to say!* I slammed my notepad down onto his desk and stormed out of the building before I really let him have it—before I could spit out my true wrath.

Chapter Eighteen

Stage Two - Anger

BLIND WITH RAGE, I'D MARCHED OUT OF Antonio's office only to find myself sobbing in the middle of the agave field, blinking hot tears. I screamed as if I might empty the toxins from my body. Exhausted, I wiped and then rubbed my eyes, in an effort to tease out a massive headache, and then I plopped down onto the crimson pathway. Waiting for my heart to slow down, I buried my head in hands.

I thought about praying and looked up. It had been years since I got on my knees. *Pray to whom? Where do I start?* I strained to listen for an answer, but only heard some crickets. I heard the whisper of the wind whistling through the plants. *Oh, dear God, I'm really scared. What's going to happen to me? What am I doing here?* I looked up and saw the mountain looming before me and in a flash, I remembered the story I'd heard in Catholic school about the long, hard road Jesus had traveled up the hill where he was finally nailed to the cross. Well, if crucifixion was the ultimate destination for being good, it's a wonder I wanted no part of my old religion. I got up, rubbing the stone-dimpled imprints out of my knees and headed back to the hacienda.

LATER AFTER NIGHTFALL, Lily and I joined Don Pio and the others for the evening meal. I'd just sat next to Lily when Antonio strolled in.

He saw us and my stomach clashed with my heart. In a few long strides, he stood by our table. *This is strange. What's he doing here?* And then he took a seat directly across from Lily. "I didn't get to tell you how sorry I was about your grandfather," he said. "It was inconsiderate of me."

He's being nice, but I'm not buying it.

Lily nodded. "Thank you. Did you know him very well?"

Antonio shrugged his shoulders. "I remember him from—" He looked at me a bit perplexed. "You look like sisters," he said to Lily.

Lily's eyes narrowed, her nose wrinkling up, obviously not appreciating the comparison.

Don Pio seemed to pick up on the tension and stepped in to try and help. "You are all your mother talks about."

"Well, someone needs to get a life," Lily answered with more than a hint of annoyance.

"Perhaps, she can find one here in the next couple of weeks," Don Pio added.

Lily turned to me. "But, Mom, I thought you were going home."

I opened my mouth to speak but got cut off.

"What about the funeral?" Lily asked.

"There isn't going to be one. I already arranged to send his body home. He's being cremated."

"No memorial? What the fuck!"

Embarrassed, I looked around the table apologetically, before addressing Lily.

"It's the way Grandma wants it."

"But this is his home. Besides, Grandma hated him. This is just shitty!"

I reached out to touch Lily's arm. "Maybe we can have our own serv—"

She pulled away. "Whatever." Standing, she excused herself before stomping away.

"She really does remind me of you when you were a girl," Antonio said.

I shot him a look I wished could knock him down to an average height and then I turned to watch my daughter join a couple of young farmers at another table.

"Am I to understand you are staying here?" Antonio asked, pouring two shots of Tequila, then scooting a glass across to me.

116

"I haven't made any final decisions," I responded, knowing I was going home. But I wasn't going to tell him that—wouldn't give him the pleasure. I hadn't really been planning anything and then—the cancer call. Everything just seemed to be unfolding a certain way; almost as if something else had taken control; something quite mystifying.

Magdalena set down two steaming bowls of food.

"I've invited her to stay here awhile," Don Pio said, ladling himself some arroz con pollo.

"Let me know if there's anything I can do to make your stay more comfortable," Antonio said, raising his glass to toast me.

Like putting a tarantula in my bed? I didn't trust what he said was genuine, but responded politely, "Thank you," I said, raising my glass to take a sip.

Antonio, peering at his uncle, ripped off a piece of tortilla and wrapped it around a piece of chicken. Before putting the tortilla into his mouth, he turned to me. "Not to your liking?"

I hadn't finished the Tequila and the dinner wasn't settling well with me. I could feel my stomach roiling. My body exuded sweat as if the small sip had awakened all of the poisonous toxins in my body now screaming to be released. I mopped my forehead with a napkin. Pepita was awake.

"It can't be this cool weather," Antonio said. "Is Magdalena's chili too hot for you?"

I shook my head, pushing away from the table.

My uncle stared at me. "You don't look good, Maya," he said. "Antonio, help her back to her room. I'll send Magdalena over."

Antonio wasted no time taking my hand. Too sick to protest, I let him wrap his arm around my waist. As we walked across the courtyard the short distance to the hacienda, I saw Lily seated near the fountain with the two young men. Too old to be told it was time for bed, I asked instead, "Lily, are you ready to turn in?"

She looked at me, coolly. "Just a little while longer, Maya," she said, slipping an arm through one of the young farmer's and walking away again.

I knew she only did that to annoy me, but *since when does she call me Maya?* We needed to talk—in the morning when I felt better.

PREDAWN AND I awoke to the strange sound of birds cheeping. I held my breath, tilting my head and listening more intently. And then I heard a child giggling. I turned to look check on Lily, but once again, she wasn't in the adjoining twin bed. More giggling and I scanned the room, the noise came from outside. *What is Lily doing out there? Who is she with?* I yanked the blanket off my bed and wrapped myself in it before stepping to the window. Lily wasn't out there. But then, something caught my eye. At the edge of the property, two pinpoints of light, like eyes of fire stared back at me. As I strained to see, I heard more cackling and stepped outside into the dark where the air felt like a cool, damp blanket. Cinching the bed coverlet tighter, I trekked across the patchy crabgrass to the edge of the field where I halted, slack jawed, wondering if I might be only dreaming.

Surprisingly calm, I followed the eyes of fire luring me into the field like a giant bowl that had been shaped by the surrounding hills. The area filled with a fog so thick bats were confused and even the nightingales warbled uncertain as to whether it was night or day. And then, through a clearing in a blue hazy mist, I stood enchanted, witnessing a fog of tiny crystals, like stars smudged across the Milky Way taking shape into something liquid-like. The brilliant atom-like points of light then consolidated into a spritely tinsel before morphing into a life-like, fair-haired luminescent little girl. Her eyes were an iridescent blue-green. I sucked in a breath when I recognized the shadowy antithesis of myself. I was that child.

And then the little girl started to pirouette around me, leaving a trail of azure sparkles.

I hugged my smaller self.

The youngster, braids bouncing, danced around me in a light, whipping up a sort of calm I'd never sensed. As the little girl skipped around me, I was beguiled deeper into field.

But I stopped, tilting my head when I smelled a cigarette. A tendril of smoldering turquoise slowly began shaping itself into something denser. A man. The little girl's smile ran away, and I screamed when I recognized my father as I'd seen him in the morgue, grey, toothless and skeletal.

Clenched between his teeth, dangled a burning cigarette. The little girl screamed, too, as she hurried to hide herself behind me. I took the girl's hand and spun around to run.

"Don't go," the specter said. "Please, Maya."

Stopping in my muddy tracks, I heard my father's baritone voice.

"Papá, what do you want?"

Next, I heard a moan and turned to see my father evaporate behind a veil of fog. The little girl was gone, too.

THE RISING SUN appeared like a golden halo shimmering around the silhouette of jagged mountaintops. Beneath my feet, the ground felt damp and cool, mud oozing between my toes. How could this be a nightmare when I could also hear the crickets chirping and the rainwater trickling toward the river across the fissures in the parched ground? I shivered, hugging the blanket tighter as I headed back to the hacienda. And then, out of the corner of my eye, across a row of agave, I noticed a refraction of light. I stepped off the path and inched toward the glow.

Behind a tall plant, I spotted Gabriel already up and working on his painting. Seated and without turning to acknowledge me, he said, "You are up early."

"Yes, and I shouldn't have gotten out of bed," I said.

"He is in a better place," Gabriel responded.

"Well, if that doesn't sound cliché," I answered. "We missed you again last night," I said, just as something stung the bottom of my foot. I reached down to smash away a fire ant. "Damn! Amazing how much pain such a little creature can inflict."

"Had it known its destiny, I don't think it would have bitten you."

"Small brains, little suffering."

"That's your perception," he said.

Since when did you go all Gandhi? I was annoyed and too tired for the banter we'd enjoyed as kids. "Well, maybe it's like the Tequila. You take that first drink, you don't know it's going to kill you."

"Tequila doesn't kill people," Gabriel said, twisting around to face me with a smile.

"Okay, Gandhi, now you're really irritating me."

And then as the magical images came to life on the canvas, and just like the last time I'd watched him paint, or rather watched the work paint itself, his creation erased everything around me, including my reality.

"You'll find all of the answers right here," Gabriel said, pointing to the painting.

LATER, I RETURNED to our room to find Lily in bed asleep. Sighing, I climbed back into my own bed to stare at the shadows dancing on the ceiling, pirouetting now like the little girl I'd seen the field. I was that little girl, but what had she been trying to tell me? I remembered reading about a person on her deathbed. The dying woman had talked about seeing her little sister.

After a while, all I'd done was toss and turn, unable to get back to sleep. *What's happening to me? Is this all just a dream? Is this because I have cancer? Am I dying? Are these visions because the line between life and death is so thin now? Am I somewhere in between, walking toward my destination? Am I having a breakdown?* And then my stomach started to burn, and I knew I wasn't dreaming. The pain was real. I wondered when I'd last taken my medication. I got back out of bed to get my pills, then grabbed a Tums. Quietly I got dressed and left the room.

WITH ONE OF Magdalena's homemade tortillas and a mug of tea sweetened with agave sugar, I swallowed my pills. Early morning, and the field called to me. I wanted answers, but to what questions? Gabriel said I'd find the answers in the painting.

I looked for Gabriel, but when I arrived at the spot where he'd been working earlier, he was gone. Noticing he'd left some things behind, I stepped closer and saw a blank canvas, a brush, and some paint. Smiling, I looked around before taking a seat on the ground. I picked up the board, running my fingers around the edges and then set it upon my lap. My hand trembled as I opened the little tubes of paint. I brought the lip of the container to my nose and breathed in. Oh, how I missed the smell of the paint. Funny, this should have made me feel nauseous, I thought as I picked up the brush.

I dipped it into the brown paint and then set the tip onto the white canvas, but still I had no idea what I might create. I closed my eyes and felt a heat travel down through my veins, seeping all the way into my now tingling fingertips. When I opened my lids, I noticed the paint-by-numbers as if for a child. In the middle of the white borders, tiny pinpoints began to dot the canvas, like immigrants to a new land, I thought with a laugh. Startled and uncertain, I squeezed the brush as I connected the dots, tracing each now with vivid colors until an image began to take form.

Swelled with anticipation, I jumped when I heard footsteps, and turned to see an elongated shadow stretched across the pathway.

"Who's the little girl?" Lily asked, as she walked up.

"I'm not sure," I said, happy to see my daughter. I turned to study my painting. "I think she's me." I stood.

"She does have your eyes," Lily said, her own eyes glued to the painting.

I then gathered my things. "Walk with me," I said. "We really need to talk."

"Oh Mom, I'm *really* tired. I watched you get dressed this morning and leave. You never came back to the room, so I came out here to see if you were okay. But I can see that you're fine."

"I just need to talk," I said. "Why am I the only one that ever wants to talk?"

"Because you're the only one that thinks she has all the answers."

"Well, not anymore," I said. "Where did you sleep last night?"

"Me? Oh my God! I was in the hammock on the porch. What about you? I saw you and Antonio head back into the room."

"He was only escorting me. I wasn't feeling—"

"Whatever." She started walking away. "Please, I'm not in the mood to be put on the stand."

"Lily, I'm worried—"

"And that's just another thing you're really good at, Mom."

Oh, really, I thought, following Lily. As a mom, worrying had been my job, and I'd been well groomed for it.

121

We reached the edge of a narrow riverbed intersecting the field. Only a rivulet of water trickled through after the rain. Not enough to end the draught.

"My father and I fished here when I was a small girl."

She stopped to look down into the dry arroyo.

"Your dad took you fishing once," I said.

Her face shadowed over. "I'm not in the mood to get all nostalgic about the dead," she said, turning to walk away, but then she pivoted and faced me. "This was a mistake. You were right, again. I shouldn't have come here. Well, you don't have to worry about me; I'm going back to school."

"Honey, I never said—"

But she'd already stormed off, a cloud puff trailing in the wind.

I knew better than to chase after her. Besides, my little girl would only run away faster.

I slumped down onto the edge of the riverbank, I never knew what to say to Lily, how to say it. I'd wanted to talk to her about her father and assure her that he'd loved her. Fathers—*at least he never physically hurt you.* Staring at what used to be the farm's abundant water source, I remembered how, as a girl, I'd lie down on my stomach, elbows propping my chin, and stare into the cocoa and strawberry-colored pool to see the reflection of clouds passing by. "There's your puppy," Papá told me one time, and I'd flipped over to see him pointing up to a cloud stretched out like a misshapen piece of cotton. Another time, he'd pointed out La Virgen de Guadalupe. It had to be in May because I'd been gathering flowers for Jesus's mother, Maria. Every year, the girls at Sagrada Familia would fashion their own wreath of flowers and don them for the May crowning.

"Maya. ¡Mira la Virgen!" Papá shouted, jutting an index finger to the sky as he came in from the field. It had been just before sunset and the sky had set against a canvas of blue with splashes of pastels in yellows and mints, purples and pinks, a veritable Easter pallet. Papá pointed up to the western sky and there, sure enough and formed out of a cluster of puffy, rose-colored clouds, I could swear to God and all the martyrs and saints that, I too, had seen her in all her glory—La Virgen Maria de Guadalupe.

I chuckled now, growing a little despondent. But what about when he told me he was the son of Pancho Villa? Might I have misunderstood that, as well? Oh, Papá tan loco. If nothing else, I'd have him to thank for my interest in clouds—the only silver lining.

Looking up now, I suddenly smelled a cigarette. I saw nothing around me and reached into the pocket of my sweater to pull out a smoke of my own. I lit it, noticing the canvas lying on the ground. I reached over to pick up the painting and suddenly more numbers popped up until the image of the little girl came to life. A young me now appeared wearing my father's white sombrero, clearly too big for me. In the picture, I fished with my father, a cigarette between his lips. I remembered bringing some paper and crayons. He'd shown me how to draw a puppy. I'd wanted one so badly; I imagined drawing one would somehow make it real. "The next time we go back to the states, I'll get you one," he'd promised me.

I looked closer at the canvas now and could see the bottle of Tequila propped between my father and me.

And then, it appeared as if the painting had come alive. I recalled catching a small fish, feeling so excited as I reeled it in. But sadly, I'd accidentally knocked over his bottle. I watched, horrified, as the liquid gold spilled across the ground, getting sucked up by the thirsty soil before I could recover any of it. In a flash, my father morphed into some sort of giant blue genie.

That's my recollection. He'd roared at me and then he grabbed me by the arm and slapped me across the face, knocking me to the ground. I'd placed a hand over my eye, feeling something thick and warm oozing down my cheek. Blood. I wanted to run, but where to? And then through my bloodied fingers, I saw the black work boots, my heart pounding away as he approached. I flipped over to crawl away, but he grabbed me by my ankle, and pinned me to the ground, his sick breath so close to my face. *I'm sorry, Papá,* I'd screamed, his hot hand reached up my blouse, touching my tiny breasts like bruised knots on my chest. His other hand unbuckled his belt. I couldn't understand. *¡No, me pegas! Don't hit me, Papá! Why are you doing this?* And then he was on top of me. I couldn't breathe. I flicked in and out of being, kicking and screaming until he rolled off. He cried as if he'd just realized what he was about to do. Somehow, I scrambled to my feet and ran away.

In the shade of a giant agave plant, the spikes poking out all around me like a crown of thorns, I sat trembling, hugging my knees. I'd wanted to tell, but whom? How could I put into words what had just happened? Later, crying would be the only way and as the tears spilled, my eyes would speak when my mouth couldn't explain. But who would listen? I'd felt the flush of shame. And then I'd heard the sound of footsteps, softer now, and through my one good eye, I saw Gabriel. Had he seen what happened to me? He approached, kneeling next to me, and handed me a flower from a shoot out of the agave. "Chew on it," he said, motioning for me to take a bite from the stem. I opened my hand and the crumpled drawing of the puppy fell to the ground. Gabriel picked it up as I chewed on the plant. It tasted sweet and I felt my lips spread into a smile.

"The picture is good," he'd said, looking at my puppy drawing.

I remembered that even though my eye throbbed, Gabriel and I had skipped out of the field hand-in-hand, only to be halted by Antonio who stood rigid, gripping a scythe. And to think, Papá had warned me to keep away from *him*.

"Must be nice to play all day," Antonio had said, before chopping down on the head of an agave.

Now, as I stared at the painting, flitting in and out of understanding, the tears slid down my cheeks. *How had I been able to bury the memories and simply skip through life all of these years?*

The next day, as I got ready for school, I heard the sound of a gunshot coming from my parent's bedroom. I ran in and screamed when I found my father sprawled on the floor with the gun in his hand. In that moment, I knew how gut wrenching it felt to lose my father forever. But then, he opened his eyes, and I threw up. He'd only pretended to be dead. "Tell me you forgive me, Maya," he said sitting up, pleading. I could see the tears in his eyes. "Okay, Papá," I said, wiping my mouth with the hem of my dress as I stared at the bullet lodged in the back wall.

I SET DOWN the canvas and got ready to head back to the hacienda when Gabriel approached on Chuey. Startled, I could feel my insides reacting and I clutched my stomach as he regarded my work.

"You were a good little girl," Gabriel said, handing me a flower cut from a shoot like he'd done when we were kids.

"Thank you."

"For your stomach."

I then looked at the painting. "Was I so bad? And now I'm a terrible mother."

He smiled at me kindly. "Lily is your masterpiece. She is the art you've transformed from the pain."

A smile spread over my face.

"It wasn't right what he did to you," Gabriel added.

I gasped. "Oh my God! You did know."

"Who do you think told your mother?"

The tears stung the corners of my eyes before escaping.

"You?"

All this time and I'd never said a word. I'd kept the secret. After a while, I started to doubt my own memory and then buried it so deep, I could believe it never happened.

Gabriel stared at me. "It broke my heart to see you go and then to know I had something to do with it."

"You had nothing to do with it," I said, sobbing now as I wrapped my arms around him.

"I know that now," Gabriel replied. "We both do."

"I really tried to forget, but it's like that underpainting of blue that just always creeps through." After a few moments, I pulled away. "Thank you for the canvas and supplies."

"Thank Don Pio," Gabriel said, staring now at the empty canvas. "Keep practicing not doing and everything will fall into place."

"That sounds quite contrary," I said, biting off a chunk of stalk and as I chewed, eyes closed, I remembered the sweet taste, surprised now at how it really seemed to soothe my stomach. I'd try to recollect only the good from now on.

Smiling, I opened my eyes to find that Gabriel, like my pain, had vanished into thin air.

I RETURNED TO the hacienda and found Lily seated on the porch, bag packed.

"I'm ready to go," she said.

Still feeling raw after my episode in the field, I rushed up next to Lily. "Are you sure? Honey, I wanted to spend more time with you." I wanted to cry but wouldn't in front of my daughter. "Please don't go. Please stay."

"What for? So you can preach some more?"

I tilted my head. "Do I preach, really?" I scratched the side of my head. "Lily, I'm your mother, but can't we please try to be friends. This Mexican standoff is ridiculous."

"Ridiculous?"

Don Pio walked by and stopped to stand in the shade of a lemon tree.

"Maya, will you be available to come to the office this afternoon?"

I wiped the corner of my eye. "I don't think I can this afternoon. Maybe tomorrow."

He picked a lemon, looking back and forth between Lily and me. "Well then, enjoy your day. We'll see each other at dinner."

"Don Pio," I called out. "Thank you for the canvas and supplies."

"You're welcome," he said, waving the lemon.

Desperate, I turned to Lily. "Honey, please don't go. I don't know when we'll see each other again."

She looked at me. "I'll think about it," she said, crossing her arms over her chest, punishing me.

"Is there anything you want to do today?"

"I think I'll go into town," she said, standing and then walking away.

"I'll go with you."

"That's okay, Mom. I think I'll call Ofelia and hang out with her." She stepped off the porch.

I clutched my stomach anticipating the conversation I needed to have with my daughter. "Lily?"

She turned around and saw me holding my middle. "You okay? Is your stomach acting up again? Have you eaten anything today?"

"Yes, I've eaten and actually—" I said, inhaling some strength. "I can't keep this from you any longer."

My baby's eyes grew large, already misting up.

"My doctor says I have cancer."

Her eyes flashed in panic. "Oh, Mom!" She burst into tears and ran up to hug me. "Are you going to die?"

"No. No. Hey, it's gonna be okay," I said, patting her back. "Dr. Vaisman says we caught it early," I said, hoping it was true. "Besides, I didn't come down here to die."

"Goddammit," Lily said, pulling away, her eyes glassy with tears, her voice cracking. "So what are you still doing here? I told you that you needed to slow down. That you needed to rest." She sobbed now, her face scarlet.

"I'm trying and once I get back to the states, I'll start more treatment."

Lily wiped the tears with the back of her hand. "Well, I'm going home with you and I'm going to make sure you stop everything."

"That's really not necessary, honey. Trust me. It's going to be okay."

"That's what you say about everything. You're not God!" She snorted. "You think you can control everything."

I was struck silent.

"You never tell me the truth. You keep things from me. Secrets. Like about my father and my grandfather."

"I've tried to tell you about your—"

"Yeah, but only on your terms." She stomped her foot. "It's not fair. It's not right. And why the fuck did you never tell me I was a twin!"

I gasped.

"Yeah, that's right. I know. Grandma told me. Sometime ago."

Instantly I felt both a betrayal and shame. I wasn't surprised that my mother had told her. Like a lethal concoction, Mamá loved stirring things up, but damn it, this had been my secret to tell. And although knowing this helped to unravel another thread in Lily's anger and the distance, I felt from her, I still felt some humiliation.

"I'm so sorry. I was waiting for the right time. I've wanted to tell you things, but it's just that I also want to protect you. You know that."

"Yeah, so then what about the Crohn's? What else haven't you told me? You know I've done my own research and it's hereditary." Hands on her hips. "Don't you think maybe, you should have told me? Do you think I enjoyed finding it out from Zane?"

More betrayal. "What do you mean?"

"He picked up the phone when I called the house. He was freaking out— saying stuff like he didn't know how much longer he could handle it."

"Handle what? He never even—"

"Believe me, if I hadn't gotten the news about Grandpa, I would have come home and ripped into you a lot sooner."

"I'm sorry, please don't be mad at me. I'm trying here. I want to be forthcoming with you from now on."

"For God's sake, Mom, you have to be! I need you," Lily said, covering her face with her hands as she wept. "You're all I have."

I reached out to hug her. "It's going to be okay," I said, rubbing her bony back. How I wished there was something more I could say or do to comfort her. I could feel the tiny sharp ridges of my baby's spine like a little trembling bird. "I'm going to do better."

"You're already the strongest person I know, but maybe that's not such a good thing."

I thought about it. "Maybe you're right. You know, there's something about this place—the field—and since I've been here, I'm not sure what it is but I've started feeling a little better."

"I'm not going with Ofelia. I'll stay with you," Lily said, pulling up her chin and then pushing away.

As much as I wanted her company, the last thing I wanted was her pity. "That's okay, maybe I'll head back into the field and try to do some more painting. You go and have a good time with Ofelia. I'll catch up with you later."

And then I hated to do it, but I asked her for a favor. "Lily, can you please keep this between us. Just for now?"

Chapter Nineteen

Intuition

I DIDN'T COME DOWN HERE TO DIE. My father did and I'm not following in his footsteps! Late in the afternoon, there were grey sheets of rain in the distance as I made my way out to the field, but I wasn't going to turn back now. A little rain wouldn't hurt me. I felt better, or perhaps I was too good at denial. Before, whenever there'd been a period of remission, I'd try to forget I had a disease, and now even though the doctor said I had cancer, nothing had changed about the way I handled the truth. And as much as I knew pain and remission—like happiness—were only temporary, I also knew denial and its consequences could be forever.

Sitting in the middle of the field tangled in the mess of my situation, slowly I twisted my anger, fear, and depression into one thick braid of denial. The rain was still off in the distance and there was always a chance it might pass altogether.

I set out my art supplies. As a young girl, I'd discovered the therapeutic qualities in painting. No matter how uncomfortable the situation seemed, I'd always been able to create a different outcome. If there was a problem at school with a friend, for instance, I'd get home and then simply pull out my brush, create the scene and then paint a smile on that person, or more often, paint a new friend altogether. I'd even dared to paint a new family for myself, complete with a puppy and the blonde Barbie doll I'd always wanted. After I'd started practicing law, however, I'd lost my passion and the place to hide my pain.

Until I met Zane, I hadn't painted again, I thought, as the memory surfaced like a splinter. I picked up a brush now and with each stroke, I covered the canvas in a shade of grey, the color of grief.

And then a drizzle swathed the field in an amethyst fog, so that everything seemed ethereal and enchanting. I turned to the canvas as the light rain began to fall, making the sound of cymbals; the droplets tapped on the leaves and the canvas like a drum. The soil was so hard and parched that the earth could no longer swallow, and the water trickled into spidery cracks like tributaries pooling into greater ones. Like puddle canvases, I thought taking my brush, still heavy with grey, and dipping it into the crimson wet patch. The paint spread iridescent like an oil slick across the watery surface and upon closer look, I saw a phantasmagoria of different shadowy creatures, of all shapes and colors blooming through the watery backdrop. The rainwater had diffused the color of grief, layering it over with colors of hope. I hoped I'd be able to recreate all of this, including somehow, the song of the crickets and sparrows chirping as they rushed for cover. What was the color of nature singing? A tiny lizard came out from under a plant, lifting its head as it flicked its tiny tongue in and out. I raised my head, mimicking it, my face being misted as a dragonfly brushed past my nose. I felt so tiny in this field, not insignificant, but an atom in the universe related to the lizards and the rain and the agave plant I gazed at now, the most perfect one I'd ever seen. I had the feeling of being enough, of being okay. And then the rain stopped. Nothing lasts forever, but if I could put it all down on the canvas, I just might have a chance.

And now, fixated on the agave plant directly in front of me, the water streaked into images I'd try to recreate. I blinked, the raindrops heavy on my lashes, and looked around now, soaking up all the beauty surrounding me, like baby Lily after a bath. I felt peaceful—or was I finally in acceptance? Whatever it was, I wasn't ready to give up on life. I had so much more to give. But wasn't that what got me sick? All the giving—all the doing.

So grateful to have this opportunity to paint before returning home, I remembered to say, "Thank you, God," and sat quietly in the hopes of finding some inspiration. And as I stared at the grey backdrop on the canvas, waiting for some sort of muse, an image cast a darker shade over the board.

"What seems to be the problem?" Don Pio asked.

I turned to look up. "Gabriel told me to practice not doing, to just be, but this is ridiculous. I'm really stuck."

"A good artist let's his intuition lead him wherever it wants," Don Pio said.

"Yeah, well I seem to have trouble with my intuition," I said, holding my stomach. I laughed. "So far, my gut just gives me trouble. I was hoping your would inspire me."

"Sí, this field is proof of our faith. It's what connects us to our past. Everyone who planted here was also nourished by what they planted."

"Well, I sure would love to know more about those misty figures of the past."

"You just need to open up for the seeds to be planted and just keep coming out here," Don Pio said, adding, "but, I must warn you not to wander off into the north field."

I peered at him.

"Snakes," he answered.

"Really?" I asked, startled at the sound of a child laughing. I turned to Don Pio. "Who is she?"

With rein in hand, he pointed to the canvas and grinned as he hoisted himself up onto Chuey. Both Don Pio and the donkey turned to look at me as he spoke.

"Your intuition."

Man and donkey trotted off.

And then out of the corner of my eye, a scintilla of specks appeared on the canvas, slowly, one by one. Fingers trembling, I grabbed the brush, quickly dipping it into the paint. In a frenzy, I traced the dots and with each new marking, I grew more excited.

A grey-blue mist surrounded a little indigenous girl in braids. I sat back, wondering who this little girl might be and then I turned at the sound of bells in the distance, and then a rooster crowed. I smelled smoke and then I heard a woman screaming.

I looked back at the canvas, but the image of the child was gone.

AGAVE NORTH FIELD – PRE-DAWN – 1913

Through a haze of blue grey, I heard a woman screaming. And then I smelled smoke and saw the fire in the north field. In a panic, I ran toward the scene, but stopped in my tracks when I heard a gunshot. I heard the blood pulsing in my ears, my heart thumping in my chest and then when I heard the sound of a baby crying, I started to run again toward the sound. Soon, I came upon a little indigenous girl—the one from my painting, except that now her head was newly shaved. Nestled in between the rows of agave, the child was huddled in the fetal position next to a dead woman and a crying baby. The little girl looked up, eyes welling with tears, in which I could see a reflection of a man in uniform hovering behind her. I turned, but he was gone and then there was another gunshot. I ran to take cover beside an agave plant where I peeked through and saw a couple of dead men in uniforms, soldiers. A horse neighed, rearing up with a man on its back. The soldier's white sombrero blew off. I stopped breathing when I thought I recognized him. Pancho Villa?

And then as he galloped off, a farmer, weathered and middle-aged, rushed in. As soon as he saw the dead woman, he dropped to his knees and scooped her into his arms. He buried his head in her neck and sobbed. The frightened little girl then reached over to pick up the crying child and hugged him close. She then patted the sobbing man, her father.

From the direction Pancho Villa took off, a young farmer ran up carrying back the white hat that had blown off Villa's head. The young farmer walked toward the little girl to help her with the baby.

Slowly, I stood to look all around me. Through the smoke, in the distance, a blaze shot up to the sky. The hacienda was ablaze. And like a pinecone opening up after the fire, my eyes opened up, and I could see that inside the distillery there was an oven where an old woman had taken cover as fire surrounded her. Flames licked the sky and burned down the property.

HOVERING ON the tops of the agave points, the sun was low, and my heart weighed heavy as I stared at the empty canvas, the smell of smoke hanging in the air like a warning. Unable to process what had just taken place, I made my way back to the hacienda.

In the distance, I heard the workers whistling in the fields, some crooning to the high heavens. I remembered how the workers used to sing when I was little and would come into the fields with my father—such a joyful sound. My heart soared and for a moment, all was well.

On the way back to my room, I found Don Pio working just outside the distillery near the ovens. Chuey, hooked up to the mulcher, clomped around the circle, tail swishing some pesky flies. Don Pio walked over and offered me some agave.

"Thank you." I bit off a piece and chewed. As the liquid flowed down, my insides began to warm.

"Any inspiration?" he asked, eyeing the canvas.

I stopped chewing and looked down at my empty picture and then slowly raised my eyes. "I painted a little indigenous girl with braids, but then the image was gone and then I saw her again out in the field, but now with a shaved head and there was a baby and a dead woman and—"

Don Pio's eyes widened, his pupils dilating, and he seemed to wobble slightly as he brought his hand to his heart. "My mother and me," he whispered.

I narrowed my eyes.

"They shaved my sister to make her look like a boy, hoping the soldiers would leave her alone. My grandmother survived by hiding out in there," he said, pointing to the oven. "Eventually, she raised me."

"But why was Pancho Villa in my painting?"

As I searched his face for answers, I could see his eyes blurring now like raindrops on the windows to his soul.

Chapter Twenty

Two Little Altars

THE NEXT MORNING, SEVERAL TOWNSPEOPLE had already lined up at the bus stop waiting to depart to the city of Guadalajara. I reached out to tug on Lily's straw-colored ponytail. She turned and grinned. "Ouch."

"You used to hate when I brushed your hair. It was so thick and curly when you were little. You'd scream and then you'd rip out the ponytail I'd made and make me start over."

Lily laughed. "Yeah, well I wanted it smooth and perfect. I didn't like bumps."

"I never blamed you. Besides, who likes bumps?"

Lily looked at me, her smile waning. "I'm sorry, Mom. But I really need to get back to school."

"I understand."

"I want to stay a little longer," she added, "but as long as you're staying longer—and you're in good hands. When are you headed back to the states?"

"Soon. Dr. Vaisman wants to run some more tests before surgery. But I think it can wait a little. In the meanwhile, I still want to check some things out around here."

"I thought you were going to slow down. You can't be thinking about taking over the Tequila business."

"No, the last thing I need is another headache."

"But I thought this Tequila didn't give headaches," Lily said with a laugh.

"Yeah, right?"

Truth be told, I knew a story was being revealed to me out in the field and I anxiously wanted to know how it all ended. I needed to know if there

134

were any answers for me out there. But I also knew I needed to go home to my doctor—except for the fact I wasn't quite ready to return.

And I wasn't ready to let go of my daughter. "You know, maybe before I go back to the states, I'll swing by the city first and visit you at school."

"Really? Oh, Mom, I'd like that. Please, promise you will."

"I promise." I wanted to reach out and hang onto her forever.

The bus driver opened up the door and the people started boarding. Before stepping on, Lily turned to wrap her arms around me. I thought I'd melt. I squeezed her back so tight, I might have broken her ribs.

"Ouch, Mom!"

"I just love you so much," I said, and she pulled away to embark. I wiped my eyes, watching as my little girl stepped up. I couldn't help but notice the tattoo and then a memory of a little Lily heading off to kindergarten with a "unicorn" backpack, and her Care Bear in tow. And now she was off again, this time back to a college in this land that was no longer feeling so strange to me.

"Goodbye," I shouted, waving to my only child.

Through the bus window, Lily stuck out her head. "I love you, too, Mom!"

I walked away and headed back to Antonio's truck. Don Pio had moved to the back of the cab leaving me the front. I stepped up to the front seat. Swiping my tears as I watched the bus pull away, I then felt a warm imprint on my shoulder. I reached up to pat my uncle's bony, calloused hand.

"She'll be safe," he said in a voice so gentle, I had no doubt. "She has her wings."

We both laughed as Antonio cleared his throat, reaching over to turn the key in the ignition. The truck pulled out onto the main highway. Always a person who seemed in control—so sure of himself—I wondered what made him tick. I wondered about the hidden recesses of his mind—the spaces like mine—where he managed to bury his turmoil. His left elbow resting on the window frame, fingers dangling inside the car, the other hand gripping the steering wheel, I remembered him as a serious, hardworking boy—never seeming to take time out for leisure; nothing like his brother, Gabriel. The fact that he had taken a break today to drive us to the bus stop said a lot—but what?

After a while, the air inside the cab of the truck had grown heavy with the musky smell of earth, sweat and perhaps a hint of shaving cream or was that aftershave? Except for the muffled sound of music playing on the radio, the ride back was silent. The white knuckle-tension inside the truck was palpable. Holding my breath, until I could safely come up for air, I felt as if I were enclosed in a bathtub, submerged under hot water.

Finally, I inhaled, turning to face Antonio. "Thanks for driving," I said, noticing the strong jaw line beneath a freshly shaved face. *Is he wearing cologne?* "That was so—"

"No problem," he responded curtly, eyes ahead like a sailor on watch at sea.

Well, at least he didn't grunt. I looked out my window and noticed two little shrines erected along the side of the road, flowers and candles laid reverently inside and around the structure. "They're everywhere. How sad," I said, noticing the muscles on Antonio's face constricting like a snake swallowing its prey, his knuckles on the wheel turning white. A flash of heat overwhelmed me, and I wondered if it might be coming from him. I swerved around to ask Don Pio about the tiny altars but noticed him staring out the window like a sad puppy waiting for its owner's return. When he turned back, I noticed a teardrop at the corner of his eye. I decided to hold my tongue.

During the rest of the drive back, it felt as if I was riding in the front seat of a hearse during a funeral procession.

LATER, AROUND dusk, after an afternoon spent wandering around the field, wondering about my future, I entered the courtyard where the workers and their families had gathered for an evening meal.

Don Pio sprung from his seat to welcome me.

"So, have you decided?" he asked, clapping his hands together.

Before I could give him an answer, Antonio approached and took a seat across from me. He poured me a shot of Tequila. "Decided what?"

"How long I'm staying," I answered, reaching for the glass. "Gracias."

"Salud," Antonio said, holding up his cup.

I thought I could see half a smile playing on his face. "Salud," I answered, bringing the drink to my lips as he tossed his back.

I took a sip but paused before finishing. "Again, thank you for today. That was very considerate."

"My pleasure."

Without moving his lips, his eyes seemed to smile; something warm and inviting about the way he looked at me, I thought. But maybe it was only the Tequila talking to me.

"So, those two little altars on the side of the road—"

Nostrils flaring now, he slammed down his glass. "I don't want to talk about it."

I turned to Don Pio who merely shook his head. I couldn't understand. Had he been in an accident? *Oh shoot. Is that the reason Gabriel is disabled? Maybe there's something I can do?*

"You know, I've learned that it helps to talk things out," I said, and immediately felt a heat searing my face.

Antonio glared at me before pouring himself another shot. "This helps too," he said and threw the drink back down his throat before walking away.

I turned to Don Pio who took a deep breath as he pulled his hands together and wrung them. "Maya, walk with me."

I got up and followed him across the courtyard to the fountain where he took a seat. He patted the spot next to him and I sat down on the edge.

"There's something you need to know about Antonio."

"Like he needs to learn anger management more than business management?"

"He was supposed to get married to Camela when he found the time. She and Gabriel were actually school friends first. Gabriel brought her out here to visit. Bruno was smitten with her, but once she set eyes on Antonio, she would visit a lot." Don Pio was smiling now. "Something changed in both of them. Antonio especially. You could see it in his eyes."

"So, did he scare her away?"

Don Pio turned somber. "Anyway, they were driving back from Guadalajara after a graduation ceremony when a truck hit them head on. She was killed on impact."

"Oh my God! That's horrible." I put my hand on my forehead. "I'm such an idiot. No wonder he doesn't want to talk about it," I said, lifting my chin. "Was Antonio driving?"

My uncle brought his hand up and squeezed his brow. "No, Gabriel was. Antonio was too busy to attend"

"What? Oh, poor Gabriel. Poor Antonio. I had no idea. That's just awful."

"Yes, that day marked the worst day in his life," Don Pio said. "He blames himself."

"But why?"

Don Pio shook his head.

"I don't understand. Wait. There were two little altars," I said and watched as my uncle looked across the courtyard at Antonio who had picked up his guitar.

"Yes, two ofrendas."

"I still don't understand."

"In time you will, Maya. I'd love for him to find happiness someday," Don Pio said.

"Like Gabriel who finds it in his art." I finished my drink and looked at my empty glass. "I guess this is cheaper than Dr. Phil."

I turned when I heard the singing, Antonio's music coiling around the sound of pain.

And then in the distance, the sky lit up in an explosion of color followed by the sound like machine gunfire. I jumped.

"Día de los Muertos," Don Pio said, "The town is celebrating our dead.

Chapter Twenty-One

Stage Three – Bargaining with God

LATER THAT NIGHT, A LIGHT RAIN MISTED the earth, not enough to end the drought—most likely too little and too late. What it did do was cool things down and clear the firework smoke from the sky.

I sat in a rocker on the veranda, thinking the more I learned about the past, the more I hoped it wasn't too late for me. I prayed I'd find some answers before going home to all the tests, surgery and chemo.

The air chilled me, and as I wrapped a shawl around my shoulders, I found myself humming the tune Antonio had sung earlier. "*Tú eres la tristeza de mis ojos que lloran en silencio por tu amor.* You are the sadness of my eyes, crying silently for your love."

I warmed my hands around a mug of hot coffee, watching the swirling steam create an image of Antonio. Not only could he play the guitar, but the soulful way he sang *Amor Eterno* tweaked my heart. I'd thought he was singing about Camela, but Don Pio had explained that *Love Eternal* was written about a mother's love.

Now, I looked across the hacienda, wondering what it must have been like for Antonio and Gabriel growing up around here. I scoured my mind for a memory of their mother. I had none. I tried to recall other faces, but only came up blank. Now I wondered about all of my relatives. I knew times had been hard and many had gone north just to survive, sending back money to those they'd left behind. What must it have been like for them? I had some indication. And when the idea of my own mother and father stumbled across my mind, I slammed closed my eyes, pushing away the memories.

STRAIGHTENING MY back, I looked across to the distillery and then a crazy notion came skipping through my brain. It wasn't the idea that I could run a Tequila business, rather, that I'd never be able to. Somewhere, somehow, I'd grown up telling myself and believing there was nothing I couldn't do. But this fantasy would never take root, and now especially since I was really sick, how could I ever be able to run a Tequila business? *Oh, what must my uncle be thinking? Silly old man. He wouldn't be pushing it if he knew I had cancer.* And then a kernel of an idea popped into my head—after all, I really wasn't feeling so bad; actually, I felt better. What if there'd been a mistake? Or, what if there's a cure—a miracle—I thought as the door from the distillery opened up. Out stormed Antonio, with a determined look, or as if he were late for something. He marched toward his truck. I set down my coffee cup, bolted out of my rocking chair and scrambled toward him.

"Antonio," I said, short of breath, "about last night—I'm really sorry about Camela."

Hand on the truck's door handle, he turned toward me, glowering. "I thought I told you I didn't want to talk about it." In the cold, I could see his breath like dragon smoke flare out of his mouth. I stopped in my tracks before stepping back. I wasn't going to get anywhere.

Don Pio came walking up from the hacienda and he wasn't wearing his work clothes. All dressed up, he headed toward the truck.

"Where are you going all slicked up?" I asked.

"A misa."

"Mass, today?"

"Día de los Muertos."

"Oh, that's right." And then I came to another realization. Yesterday, Halloween, would have been Papá's birthday, but he hadn't made it, not that we'd ever celebrated him. "Halloween is for your American kids," my mother had told him, and I never recall her even baking him a cake. Had I played a part in turning him into the monster he was? I do remember sharing my candy with him. Reminiscing now, I wanted to cry.

One time, after a night of trick-or-treating, I'd attended mass for All Saints' Day at Our Lady of Guadalupe with my classmates in the states. So full of sugar, I hadn't been able to sleep the night before and in the morning in church, as we prayed for the souls of the dead, I hadn't been able to keep my eyes open. I'd been nodding off when Sister Bernadette walked up and pinched my arm. I never understood the notion of praying for the dead. But then again, in the church, we were always worried about death or going to hell and so I'd never wanted to risk not praying. Only later, did I stop fretting.

"Maybe saying a novena will help," I said. *Maybe now that I'm facing death, I should start praying for a miracle.* "Can I tag along, Don Pio?"

ANTONIO SLAMMED on the brakes the moment we crossed through the iron gates of the property. Ahead of us, along the road, idling on the left side of the entrance, I noticed a dark Cadillac Escalade. The driver in a black sombrero stood just outside his vehicle scanning the property through a pair of binoculars.

From the back seat, Don Pio grabbed Antonio's arm as he reached for the door handle.

"Hijo, let it go," my uncle pleaded.

But Antonio yanked away, exited the truck, and marched toward the man who by now had lowered his binoculars to turn and face Antonio.

Staring out the window, I asked Don Pio, "Who is that?"

"Bruno."

So that's him. Antonio approached Bruno, a bit stockier, but standing shorter than Antonio. I couldn't hear what the exchange was between the two agitated men, but I heard the frantic beat of my heart when I saw Antonio shove Bruno. Bruno merely laughed at him. My first instinct was to get out of the vehicle and run to the aid of Antonio, as if he needed my help. But before I could open my door, he was already tramping back toward the truck. He got in, put the vehicle into gear and tore away, gravel spitting out behind us. Out of the corner of my eye, I could see the snake in Antonio's face constricting, ready to pounce.

Chapter Twenty-Two

Día De Los Muertos

I'D NEVER UNDERSTOOD—NEVER TOOK THE TIME to understand—the concept of death, much less the whole Mexican custom of mortality. And now with the thought of cancer weighing on me like the elephant that used to sit in our living room, I couldn't help but wonder if there was some connection. During this visit, I'd try to pay attention, ask questions and look for answers. Perhaps I might learn something helpful from my family.

Antonio got as close as he could to the church before dropping us off on the perimeter of the plaza. Hundreds of people were already gathering, some to erect makeshift altars and gravesites and others just to observe. By evening time, every inch of the plaza would be covered with ofrendas and gravesites covered with flowers, primarily marigolds whose scent and vibrant colors would guide the spirits to their gravesites. Dolls, toys, candies, and the favorite foods of the deceased were placed around the shrines where candles burned. And, of course, there was also Tequila! Family members and friends knelt in prayer; some beat their chest. Beneath the arches, around the plaza, streamers swung in the breeze, underneath which vendors sold their wares. Blasting the area like an air freshener were the mouth-watering aromas of the favorite staples: frijoles, cebolla, arroz con pollo, nopalitos and elote. Platforms had been set up for people to make speeches and sing folksongs. All around were pictures of relatives who had passed.

Across the square hung all sorts of papier-mâché creatures. Aztec dancers jumped up and down with offerings of incense as several women and children, dressed in peasant costumes, carried crosses, re-enacting a death scene, all against the backdrop of sad ballads sung by guitar-strumming mariachis.

Children scampered around in colorful get-ups. I noticed one little girl dressed as a skeleton princess, and it took me back to the time I took Lily out trick-or-treating. She was around six, dressed as Jasmine from the Disney movie. She'd insisted I could only accompany her if I dressed as Aladdin. The next year, she wanted nothing to do with me. She wanted to be with her friends.

Another group of children were on their knees chalking colorful messages to their abuelitos; others drew flamboyant skulls with giant empty eye sockets. Families carried flower arrangements: some simple bouquets, others ostentatious creations on easels. Morbidly, I wondered how Lily might react when my time came. As strained as our relationship had been and as angry as she seemed, would she visit my grave?

And all of this took place in the plaza at the front of the church. Behind the cathedral in the graveyard, the same event was also happening, just as it was at the local cemetery, in private homes throughout the town, and even throughout the country.

Alive and well stood my cousins at the entrance of the church. "How are things going out at the farm, Papá?" Angela asked, reaching out to embrace her father. She then let go and smiled as she reached out to hug me.

"You're looking much better. The color has returned to your cheeks."

Seriously? I touched my face.

Ofelia smiled. "I told you it was the agave."

Hmm? I laughed.

All together, we stepped into the church and entered a pew where I bowed my head before kneeling and making the sign of the cross.

The smell of incense overwhelmed me, the whole scene overpowering. Sure, I remembered when I was a little girl, the village had all turned out to pay their respects. I couldn't remember this day ever being so grand, like some sort of Hollywood production. I'd taken it all for granted. At night, there'd be singing and dancing. There'd be contests for the best costumes and the best decorations in various categories—like a night at the Oscars. I followed my family out after mass.

"Let's pick up something to eat," Angela said, pointing to a stand advertising *Esquites*—creamy corn in a cup. "And then we can go back to the house for some coffee and dessert."

"More flan?" I asked. "Wild caballos couldn't keep me away."

143

I smiled thinking the reason I'd come down here was to take care of the business of death, but here death wasn't treated as a business. Death was a celebration.

THE SOUND OF mariachi music filled the air. Through a rain of confetti, we carried our lunch, following the children as they ran through a procession of figures of los muertos. We'd just reached the end of the plaza where things were a little quieter.

"Joaquin sure loved the music," Don Pio said, arm hooked through his daughter's. "Every once in a while, they would let him join in."

Leonardo, one long stride ahead of us, turned his head. "I remember the night Tio Joaquin nearly gave old Doña Paola a heart attack," he said. "It was after a night of singing."

"And drinking I'm sure," I added with a sad smile. "Wait, Doña Paola? Domingo's wife?"

"Sí, Doña Paola Montoya, your father's stepmother, "Angela said, shuffling behind with her father. I waited for them to catch up to me.

"Your papá used to go there quite a bit when Domingo was alive."

"Well, of course, that was his father's house," I said.

Angela added, "It was a little after two in the morning when he was walking home. He was confused—"

Leonardo pretended to stumble down the street.

"Borracho," I said.

"He started pounding on her door," Angela said. "'Vieja, let me in!' he yelled."

Leonardo punched the air. "'What do you want? Go away!' she yelled back. 'Go away! We buried you many winters ago in the plot next to your brother!'"

Now looking at me, Leonardo added, "You see, Doña Paola thought it was her husband Domingo and she was so scared, she almost got to join him in heaven that night."

Their infectious laughter made me laugh, too, even though I couldn't imagine what was so funny. "Papá had a way of haunting people even when he was alive."

"Anyway, he finally realized his mistake and went away," Angela said. "It's funny to hear Doña Paola tell it."

"Papá was always someone to laugh at or about. I'm sorry. He must have been drunk."

"There is no need to apologize. You have no control over the actions of others, especially not your father's," Angela said.

I saw the kindness in my cousin's eyes, but as I looked around to see everyone staring at me, I felt uncomfortable.

"You have nothing to be ashamed of," Angela added.

Oh, how I'd always been ashamed of my drunk father. It would take a miracle to let go of the idea that I had something to do with his behavior.

"Is Doña Paola still alive?" I asked.

Angela narrowed her eyes, shaking her head. "Yes, she's still alive."

"Dios mío! We still talk about it," Leonardo said, bent over, one hand on the back of his hip, the other pumping a fist as he pretended to hobble down the street like an old man. "Let me in, vieja!"

Everyone laughed and now even Ofelia mimicked the old lady. "Go away! Go away!" she shouted, waving her arms in the air.

Heading toward home, colorful streamers zigzagged the village rooftops. We turned the corner, but I felt so left behind.

DON PIO FOLLOWED Leonardo and Sylvia, and his great-grandchildren out into the courtyard while Ofelia and I stayed inside to help Angela, already busy at the stove.

"So, Angela, you never go out to the hacienda anymore?" I asked, setting some napkins and flatware down on the table.

"She doesn't like where she grew up," Ofelia answered for her mother as she pulled out some plates from the cupboard. And then with a snicker, she added. "Too many ghosts. Especially after our grandmother died. It was uncomfortable around there. Too much fighting and arguing."

Angela then turned to face me. "De veras, mi padre, él es un santo," she said, pointing a spoon.

"Yes, I really like your father. He is a saint. My life would have been a lot better with a father like that."

"Y podría haber sido peor," Angela replied.

"How could it have been worse?"

Angela had returned to her cooking. *What could be worse than growing up with a father who was a drunk?* I thought. *A father who beat his family—hurt his daughter? And then with a father who wasn't with it all of the time. I was grateful for the times he abandoned the family—days, weeks, months at a time.*

"Papá never stepped in," Angela said, bottom jiggling as she stirred the pot.

I could smell chocolate now and cinnamon sticks, taking me back to the kitchen in the hacienda years ago where Angela had been stirring chocolate on the stove.

There'd been an argument between—it was all coming back to me now—between Antonio and the other boy, Bruno. Don Pio had taken off. "He'll be back when he smells the canela," Angela had said to me with a wink, and then she turned to the boys. "Ahora, Antonio y Bruno, dejan de pelear."

"Why would they fight?" I asked, observing how Angela added the agave sugar. *So that's the secret ingredient.* I slid my tongue across my lips.

Angela shrugged. "Boys will be boys."

I watched as she added even more sugar. *Yes, let's just shrug it off—add more sugar. Oh, who am I to judge?* "What do you mean—worse?"

"When the boys would fight, Papá would just leave the room and go out into the fields," Angela said.

"My uncles were always arguing and getting into fights with Antonio. He was such an angry boy," Ofelia added, as Sylvia came running in from the courtyard, pulling Mateo by the hand, his other hand holding his crotch as they rushed across the kitchen.

"Talking about the monster again?" Sylvia asked, entering a tiny room off to the side. "Antonio stole Bruno's girl."

"She was never his girl," Ofelia said.

"And now Bruno is going to steal the distillery to get even with Antonio. But then—"

"Silencio! Hijas, that's enough," Angela shouted.

"Mamá doesn't like to talk chisme," Ofelia said. "Anyway, everyone left except Antonio. The town is afraid of him."

"Why?"

"He was always very serious and yet, for a time, he had been happy. But now, saddled with this anger and the sadness buried deep within, it makes it hard for people to get close to him. He's become a phantom of sorts, isolated. Life has sure dealt him a hard hand."

Sylvia closed the door to the bathroom and returned to the kitchen where she leaned on the counter. "How Camela chose him over Uncle Bruno is still a mystery."

"Hija, we cannot help who we fall in love with," Angela added, "and again, she was not his girl."

Ofelia looked at me. "Your being out there is even more of a mystery to me."

"Really?" I answered. "Maybe I want to learn the business," I added, suddenly realizing how crazy that sounded, especially now that I had cancer.

Angela slowly twisted around, peering at me, and then smiled.

"Seriously, Angela, I think there might be something there for me."

Ofelia had left the room and returned quickly carrying a folder. "You know, I'm working on my master's at the University of Guadalajara where they're doing a lot of research right now with agave." She handed me the folder. "You should read about it."

"Ofelia says it can help lower my cholesterol, too," Angela added with a chuckle. "Maybe even help with my arthritis."

Ofelia reached out and touched my arm. "Lily tells me you have ulcers."

And now since Lily had already let the cat out of the bag, I thought about telling the truth but not the whole truth. "Actually, it's a little worse."

Ofelia gave an almost knowing look as she squeezed my arm. "You really should check out the study," Ofelia said, pointing to the folder. "Agave was used for so many things," she added. "Mats, fabric, paper, medicine."

"What about erectile dysfunction?" I asked with a laugh.

Ofelia's brow furrowed and then the creases on her forehead turned smooth as añejo when she caught on. She laughed.

"There are so many uses, but Antonio won't listen. Maybe that's why you're here?"

I shrugged my shoulders, shaking my head as I finished setting the table. "Or to rediscover a passion of mine. Gabriel taught me a lot about—"

Don Pio entered the room and took a seat at the kitchen table.

"—painting," I said.

Slack-jawed, the cousins stared at each other as if they were so surprised I'd ever consider any sort of artwork—anything other than work.

"She has seen his creations," Don Pio said, matter-of-factly. "Is lunch ready?"

"Speaking of painting—" Angela said, setting down a cup of coffee for her father and then wiping her hands on her apron before leaving the room.

Ofelia brought over some milk from the refrigerator and poured it into her grandfather's cup as her nephew dipped his finger into the sugar bowl.

"I hope you washed your hands!" Don Pio said, and his great-grandson smiled before kissing him on the cheek. The old man was on his third scoop of sugar when Angela shuffled back into the room. "¡Ay, Papá, that's enough! You're worse than Mateo with your sweet tooth."

She carried something covered in a small, flowered cloth or pillowcase, but managed to pat her grandson on the behind before he re-dipped. Mateo skipped back outside. Angela then pulled the cover away and handed me a painting.

"Guess what the canvas is made of made of?" Ofelia asked with a lilt in her voice.

"Agave?" I said. *Of course, everything else seems to be.*

Ofelia nodded with a smile.

Surrounded by a family who treated each other with such tender kindness, I'd been feeling so calm and then I saw the painting. My whole body shook when I looked at the picture of the same little bald indigenous girl standing before a tall agave plant. Shocked, I felt as if my legs would no longer support me. I sank into a seat at the kitchen table, setting the picture down and looked up at the caring eyes all staring at me from around the kitchen. Don Pio grinned. Angela steepled her hands to her lips and Ofelia stood, hands-on-hips. I inhaled, daring to look back at the painting, and then when I did, I noticed the man my father had always said was his father. In the background, a horse reared up and standing in the saddle, waving a sombrero overhead, was Pancho Villa.

I exhaled, lifting my head. "What is this? Who did this?"

"Your father," Don Pio answered.

He saw them, too. I grabbed onto the edge of the table as soon as I felt the kitchen spin. I tried to focus on my uncle's moving lips, but it was as if

I'd been sucked up by a wind tunnel. Their voices were muffled and all I could hear was the whirring sound of a tornado. In an effort to compose myself, I closed my eyes, but on the backsides of my eyelids, the memories of what I'd witnessed earlier in the field came to life—this time in a montage of still shots whipping by like flash cards.

Set in a backdrop of smoke across the agave field were a couple of dead men in uniforms—a frightened little indigenous girl beside a dead woman and a baby—a horse rearing up with a man on its back—a white sombrero— a farmer scooping up the dead woman—the little girl hugging the baby—a young farmer holding the white hat—the hacienda on fire—flames licking the sky—and the property burning to the ground.

MY STOMACH burned. I opened my eyes to see that someone had brought me a glass of water.

"Are you okay?" Ofelia asked. "Is it your ulcer?"

"Yes and no. Thank you," I answered, as Ofelia offered me a little pill. "What's this?"

"It's like a sugar pill made from agave. It might make you feel better."

It couldn't hurt, I thought, popping the pill into my mouth before draining my glass.

Wiping my sweaty brow, I turned to Don Pio wanting to ask about what I'd just experienced, but Angela walked up. "Are you okay?"

I nodded.

"I have another painting to show you, but only when you're feeling better."

"I'm okay. Please, show me."

"Your father wanted to finish this when he returned someday," Angela said.

So Papá painted? I looked up to accept the next piece of work. Anxious to see what else my father could have possibly created, I looked down and quickly placed a trembling hand over my mouth. Even though the painting was unfinished, I was still able to recognize myself as a child running through the field of agave. The same photo I'd found in his wallet. Papá had cared enough to paint a picture of me. Was this his amends to me?

I burst into tears. It was all too much. To see myself as a child, I couldn't help but think of Lily and feel just how much I loved her. I couldn't leave her. I couldn't die on her. At that moment, I wanted to reach in and love that sad, scared little girl in the picture; I wanted to hold her and let her know everything would turn out okay.

Through watery eyes, I stared at Ofelia, Angela and then at Don Pio, still grinning.

"You see. He did love you, Maya," he said.

I looked at the painting again, sadly being loved was not what I remembered.

Chapter Twenty-Three

You Should Go Home

MOTHS DANCED AROUND THE DIM STREETLIGHTS. A rowdy crowd of skeletons and other face-painted revelers bopped around me as I tried to make my way across the cobblestone road. A cool wind tumbled in off the nearby mountains and I clutched my sweater at the neck. Only a block away from my cousin's house, I found the place I'd been looking for. Standing on a porch step, I knocked on a weathered, wooden door.

"¿Quién es?" came a high, squeaky voice from the other side.

Lips only an inch away from the splintered door, I answered. "Soy hija de Joaquin. Maya Hidalgo Miller. ¿Eres Doña Paola Montoya?"

The door creaked open to an aura of musty darkness surrounding a tiny toothless, old woman. Hugging a black shawl around her bony shoulders.

"Sí, soy Doña Paola," she said, peering at me curiously. Humbly, she invited me into a little dank, dusty room illuminated only by a couple of candles. She asked me to take a seat. The candlelight distorted her already severe features. This stranger, my step-grandmother, looked as dried up as a roasted chile poblano. I examined her cloudy eyes searching for answers about my father.

"Joaquin always wanted to know the truth about his father," Doña Paola said, wringing her sparrow-like hands.

"I know," I responded. "He was obsessed."

With tremulous hands, Doña Paola reached into her apron pocket and pulled out a rosary necklace. She passed the beads through her fingers. "Your grandmother Lucia was already pregnant before she married Domingo."

151

"Really?" I asked.

Doña Paola nodded. "Domingo always swore the baby wasn't his and I believed him." She peered at me, and I could see the candlelight reflecting a truth in her overcast eyes.

Grandma Lucia was already pregnant. So, then it's true—Pancho Villa was Papá's father.

"Domingo worked on the farm. After Pancho Villa's raid, Lucia's father paid Domingo to marry her and move north. Later, Domingo left her up there and came back to me. We had Victor months later."

Victor. Victor Montoya? I looked away. I'm confused.

"Victor, our son," Doña Paola said. "Sad, but Joaquin's own mother didn't want him around. He was a reminder of his father, and it wasn't Domingo, but still we'd let Joaquin stay with us. He'd go back and forth between here and the hacienda. He liked being around Victor and our daughter, Estella."

Poor Papá, rejected by his own mother, I thought as my eyes fixed on a hat rack in the corner. "Hey, es mi sombrero!" I said, recognizing the hat on the hook, the one the woman in the plaza wore; the one with all of the kids. The woman rumored to have killed her abusive husband.

"Estella gave it to me. She told me it was too fancy for her," Doña Paola said, removing it from the hook and then handing it to me.

Estella, Victor's sister, my father's stepsister.

"No, please you keep it," I said. This was all too much.

I watched as she hung the hat back on the hook and then noticed a picture hanging on the wall next to it.

Holding up a candle, I inched closer to the photo. In the picture, a young man stood wearing a white sombrero like the one I took from the morgue.

"Who's that in the hat?"

"Mi esposo Domingo in his younger days," Doña Paola said, chuckling softly. "He used to say the hat belonged to Pancho Villa." She peered at me. "Joaquin, your papá, took it."

My jaw sagged as the woman stood, simply gazing at me until the sound of rapping on the door broke the silence.

Startled, she turned to me before edging toward the door. "¿Quién es?" she asked.

I couldn't make out what the man said on the other side as Doña Paola quickly unlatched the door. "Oh, you've come home to me!" Making the sign of the cross, her rosary beads swinging from her neck like a pendulum as the man stood in the doorway, the streetlight casting a shadow across the threshold and spilling onto the floor, at my feet. The man then reached out to hug Doña Paola.

I came closer, catching my breath as I recognized the man who'd just stepped into the light.

"Antonio, what are you doing here?"

"Come in. Come in. Silly me," replied the old woman. "You look so much like your father. It's unbelievable."

His father? I don't see it.

"I'm sorry Abuelita, but I left my truck running," Antonio said, "and I've got to get back." He then turned toward me. "Don Pio told me you needed a ride."

"Ay, Hijito, it's been so long," Antonio's old grandmother cried, stretching out her arthritic hands. "Promise you'll come and visit me soon."

"I will," Antonio said, guiding me out of the tiny house.

At the doorway, I hugged the woman goodbye, thanking her for the new information I'd already started to process.

IN THE TRUCK, I turned to Antonio. "I don't get it. It's just so hard keeping track of everyone and knowing who's related to whom. She said you look like your father. But I really don't see it. You're much taller than Don Pio."

Antonio grinned. "All you need to know is that everyone around here is either an hermano, a primo, a tío, or an abuelito."

"So, how was your day, Primo?"

His hands on the wheel, I thought I saw a smirk. "Let's just say I managed to keep the farm from going under if only for one more day."

I laughed, liking this side of Antonio. He seemed almost like a normal human being.

"So, Bruno—now, he looks more like—"

"I'd rather not talk about him right now," he replied, still looking forward. "Did you enjoy yourself today?"

"Yes," I answered, turning to see him in profile, his jaws clenched. "It was an interesting day. I don't remember ever knowing about the customs or the history behind Día de los Muertos."

"It's just a strange gothic fairytale, that's all."

"Well, anyway I thought it was an extraordinary celebration of death. It makes the line between life and death seem almost non-existent, as if there's nothing to fear by crossing over," I said, wanting to believe it could be that simple.

Antonio screwed up his face as he turned to look at me. "Loca."

"Do you know how much I hate when people call me that?"

"It happens a lot?" Antonio asked.

Under my breath, I counted to ten.

"That's your only free pass."

After we drove in through the gate, Antonio pulled over to the side of the dark road. I instinctively grabbed the door handle, waiting for him to make a move and then I'd bolt. Minutes went by and as I looked out the window across the field, I could see the high moon and brilliant stars blanketing a cerulean sky like Van Gogh's *Starry Night*. He cut the engine but continued to stare straight ahead. All was quiet except for the sound of crickets and the wind whistling through the field. I turned to see the blood in his temples throbbing as I tried to follow his gaze, wondering what he might be thinking or looking for. Or, I wondered, was he waiting for Bruno? The glands in my armpits secreted a stinging moisture and, in an effort to drown out the sound of my pounding heart, I whispered, "Such a breathtaking night."

"And I'm with such a breathtaking mujer," Antonio said, surprising me.

I take his breath away. Is that a good thing? I felt myself get hot even though the night was crisp and getting colder. As I reached over to roll down my window, Antonio stretched out to touch my arm. He stared at me now.

"Maya—"

"Yes," I answered—neurons firing—unsure what to expect. I couldn't deny I felt some sort of an attraction to Antonio—always had since I was a kid. But whatever feelings I had for him were mixed with shame. *Remember, he's your cousin,* Papá would say, as if liking him at all would be a sin. And the way Antonio had always treated me was no indication that he ever felt anything but annoyance. Or maybe he was like a grade-school boy; too shy to say he liked me, so he tugged on my braid, instead. When it came to Gabriel, my father also had some choice things to say, but then he'd laugh and call him a *maricón*. I had no idea what faggot meant, but I had the feeling it was someone pretty harmless.

I heard the bats flying across the front of the truck and then Antonio said, "You need to go home."

I CLOSED THE window in my room, hoping it would keep out the sharp bite of the chilly evening. Still reeling from my episode with Antonio, I slumped onto my bed. *What a pompous ass!* I took off a shoe and threw it to the corner. *How dare he tell me what to do?* I threw off the other shoe. *He's not even the boss of the farm.*

The radio in my head wouldn't shut off. I couldn't go to sleep with the sound of Antonio's voice booming: "You need to go home . . . you don't understand . . . much less how to run a Tequila farm . . ."

"That's none of your business," I'd replied.

"Well, the farm is my business, mujer," he'd responded calmly, leaving no room for debate, "and when you run a business, you can't just take off."

Heart racing, that's when I'd again reached for the truck's door handle. This time I opened it, got out and slammed it shut. I walked the rest of the way back on the dusty road with the light of the silvery moon—and the headlights from Antonio's truck searing into my back.

Chapter Twenty-Four

Stage Four - Depression

I SAT ON THE EDGE OF MY BED, MY ANGER teetering now on the precipice of depression. I pushed myself up and shuffled down the hall to brush my teeth and take my pills, including the sugar pill Ofelia had given me because why not? No harm, no foul. When I returned to my room, I noticed the canvases leaning up against the desk. Don Pio had obviously delivered them to my room earlier. I turned the switch on the little desk lamp and took a seat to get a better look. And then next to my laptop, I saw the hat. *Pancho Villa's hat, indeed.* I opened my computer and waited for the slow connection. *Every farmer in town wears the same damn hat.* By the time the screen lit up, the adrenaline had kicked in. *For God's sake, every ranchero across the State of Jalisco wears* . . . clicking furiously across the keyboard . . . *the same* . . . my heart stopped when I saw the image appearing on the screen. There in black and white with ammunition strapped crisscross over his shoulder, sitting erect on the back of a horse was Pancho Villa. He wore a white sombrero. My eyes darted from the screen to Papá's hat, and back again.

Fingers trembling, I reached over for the bottle of añejo I'd been saving for a special occasion. I uncorked it, poured myself a glass and then re-corked the bottle before taking a sip. Instinctively, I squeezed my eyes shut, waiting for the burn that never happened. Springing open my eyes, *so what if he wore the same hat?* I contemplated the painting of the girl with the shaved head.

"Chica? What are you trying to tell me?"

I stared at the baby lying next to the dead woman in the painting. "Are

156

you baby Don Pio?" I took another sip and narrowed my eyes to stare at the man on the horse—Pancho Villa.

It had been a long day and my head swarmed with so much information. The Tequila did a fine job relaxing me and as I gazed at my father's paintings, I tried to process everything, but began to nod off.

Drifting off, I nearly fell out of my chair when I heard the sound of a bottle cork popping. *Oh shit!* I was terrified the blue genie would make another appearance but noticed that the cork was still in the bottle.

Calm down, Maya. Remember, tu imaginación no es bueno.

Keeping my eyes on the bottle, cautious as a cat, I inched away until my calves touched the edge of the bed. I felt the small foot blanket, and then snatched it to cover the bottle. Satisfied now that the genie couldn't make an appearance, I sat on the bed, heart racing, and stared into my lap, clasping my shaking hands to my chest. *Oh God. This is so crazy.*

I twitched when I noticed a blue light, thinking it came from my laptop, but then realized the flashing came from the canvases propped up against the wall. Peering at the paintings, I shrieked. The canvases were blank. I stopped breathing as I looked around the room to see if the subjects might be hiding and then I heard my name being called from outside. "Maya, ven."

Breathing in some courage, I tiptoed toward the window to look out. At the edge of the field, I saw four pinpoints of light this time, like two sets of fiery eyes staring at me. Beyond, the north field seemed to be illuminated by a pulsating azure mist. I opened the door and fear ran away. I exited my room to chase after it.

LURED DEEPER into the field, I sensed the fire eyes belonged to both the little indigenous girl with the shaved head and to the younger me in braids. I got close enough to the little bald-headed girl who stood crying, tears dousing the flames in her eyes.

"Lucia, what's wrong?" I asked, moving toward the little girl, but she turned and scurried off. I gave chase until I slammed into a titanic block of blue dry ice and bounced off the cold slab onto my bottom. Dazed, I looked up at the massive cool gem, shining intensely with its own scintillation and then I looked down at my feet, so small in comparison. But when I stretched my arms out in front of me, baffled, I opened and closed my fingers only to see that they were small like those of a child—my young hands. *Okay, this is totally out of control!* Angry, I stood dusting off my hands and then placed them on my hips, ready to take on the blue giant or whatever the hell it was, but then a light began to whirl, swirling around the little indigenous girl whose features now began to soften then wrinkle into the face of an old woman.

Frightened, I tried to back away, but the liquid light enveloped me, calming me like a soothing balm. "Abuelita Lucia?"

"There, there, Hijita. It's all right," my ghostly grandmother said. "He didn't mean it, he was drunk."

I kicked up dirt. *That's no excuse!* And then I felt the old woman's arms tightening around me as they turned into sharp bones. I pulled away, sucking on dry air, when I saw the transformation. The old woman had morphed into a skeleton figure. *Here we go again. I'm hallucinating! I shouldn't have gone to the Día De Los Muertos celebration.*

And then, the blue wall of light consolidated into another figure with the face of an old man. He shuffled over to address the old woman who suddenly transformed back into the little indigenous girl.

"Lucia, I am sorry for making you with child," the old man said, and, in that moment, I understood him to be Lucia's own father. My grandfather.

The small, braided figure looked at me, the fire having returned to her beaming eyes. "Papá was very unwise," the young Lucia said, her voice deepening. "But we become wiser when we cross over. I've learned forgiveness," Grandmother Lucia said. "It is never too late to learn that."

And then another ethereal skeleton appeared, cigarette dangling from his lips. I recognized him. "Papá?"

"Hija," my father said, and my heart stopped. "I was such an angry soul believing I was the son of Pancho Villa.

What? Knowing your father was your own grandfather made things better?

"I wasn't in my right mind. Maya, I'm sorry for hurting you. Please forgive me."

I didn't know what to say. I'd always worried that by forgiving him, I was saying, "What you did to me was alright."

"Have you let go of the shame?" the old woman skeleton asked me.

I thought about it. As a child, I'd taken on the shame of what he had done to me as my own shame.

I nodded.

"What about the anger? Anger will make you think you have control. Do you continue to suffer to punish those you've allowed to hurt you?"

"No!" I screamed as yet another skeleton appeared.

"Maya, I'm sorry," the skeleton said. "I never wanted to hurt you and Lily."

"Oh, Elliot!" I bawled. "How could you leave her?"

"Speak your gut, Maya," the old woman said. "Liberate your mouth! So that we no longer are women who are silent—just surviving until we collapse. But remember that we all want forgiveness. Maya, forgive us and let go. Be happy!"

"But how?" I asked as yet another figure walked in. This time it was like looking in the mirror. "You're me?"

"Forgive me, Maya!" the figure said.

I covered my face, scrambling to think and then suddenly filled with a sense of shocked euphoria, I wanted to laugh and cry.

Overwhelmed, I fell to my knees, sobbing uncontrollably, but this time it was for the little girl I'd never taken care of. Me.

Chapter Twenty-Five

¿Soy Loca?

I GOT BACK TO MY ROOM AND STUDIED PAPÁ'S paintings again, looking for more clues about the relatives who'd just paid me a visit in the field.

I thought about what I'd been told—other than the identity of Papá's father, it was nothing new, just more of the same. Hadn't I been told over and over to let it go, get over it. Hadn't I been trying to be happy? Hadn't I forgiven?

I then picked up the painting I'd been working on, realizing now I'd given it an underpainting of truth that would shine through no matter how many layers of memories mixed with history, both fact and fiction, were laid down. I tried to tone down the shades of black with a dab of grey. I added a little white to the lies, but the fact was that the truth would always shine through and prevail in a true work of art, no matter how many coatings of paint—washes, so thin and transparent—I could see the film underneath. My eyes were no longer glazed over as I focused on the young Lucia in the painting—already pregnant with Papá. Nausea overwhelmed me. Still, I felt sorry for all of them. Since I was young, I'd made excuses for my father, for his drinking and for the abuse. I'd forgiven him a long time ago; it was the Christian thing to do.

But it was no secret I'd wished him dead. I'd taken on his coat of shame and guilt, wearing it like a heavy hand-me-down—like a cancer that had ravaged my body. And it was my molestation that broke the family up, turned Mamá away from me. *He was sorry*. Mamá would say later. *How do you think I felt?* I'd looked my mother in eyes, so dark. I was frightened into letting it go. *He was my husband*. It was what silenced me, froze my tongue, and eventually scared my little brother away from me.

Oh, Rudy, I'm so sorry I was such a little bitch. I'd turned into a very angry, frightened and lonely little girl. I drifted away from Rudy and lashed out at him, all because of the shame and the burden that I carried. And now that I'd learned the truth about my father, I was almost tempted to make more excuses for him, again. Pobrecito. He was a bastard child, unloved and unwanted by a mother too young and ashamed of his presence. But that was his shame to carry, not mine. I'd done nothing wrong. He should never have burdened me with that weighty cloak. None of this had been my fault!

I fixated on the painting of myself as a child—so innocent. How could anyone want to hurt me? Why would anyone do that to me?

I hadn't been able to talk to anyone back then, having been told to get over it, let it go, be quiet. Words pounded into my head by Mamá. She'd even told me I was a liar. *I'm not a liar!* And now these ghosts were telling me to forgive. Forget that shit!

I'D ALWAYS been so busy treading water, too blind to see myself drowning in a sea of despair, and even if I took the time to be introspective, I got bored of myself, besides I wasn't one for pity parties.

Like many cultures that immigrate to America, there is a stigma, including shame, about being labeled *loca* if you were to ever seek psychiatric help. Fortunately, there were plenty of self-help books on the shelves at Barnes & Noble, but they were all just so touchy feely. In my Mexican community, the tendency was to keep your problems inside, and in my case, I was to bury any troubles way down in the bottom drawer of my gut. While some did not have the means to access appropriate mental health needs, seeking psychiatric services was a luxury I'd never afforded myself, even after I started making good money. Besides, it was a sign of weakness if you couldn't handle your own affairs. Fortunately, I was strong. I'd proven it time and again; a smart woman who'd come up the hard way and I'd done a damn fine job. Besides, I never really believed I had the problem. It was everyone else. My head used to spin thinking that it was my father, my mother, my brother, Elliot, Lily, Zane, the butcher, the baker, and the candlestick maker. I was the victim; never mind I was also the common denominator.

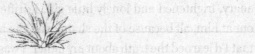

AFTER THE CRAZY incident in the field, I ran into Gabriel on my way back to the hacienda. It would be such a relief to talk to someone, not just about my shame, but about Elliot. I'd always been so good at diverting attention from the real issues, the root of the matter.

"Ay Dios," he said. "You are as white as a sheet—like you've seen a ghost."

"Lots of them. They came to me." I started to cry. "It was horrible, but wonderful. Elliot was there, too, and he wasn't even from this area."

Gabriel squinted up at me, a question hanging in the air. "Those who love you will always find you."

"I never forgave him," I said. "He was just a boy who loved a girl the best he knew how, a girl who didn't know how to love in return. A girl who didn't know how to love herself."

And I came undone, pulling up the hem of my dress to blow my nose into it, and letting my words stumble out. "Even though I was the one to leave the marriage, he threw the baby out with the bath water and never wanted to see Lily again," I cried. "You think you know someone. I thought I knew him. I thought that since he loved me so much, he'd understand and let go. We were both so miserable. We were so young."

My anger rose. "But just because you're too young doesn't mean you have to be immature about things. He couldn't think about anyone's feelings but his own. He wouldn't see Lily, because it would be too painful. She was a reminder of me and the baby boy we'd lost." I sobbed. "And then one day I found out he'd died in a ski accident. I was devastated. I really did love him. We never even talk about him." A consequence of the walls I'd been taught to erect. My daughter, my pride and joy, Lily, grew up with this impenetrable wall erected around the memory of her dad.

I stared at Gabriel, waiting for him to say something, but he remained silent.

I looked down at my feet. "I'm the one who needs to apologize to him. I used Elliot as an escape. I might have run away from home sooner, but he'd been nice to me and made my life bearable. He rescued me from my home." I wiped my eyes.

"And Papá was there, too. They all told me to let go," I said. "To forgive and be happy."

Gabriel reached out to hug me. "Maya, they were talking about you. You must forgive yourself."

I pushed away, sucking in a ragged breath, holding it in as I peered into his blue green eyes.

GABRIEL'S EYES are the same color of the agave in my painting, I thought, as I worked on my landscape the next morning. The agave looked quiet and so serene against the grey backdrop. I gazed at the canvas wondering if I was supposed to just go back home and start a new life. To live, love, and laugh; to forgive and forget—all against the backdrop of cancer? Was that the answer?

No! I was a fighter. I'd attack this like I had every other challenge in my life. Challenge was opportunity, after all.

A logical person, that's me. Surely there were rational answers for what was happening to me out there in the field. Most likely, what had happened was I'd returned to this place where my mind, like a blender, had filled with the mystical legends mixed into my culture together with the stories Papá had muddled for me as a child. Add a lot of Tequila and you end up with quite a crazy concoction—a hell of a cocktail!

I reached over, turned the paintings over, and then went to bed.

AGAIN, THE NEXT morning I woke up thanking God that it was all just a crazy nightmare, and then I rubbed the gritty reality into my eyes. But this morning, I felt so good, I refused to believe I was sick. I thought about it for a moment, comparing it to the pain of the molestation that had thankfully lessened as time went by. Time was a healer. But I also knew now that the denial and its consequences had indeed taken a toll. At the moment, I was happy to hang it all up in the back of the closet of my mind as if it were just last season's old dream, so out of style. I'd spend no more time thinking about it and got out of bed.

Chapter Twenty-Six
Under Clear Skies

THE SUN CRAWLED UP OVER THE MOUNTAIN, scratching its fingers of light over the sides. I heard the sound of a burro braying and looked up to see Don Pio riding up on Chuey. Behind them, down the row, the farmers were already swinging their machetes, whistling at work under a clear sky as if it were just the dawn of another day in paradise.

"Buenos días."

"Buenos días," I replied. "The sky is so blue here."

"It is the same blue everywhere," he answered with a wink. He slid off the donkey and stomped his legs. "The agave when first distilled is so pure. It is when we start adding things that you get hangovers—same as polluting the sky."

I nodded as a couple of burros clomped by laden with leaves. Behind them, a group of workers sang to the heavens, blossoming with white wisps of clouds.

"We have rainy days, but those days pass as do the clouds," Don Pio said. "But always, behind the clouds, the sky is blue. Same everywhere. Same yesterday, today and tomorrow."

Placing a hand over my stomach, I wondered how or whether I should share yesterday's experience.

"Are you all right?" Don Pio asked.

"Yes, yes. It's just that sometimes when I think of things that are painful—it's just a habit."

"Like what?" Don Pio asked.

I'd been able to talk easy enough with Gabriel about the blue monster and all the ghosts, but then hanging in the air like a cloud filled with the scent of misconception, the hint of a question about my father still lingered. And then suddenly, things that happened yesterday weren't as important as the reality of today. Today, I had cancer and tomorrow I could be dead. What would happen to Lily?

"Like, I'm concerned about Lily," I said. "I have to do something. I haven't been able to do anything about the men in my life, but she's—"

"Life is too short to try to change someone else. Put yourself first."

"But Lily's my daughter."

"She's God's daughter, too."

Struck by the words, I wanted to cry. I'd never thought about that. What a concept to think that someone else could actually watch after my baby, better than I could.

Don Pio clapped his hands together. "Now, what else is causing you pain?"

"Well, so—my father," I said, giggling nervously. "He died thinking he was the son of Pancho Villa." I picked up the quiote. "Quite a legacy, wouldn't you say?"

"It's just tragic, that's all," Don Pio said, dipping his head and then quickly spreading his arms wide and beaming. "This is the legacy. This field. The future of this field."

"But what if Bruno succeeds in taking away this field?" I asked, chewing now on the flower.

"And it could happen any day."

"What about Antonio?" I asked, anticipating pain in my gut at the mention of his name. It was if I were standing on solid ground, and then just the thought of him, I would feel the treacherous undercurrents. Something always moved underneath him, shifting all the time. "He is a mystery," I added.

"But not hard to understand," Don Pio said. "He is threatened and lives with anger and fear. Blind and stubborn like Chuey." He looked up to the sky. "God's will be done."

I swallowed the juice from the flower, feeling the soothing nectar trickle down my throat.

"How long will you be staying?" my uncle asked. "This place could use a woman's touch.

"You like paisley and polka dots?" I asked, feeling a little better as the juices soothed my stomach.

He smiled. "Seriously, we can probably use some of your business sense, too. Antonio seems to be resigned to let things go."

"Just because I'm an attorney, doesn't mean I have a head for business," I said. "Besides, I need to get back." Even though the pain in my belly was now entirely absent, experience told me it was only temporary. I'd better hurry and get home. Nothing good ever lasted.

He picked up the coa and I noticed the gold ring on his finger sparkling in the sun. "You still wear your ring. How long has Arisel been gone?"

Don Pio brought his hand to his heart. "She's still here."

I slipped my left arm behind my back when I saw he'd caught me looking at my own bare hand.

"We face so many other disasters with courage, why not marriage?"

"It's complicated, Don Pio," I said and kept walking.

Sweating in the noontime sun, the hat-covered workers chopped around the plants with their machetes and scythes. All the while, singing like cheerful little parakeets set free from their cage.

"I couldn't walk away," Don Pio said.

"You don't understand," I replied. I had to walk away, both times. It was something I learned from Mamá, even though she always took him back. I'd be different.

"Gabriel, when he *could* walk, didn't walk away," Don Pio said, pointing to the fallow north field. "Every day I went out and prayed for an answer, and after a while, the agave began to look healthier." He looked at me. "Sometimes when our lives seem so out of control, we forget to kneel."

"I don't forget. I just don't believe anymore."

"And I don't believe you, Maya," he said, peering at me now. "Have you not known love in your life?"

"Of course."

"You have loved someone more than yourself?"

"I have a hard enough time loving myself."

"Well, that's the problem." He stomped his foot. "When the ground is so hard and unfertile, there is no room for love to grow."

I smiled, stamping my foot. "I do love Lily more than anything in the world. As for the men in my life—" I thought about Elliot and how at seventeen, I'd thought I loved him. Nothing like my father, he was responsible and hardworking—just like me. A year older and a senior in high school, he played on the football team and already had two jobs: one at Tastee-Freez and the other, a seasonable position at a ski shop. He saved for a car. But at that age, what do you know? And then when you end up pregnant. And then you get married. And then when a baby dies—what's love got to do with it? He'd tried to do the right thing. How could I hate him for that? Besides, his ghost just apologized to me out in the field.

And then I thought about Zane and how he was everything Elliot was not. Artistic and passionate about life; he'd teased out the creative side of me, both on canvas and in bed. He'd also been the only one who could beat me consistently at tennis. He liked to live life on the edge—paint the lines—as they say in tennis. But then the lines got so blurred, and things got out of hand. Besides, sometimes you do need to come in off the playground.

"I sure know how to pick 'em," I said. "I've really hurt Lily."

"You thought they loved you. Imagine how much more God does," Don Pio said. "More than you can ever know."

The tears streamed down my cheeks.

"Why don't you let your heart do the picking next time."

"But love shouldn't hurt." I wiped my face.

Don Pio shook his head. "Sometimes, you must squeeze the plant to get the juice."

I let out a hearty laugh.

"Why don't you open up your heart to God?"

"Don Pio, I'm trying, but the words God and father have always been synonymous with pain and suffering and with a father like mine—well let's just say that if God were anything like my father—I say the word God and conjure up images of people speaking in tongues or the moral majority, or the war in the Middle East. I used to pray for a simpler life."

"But life is simple. People tend to mess it up."

I smiled. "Like a good Tequila?"

Don Pio nodded and then crouched to the ground. Using a knife he pulled from his pocket, he cut a rosette off from the agave. He trimmed around it, examined it, and then rejected it, tossing it onto the ground.

"Not ready for picking. Time for siesta."

"Reposado," I said.

Chapter Twenty-Seven

Pedos

AFTER I'D CARRIED IT DOWN THE HALLWAY, I stood with the phone to my ear.

"Damn it!" I said, immediately sorry for having raised my voice. I knew better than to shoot the messenger, but I was frustrated. Poor Betsy. How was I supposed to handle everything, especially now with this cancer thing hanging like a heavy crucifix around my neck?

I twisted the cord around my finger. "I'm sorry, Betsy," I said, lowering my voice. "Just file it with prejudice. Have Jim sign it." I paused, straining to listen. "I'm sorry. I don't know when I'm coming home. I've kind of got a lot on my plate right now."

"And your doctor called again," Betsy said. "She said it was important. Maya, you can't ignore your health."

"Gracias," I replied, slipping into Spanish. I wasn't ignoring my health; I just needed time to figure out a different way—another solution. Maybe surgery and chemo weren't the answers. Besides, I felt pretty good, as a matter of fact, better than I had in a long time. I'd call my doctor later. "Hasta luego, Betsy."

I PUT ON THE straw hat one of the girls in the field had given me earlier and left my room. Crossing through the courtyard over toward the distillery, I came upon the mulcher and reached in for a handful of the roasted mush before heading out to the field. Chewing on the sweet treat along the way, I imagined the organic juices, like a Tequila drip working their magic throughout my body. My mood lifted with the pigeon-gray fog and as I scanned the landscape, I noticed a burst of blue sky and the dew glistening like a prism refracting light onto the tips of the agave. The meadow was alive with life. The insects appeared larger; the butterflies, more colorful and the bees buzzed louder. The field surrounding me vibrated, infusing me with an energy I'd never known except, perhaps in pill or alcohol form. I took another bite of the maguey and as I walked past the young girls busy chopping away at the agave leaves with their scythes and machetes, they stopped to wave.

"Buenos días," a young woman said. "¿Vienes a trabajar?"

I felt a twinge of guilt that I wouldn't be helping today. But today was my day and I'd prescribed myself a break.

"Buenos días. Not today," I replied, wondering now how I might have been destined to work the fields, too, like everyone, had my family not gone north. Everyone, that is, except Gabriel—it seemed—who'd been able to break the pattern and do his artwork, what he loved.

I loosened the hat strings around my neck and kept walking. A little further in the field, I came upon Gabriel. He seemed to have been painting for a while. Looking at his work, I gasped. The images of nature's creatures coming to life through the translucent yellows, golds and oranges in the backdrop and then layered with opalescent hues of turquoise and shades of cyan and garnet. I couldn't help but envy his work. Quietly, I set up my easel next to him.

"How is life treating you today?" he asked, without looking up.

"Pretty well," I responded, mesmerized by his work. "I thought I'd try to get one last painting in before going home—a painting of this field so that I can take it home and remember."

Gabriel nodded.

"I also hope I can remember everything you've taught me," I added.

He smiled holding up a brush. "Recuerda, it's all in the brushes—big shapes first, small details last."

"Got it, don't sweat the small stuff," I said with a laugh. "And I want to remember everything Don Pio has taught me. He's also full of good advice. Lots of knowledge—such a pragmatic outlook on life."

"Yes, he is very wise," Gabriel responded. "Like the time when I told him I wanted to go to school to learn more about the agave, he said, 'Hijo, I suppose knowledge of something as simple as the agave might make it possible for you to see into the depth of things.'"

"Wow. I wish I had someone like that to guide me growing up."

Gabriel nodded. "I was blessed to also have Antonio."

I peered at him as I picked up my palette.

"In the end, they all just wanted me to walk again," Gabriel said.

"I'm sure you want to walk again," I said, squeezing on some yellow and gold. I'd try to imitate the work Gabriel had done.

"I walk in my dreams."

I tilted my head. "You happen to be a great artist, Gabriel. There's a market for this sort of work. I know—"

"I'm not in the market. My creations bring me joy and since this is also my dream, my life, only I need to be amused by myself," he said, waving a hand over his work, which suddenly came to life.

I laughed as colorful birds and butterflies came flying out of his painting and then a green gecko crawled out and scurried across my feet into the field.

I'D BEEN WORKING on my painting awhile when my hand started to cramp. I shook it out, waggling my fingers.

Gabriel looked over and shook his hands, too, and then stretched out his arms. "There was a time when I was angry with God," he said, breaking the silence. "I was so grateful She spared my arms—my hands."

"Pain and loss I guess are just a part of life," I said, thinking about my cancer. Perhaps the time had come to just accept that it could be worse; that this was the card I'd been dealt. I could either be all in or just fold.

"Claro, and there's nothing we can do to control or change that fact."

"You can't say I don't try," I said, thinking I wasn't ready to give up.

"You've got a good heart," he said, looking at me now. "But it is not open. Your consciousness is focused on fear, not love. You must be open to change."

He was right and as logical as I was, my rational mind was disengaged, but it was my survival method. My whole life had been a series of short-term emergencies on which I focused for short-term survival. I'd lost the ability to relax and enjoy the moment. I'd lived from crisis to crisis, with no relief in sight.

In front of me, a farmer carried a giant trimmed agave heart on his head. I notice even more piñas saddled onto burros crossing my path. I'd love to be able to open my own heart and follow it, but soon I'd be going home and getting down to the business of fixing my problem.

LATER, I SAT back, pretty pleased about my creation until I made the mistake of turning to compare my work with Gabriel's. I heaved a heavy sigh when I saw the yellows and golds in his underpainting glowing, and the reds like molten lava coming through layers of paint so fine and translucent I could almost see the glistening field before time. "Oh Gabe! It's out of this world."

And then I looked back at my own work, like a preschooler had painted it. "I suck."

"Quit being so hard on yourself," Gabriel said. "Colors blind the eye; thoughts weaken the mind."

"Now you sound like Don Pio."

"And where do you think I learned that," Gabriel said, pointing his brush at me. "Look into your own heart, trust your inner vision."

I laughed. "I barely have any outer vision."

My head was thrown back in laughter as Antonio approached on horseback. Earlier, carrying my art supplies, I'd walked past his office window and sensed his eyes following me. I'd hurried along, turning a flushed face away, feeling uncomfortable as if I were doing something wrong, as if it was shameful for me to be taking a break and enjoying myself. I remembered feeling that way when Gabriel and I would play together. Antonio would always be lurking around, casting aspersions with only a look. My heart clanged now in its tower and when our eyes tripped upon each other, I looked away and he quickly trotted off.

"So what's your dream, Maya?" Gabriel asked, interrupting my thoughts.

I giggled. "I used to think about being a teacher or a nurse and even marrying a prince. But the truth was I wanted to be an artist and a Tequila farmer and—" I looked at Gabriel, "and to marry Antonio."

Pouting, Gabriel asked, "What about me?"

I pointed at him. "You? Seriously?"

Striking a pose like a fashion model, he batted his eyelashes and we both busted up laughing.

"You and I were best amigos," I said with a look reserved only for friends who understood each other. And then suddenly, I felt the old pain that had sunk down like sediment into the memory of my mind; the ache over the loss I'd experienced when my family had moved away. *Besides, I don't want you hanging around with queers*, Mamá had said, referring to Gabriel. Again, I hadn't understood the term back then. But once I knew better, I realized that both Mamá and Papá weren't accepting of Gabriel's identity. Blame it on culture or Catholicism, but while Papá viewed Gabriel as harmless, Mamá preferred I not associate with him to save my soul from damnation.

I'd lost my best friend—the boy I sat with in the field full of honeybees. The boy who'd taught me how to pet a bee by putting a bit of the sweet agave nectar on the tip of my finger and letting it land there. "It tickles," I'd whispered. "Now gently pet its back," he said. "Like this." Gabriel was the boy I swam with in the river where it pooled beneath the waterfall, cascading red velvet chocolate (we pretended); the boy that I chased after geckos with; the boy I chased butterflies with, hopped shadows of the clouds with; the boy I laid with in silence on the tall, cool grass, watching the clouds like woolly lambs, drift overhead. We'd listened to the quiet language of the lazy lizards, a language more meaningful than a world of sophisticated adults. Gabriel and I knew everything about each other without having to use words, especially when there weren't words to describe such unhappiness. He was the only male—the only person, actually—I'd ever really trusted. Ours was a friendship that would only be ruined with marriage.

"Besides, you're my cousin," I added now. "Just like Antonio, and you can't marry a cousin."

Gabriel laughed. "Tell that to some of our primos."

"I know, right?" I smiled, glimpsing at his legs now and thinking I already knew the answer as next I asked, "Why haven't you married?"

"I never found a man who didn't want to change me." He chuckled. "Once a *Chivas* fan, always a *Chivas* fan."

"You're such a diehard!" I said, laughing out loud. "Well, anyway, now my dream is for good health and for Lily to be happy—that would make me happy."

Gabriel peered at me. "And so it is. You must believe that."

I smiled. "Oh, and I do like to paint," I said, squeezing a little white paint and mixing it with the yellow on the palette.

"And it's as simple as that. Let go of everything that's keeping you from realizing this and follow your heart," Gabriel said.

I peered at him. *Yeah, right.* "I'm going to miss you, Gabriel," I said just as Antonio rode by again, this time tipping his hat.

I waved and then watched him ride off.

"Is he checking up on us?"

Gabriel shrugged his shoulders. "Sometimes, it's just good to get out of the office."

I yawned and stretched. "You're right. All those years working inside and now I wonder how I even stand it."

"I'm not much use to them inside." He waved a crutch over his head. "At least out here I can scare away the bats and buzzards. What's it like being an abogada in Los Angeles?"

"Well, things are pretty stressful, that's for sure." But I lived for stress. If I wasn't stressed, I wasn't challenged, I wasn't going places, and I wasn't alive. That was the mantra I'd fed myself. And now what could be more stressful than cancer? "But I'm not a quitter," I said. "I've been thinking about switching fields."

Gabriel tilted his head slightly.

"But once I make partner, which I should, there will be more money," I said, as if making more money was a good goal.

Gabriel faced me now, pointing his brush.

"You americanos chase after money and then wonder why your hearts are clenched."

"You mean it shows?" I laughed, leaning back on my elbows to warm my face in the sun.

So many times when I was unhappy, I simply checked my privilege at the door. I'd been doing what I loved, after all. That's what I told myself. I'd come a long way as a single mom, and I was damned lucky to have the position at this firm. I'd make partner soon, if I could stick it out just a little longer. I told myself to be grateful because I probably wasn't even qualified. I probably didn't even deserve the job. But all that was before I got cancer. Everything was changing now.

"That doesn't mean I don't take time to daydream or fantasize about quitting and disappearing into the sunset."

"Can't you see this as a sign?" Gabriel said.

I turned to look at him, his face so serene and yet, deadly serious.

"You know, God sometimes does for you what you cannot or will not do for yourself," Gabriel said.

"Yeah, maybe they'll just fire me." Or maybe, I thought, the cancer will take me out. That's one way to leave.

"The fields look like the sea or an ocean of blue green," I said, legs crossed in front of me, wondering how many of these workers had ever been to the ocean. "The peace, the tranquility of it all," I added. "I used to go to the beach and paint with Zane—" I stopped and tried to drown the memory. But the truth was that there were some good times and if we could have, we'd have spent everyday painting on the shore. It was calming. But that's not always the way life was. Life was full of ebbs and flows.

"I'd love to paint the ocean," Gabriel said.

I sat up as a recollection came swimming up from a dream. "Hey, do you remember the time we went to the beach in Puerto Vallarta."

"I do," Gabriel said. "Everyone went, except for Antonio. I so wished he would have come along, but he said he needed to work."

"Even back then, huh?"

"Later, I told him how we snuck out to watch the baby turtles hatch and then scramble back to the ocean," Gabriel said.

"They were so cute. I'll never forget. I wanted to bring one home."

He nodded. "Yes, and you would have, too, except the moon was so bright, we were afraid we would get caught."

"They were going home, back to the sea," I said. "I wondered how they knew." Does the saying, *la sangre atrae,* also apply to turtles, I wondered?

"I remember how sunburned you were the next day. Your nose peeled off like snakeskin."

I pinched my nose. "Remember the coconut juice we drank straight out of the shell?"

"And the fish-on-a-stick."

I licked my lips. "I'm thinking about taking Lily there before I go home. I've told her so much about the place. Come with us! You'd be a great companion. That is if the old grump can part with you."

"Don Pio?"

"No. Mr. Stick-Up-His-Ass, Antonio."

"My brother is harmless." Gabriel grinned. "It's like working with the agaves. You just need to know how to get near without letting them stick you."

"So, that's what you do."

"Pretty much. I learned to enter the thickest, thorniest rosettes without getting hurt."

"Your threshold for pain is much higher than mine."

"Don't take the pain personally." He chuckled and then using a paintbrush, he pointed to his eyes and then mine.

I giggled but then accidentally let out some gas. "Oh my God! I farted. How embarrassing. I'm so sorry." I covered my mouth.

"Maya, everyone makes pedos. There's nothing shameful or unhealthy about that."

Nothing unhealthy, I thought, wishing that were true. "Stomach problems."

He squinted at me. "Denial is a dangerous thing. You've got to take care of yourself," he said, handing me the flower from an agave. "Chew on it. You know you'll explode if you hold that in for too long?"

I laughed but then became somber. "Everything in my world is falling apart. I thought I had a grip on life. I thought I could handle it."

"What, the pedo?" he asked as Chuey approached.

I had a feeling somehow, he already knew about my cancer and wasn't going to mention the "C" word until I did first, but we'd had such a lovely time I'd wait. I'd continue to hold it in.

We gathered our things to leave. "You know my stomach feels better. What's in that agave anyway?"

Chapter Twenty-Eight

Mayahuel

I FANNED THROUGH THE FOLDER OFELIA HAD GIVEN me and then set it down next to my computer as it booted it up. I found myself falling down a rabbit hole, browsing the web for answers to my condition, as if cancer were only a condition. I knew I could no longer avoid my doctor. The time had come. I got up to go use the phone down the hall.

"When will you be home?" Dr. Vaisman asked from the other end.

"Soon," I said. "You know, I'm feeling much better. I've been watching my diet—lots of choices down here." I giggled nervously. "I've slowed down, and you'll be glad to know that I've finally quit smoking."

"Again?" Now, the doctor laughed.

"Yes, but this time for good," I answered. "And I'm even thinking about a vacation."

"That's all great, Maya, and it will certainly help, but right now you need to come back for some more tests and we need to get you prepared for surgery."

"Okay, I'll be home next week. But first, I promised Lily a vacation."

IN MY ROOM later that day, I stared at the work I'd created, a landscape of the agave. Feeling good and so grateful that my passion had been reawakened, I felt alive for the first time in a long time. Knowing I'd found something to bring me contentment, I'd be able to go back to Los Angeles. I promised myself to take time out to paint again. Holding the painting up now to compare, I looked out the window and saw Antonio heading into the distillery. I slid into my sandals and then left my room to hurry across the courtyard.

Slipping into the distillery, I tiptoed down the hallway and then knocked before entering Antonio's office.

"Shouldn't you be out there finding a life?" he asked, looking up from his desk.

I gnawed at the inside of my mouth, thinking there's no way I'd let him beat me down.

"I think I have. I was just coming here to tell you—"

"Tell me how to live mine," he said with a sneer.

I screwed up my mouth. *The hell with him.* He didn't deserve the courtesy of a goodbye.

"No, Antonio," I said with a smile so smug, I hoped he couldn't tell how deflated I was now. Lifting my chin, I turned to leave. "You seem to be surviving just fine."

Once outside the veranda, I took off into the field, running like a mad woman. Heart racing, I let out a scream so loud, it could wake the dead.

IT WAS IN THE heat of the day that I'd wandered into the field, noticing a small wisp of dark smoke curling up to the sky. There was whistling and singing and as I got closer, I noticed the workers gathering twigs and using cut agave spikes for a fire. They roasted corn and then used a little saucepan to heat their lunch. Together with the woodsy, sweet smell and whatever was in the little pan, my stomach gurgled. Amidst the worker's tools, a couple of scraggily dogs waited for handouts. "Ven a comer," a young women said to me, patting a spot next to her on the ground.

"Gracias," I said, suddenly ravenous from the aroma.

They shared their lunches with me, talking and tittering quietly amongst themselves until there was nothing left but a spoonful of humble silence. After all, I was still a stranger and they probably wondered what I was doing here.

"Tan sabroso. Gracias," I said, holding up a tortilla stuffed with the most flavorful beans I'd ever tasted. I looked around at the sweat-stained faces, wiping my mouth with the back of my hand. "So did you hear the one about the jimador, su hija fea and the parched traveling Tequila salesman who asked for a drink of water?"

The young workers stared at me blankly.

"So," I said. "The jimador's daughter came to the door with a jug of water and after the salesman took one look at the ugly daughter, he pulled out a bottle of his Tequila and guzzled it back. He then asked how far it was to the next farm."

I'd never been a good joke teller and there was definitely something lost in the translation, but the workers all flashed a respectful smile, nonetheless.

After a while, I watched them all curl up like day lilies at evening time, shading their faces with their hats, as they got ready for siesta.

THE AFTERNOON thunderclouds moved in rapidly, casting dark shadows across the plain. I worked quickly alongside the others, through the muggy afternoon. On my knees, face smudged with red clay, I pulled back a plant to examine its thin, pointy leaves. I noticed a slow moving, elongated shadow stretched across the path and turned to see Don Pio standing behind me. Looking like the Grim Reaper, he was holding a long pole at the end of which was a flat-bladed circular knife.

"What's that for?" I asked.

"This is a coa de jima. The jimador uses it to first remove the flower center, so that the agave can put all of its energy into swelling the heart—the piña."

I looked at the plant I was working on and noticed the flower shoot had already been removed.

"Very good. This one is ready to flower again," Don Pio said. "Let us take it back."

He raised his hand and clicked his fingers, motioning for a worker to come and help. The girl was young, but strong as an ox as she raised an axe over her head and came down at the base of the agave plant, prying loose what looked like a giant pineapple. Smiling, she rolled the plant toward Don Pio who used the knife from the end of the pole to trim up the piña, exposing the pulpy center.

Lightning cracked in the distance and the workers stooped to pick up the harvested piñas, tossing them overhead from person to person, by back and by burro, to take to the distillery.

Finally, there was a cloudburst, and a shower of rain came splashing down from the skies. I watched as the streaks of mud washed clean off my arms and then I held my face up to rinse it off. Refreshed, I opened my eyes to see Don Pio holding the piña out to me. Thanking him, I heaved the giant heart onto my shoulder and then onto my head. I hurried toward the distillery, but after a moment, because of the weight, I had to stop and set it down, and as I lowered it across the front of my chest, I felt a heartbeat. Whether it was mine ricocheting against the heart of the agave or not, I suddenly felt connected.

THE NEXT MORNING, I couldn't pull myself away. I tried to say goodbye again to all of the workers who by now had also become my family, but as I approached the factory, I heard the music—too lively for this time of morning. I hadn't even had my second cup of café, but once I walked through the door and saw the young girls bumping hips along the conveyer belt, I didn't need a second cup. The electric energy in the room was palpable. I donned a hair net and mask and stepped in next to a worker, grabbed a bottle and slapped on a label. As I handed the bottle off for another girl to pack, I noticed a baby sitting up in a box lined with blankets. The infant was chewing on a rubber toy. I looked closer at the young woman standing next to me, recognizing her from Antonio's office. Her name was Teresa. Teresa, the daughter of the toothless woman from the plaza? The girl who worked to help her family? I looked at her more closely, she stared back, and I could really study her. She looked eerily familiar, like a sister even. But then again, as had been said, everyone around here was related somehow. I then walked over to play with the baby before getting back to work. I loved babies. Zane and I had even talked about having one together. But then—and now—

I pushed the crazy idea out of my head and continued to label, taking sneak peeks at Teresa and wondering about her mother Estella, Doña Paola's daughter. My step-cousin once or twice removed?

After a while, my brain and my body grew tired. My feet and hands hurt, my back ached. I turned to Teresa.

"When's the break?"

All eyes were on me. Teresa shook her head, shrugging her shoulders.

"Seriously? That's not right," I said, stepping over to flick off the switch to the conveyer belt.

The girls grew wide-eyed and turned to whisper amongst themselves.

"Síganme, por favor," I said, and the girls tentatively followed me out the door.

Outside, on a patch of dried grass, I stretched my arms to the sky. "Toca el cielo." I lay my hands flat on the ground, wishing now I'd kept that Yoga book Lily was studying. "Toca el suelo." The girls giggled, but eventually mimicked my moves.

My cell phone went off and I looked to see that my office was calling again. I'm on my break, I thought, smiling, ignoring the call.

And then as I pushed my tush into the air—downward-facing dog—I heard the door slam and looked up to see Antonio marching toward us.

"*Que la chingada!* Maya, what's going on out here?"

I sprang up as the young women all scattered, scurrying like little mice back into the warehouse.

THAT EVENING after I'd finished packing, I poured myself a small Tequila and took it with Ofelia's folder to sit out on the veranda. Maybe there was something I'd missed in the reading. I'd tried to read between the lines, but every time, I came up with the same conclusion; it's not a cure. It was looking more and more like I'd end up having surgery and then chemo. I set the folder down and saw Don Pio strolling toward the house. He was whistling.

He stopped when he saw me sitting on the porch. "Too lovely an evening. Why do you look so down?"

"I'm just really going to miss this place." It wasn't a lie, but it wasn't the whole truth.

"Why not take a break?" he suggested.

I raised my glass. "I've been taking lots of them, and it's been wonderful."

He reached out to pick up the folder I'd set down. He looked it over before setting it back down. "Sabes, in times like these, I go to sleep and ask God to send answers in my dreams."

I wondered if he knew about my cancer. And if not, perhaps now might be the time to tell him.

"Don Pio, I have been praying and you know, I've already had some pretty interesting dreams." I peered into my glass. "Visions," I added, looking up at him, his eyebrow arched now. He took a seat next to me.

"You and my dad—you were brothers."

Don Pio tilted his head slightly.

"You shared the same father, and it definitely wasn't Pancho Villa." I hesitated now, afraid to tell him the next part. "Your father raped your sister."

Don Pio's face fell like a window closing as a single tear like a raindrop slid out of the corner of his eye. "That is your truth."

"Mine? What about yours?"

He pushed up on his knees and stood. "It never mattered to me who his father was. In my heart, he was always my brother," Don Pio said, walking to the edge of the veranda.

"But didn't it matter what happened to your sister?"

He turned to look at me. "Of course it did, but it's over now and soon, I will go to be with her. She waits at the door for me," he added, looking out across the clearing. "But this field will go on, it must not die."

"You're right. It can't die."

"Antonio does what he thinks he must. Bruno only sees pesos," Don Pio said, turning now to me. "It was important for me to see that you love this place. Your truth makes this farm yours, too."

"I do love this place. I feel like I'm home, but I also feel so lost."

"Those who love you will always find you," he said before stepping off into the night.

I remembered Gabriel telling me the same thing.

I ROCKED FOR a while after Don Pio left. *Those who love you will always find you.* A lovely notion I thought as the sound of twilight called out to me. Crickets chirruped and, in the distance, an owl hooted. And then I heard my name being whispered on the wind.

STANDING BAREFOOT now just inside the field, I reached out to touch the waxy leaf of an agave and rub it between my fingers. I closed my eyes, and then as if an oxygen mask had been placed over my nose, I breathed in the earth's sweetness and settled into a foreign calmness. Toes digging into the cool crimson earth, I felt rooted, an agave plant.

Arms outstretched, I lifted my head to soak in the energy of the field.

It began as an ember in the pit of my belly, then little charges fired through me, kindling an energy igniting a forest fire in my soul. I felt I might be glowing and opened my eyes to see the bluish pulsating stars outshining the dying yellow ones. This light was more than an illusion that would continue to shine for eternity. It was a reflection of me and the stars together with the moon, glistening across an emerald ocean—where beneath the surface, a whole infrastructure of life and fossils existed. A swarm of fireflies flitted across the field. This land was breathing life back into me. The field, a giant altar to the dead; a holy place to come and worship and lay down treats and dance and sing.

"I used to think her young spirit had returned to enjoy her childhood."

Startled, I turned to see Don Pio standing next to me, his face turned up toward the heavens.

"You mean your sister, Lucia?"

He nodded.

"You've seen her? Did my father know?"

"I do not think so. He was too full of fear to find the truth."

I looked up at the dazzling heavens. "It really is a lovely evening. So many stars."

Don Pio raised his head and blessed himself. "Our ancestors. There's my angel Arisel," he said pointing. "But see that star?"

I followed his direction. "That one?" I asked, pointing now.

"That's Mayahuel."

"The goddess of Tequila?"

"You see," Don Pio said with laugh. "When the world began, there was a goddess in the sky who devoured the light . . . Quetzalcoatl got tired of living in darkness and went up there to fight her."

I watched as a bright star appeared. I imagined it slowly transforming into a starry goddess, blanketing the heavens with light.

"Instead," Don Pio continued, "he fell in love with her granddaughter, Mayahuel. He brought her to earth. She was also god of fertility with four hundred breasts."

"Four hundred chichis?" I laughed. "Lucky Quetzalcoatl!"

"That is just a number the Aztecs used for many." Don Pio chuckled. "Maybe she had only three. More than two anyway."

I threw back my head, really laughing now.

"So, anyway, this evil goddess came to earth and killed Mayahuel. Quetzalcoatl grew very sad. The other gods saw—"

I stared at the heavens. "Because now there was light?" I said, facetiously.

Don Pio looked at me askance, as if I wasn't taking this seriously. "They planted a plant with special powers where she was buried to comfort the soul of Quetzalcoatl." He turned toward the heavens. "The people believed that was how agave came to be and why Tequila comforts the soul of those who have lost someone dear to their hearts."

I gazed at the star. "So that's Mayahuel. She sure gives comfort to a lot of people."

"Well, it's not a cure," he said, now bowing his head. "I think it's time for me to call it a night."

"Don Pio?" I asked and could see his profile as he turned slightly. "What about Antonio? I mean if I should decide to stay."

He faced me now with a smile that couldn't be contained.

"Dream your answer for tomorrow and if you wake up feeling differently, may I recommend something else I do before I enter the distillery?"

"What's that?"

"I usually send God in before I even cross the threshold."

I raised my arm. "What about your angels?"

"Ay, they go in without asking." He laughed, spreading his arms wide. "The bigger the army, the better."

Chapter Twenty-Nine

Business Con Bruno

THE NEXT MORNING BROKE THROUGH, RUBBING its sleepy eyes as I exited the hacienda carrying two mugs of coffee. I'd been able to dream and like Don Pio said, I'd come up with an answer. Feeling wonderful, I wanted to believe there was something special about the field, about the agave. I'd always felt a kinship with the agave field and when I returned from el norte, I was parched with a cracked terrain and thirsty for knowledge that might mend the fissures; full of secrets ready to be tilled and unearthed, and with a child at my core rumbling to be heard at last. I decided it wouldn't hurt to stay just a little longer to find out more. I called my office to let them know I was extending my stay. As for my doctor, I didn't want to think about that right now, besides from all that I'd researched, right now I wasn't even sure chemo was the best answer.

Through the morning mist, I could see the workers, like sleepwalkers, headed out to tend the plants.

A little closer to the distillery, I yawned and then looked up. "God, it's me, Maya. If you exist, please go in and sweep for land mines. Gracias."

Down the hall I shuffled, until I saw Antonio's office door slightly ajar. I inhaled, gripping the cups tighter and then before entering, I uttered another prayer. "Please God, help me." Holding my breath, I bumped the door gently with my hip and it swung open. Seated at his desk, Antonio was just bringing a mug of to his lips when he looked up.

He set down his cup. "You're a two-fisted drinker?"

I was embarrassed, noticing the Mr. Coffee set up on a credenza behind his desk. "Uh, yes. I usually have two cups in the morning. I didn't realize—"

185

"So, I see you've returned to get back on the beast."

"I'm not one to give in easily," I said, forcing a smile as I set down the extra cup of coffee. "I just dig my spurs in deeper."

Antonio reached across to the side of his desk and grabbed a stack of papers. "Let's see what you can do with this," he said, shoving the heap toward me, and then he swiveled back around to face his computer.

LATER THAT MORNING, I pushed away from my desk in my room and returned to Antonio's office. I handed back the stack of papers.

"So soon? Did you have some questions?" he asked.

"Nope. Looks like you should hold off on new barrel orders until next year, at least until you get the north fields back in production. Anything else?"

"No, and who said anything about the north fields, mujer?"

Biting into the soft flesh on the inside my cheeks, I thought better than to engage with Antonio. "Well then, if that's all, it's time for my siesta," I said, pivoting to leave.

I left Antonio's office, victorious, as if I'd been in the middle of a trial where sometimes the causes of action could only be addressed one count at a time, and sometimes, only one day at a time. For the moment, it felt as if I'd just won a momentous motion in court—not the whole case, but a landmark for today, nonetheless. I walked out of the distillery and into the bright sunshine. I lifted my head and whispered, "Thanks, Big Guy. I owe you one."

ON MY WAY out to the field, I was thinking I deserved this break when, all at once, the earth rumbled beneath me. I planted my feet on the ground at the roar of an engine in the distance. Raising a hand up to shield my eyes, I squinted down toward the entrance of the property. Whipping up the road, something akin to a red dust devil approached, getting noisier. The earth shook even more violently. And then I could see that the whirling dervish was merely a blood red tractor spitting out the chili pepper dust powder and gravel. But why was it traveling so fast?

A door slammed behind me, and I turned to see Antonio running out of the distillery, crimson-faced and carrying a rifle. "Te voy a matar, Bruno!" he yelled, bolting toward the John Deere.

Don Pio came rushing out of the mulching area and hobbled over to where I stood. "*Qué pasa?*"

"It's Bruno," I replied. "Antonio says he's going to kill him." I took off running toward the commotion but stopped in my tracks when I saw him mounting the machine. The tractor slowed down and then he pulled the driver out by the scruff of his neck, slamming him down onto the ground, leaving the vehicle in idle speed. Antonio then placed his boot on the man's chest and held the gun to his head. I heard a shot and screamed, but then realized it was the tractor that had backfired before finally sputtering off.

I stood watching in a panic. Antonio said he was going to kill Bruno. Was he capable of that? Of course he was. In a rage and when it came to your property, lots of people might be capable of murder. I looked at the man on the ground, but it wasn't Bruno—perhaps, one of his workers. I felt helpless, wondering whether I should call the authorities. When I turned to go back to the house to use the phone, I noticed Antonio's truck parked on the side of the building and ran toward it instead.

SPEEDING ALONG the outskirts of town, I was operating the truck on an adrenaline cocktail, mixed in equal parts with Antonio's murderous look and the face of fear on poor Don Pio.

As an attorney back in the states, I knew that certain measures needed to be taken to keep intruders out. Signs needed to be posted everywhere with the penalties for trespassing posted clearly. Some states recognized the Right to Stand. And in California, the Castle Doctrine even allowed the homeowner to give chase or if someone were to unlawfully break in and the owner feared imminent death or bodily injury toward themselves or their family, they're allowed to use deadly force. But it's always a gamble to shoot. This, I knew all too well. It had been the bad luck of the draw a couple of years ago when I represented a client who was trying to protect his home. After shooting the intruder, he'd been arrested for homicide and after a period of agony, I was able to paint a picture of justification, and the jury acquitted my client. But again, that was in California.

I knew the best thing to do in this situation was to call the police, but out here in this rural part of Mexico where not too long ago intruders came onto the land to rape and murder my ancestors, I wasn't so sure Antonio would be capable of simply standing his ground.

Just ahead off the side of the main highway, sticking out like it didn't belong—like someone hadn't taken business seriously—I saw a flat, plain-looking white stucco building facing the road like some sort of makeshift façade. It reminded me of a kid's lemonade stand, set up just that morning to do business. Further giving it a temporary look and standing sentry were a couple of telephone poles with wires looped loosely across the building. Stretched across on either side were chain link fences. Along the face of the building was a row of tall shapes like Moroccan arches—an afterthought, perhaps—on every other a window. There were half a dozen vehicles parked in the lot carpeted with crabgrass. I knew I'd found the right place when I spotted the black Cadillac Escalade parked under a tree on the right side of the building. It was the same vehicle I'd seen loitering around the perimeter of *Los Olvidados*. I pulled into an empty space and got out of the truck.

Except for all of the cars parked out front, and especially with no sign posted, you'd never know it was a place of business, much less a distillery. I walked up the couple steps to a small arched doorway and pressed a buzzer. No sooner had I taken my finger off the button, than a middle-aged man with a moustache opened the door.

"Bienvenidos. How can I help you?"

"Soy Maya Miller. I'm here to see Mr. Hidalgo. Mr. Bruno—"

"He is expecting you," the man said, leaving me alone in the strange makeshift foyer.

Expecting me? How is it that everyone down here seems to be expecting me? "But I don't have an appointment," I said as he walked away. And then in the same moment, a stout dark man in cowboy boots came walking up the hall. He wore a grey shirt and jeans and under his dark cowboy hat, I could see his face was badly pitted as if he'd suffered chicken pox as a child. Around his waist he wore a huge gold medallion like a *Lucha Libre* championship belt. I wasn't here to do battle, merely to negotiate. When he came close enough, he stopped and removed his hat.

"Soy Bruno Hidalgo, a sus ordenes. I've been waiting for you, Maya."

I wasn't here on a social call. "So, what's up with the tractor?"

He laughed. "Simply a reminder that I mean negocios. Surely you noticed that old junker growing weeds out back? They could use a new one."

I thought about it, recalling Antonio tinkering behind the distillery where it was like a bone yard full of old farm equipment.

Bruno opened an arm, motioning for me to follow him. "I see you got my emails," he said leading the way.

"I thought they were from Don Pio."

Bruno laughed, turning to face me. "They still use burros to mulch the maguey, and brick ovens. You think he's going to know how to use the computer?"

I shrugged, except for Antonio's prehistoric computer, he did have a point. "So why did you email me?"

"Puro negocios," he said, all jaw and determination. "I can't talk to them. Victor told me you were a good attorney."

"Victor?"

"Yes, you represented my uncle fairly."

Your uncle?

Still trying to process the relationship, I followed Bruno outside. A warm breeze blew across the hill where his property was situated, and I tried to pull the hair out of my face. As we stood on the precipice overlooking a sea of agave, Bruno pointed to a speck in the valley below, beyond a steepled village. I could see the bell tower from the church. "That's where I was born and that's where I was baptized. And now from here, I can look down on all of them."

I held my tongue and turned to see a snide smile spreading like wildfire across his scarred face. How bad could it have possibly been down there with a father like Don Pio, I wondered? Again, I suspected my life would have been a whole lot better with a father like him.

I then followed Bruno around to a tall hangar-like building outfitted with modern conveyer belts, vats and other equipment. Once we were back in the main building, he turned into an office that looked like a boardroom with its long table and half a dozen leather chairs. He took a seat at the head of the table.

"Siéntate, por favor," he said, pulling out a cigar.

I took a seat and looked around the room. Hanging on the walls were pictures of him with all sorts of dignitaries. In one photo he was shaking hands with the president. In another, it looked like he was in Japan with some businessmen. After a moment, a worker came in carrying a couple bottles of Tequila.

"Gracias, Miguel," Bruno said, dismissing the man. He then reached for the bottle and poured a shot and slid the glass in front of me.

"This is our añejo," he said, unlit cigar dangling from his lips.

"Where's yours?"

"Strictly business. Don't normally touch the stuff," he said, pointing to a picture on the wall. "Oh, every once in a while, I'll drink a toast or something like there con el presidente."

"And so this isn't a business call?" I said, pushing my glass away.

He nodded ruefully but grinned like a fiend as he poured himself a glass. "Your being here calls for a toast."

Curious, I arched an eyebrow, and he slid my glass back, as if we were playing some sort of chess game. He set down his cigar and raised his glass. "Salud!"

I kept an eye on him as I lifted my glass. "Salud." I drank the shot, surprised at how good it was. Almost the same as Los Olvidados, but different, a little less earthy, perhaps not as pure. "Smooth."

"Now, try this one," he said.

I couldn't imagine anything could be better on this farm as I brought the glass to my nose. I took a whiff, and the smell stung my nose causing me to cough. Not wanting to be rude, I took a moment and then tried it again. This time I held my breath as I sipped, but then I started choking. My chest burned. Bruno was laughing and when I wiped the tears from my eyes, I saw his gold-bordered teeth glinting under the fluorescent lights.

"So, what do you think?" he asked.

"Um, honestly. This tastes like polish remover."

He slapped down his hand, laughing even harder. "It's Cuervo. Your gringos love it with a beer chaser or in a Margarita."

Thankfully, Miguel came in to offer me a glass of water.

"Now you truly taste the difference," Bruno said.

I nodded. "I understand you think you can take over the family's farm."

Bruno smirked. "As the one true descendent and oldest son—"

"Are you so sure about that? What about Victor and Antonio? And—"

"Antonio has always been hardheaded, nose to the grind, but he's bitter." Bruno's face seemed to melt. "Ever since Camela was killed, he's worse. As for Victor, he walked away a long time ago. I can simply take it over. But I am a fair man and am prepared to make them quite an offer. I need to be able to fill the orders. I need more plants."

"I see. But what will happen to their local business?"

Bruno held up the palms of his hands, shrugging his shoulders.

"It's important to the livelihood of the people. The field means so much to Don Pio," I said. "You don't even like Tequila."

Bruno sneered now. "My business is growing so fast, I can't keep up. I need three times more than what we are already producing. Orders for Europe and Japan must be filled. I am looking at other farms, too."

"But what if they simply got the north fields up and running and sold you what you needed? Antonio is thinking about plowing it all under, but I have some ideas. This could be a win/win situation."

"I know how hard my father has worked," Bruno said. "I thought I could lessen the burden."

I doubted his sincerity. "You Hidalgos are proud, stubborn people," I said. "This isn't a burden. It's their life. Your legacy." I set my elbows on the table and then massaged my temples. "Listen, you've already provided tractors, now if you can provide the capitol, they can provide the labor."

"Let me think about it," Bruno said, smiling slowly. "I had a feeling about you when you first walked in."

"Remember," I said, hooking a thumb toward my heart. "I, too, am a Hidalgo."

He nodded. "You know, I am not the bad man they make me out to be. I do have the heart of an angel," he said with a laugh. "Call me a philanthropist."

"I see you inherited your father's pragmatism," I said. "They might be able to use some of your philanthropy, too."

I thought I'd made a breakthrough. And then Bruno burst out into an almost devilish laugh. "Those people are simpletons. There is no getting through to them and there is no stopping me from doing what I must."

"So then why did you contact me?" I asked, pushing away from the table.

Bruno stared at me, his eyes black as his soul, and then he smiled. "Ah! You're right. You are a Hidalgo and with you in charge, I might reconsider how I do business. I'll give you a week to talk some sense into those tontos."

In charge? I can't be in charge. I'm sick and I need to go home. But, if I leave now, Bruno will have a stronger foothold in the family business.

He raised his glass. "Salud!"

We stood and feeling like some sort of Judas, I shook Bruno's hand, so soft, as if he'd never lifted a shovel in his life. I paused a second, trying to figure out whether my next statement should be calibrated to please him or my own good conscience. "Nice doing business with you," I finally said before departing.

Chapter Thirty

Shadow of the Wind

THE NEXT MORNING, I WANDERED INTO THE KITCHEN after everyone had left for work. I poured myself a cup of café con leche and grabbed a pan de huevo. Through the window I could see Magdalena watering the red geraniums in the courtyard as she also tossed some scraps to the chickens. What a multi-tasker, I thought chewing on the sweet bread. I can barely walk and chew gum. How would I ever be able to handle this farm especially if I had to battle cancer? There was no way. I rinsed my dishes and walked outside.

I crossed the courtyard, making my way toward the office when I noticed the plume of red dust coming up the road—Antonio's truck. Good, it was time to have a conversation with him and Don Pio—perhaps two conversations. I watched him pull up and then get out. As soon as I saw him holding a bouquet of flowers, I changed my mind about having any discussions just yet. Bewildered. This called for some meditation out in the field. But first I walked back to my room to gather my painting supplies.

THERE WAS A spot with plenty of shade near an old oak tree that had probably been rooted there for centuries. Oh the stories you could tell, árbol, I whispered, setting up my canvas. I squeezed out a little brown paint for the tree trunk and then before I could lay it on, the little indigenous girl in braids was back. She reached out to me and took my hand.

SHE LED ME into the fallow north field where I noticed a short stone wall. I got closer and saw the crosses sticking out of a small cemetery and then I noticed the fresh-picked flowers—*the ones Antonio had carried?* They'd been placed near a headstone.

Amelia Marquez – 1982, it read. "The mother of Gabriel and Antonio," I said out loud.

I stepped around to read the inscriptions on the other headstones: Maria Vargas Villaseñor – 1914; my great grandmother; and then, my grandmother, Lucia Hidalgo Montoya – 1968. My father hadn't kept the name of his stepfather, Montoya.

I moved to the next marker and shrieked when I read the inscription. My legs wobbled. I reached out to lean on the cold stone. I then traced the marker with my fingers before dropping to my knees and burying my head in my hands.

After a moment, I raised my chin and noticed that the little girl was gone, but Gabriel now stood there. I shook my head, pointing to the marker. "What does it mean?"

He reached out to cradle my chin. "There's nothing to be afraid of."

"When? I'm not ready."

Gabriel simply smiled and turned to walk away.

"But Gabriel, I'm not ready," I said again, calling after him.

I GOT UP AND followed Gabriel. He didn't stop until he reached the house on the hill. Winded, hands on my knees, I watched him disappear inside.

At dusk, I wandered around the perimeter of the small house. Antonio lived there. I peeped in through a window where I saw a room full of textbooks, probably belonging to Gabriel from school. I tried the door and entered. There was literature from the University and next to a computer, I found a book on the *Agave Azul*. I was surprised when I came across a picture of Antonio with his arm around a very pretty girl. I picked it up and examined it more closely. *Camela?*

I wandered into a bedroom and handled items like I was reading braille; like I'd been so blind when it came to Antonio. On the nightstand was a book entitled *La sombre del viento: Shadow of the Wind by Carlos Ruiz Zafón*. I opened it up where the marker had been placed and read:

"There are no second chances in life, except to feel remorse."

Intrigued, I read a few more paragraphs before realizing I was sitting on his bed. I bolted up, smoothing my impression out of the otherwise and surprisingly, neatly made bed. I continued to peek around a little more before opening an old armoire, and then I riffled through his clothes until my fingers caught on a white guayabera shirt. I brought it to my nose and inhaled, closing my eyes and imagining Antonio standing next to me. I opened my eyes and next to the cupboard, on the wall, I noticed another picture of him and Gabriel in the field as boys. In another picture, they stood on either side of Victor Montoya, as if he were their father.

Carefully, I returned the shirt, smoothing down the sleeve, and then I exited the room before I could get caught. Wandering to the other end of the veranda, I tried another door. I turned the knob and the door opened to a very dusty, cobwebbed room.

"See anything you like?"

I grabbed my heart and screamed when I saw my cousin.

"Gabriel. I'm so sorry. It was open."

After I calmed down a bit, I surveyed the dark room. "So, this is where you've been hiding your masterpieces," I said, scanning the hundreds of sooty paintings.

"Have a seat," Gabriel said.

I looked around the monastic-looking room but couldn't find a place to sit. "Don't get many visitors, do you?"

I found an old steamer trunk and brushed off the dirt before taking a seat. Dusting my hands back and forth, my jaw dropped, and my eyes widened when I noticed a newer painting leaning on the wall. I peered closer, noticing a spotted eagle ray, an octopus, and a puffer fish swimming across a turquoise backdrop. And then across the right corner, I noticed a giant sea turtle paddling toward me as if it were going to swim right out of the picture. The turtle winked at me.

I turned to Gabriel. "Oh my God. That's the ocean. How did you—"

"My imagination," Gabriel said. "That's the turtle from when we were little. It's grown-up now. Aren't you glad you didn't take it from its home?"

I nodded, looking around the room, noticing another painting. I was even more astonished. "When was I—but that's me?"

In the painting, a young me held out a flower and then magically, a grown me rose up out of the heart of an agave plant.

I blushed, the color of a rose, mouth agape as I stared at the naked picture of me, my heart pounding now, afraid to face Gabriel.

"It's beautiful, but I'm naked."

"Look at me," he said.

"I'm confused," I said looking at Gabriel. "This is sort of making me nervous. Got Tequila?"

"What are you afraid of? Of being told you are beautiful? Of being naked?"

"It usually leads to something else," I said.

"Maya, you know you're not my type. Remember, I'm a *Chivas* fan."

I laughed and then looked back at the painting.

"This is the pure Maya," Gabriel said. "You have got to start believing that you are good and smart and beautiful," he said. "Love yourself."

I shrugged my shoulders and then wagged my head. "Stop it. You're making me laugh."

"And you are afraid of laughing—of feeling good."

"It doesn't last. It never does." I caught myself speaking in my old negative language.

I sensed the warmth in his eyes as he smiled at me; the same as always. That had never changed. He was as consistent as a sunrise.

"Well, that's just sad," he said. "What happened to your dreams?"

"Remember, I stopped dreaming, I never followed my heart. I was afraid, but now—" I said, jumping when I heard the sound of a vehicle outside.

I ran to the window, peeked out and then screamed, bringing my hand to my mouth. "It's Antonio," I said. "He's on that old tractor. He must have gotten it to work." I hurried toward the back door.

"There is nothing to be afraid of. He never comes back here."

I stopped in my tracks. "Well, he's always scared me." And now that I'd seen how he lived, I grew even more bewildered.

"My brother is a good man. Self-taught. See how he fixed that old machine?"

I went to the window again and watched as Antonio traversed the area in front of the house. "Your brother is even more of a mystery to me now. More mysterious than the dark side of the moon," I said, pushing the curtain back further. "Is he really going to plow down the north field?"

"I'm not sure," Gabriel said, seemingly unperturbed. "Anyway, he was the one who urged me to follow my dream of going to the university. My greatest benefactor," he said and then pointed to the painting of me. "Why don't you give it to Antonio."

"The painting? Why?" I asked, taking the brush and swiping some war paint across Gabriel's nose.

"Because I know he'd love it."

I narrowed my eyes, searching Gabriel's face. *Seriously?*

"But first she needs some clothes," I said, handing him the brush.

Gabriel took the brush and instead, swiped my nose. I picked up another brush and the paint fight was on.

Later, with a face full of paint, I looked around for something to clean myself.

"There's a water pump just outside," Gabriel said.

I glanced out the window. "I'll wait until he leaves."

ANTONIO HAD worked late into the night, and I'd been too afraid to leave. As time ticked away, I grew hungry and tired, dozing off occasionally. Finally, I was able to sneak out to try and head back to my room unnoticed. I tiptoed across the porch, as if I were on some clandestine mission—*well, I had been nosy, looking for clues about Antonio*. I walked down the road as a shooting star crossed my path. I stopped a moment to look up to a full pearlescent moon balanced in a sapphire sky full of twinkling stars. In awe of the smudge of diamonds called the Milky Way, I felt a hand slip into mine. "Close your eyes."

I felt the gravity pulling as Gabriel and I ascended like a rocket ship into the cathedral of sky. Piercing through, together we soared through the galaxy until we floated hand-in-hand through the heavens, giggling like we did when we were children. I breathed in the sky as if I were a baby taking my first breath. And then I saw my name spelled out in edible stars across the constellation. I saw my mirrored reflection and reached out to trace my heart.

Sticking out my tongue, I tasted the bubbles of light as we hovered above the earth. We then rocketed beyond the backside of the moon that no longer seemed so dark.

"Now, what were you saying about your problems?" Gabriel asked.

"From this perspective? I really can't remember. At least, they're not worth hanging on to," I said, looking all around "my world" which seemed so small and insignificant in comparison to the universe. And then I homed in on the little house in the middle of the field. "You know, you should show Antonio this view," I said. "Maybe he could let go of his anger."

"I leave that mission to you," Gabriel said.

WE'D RETURNED to the room where I fell asleep on the floor. I woke up to the sound of a rooster crowing the next morning. Dogs barked in the distance, and then the sound of the truck's engine revving up. Antonio must have been on his way to work. Disoriented, I looked around the room, but didn't see Gabriel. He'd probably already gone out to paint. I walked to the window. It was still dark. I saw two headlights approaching and watched as the truck pulled up, gravel pinging like an oncoming hailstorm.

Out of the cab, Antonio's long leg emerged before he got out, leaving the vehicle idling. I shrunk away, mouth open, hand on my charging heart, as I watched from a corner of the window. He strode around searching the surrounding area. I panicked when I saw him headed in my direction. Hide! How would I ever explain my being here, especially at this time of morning? I saw Gabriel's giant ocean picture and hid behind it. Peeking around, I first saw his hands, cupped against the window, and then his face, eyes tapered. I put my hands over my mouth and then he was gone. His boots stomped along the porch and then I heard the doorknob being tried. I could taste my heart in my mouth as if I'd just run a marathon. The door was locked. Why had Gabriel locked it? And then, after a few seconds, I heard the truck rev up and pull away, gravel pinging behind it like a weakened storm.

Chapter Thirty-One

Antonio, I Had No Idea!

LATER THAT MORNING, I FOUND MYSELF WHISTLING, the birds chirping in harmony. Still feeling buoyant after my trip out of space, I passed workers along the way. Even they seemed happier, their smiles wider, their teeth more sparkly. Before entering the distillery, I looked up to the heavens, made a sweeping motion with my right arm, and bowed.

"After you, Big Guy!"

And then I sort of sauntered in and greeted Antonio.

"Buenos días, Antonio. Isn't it just a glorious day?"

Antonio raised his head from the computer to peer over his reading glasses. Even he seemed a little friendlier, if not suspicious looking.

"Buenos días," he replied.

Like a ballerina, I did a pirouette to leave.

"Maya?" Antonio said.

I spun back around. "Yes, Antonio?"

"You have some paint on the back of your shoulder."

I quickly slapped a hand over my shoulder, covering it. "Oh yeah, I got up early to do some painting."

He arched one eyebrow. "A little dabbling, eh?"

I smiled coyly. "And not just by the number, either."

This time as I left his office, I paid more attention to the paintings hanging on the wall, peering even closer. They were all signed by Gabriel.

"Isn't his work just heavenly?" I was killing it with the sappiness and cringed. I sounded like some old-timey actress.

Antonio nodded. "He went away to study botany but ended up spending more time detailing the intricacies of the different species of the agave."

Antonio stood and walked over to a painting. "From the pistil," he said, pointing to the stalk growing from the center of the plant, "to the tepal or petals and the leaf, to the blue green rosette."

"So, there are different species?"

"Many, but the most common and the only agave permitted by Mexican law to be used for making Tequila is a particular variety of *Agave Tequilana*, 'Weber Azul'," he said, now standing beside me, his earthy smell making me dizzy. "The blue agave."

I steadied myself, remembering guiltily, sniffing his shirt back in the inner sanctum of his room. I turned now to look up into his eyes. From the close proximity, I could see a red speck in his left eye. *Had he strained it from reading so much about the blue agave?* I had no idea he'd taken such a keen interest in the plant. *More likely, he'd broken a blood vessel from getting so pissed at the world.*

"Maybe you will show me what you've been working on sometime."

I stammered. "Of course. I—" And then I stopped, suspecting a trap.

I was just about to leave when I remembered. "By the way, I have something to give you."

Antonio raised both eyebrows this time.

THAT EVENING as I got ready for dinner, there was a knock at my door off the courtyard and when I opened it, I was surprised to see Antonio standing there, a giant silhouette in the setting sun.

"Antonio, well this is a . . . I mean that was quick. Come on in."

He removed his hat, stooping a little as he crossed the threshold, but it was the sweet smell of *Tres Flores* that made its entrance first. The hair tonic, blended with chrysanthemum, jasmine and a third flower—I never knew the name of—was a cloying reminder that zapped my nerve endings. *What was my gut trying to tell me?* My father used that hair stuff, but then again, I rationalized, so did every other male this side of Tijuana.

Antonio's hair was slicked back, and despite the hour, he had no five o'clock shadow. He wore the fresh white guayabera shirt as if he was on his way to church to get confirmed.

"Here," he said, handing me a bottle of Tequila. "It's our premium añejo from the new harvest. I would have brought flowers, but I don't know what the protocol is for—"

"For coming to look at paintings," I said, smiling. "I think Tequila is a good choice. This is so thoughtful."

I set the bottle down on my desk. Antonio didn't know what to do with his empty hands. Stuffing them into his pockets finally, he searched the room like a trapped animal looking for a way out. *He's on my turf now*, I thought, feeling a little less threatened, yet probably more exposed.

"So, yes, I've come to look at your work."

"Oh right," I said and took a few steps over to where a couple of my pieces were leaning up against the wall. "Are you sure? They're not very good. This is what I've been working on."

In the room, small as a closet, I could feel his damp breath now on my neck as he stood behind me, the scent of the three flowers even sweeter and yet more ominous. My heart raced. His arm jutted out in front of me.

"Very good. Who is she?" he asked, pointing to the little girl in the picture. "Children are not allowed around here."

"Oh no? What about the baby in your office?"

He cleared his throat. "Teresa couldn't find anyone to watch her."

So he has a soft spot.

I smiled, admiring my work as if it were my own child. "Don Pio calls her my intuition."

"And what about this picture of the agave?"

"I was trying to capture the heart."

"The piña," he said.

"Yes, that's right," I replied, walking over and grabbing the back of my desk chair. "Here, take a seat," I said, turning it to face the room. I brushed him accidentally and felt a surge of electricity jolt me. "I'm going to the kitchen to get us some glasses."

I stepped out of my room not knowing what to think. Steeling myself up against the wall, my mind reeling. What was I doing? What was he doing? Was he trying to make things more civil between the two of us?

Magdalena stood in front of the stove and looked up to see me taking two glasses out of the sideboard. "I have company," I said just as Don Pio came into the kitchen.

He lifted his eyebrows.

"It's just Antonio. He came to look at my paintings."

"Is he staying for dinner?" Magdalena asked, wiping her hands on the front of her apron. She looked at the glasses. "Or is he just drinking?"

"I—I didn't even ask."

Don Pio walked over to the cupboard and removed another plate and set it on the table.

By the time I got back to the room, I'd already forgotten about dinner. "It was so nice of you to take time off from your busy schedule," I said, setting down the glasses.

"No trouble," he said.

"I know how hard I work and often think who else is going to run things and pay the bills, right?" I said. I'd clung tightly to the 'workaholic' badge like a life vest—it was my salvation, confirmation that I wasn't drowning. "I'm thinking of just letting go."

"So you're running away," he said, opening the bottle of Tequila.

"No, I'm not running away. I raised my daughter, worked hard, paid my taxes. Hell, I haven't had a day off since Lily was born. Maybe, I've come in search of something different. Change can be good, you know." The last thing I'd do was share with him about my cancer. I wouldn't show any signs of weakness.

"Again, I don't need your help." He poured two shots.

I didn't wait for him to hand me a glass. "You're right. You're in control," I said snatching my drink. "You don't need anyone's help."

He grabbed his glass. "Listen, I didn't run off to el norte like everyone else. I stayed."

"Oh, here we go. And you resent that. I happen to think it took courage for them to leave."

"It takes cojones to stay."

He looked so serious, but I couldn't help myself. I laughed, raising my glass for a toast. "Balls to the wall, I say. Salud!"

He raised his glass. "You make me laugh, too."

Antonio gulped his drink, and I recalled my conversation with Gabriel only hours earlier. "And you're afraid of laughing—of feeling good?" I said. I'd told Gabriel, feeling good never lasted and it would never leave the room. But here in this moment, in this room, I laughed and felt pretty good.

Like little golden orbs layered in cyan onto the backdrop of a white canvas, a warmth glowed in his eyes where I saw my own reflection and sensed the heat as he smiled at me now. Coming from him, this was something completely foreign. Again, perhaps it was only the Tequila.

"This field has been in the family for generations," Antonio said. "Through good times and bad. It's not like a marriage you can just run away from."

And just like that, the good feeling evaporated out of the room. "Ouch. Was that supposed to hurt me?"

"If the *huarache* fits."

"At least *I* wasn't afraid to get married," I said, pushing back a loose tendril of hair.

"¡Ay, ay, ay! Now that hurts."

"After I divorced Elliot, who died later by the way, there was another guy." I glared at Antonio. "That guy, a study buddy from law school, was only a rebound. As for Zane and me, we weren't married—yet."

"I'm sorry. That was uncalled for."

"Yeah, whatever. Let's just start over?" I said. "I have no right telling you how to run your business."

Easing into a smile, he raised his glass and clinked mine. For a moment, our eyes locked like small marble magnets.

I blinked first, breaking the force. "This really is delicious."

"It is the blood, sweat and tears of the people that give the flavor," Antonio said, turning to look out the window. The sunset was now like an explosion of crimson, salmon and rose colors. "I love this farm and want to see it continue for generations."

"That is not the impression—"

He cut me off. "My concern is not what others think. I just know no other way, right now."

Impressed, I gazed at him as he walked over to look at the picture of me as a child.

"That's you? I really like it. You were a funny muchachita flacita."

"I wasn't that skinny," I said.

I sipped my drink, nervous now as he moved closer. Closing my eyes briefly, I took a deep breath and suddenly felt his calloused, yet warm and gentle hands caress my face. I opened my eyes and found myself peering straight into his. And then he kissed me on the forehead.

"Who would have thought such a skinny girl would turn into such a mujer tan bonita?"

I could still feel the imprint of his lips on my fevered brow. "I've been told I have un corazón muy bonito, también."

"My own heart is beating like the wings of a hummingbird," he said, surprising me and perhaps himself.

I was playing with fire and without thinking, I reached over to place my hand over his heart. "Why Antonio, I had no idea," I said, playfully, at once snatching back my hand, hoping I hadn't come across as coquettish. We were after all, cousins.

I didn't know what the hell I felt. Gabriel and I had play acted like this when we were kids. But now what kind of dangerous dance were Antonio and I doing? What kind of fallacious thinking was I doing?

"You don't see how you drive me loco?" Antonio asked.

"I have that effect on most people. You should hear what—"

"Silencio, mujer."

"You see. I always thought you—"

He reached out and with a finger, gently tapped my lips.

"You think too much."

"And I thought I talked too much."

He pulled his hand away and I snatched it back, his body smashing into mine. I lifted my chin and my lips found his like long lost cousins, and I was silenced. I lost control of all thoughts, including any notion of resistance. But my mouth already had a memory of what this kiss would be like as it opened up to him. My tongue, like a little glistening red carpet, rolled out, swirling itself around his. Still lingering, I tasted the sweet Tequila. Caught now in a maelstrom of emotions—being scared to death was one—but also the realization that I'd been waiting all of my life for this. Suddenly I remembered it being wrong and pushed away, panting for air. I opened my eyes to find myself staring at the agave painting propped up against the wall. The piña as a focal point seemed to shore me up. And as the heart of the agave opened up, all of the sweet nectar was exposed and glistening in the sun. *They're not the same. It's not the same. He's not like the others.*

As if I'd given him the permission he needed, Antonio kissed me again and we dropped back onto my little twin bed. My body feeling as if it whirled up through the heavenly galaxy. I pulled away and went to sit opposite him on the other twin bed, just staring at him. "Would you like to stay for dinner?" I asked, gasping for air.

MAGDALENA ACTED giddy as a teenager when Antonio walked into the kitchen behind me. "Oh, good. You're staying."

"I do miss your cooking, Magda."

"Well you know where you can always find me," she said with a wink. He then bussed her on the cheek.

I took a seat with my back against the wall, looking out the window at the inky sweep of the sky. A fleet of dark clouds sailed across a thumbnail of a moon that already hovered just above the mountains out past the field.

Magdalena served bowls full of steaming soup, nopalitos, tortillas and then she set down a bowl full of roasted elote.

I reached for my glass of water and took a drink as Antonio turned to Don Pio and leaned in. "I got a call today from a company who will buy our corn," Antonio said.

"Corn?" I asked, setting down my glass.

"Yes, it's what's for dinner," Antonio replied, holding up an ear of elote, exposing a brilliant set of teeth before munching down on it.

"What are you talking about? You can't do that. Don't you think you're being a little desperate?" I said.

"Desperate? What do you know? People around here are *desperate* for work. Do you think everyone wants to go north? Not everyone can. Corn is worth more than Tequila."

Don Pio held out his hand, gently setting it down on the table. "Please, no business talk tonight."

"This isn't just business. It's our life." Antonio said, raising his voice.

"But your life is Tequila," I responded.

Don Pio quieted me with just a look.

A long silence filled the air as Magdalena filled soup bowls, ladling big chunks of papas, calabacitas and pollo. Don Pio and I raved about the dinner, moving things around quietly. And then Antonio spoke, almost spitting now. "You know, I came here to try and be nice to you."

Taken aback, it embarrassed me to think that he'd paid me any attention at all. "Well, I hope you didn't strain yourself," I said, lifting my spoon. "So you weren't really interested in seeing my paintings?"

"Magdalena, el caldo es tan sabroso," Don Pio said as Antonio stood, scraping his chair. But he sat back down heavily when Don Pio reached for his hand, inadvertently knocking his glass of water into Antonio's lap.

"Ay Dios. Lo siento," Don Pio said as Antonio jumped back up again nearly bumping Magdalena over as she brought him a dishtowel.

"No need to be sorry. Accidents happen," Antonio said, dabbing himself. He then took his seat.

"I'm sorry it's so hard to be nice to me," I said.

"You just make it impossible," Antonio replied. "And, of course, I'm interested—in seeing your paintings. I apologize. I can be a jerk sometimes, please forgive me."

We were all under a lot of stress. His lips, like a tight rope, began to loosen up and then loop into a smile. Now under the light from the rustic chandelier, I noticed how young he looked and again just how good he looked—his hair slicked back, well-shaven and wearing that pressed white shirt. If I closed my eyes, I could make out his scent from across the table.

"You know." Don Pio stared at me as I opened my eyes. "Years ago, when you left, Antonio actually chased after your car."

I sat up straight. "Wait. That was you?"

"Obviously, there was nothing I could do to stop it," Antonio said, screwing up his mouth like a little boy.

I almost wanted to reach over and kiss him—on the cheek—right then and there, but I put the thought on hold as Don Pio added, "I never knew who was sadder."

"It killed me to know that Gabriel would be broken hearted," Antonio said. "You two used to laugh a lot. He didn't laugh again for a long time after you left."

"Believe me, I didn't do much laughing anymore, either," I said. "Once we returned to the states, I had to take care of my brother so my mom could work two jobs."

"I miss his laughter," Antonio said.

I nodded. "Me, too. I remember the time—"

"Magdalena, what's for dessert?" Don Pio asked, suddenly, and she hurried over with some flan.

Antonio had just put the spoon into his mouth when I said, "Oh, speaking of Gabriel—"

Antonio looked across the table at me with interest.

"After you're finished," I said. "I have something to give you!"

Don Pio set down his spoon and reached for his glass of water. The way his eyes widened to the size of small saucers, I sensed his apprehension.

ANTONIO CLOSED the door once we got back to my room. Before I could say anything, he'd pinned me to the wall to kiss me, but just as quickly he pulled away. "Lo siento. I'm not good at this."

"Oh." I took a breath. "Something you're not good at. Let's see. So, if you'd like to kiss me, you should ask. *May I kiss you?* But seeing how we're cousins—" My mind went blank, any notion of being related erased, as I returned the kiss, pushing him down onto the small bed. He pulled me beside him, his hot rough hand on my stomach, sliding up as I worked feverishly on the buttons of his guayabera shirt. The sound of the bed squeaking returned me to my senses. I pulled away.

"Probably not a good idea in your father's house." I sucked in a sobering breath. *No importa que somos primos.*

"My father's house?" Antonio laughed, shrugging it off, tugging me back toward him—my heart beating in places I didn't know I had a pulse anymore.

I stood, smoothing my blouse. "They're probably standing just outside the room," I whispered.

"With a glass to the door," Antonio said, cupping his ear, as he got up and took a seat at the desk.

"I think Magdalena's flan is even better than Angela's," I said loud enough for the whole house to hear. And then I turned to Antonio and whispered, "Actually, Lily said Angela's was better than an orgasm."

Antonio laughed loudly and we turned at the creak of a door opening out in the kitchen. It was probably Don Pio headed out for his nightly stroll.

I followed Antonio's gaze as he looked around the room. His eyes stopped when he saw all of my medicine bottles lined up on the nightstand. I'd just finished taking my pills when he knocked at my door earlier and I hadn't thought to put them away. Now, so nervous, I wasn't prepared to explain.

And then as if he sensed my discomfort, he looked away. "You wanted to show me something."

I got up and walked across the room to retrieve the canvas now wrapped in a red ribbon.

"Gabriel asked me to give it to you," I said, handing him the naked Maya painting. "I told him to paint some clothes—"

Eyes narrowed at me, Antonio seemed breathless, and I saw his expression cloud over like an oncoming thunderstorm. All the light left his face, as if he'd stepped into a dark shadow. He sprang up. "Stop!"

The picture slipped out of my hands.

"You and Don Pio talk about him as if he is still alive! To torture me!"

"What—no," I said, feeling suddenly as if I were swirling down a drain. And then, a blue mist filled the room as he moved toward me, and I screamed. "No. I don't understand!"

I backed away into the corner, slumping into a huddle, sticking out my arms as Antonio approached me, but when I saw my small hands, I realized they belonged to the young Maya. I tried to take a deep breath, but the air in the room seemed to vanish. I looked up, confused when I saw the image of my father getting closer, a smile chilling me to the marrow. I screamed, "No Papá!" My eyes flooded with tears blinding me. I swiped my eyes with the back of my hands, and then I noticed the rifle on the wall. I catapulted myself over to it. I took it down and pointed the gun at him.

He burst out laughing. "What are you doing? That antique has not been fired since the revolución."

My mind tangled, I thought I was looking at my father, but it was Antonio's voice that triggered me. "It's not even loaded."

I cocked it. "Get out!"

And then it fired, sending me crashing back against the wall.

DON PIO HAD been out for a stroll, before dinner, he'd tell me later, talking to the stars when he heard the gunshot and came running. He'd watched as Antonio stomped toward his truck and took off. Winded, Don Pio then bolted into the room to find me in tears slumped against the back wall with a rifle in my hand. He looked around the room, noticing the giant hole left in the ceiling.

"I don't know what happened—it wasn't like me—I didn't think it was loaded," I cried.

He then leaned down in front of me, cradling my chin.

"Why have you let me carry on and on about Gabriel?" I said. "I've got to go home!"

"All right." Don Pio gently wedged the rifle out of my hands.

THERE WAS indeed a storm coming. The sound of thunder and lightning cracked in the distance as I made it back to my room to cry myself to sleep. I dreamed about a fire and saw the agave heads like faces burning in the ovens and then I heard the sound of bells clanging and people screaming. I started to cough and woke up to the smell of smoke.

Bolting out of bed, choking on smoke, I heard the bells clanging. I looked out the window. Against a backdrop of vibrant reds and oranges, the sky looked as if the sun had just set. I saw the flashing blue and the eyes of fire summoning me out to the north field. Petrified, I was then rocked by an explosion and ran outside to see that the north field was on fire.

From all around, the workers came running with hoes, shovels, scythes and buckets of water splashing over the sides.

I grabbed one of Magdalena's watering cans and followed the workers deeper into the field. A blue vapor hovered above the field as the wind howled, stirring up chaos. The old tractor blazed.

"Look, the fire is headed in that direction," I shouted, turning to see the fire eating up the dry, dead plants and moving now toward Antonio's little house at the edge of the north field. The workers darted back and forth with pails of water from the pump just outside Antonio's little house. And then the silhouette of a tall woman came running out of the smoky house carrying items from inside and screaming. The rains started but it wasn't enough. People from the nearby farms arrived to help. Frantic, I ran toward the house.

"Gabriel! Gabriel, get out! Get out!" I screamed, feeling my feet leave the ground. Someone had come up from behind and swooped me up. Kicking and screaming, I was pulled off the ground. Another explosion rocked the earth, ripping my body away, rattling my molars. Something came crashing down over me and I fell face down. I felt a heartbeat on my back and a warm breath at the top of my spine. I turned enough to see Antonio on top of me. Debris came showering down on us as I pushed him off.

"He's gone," Antonio said. "I will not lose you, too."

Tears and ashes, smeared with crimson grime, we stood dripping wet, a couple of shipwrecked passengers, clinging on like each other's lifesaver, as the house burned to the ground.

THROUGH A CHARCOAL gray haze, the sun came up as I stood hugging myself at the edge of a smoldering field with a face-smudged Don Pio surveying the charred remains, Antonio hunched over, shoveling in the distance.

"I knew Gabriel was dead," I said, mucous dripping from my nose. Don Pio handed me his handkerchief. "I just didn't want to let go. He's been my angel." And now that I'd had the chance to hang out with him, even if he was dead, I was going to miss him.

Don Pio patted my shoulder. "There's no need to let go. I never will. The experience is good."

"He was teaching me how to live once more," I said, crying again. "I suppose I knew for sure when I came across his marker at the cemetery."

Don Pio nodded. "We buried him next to his mother Amelia, and the rest of my family. Ashes to ashes. Love burns eternal."

Gabriel is dead. I sobbed as the truth finally sunk in. My legs gave way and I collapsed, slumping to the ground where life slid off my bones, puddling at my ankles like dirty clothing after an exhausting workday. And my uncle could do nothing to console me.

LATER THAT night out on the veranda, I sat wearily in a rocker, my heavy head between my legs.

Don Pio limped up and took a seat in the rocker next to me. He put a hand on my shoulder.

"Gabriel died of complications later," he said. "Antonio found him in the field where he'd been painting. It was his most stunning work—a picture of the ocean. That trip you took when you were little."

I raised my head and nodded. "He gave it to me with a couple of the others he had. I'm so glad they weren't part of the fire."

Don Pio lowered his head. "Antonio wasn't able to save very much."

I sobbed. "Oh my God. It's a wonder Antonio doesn't drink more."

My uncle shrugged his shoulders then lowered his head. "It's been the ruin of many," he said, voice weary, but then he looked up. "Quetzalcoatl's reign ended after too much Tequila. Legend has it that he ended up making love to his sister."

"Hmm, talk about incest. I guess it doesn't matter the culture or time, it happens and it's still not right."

Don Pio simply glossed over my comment. "After he sobered, he was sorry. You see, it was the Ancient Aztec who had set out onto the Caribbean. He burst into flames as he returned to heaven. Now he's the morning star of Venus until his return to earth."

"Really, do you believe all this?" I asked.

"Seguro, why not?" my uncle replied, smiling as he shrugged his shoulders.

"I thought you were Catholic," I said. "Aren't you waiting for Christ's return or the Rapture or something?"

Antonio marched across the horizon to shovel dirt on another hot spot to stop the flame from growing.

"He is so angry. Like all the men in my life," I said. "Scared souls."

"And, you haven't been able to change them. To fix any of them?"

"No, and I've hated myself for not being able to do anything. For not being able to put out all of the fires. Never good enough or smart enough," I cried. "I've made so many mistakes."

"Perhaps you should try giving up the notion that you have control," Don Pio said.

"Now you sound like Gabriel," I said, swabbing my tears with the back of my sleeve.

"Maya," Don Pio said. "The world is out of control, and yet it is orderly, it is also sacred and cannot be improved."

"But I'm an attorney. I have to have answers. I thought that by trying harder—I thought that—" As I spoke, I could hear myself. I realized just how wrong I'd been all these years.

"Papá was so angry. Mamá put up with so much."

"We all have choices. Dolores showed such strength when she left here years ago with you and your brother."

I cast back my mind to the small hand swiping the foggy backseat window. I remembered Gabriel standing at the edge of field waving goodbye. I remembered Antonio stomping away. Inside were two adults, a little girl and a small boy pulling away forever in an old station wagon. It was Victor waving goodbye from inside the car. Through the back window, I could see Antonio swinging a scythe; Gabriel growing smaller until he disappeared. My mother drove us through the gateway and never looked back.

I realized now how hard that must have been for Mamá. Back then it seemed only the men, like Victor, left to go north in order for the family to survive. I pulled my knees into my chest feeling the tears stream down my face.

"It was a sad day," Don Pio said, "but the farm was suffering, and this was Victor's chance to go north. He left his sons behind, putting Antonio in charge of his little brother."

"Wait a second. You mean they're not your sons?" I asked, my voice raising a notch.

Don Pio looked at me curiously as if he was surprised I didn't know. "Victor's, but I raised them as my own."

I tried to unscramble my brain. And then I couldn't recall either boy ever calling my uncle anything other than Don Pio, like everyone else. "Wait, so we're not cousins?"

Don Pio shook his head, sadly. "Victor *Montoya*."

I'd never thought about their last names. *Who goes around calling their cousin by their full name?*

"Victor was Domingo's son," I said, adding. "He was my father's stepbrother."

Don Pio nodded.

"What about their mother?"

"She died giving birth to Gabriel."

"¡*Ay Dios*! Does this saga just keep getting worse? It's like one of those freakin' Mexican telenovelas," I said, noticing Antonio in the smoky background, swinging a scythe. "I think I'd drink, too—well more at least."

"Again, God doesn't give us more than we can handle. There are other answers, but that is Antonio's way." Don Pio looked around. "I guess we're planting corn."

I sprang from my rocker. "Like hell we are! After my meeting with Bruno—I won't let it happen. I'm just as much a part of this field as anyone."

Don Pio smiled from ear to ear. "Esooo! Of course you are!"

Chapter Thirty-Two

Over My Dead Body!

NOTHING COULD BE AS BAD AS WHAT ANTONIO had been through. After my talk with Don Pio, I had a new understanding of him.

I wouldn't let anything ruin my afternoon, I thought as I walked into Antonio's office. It was hard for me not to smile thinking I had some answers on how to save the business—but he refused to meet my eyes. His mouth, a line, Don Pio, already seated, raised his head when I walked in, grinning.

Nervous, I thought the best way to broach the subject would be to just jump right in. And while I hadn't put a dint of sweat equity into the farm, I knew I had a right to be here, a right to speak up. I took a seat across from Antonio and folded my hands on top of the desk. "So, the way I see it—"

"All you see are dead people," Antonio said, quick on the draw, voice booming. "You sit out there all day and talk to ghosts. I've seen you."

"Antonio, let her speak." Don Pio said.

"You can start using the north fields," I said.

"Over my dead body," Antonio replied.

You mean over my dead body, the old me would have said, but I'd promised God I'd try to be a nicer person. "Many farms have gone under. But now, there's a chance—"

Don Pio pushed off on his thighs and stood to face Antonio. "I thought I was doing right by handing you the reins, but you are as unyielding as the north fields."

"We'll plant corn," Antonio yelled, stalking to the table and slumping into his chair. "We did it before."

"But that was a different time," I said. "Polyculture was definitely the way to go, but—"

"That's okay for our neighbors," Don Pio said. "But we have an opportunity for some new life around here. It's time to let go of the pain and forgive."

Antonio took a deep breath, pursing his lips. I thought his head might just explode. He pounded his desk and then stood. "Bruno with his thousand-dollar belts and ostrich skin boots can just open up his wallet and buy us off like all his government jobs."

"You don't know that. I didn't raise my sons to be that way," Don Pio said.

Antonio glared at him. "You are a blind old man."

"Antonio!" I yelled, standing now, too.

"Mujer! Mind your own business!"

Don Pio sidestepped next to me as if I might need his protection.

"Crazy mujeres," Antonio said, lumping me now with all the other women in his life. "You are the ones—"

"That what? Hurt you? Abandoned you?" I said, reaching out to touch his arm. "You've got to get over it. You're not the only one who's lost someone—"

"Antonio, no one abandoned you,' Don Pio said. "Your mother and your father loved you."

Antonio pulled his arm away from me. "Where is the cabrón now?"

"Hijo—"

"Hijo?" Antonio said. "I am not your son. Go ahead and sell to Bruno, but remember, Don Pio, I was loyal to you. Let me slaughter our finest calf for the return of the prodigal son."

"You have got it wrong. We all have. We are all the same blood. This place belongs to Maya, too."

"And the blood flows north like El Rio Grande carrying everyone away," Antonio said.

I leaned in, gripping the edge of the desk. "But you can travel the river south, too," I added, leveling my eyes on Antonio. "The sugar from the agave can also be fermented into ethanol, should you decide to go that route. But I've done my research and we can also—"

Antonio stormed out, the door slamming behind him.

LATER THAT NIGHT, I sat on my porch as Don Pio hobbled by carrying the rifle.

"Well, that's one way to talk him out of planting corn," I said.

Don Pio handed me the rifle, butt end first. "I cleaned it and made sure it wasn't loaded. Would you mind returning it to its place?"

I took it. "I didn't think I had it in me."

"Well, not if you missed."

I laughed. "Don Pio, I'll be leaving tomorrow morning. I need to get back."

Chapter Thirty-Three
Stage 5 - Acceptance

THE NEXT MORNING AS SUNLIGHT SPILLED LIKE an egg yolk over the side of the mountain, I headed out to the field to say goodbye to the place. As I passed the distillery, Antonio came out.

"Maya, can I walk with you?"

I nodded but kept walking.

"I am sorry for being so stubborn."

I slowed down and held out a hand, like a peace offering. "Did you know we weren't cousins?"

Antonio looked at me as if I were crazy. "Por supuesto."

"Well, I'm glad I didn't know," I replied.

"Why?"

I stopped in my tracks. "Because it might have been harder for me to resist you," I said, looking up into his eyes.

"Well then I'm glad, too."

"Why?"

"Because I might have had to be a lot meaner," he said, smiling. "You were annoying enough as it was."

I slapped him lightly on the shoulder.

"Ouch! You see how you are?" he said.

The sound of my phone interrupted our laughter. I looked at the screen and then held a finger up to Antonio. It had been a very long time since I'd heard from Zane, and I was just a little curious. I could wait to return the call, but chances were hit and miss that I'd get him. "Antonio, please excuse me."

Antonio turned to walk back toward the factory.

MY HEART THUMPED. Was Zane all right? *Was he in the hospital—or jail? Maybe the bank finally caught up to him and he doesn't want me to press charges?* All of the old anxiety came rushing forth.

"How are you feeling, Maya?" Zane asked and I sensed it to be a leading question.

"Pretty well," I replied, watching Antonio walk away.

"I'm glad. Well, I just want to say how sorry I was about your dad."

"Thank you."

"Plus, I wanted to ask when you're coming home."

And there it was. He needed something from me. More money than what he'd already stolen? Until the bank proved otherwise, I was convinced he was the culprit. What more could he want from me? A place to stay? I looked around. "I'm not sure where home is anymore."

"Really? Well, I hope you've been able to take it easy."

I saw Antonio in the distance and wanted to run after him.

"Anyway, I need to get the rest of my things. We're doing the sequel to Captain Hightower and—"

"A chance to play dress up again." I couldn't resist.

I could hear him laughing on the other end. "I'm really going to miss the sarcasm," he said.

Yes, I'd always loved the banter. Who didn't love a good debate? *Wait? He said, 'Going to miss . . .' So he's finally going to move on without me?*

"Anyway, I wanted to let you know that I'm getting married."

Stunned. "You're what? How—when—?" *I haven't even been gone that long.* "Touché," I whispered.

"What did you say?"

"Congratulations."

And to think, all along I'd secretly worried about him. Did he have enough food? A place to sleep? Would he ever work again? The idea that he'd ever be able to manage without me was unimaginable. I remembered all the times he'd disappeared, and I'd worried myself sick. And then when I recalled the time I found him holed up in a hotel having himself a hell of a little party without me, I got angry. Why had I ever felt sorry for him?

"Maya? Listen, I really don't want to do this. I love you and I miss you. Just say the word and I won't."

And there it was again. Somehow, he made it sound like it was all my fault. Like I'd forced him to get married? It had worked too many times before—his manipulation. But maybe this time it would be different, I thought—maybe he's changed. And then before I could really flip flop, he added, "Let me give you some time to think about it."

"Give me? You've never given me—"

"I'll call you back in a few days," he said quickly. "I've got to go now."

"But—"

THE NEXT MORNING Leonardo helped carry my bags out to the station wagon. Magdalena stepped off the porch and shuffled over to stand next to Don Pio. It broke my heart to say goodbye.

"Thank you for talking to Bruno," Don Pio said.

"You're welcome. He should be calling you within the next couple of days. I really think it's a good plan. The best plan." The solution was that they'd be able to keep producing Tequila, as long as they sold Bruno the agave from the north field. "You just have to convince Antonio. I'll be back in my office on Monday. You can call me if you have any questions."

Don Pio nodded.

"Thank you for everything, Don Pio. I'm so glad I was able to visit. I didn't realize how much I missed this place."

"You always have a home here," he replied, as Magdalena reached out to hand me a sack. "Lunch for the ride back."

I touched Magdalena's arm. "Thank you for trying to fatten me up. I haven't eaten this well, ever."

"There's some roasted maguey in there, too. I know how much you like it."

Don Pio and Magdalena grew smaller as the orange sedan pulled away. I wiped a tear. And then when I saw Antonio standing at the edge of the field, my heart split in two. I hadn't bothered to tell him goodbye. I thought I saw him looking my way before he turned to chop down on an agave head with his coa.

Chapter Thirty-Four

Puerto Vallarta

I'D JUST WALKED OUT OF THE HOTEL GIFT SHOP to wait for Lily. The lobby was filled with young tourists who watched as Lily sashayed across the terracotta floors, a mermaid out of water, headed back to the sea. I still couldn't get over those wings tattooed across her back.

"Over here," I shouted.

"Sorry I didn't recognize you. New hat?" Lily said, reaching out to pull off the price tag. She stared at me, inspecting. "Mom, I can't believe you're still in Mexico. I mean it's great and I love having you here, but shouldn't you be getting ready for surgery already? I really don't—"

"Next week. So, in the meantime, let's try to have some fun, okay." I grabbed Lily's hand. "Last one in is a rotten egg."

On the beach under a palapa, Lily lay next to me on her stomach propped up on her elbows as she texted. A cabana boy in Hawaiian shorts walked up to ask about taking our order. About Lily's age, he had sun bleached almost translucent hair, brilliant against his bronzed skin. He reminded me of someone.

"Just some water for me," I said.

"I'll take a Coke," Lily added.

"We have matching tattoos," the young man said, pulling his shirt down off his tanned neck to show Lily.

"And how did your mother react?" I asked.

He smiled, pulling open his shirt to show *Amo a Mamá* tattooed right above his heart.

My own heart felt a pull. I laughed, arching an eyebrow as I looked at Lily.

222

"There's no way I'm tattooing *I Love Mom* across my boob!" she said, and then she burst out crying. "I'm sorry, Mom. I didn't mean—I'm just so scared. You act like it's no big deal." She sobbed now. "I can't lose you. You're all I have."

I reached over to hug her. I really had no idea how Lily was handling my illness. Most of the time, I thought she acted more like me, on the surface pretending everything was fine, but underneath everything churned. To think she'd known for some time about the Crohn's and never brought it up. Then again, she'd known about a lot of things. No wonder she was even angrier with me lately. I suppose I hadn't fooled everyone.

If it would make a difference," Lily said, wiping her eyes, "I'd tattoo *I Love Mamá* across my forehead."

I laughed and then heard someone shout Lily's name. I turned to see three young people walking up, two girls and a young man in a straw hat and flip-flops.

"Lily, you didn't tell us you were coming down?" said a young girl in a small bikini top with very short cut-offs. The other girl wore a more modest mesh cover-up.

"Uh," Lily answered, putting on her sunglasses, and I knew something was up. "Everybody, this is my mom."

Lily stood, dusting off the sand and said, "Mom, I'll be right back."

WHEN SHE RETURNED, I set down the stack of reading materials including the folder Ofelia had given her from the University.

"Your friends seem nice," I said. "Are they from school?"

"Yeah," Lily answered, pulling out a magazine.

I pulled a book out of my beach bag. I'd picked it up back at the gift shop when I read it was a New York Times Bestseller. That, plus I was curious about Antonio's choice in reading materials.

"Hey, I'm reading that in Spanish," Lily said, pulling the same book out of her own bag. "*La sombre del viento.*"

"*Shadow of the Wind.* Is it any good? I asked.

"Yeah, and it's probably way more exciting than this stuff," Lily said, picking up the folder I'd set aside. She flipped through it.

"Actually, this stuff is pretty exciting," I said.

"So does agave really have medicinal value?" Lily asked.

"Says so. What they do is extract fructans from the blue agave," I said, reaching for the folder. "Then, it says here—" I opened up to the page where I'd underlined the language. "It shows promise as a new way to deliver drugs to the colon in order to treat colon diseases, such as ulcerative colitis, irritable bowel syndrome, Crohn's disease and cancer. They chemically modify the fructan compound to allow drugs to be encapsulated, making the drugs resistant to degradation in the digestive system."

"But—so then, it's not exactly a cure?" Lily asked, face scrunching into a frown.

"Even with chemo, there's no guarantee."

I suddenly recalled my conversation with Don Pio out in the field as we looked at the stars. "That's Mayahuel. She sure gives comfort to a lot of people," I'd said. "Well, it's not a cure," Don Pio had responded. Were there really any cures in life? And weren't we all just going to die, eventually?

I looked at Lily. "I'm not sure. It sounds like it's just a way to treat the disease. But I would like to know more."

"Look at the heading on this article," I said, handing Lily a paper. "Tequila Will Save You Pains in the Ass."

Lily's laughter was irresistible. She read the article more closely. After a few moments, she looked at me, pointing to the print. "Seriously, did you read where the team in Guadalajara is currently looking volunteers to perform case studies?"

"I wouldn't want to be a guinea pig. I'll be home soon where I'm sure the doctors are up on all the modern treatment."

Lily just shook her head.

THE MARGARITAS arrived just before the sun finally set over the bay, splashing brilliant shades of reds, purples and oranges. We sat on the patio outside the hotel restaurant.

"Thank you," I said to the cabana boy, watching now as he walked away. "He's cute," I said to Lily.

Lily shrugged her shoulders.

"Plus he loves his mamá," I added with a wink.

"Not really into mamá's boys," Lily answered.

Of course not, I thought, lifting my glass. "Salud."

Lily raised her glass and took a sip, with one eye on her phone. Fidgety, she took a gulp.

"Hey, what's your hurry?" I asked. "You're gonna get brain freeze."

"It's just good, that's all."

"Well just take it easy. Back home you aren't even old enough to be sipping a Margarita."

"Ha! Like that's ever stopped me," Lily said. "I'm in college, Mom. Everyone drinks."

Even though I'd never gotten to experience regular college life, I knew she was right. I nodded, staring at Lily.

"What?" Lily asked.

"Your dad and I wanted to come here for spring break."

Lily's mouth pinched up.

"But plans changed. He was so happy to be a dad. He loved you so much."

"Mom, stop," Lily said and then slugged down her drink.

This obviously wasn't the time to talk about Lily's father who had died when she was so little. Maybe it scared her to think she might also be losing me, too soon.

Lily picked up her menu. I did the same. Everything looked so good. "I'll have one of everything," I said, licking my lips.

"Mom, you really don't act like you've got can—like you're sick."

"I really don't feel sick."

"So, you really think the field is magical and the agave is miraculous."

I nodded, still studying the menu. "Well, at first I thought it was all the stress and the medicine causing me to hallucinate—I read that it was one of the side effects—but then I started feeling better and started seeing things even more clearly. I began to understand. I'd like to believe the field healed me, physically, mentally, and spiritually." I looked up; Lily's eyes fixed on me. I looked back down at the menu. "Oh this looks good," I said, pointing to the chile rellenos.

"Like how?"

"It's hard to explain. It doesn't happen overnight and it's something where you just need to be there," I said, referring now to the enchiladas. "No, this looks better."

By the time the waiter came, I'd settled on the chili verde. I set down the menu to share with Lily more about my experiences out in the field, but her phone buzzed and before I could say anything more, she picked it up to read an incoming text. Her face softened. Within a few moments, her friends came stumbling into the restaurant.

"Mom, I hate to do this." Lily cleared her throat. "I won't if this ruins any plans you had for this evening."

I smiled through the hurt. "I wasn't allowed to plan anything. Remember, that was the deal for this trip."

"We're gonna go to a club up near the Malecón. Do you want to come?"

"Sounds like fun, but you go ahead. I think I'm going to turn in early. I'm really getting into this book," I said. "Go on. Have a good time but be careful."

Lily kissed me on the cheek and disappeared into the night with her friends as the cabana boy returned to the table.

"Anything else?" he asked.

Yeah, can you bring my baby back? "No, thank you."

THAT EVENING, millions of points of light shone on the sand as I crossed over toward the shore of Mismaloya. I was rapt as billions more popped out when the waves receded.

I then scooped up the sand, mesmerized by the light I held. Phytoplankton. The first link in the food chain. *We're all made of light.*

And then something stirred in my gut. I peered closer, envisioning something painful in the palm of my hand. I watched as the sand twinkled and the reflection of stars bounced off the ocean. I tried to think good thoughts but had a sinking feeling and made my way back to the hotel to wait for Lily.

In the hotel room, I paced the floor. I'd never had to worry so much about Lily staying out late. But I knew what it felt like to wait up for my father or for Zane—for hours, for days, for weeks.

I was worried but tried to take comfort in the fact that Lily was older now, had been through so much and knew better. I picked up the folder and began to read, but I couldn't keep my eyes open and eventually I drifted off to sleep.

I dreamed I was in a duel at high noon on the shores of Mismaloya. Gabriel stood on the shoreline, holding out a slender wooden box. "Sable or bristle?" he asked me.

I reached out. "Bristle—no wait—sable."

"Flat, filbert or round?" he asked.

"Jeez. You mean I have to choose."

Gabriel smiled, shrugging his shoulders before pivoting to count out his paces. I did the same, and once I'd counted to twenty, I turned to face him, beaming.

"Gabriel, you're walking."

"In your dreams," he answered.

Suddenly, I felt distressed. "Wait! I can't do this. I can't paint. I need to go," I screamed. "Lily needs me. She needs to know."

I dreamed myself awake, bolted upright, and saw the clock on the nightstand. Two o'clock. *Where could she be?*

Pacing the room, I tried Lily's cell phone again, but her mailbox was full. I felt the pain in my stomach return, my body filling with fear. "Dear God, please keep her safe." I couldn't just wait around. I grabbed my purse and left the room.

ALONG THE MALECÓN, lovers lay sprawled out on the shore. I hurried along the cool sand, calling out Lily's name. Someone yelled at me. "Go home, already!"

On the street, a drunk boy staggered out of *Carlos'n Charlie's* and then threw up right in front of me. Frantically, I searched in and out of the bars, up and down the alleys. *Oh, please God!* And then under the glow of a streetlamp, I thought I saw her. But it was only some other young blonde girl who looked like Lily. I tried her phone again and then I called the police who only instructed me to return to my hotel room and wait for the police to arrive. But how could I wait? I continued searching for my daughter, afraid to check the bubbles surfacing on the shoreline, and then just before dawn, exhausted, I returned to my room.

The morning light already streamed through as I walked back into the suite. I didn't know whether to laugh or cry. When I saw Lily in bed I rushed over and took a seat on the edge of the bed.

"Lily, you're wasted. Where have you been?"

She turned onto her side away from me. "You know how things just get started late around here."

I stood. "I won't do this again. We're going home."

She rolled back over. "Mom, I'm sorry. I've just been so stressed and scared. And mad."

"Mad?"

"Hell yes!" She burst out crying. "I'm mad because—because you don't take care of yourself. I don't want to lose you." She sobbed. "I can't lose you!"

I scooted closer to rub her back. "Lily, I am taking care of myself and I'm doing it for you." I paused to swallow my tears. "You're my sweet girl, like the flower that grows from the agave. But you've got to keep those nasty bats and buzzards away. I love you so much. You're my greatest masterpiece."

Lily turned around to hug me and I wrapped my arms tightly around her. "You've got to start believing that you are good and smart and beautiful. You've got to love yourself."

AFTER THE POLICÍA had determined Lily to be okay—she had nothing to report—they left. Lily climbed back into bed and then she sat up.

"An angel saved my life tonight."

I took a seat next to her.

"I think it was that cabana boy—the one with the tattoo like mine."

Hearing who saved her, I now knew why he looked familiar to me. "Your twin."

"I think you're right." She smiled. "It was around two in the morning. The night was so bright, everything seemed safe," she said, mopping her tears with a corner of the bed sheet. Everyone had abandoned me after I insisted on walking along the shore, but I wasn't afraid. The shoreline was full of light. I mean the light was everywhere. In the sand I scooped up. In the water. It was so trippy."

"Phytoplankton," I said. "I saw it, too."

"Really? I'd smoked a joint—but still I knew it was so real. I just wanted to dance, I felt so happy. I threw my head back and raised my arms, twirling around. But then suddenly, I had a feeling I wasn't alone. There was this guy from the club. I'd sort of brushed him off. I guess he followed me. I was fighting him off when the cabana boy, my angel showed up.

"I just lay in the sand, real quiet, pretending to be dead. After a while, I wondered if I might already be dead."

"Oh, Lily," I heaved a sigh. "Did he—did he hurt you?"

"No. As I lay there, I noticed my phone lighting up from my breast pocket. It was like a heartbeat."

"That was me," I said. "I must've called you a million times."

"I lifted my head to look around. That's when I saw the cabana boy, his body glistening in the starlight, like he'd just come in from a swim or something. I saw these little fishing boats on the shoreline where he'd tied the dude up with some fishing line. I didn't wait around to see what else he might do. I ran back to the hotel, feeling this presence following me, shrouding over me like it was protecting me."

I got up to look out the window, tears flowing. *She's God's daughter, too,* I could hear Don Pio saying. *She has her wings.*

I returned to her bed and wrapped my arms around my daughter. "Gracias a Dios."

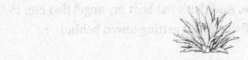

LATE THE NEXT morning, I awoke when I heard Lily on the phone.

"Okay, we'll be there tomorrow afternoon at two-thirty," she whispered, smiling at me now. "Oh good, you're awake."

"Tomorrow? What's going on?"

Lily, already in her bikini, pulled up some shorts. "We're supposed to go snorkeling today."

"Yeah, we're canceling that."

"But why?"

Why indeed? Lily had obviously inherited some sick sort of survival skill called 'denial.' But I was even worse at denying my daughter. She'd just been through an ordeal.

THE DAY COULDN'T be more luminous as Lily and I sat on a boat to Los Arcos, a giant rock jutting out in the middle of the bay. We were headed out to snorkel.

"Feeling better today?"

Lily nodded. "Thank you for not making us leave."

"I couldn't get a flight out today, anyway."

The boat was filled with a group of loud gringos singing unabashedly while pumping Tecate beer bottles in the air.

"Poor fish should any of these amateurs get sick," I said.

"Yeah, I don't think barf is good chum for even the lowliest bottom feeding sharks you work with back—"

"Watch it, matey! Or you'll be walking the plank," I said. "I really don't know what you have against my profession."

"Oh my god!" Lily shouted, pointing to a patrol boat that passed by. "That's him."

"Who?" I asked, noticing a young man seated in the back of the boat. He was handcuffed.

"The boy who attacked me. And that's the boat my angel tied him to," Lily said, as I noticed a small fishing boat getting towed behind.

WHEN WE GOT within a few feet of Los Arcos, our boat anchored. Lily and I, in our snorkeling gear, stood on the edge.

"Last one in—" I shouted, before jumping in.

On the descent I noticed the colorful sea life. A spotted eagle ray, an octopus, and a puffer fish all swam past her. It was the same scene Gabriel had painted.

Back on the surface, we paddled around the perimeter of the steep rock wall. Suddenly a giant sea turtle swam right up to me and gave me a start. The turtle stared at me and then moved its mouth. I lifted my head out of the water, pulling off my mask. Lily paddling next to me already had her mask off. "Did you see that turtle?" I asked her.

Lily laughed. "Yeah, it looked like it was talking to you."

Even out here in the ocean, I sensed Gabriel's presence. I knew from now on, he would always be with me.

THE NEXT AFTERNOON around two-fifteen, our taxicab pulled up to a tall glass building with a statue of an old Spanish friar named Fray Antonio Alcalde out front. Lily stepped out of the cab.

"But this isn't your dorm."

"No, it's the medical center," Lily said. "Starting now, I'm in charge and you have an appointment at two-thirty to see the head of the study."

"Wait a minute," I said, searching her face and then realizing I wasn't going to be able to win this argument.

Inside, we hadn't waited that long when a middle-aged man walked up to introduce himself. He had a friendly round face with short black hair coming to a widow's peak. "Buenos días, I'm Dr. Gonzalez. How are you today?"

"Just fine," I answered, cynically and then we followed the doctor back down the hall into a large open room. My spirits plummeted when I saw his office, less than a no-frills cubicle with two desktops, some bookcases, a printer, and some cabinets. *What kind of quack am I dealing with?* I looked helplessly at Lily who narrowed her eyes at me.

"Please take a seat," the doctor said with a lopsided smile, motioning to two of the three chairs. On one wall I noticed a whiteboard and across from that, a floor-to-ceiling window with a view of the side of another building. Extremely skeptical, I thought this was all just a big waste of time.

But then Dr. Gonzalez wasted no time getting down to business. He took a seat across the desk from us and folded his hands into a teepee. "Thank you for coming, Ms. Miller." He sounded eager. "So, basically, what we're doing here is working on a new treatment for these types of diseases. Our research is directed more toward encapsulation of anti-cancer drugs that will be delivered to the specific targeted site."

"Anti-cancer?" I asked, a little surprised. I hadn't read about that in the folder. "I did read how they are working on treatments for cancer."

He nodded, leaning forward now. "Yes, and we're also getting closer to a cure. We've found some special compounds and extracts that have anti-cancer properties. What we've done is chemically modified a fructan compound—"

"Yes, from the agave plant," I added. "I read how it makes the drugs resistant to degradation in the digestive system. I've been doing some research."

"Exactly," the doctor said.

"But to hear that there is also research going on with regard to anti-cancer properties," I said, "well, that is just so, so remarkable."

Dr. Gonzalez smiled, picked up a marker and then walked to the whiteboard. "Yes, we are working on a cure for cancer—many types," he said and began drawing what looked like a bunch of hieroglyphs.

"The studies are carried out here in my lab where we are also designing microspheres," the doctor said, drawing figures I might have seen in a chemistry book, "by selecting the specific size of the agave fructan, then by attaching different molecules to tailor the size of the microsphere," he said, drawing now what looked like a tiny capsule being deliver into sausage-like links of a colon, "and the ability of microbiota to degrade these new compounds and the effect of the drug on the microorganisms. We are also studying the synergy of different bacteria to degrade the microspheres . . ."

Overwhelmed, my head spun. All I'd heard was "cure for cancer" and my brain had stopped processing anything else. It didn't matter that this wasn't some big fancy doctor's office in West Los Angeles. This was million-dollar news. What Dr. Gonzalez told me was more than I expected.

Off my puzzled face, the doctor stopped talking, pen in the air. "Lo siento, this is just all so exciting, and I was assuming you wanted to be a part of our study."

"Oh yes, I'm sorry, doctor. Absolutely!"

He smiled. "Well then, first of all, we'll need to have your files sent to us from your doctor in Los Angeles. But, in the meanwhile, because time is of the essence, we'll do our own lab work. Either today or tomorrow, I'd like to see you over at the civil hospital," he said, pointing to the side of the building outside his window, "for the x-rays and an MRI, perhaps also a sonogram." He opened a file and started writing. "What medications are you currently taking?"

This was all going so fast. "Usti—ustikanumab," I replied.

"Isn't it easier to use the brand name?"

"Yes," I said with a nervous giggle. "And I'd already gotten used to saying adalimumab." The doctor laughed and I felt like I was in good hands. "I've also been taking a cocktail of different antibiotics and a whole list—I've got it written down here in my phone," I said, reaching into my purse.

"That's okay. I'm sure it will all be in the chart when we get the file from your doctor."

I folded my hands in my lap, relaxing now only a little.

"And have you been feeling any better?" Dr. Gonzalez asked.

I nodded. "All I know is that I started feeling better once I left Los Angeles, once I got to the Tequila farm. I can't explain it."

"I think I understand. I've always felt there was something special about Tequila," he said with a wink. "Agave plants definitely have some healing properties."

Lily added, "Yeah, Mom thinks that the field is magical, and that the agave is miraculous."

"Well, part of the healing process does involve having a positive, hopeful attitude," Dr. Gonzalez said with a wink.

"My mom even wants to believe that the field has healed her physically, mentally, and spiritually."

I smiled. "One thing though, I do think the medicine has been causing me to hallucinate."

The doctor stopped laughing. "Yes, it could be a side effect of the medicine, or just part of the illness." He became somber. "Unfortunately, another side effect in rare cases is cancer, and it's a very aggressive type."

My stomach lurched.

"We should have your lab results back in a week or so at which time we'll determine whether or not you are a good candidate for this study."

I felt woozy, suddenly feeling deflated. "But what about chemo?"

"We want to try and avoid that for now. In the meanwhile, I'd like you to also take this medication. It's part of the study."

"Oh, by the way, I've been taking this little sugar pill," I said. "It's made from agave."

Dr. Gonzalez raised his eyebrows. "You don't say. Where'd you get it?"

I wasn't sure I should mention Ofelia's name just yet. "A cousin gave it to me— said it would make me feel better. And it has."

Dr. Gonzalez nodded as he picked up the phone. I panicked.

He held his hand over the receiver. "The hospital can take you this afternoon. Is that okay?"

I would have to miss my flight home to start the treatments, but that was fine by me.

THE NEXT DAY after all the lab work, I stood outside the bus station hugging Lily before boarding the bus back to Sagrada Familia.

"I'm so happy you decided not to go back to Los Angeles, Mom."

"Well, it really isn't practical. And it doesn't make any sense to hang around here bothering you. So, I'll just go back and bother them at the farm a little longer while I wait for the lab results." I smoothed the hair out of Lily's face. "I hope you had a good time."

"I had a great time."

"Please be careful, Lily."

"I will, Mom. And I don't want you worrying about me anymore. It's time for us to worry about you." Lily looked me in the eyes. "I'm sorry about the other night. I'm gonna make you proud. You'll see."

"I'm already proud, sweetie."

I stepped onto the bus, making sure I had my new medicine in my purse and when I got to my seat, I leaned out the window. "I love you, Lily. Thank you for taking care of me."

"It's my turn," Lily yelled back. "Te amo Mamá!"

Chapter Thirty-Five

Volver, Volver

THE NEXT MORNING, I SAT CROSS-LEGGED BACK in the field again, chewing on some agave. I faced the sky, eyes closed, chin to heaven. "Dear God, thank you for another today. Thy will be done. And hopefully thy will is that I'm cancer free."

I stared at the canvas waiting for my muse when Don Pio approached on Chuey. "Estamos muy contentos de que hayas decidido volver."

I smiled. "I'm glad I'm back, too." I really needed to tell him the reason why.

Back in Guadalajara, I'd called my office to let Betsy know I wouldn't be coming back. "I just wanted to let you know before I told the partners," I told her. "As you know, I'm sick and the University has just accepted me as part of their medical study." Betsy had wished me all the best.

"Will you be coming into the factory today?" Don Pio asked now.

"Maybe after lunch. I'm not quite ready for Antonio."

"Don't let him fool you. I think he's trying."

I shrugged my shoulders.

"He has a huge heart but filled with pain."

I picked up my brush. "Like the worm in the agave. We've all suffered some. He's just so nasty sometimes."

"Can I share something about him?" Don Pio asked.

I nodded, painting a swath of yellow-gold paint across the canvas.

"He should have gone to the graduation, but he was too busy," Don Pio said.

"Too busy to ever marry Camela," I said, dabbing a little more paint.

"What makes matters worse was that the driver was one of Bruno's workers."

I turned to face Don Pio, setting down the brush and then bringing my hands to my mouth.

"If Antonio ever learns to forgive himself," Don Pio said, "then perhaps, he'll be able to forgive Bruno."

I shook my head.

"Well, I'll leave you to your artwork," he said.

"Have a nice day."

LOOK INTO YOUR own heart, trust your inner vision. I could hear the voices of Gabriel and Don Pio. *Clear your mind. Open your heart. Your vision will become clear only when you can look into your heart.*

I closed my eyes. *Open my heart. Open my heart.*

With one eye open now, I stared at the unfinished canvas. I opened the other and picked up my brush. Within moments, I was painting something; I wasn't sure what. And then slowly an agave plant took shape. Working even closer, I could see the heart of the agave opening up with all of the sweet nectar exposed and glistening in the sun.

Satisfied with my creation, I lay down to take a little siesta, but then my head started spinning. I couldn't get Antonio out of mind. I couldn't get over what he'd been through. I had him all wrong. The last thing I remembered before falling asleep was wiping the tears dripping into my ears.

I DREAMED I'D painted a man who was tall and strong, but I couldn't make out the face. He was reaching out for me.

"I'm so glad you came back, Maya," he said.

"Antonio!" I shouted, reaching out for his hand. In the painting, I could see us strolling hand-in-hand. I felt joyful.

"Maya." Someone was nudging me, and I heard my name again.

I woke up and rubbed my eyes. "Antonio?"

He towered over me, his back to the sun. "You must have played a little too hard on holiday."

In his gaze, I sensed a veiled and tightly contained delight. *Might he be pleased that I've returned?* "I remembered what it was like to have fun with Gabriel," I said, smoothing my hair.

He crouched down. "Yes, you two were always up to something."

"And you were always so serious. We were afraid of you."

"That's too bad. I was just glad to see my little brother so happy. He'd suffered so much as a little boy. Always being picked on because he was different."

"You mean because he was gay."

Antonio nodded.

"So you tried to protect him?" I'd never known this side of Antonio. All the times he seemed to lurk around, he'd merely been making sure Gabriel was in good spirits.

Antonio smiled. "You had a nice time?"

"Rested—like a bottle of reposado," I replied.

"And as golden as añejo."

I felt my face blushing, the color of a rose underpainting through my new tan. "Hopefully not as aged." I stood.

Antonio laughed and stood also before turning back to his office.

Shading my eyes, I watched him walk into the sun toward the distillery. Was he different or was I just seeing him in a new light? Was my heart opening up? I thought about chasing after him to tell him about my illness, but I was distracted by a dazzling butterfly as it landed on a tepal. I could add a butterfly to the painting I worked on—the one my father had started—the one I would make my own. And then it landed on the back of my hand. I let it rest there.

So preoccupied with my painting, I had no choice but to let go of all of my troubles. While the field was my own creation, I was conscious of being part of something greater than myself. The little butterfly had not flown away. For the rest of the day, I tinkered with the painting, filling in the faces of all of my ancestors I'd met in this field. I played with the images, changing Papá's expression. Sometimes he looked at me lovingly, sometimes even proudly. I painted a heart on Mamá, so full of love there was enough to shower the parched soil. I removed the cloudy cataracts from Don Pio's eyes and made the sky clear blue. I gave Gabriel a set of strong legs and made the agave plants stand firmer and taller. On Lily, I painted a real pair of angel wings. And then when I got to Antonio, all I could do was smooth out the sharp slash of his mouth into a smile.

"It's finished," I whispered after a while and the butterfly flew off.

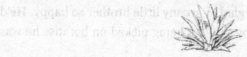

IT WAS GETTING late; the sun was already sliding off the painting when I picked up my supplies to head back, but when I heard a voice, I stopped to look up.

"Maya, you are not alone."

And then I heard a cacophony of laughter and joy filling the air. Hugging myself, I felt the arms of a thousand angels embracing me as tears of happiness flowed freely down my face. I sank down onto my knees.

"Let go, forgive," I heard the voices say, "watch the stars come out, new beginnings each one of them. All that's left now is love."

Laughing through tears, I lay on my back, watching as even more stars popped out and shot across a sky, covering me with a comforting blanket of light.

THE NEXT DAY as I headed toward the mulcher to grab some roasted agave, Antonio rode up on horseback.

"Is that your new obsession?"

"What was my old one?"

He smiled, motioning me to hop up. "I want to show you something."

"Seriously, what was my old obsession?" I asked again as we traveled along.

"To annoy me."

"That's not an obsession," I said, pinching him softly. "Annoying you was always just so easy to do." I smiled, turning to see the new tractor. "Speaking of obsessions—looks like Bruno does mean business."

I watched Antonio track the machine as if he were looking through the barrel of a rifle.

"If you're moved to stay, then I can deal with it. We'd even be the co-bosses," he said.

"Co-bosses? What are you saying, Antonio?"

"Maya, please stay. That is unless you are going back to work things out with—"

I squeezed him around the waist. "I'm never going back to Zane, but I am trying to figure my life out."

We rode up to the new tractor and Antonio slid off the horse and helped me down.

"So shiny and new. Where do you think he got all of his money?" I asked, running my fingers along the slick machine.

"As a law-abiding citizen. You might not want to know," Antonio replied as he stepped over next to me.

I hopped up into the driver's seat and took the wheel. "This will be fun to drive."

"Have you ever driven one before?"

"It's a tractor. How hard can it be?" I fired it up and the machine lurched forward, nearly knocking me out of my seat. We both bust up laughing.

"I almost peed myself," I said.

"With all the niños around here, we might even find you some diapers, chica."

"What happened to mujer?"

He laughed, not letting me go as he helped me down. I looked up into his eyes and then his lips were on mine. He took my breath away and then pulled back, taking a deep breath. "You are like a good Tequila. One taste and I'll never forget."

"Or one taste and you get that nice warm feeling, and you only want more," I said as he moved to kiss me again. But with both hands, I gently pushed his shoulders back. *I shouldn't lead him on.*

"I'm sorry, Antonio, but I need to take things slow this time. I really want to think about what I'm doing. I don't want to just react. This is not just for me, but for you, too."

Torn, also, I didn't like the feeling of lying to Antonio by not telling him about my cancer, but I remembered all the times I'd been sick and how no one had ever been there for me. When I first got sick with Crohn's, Zane had been attentive, but it didn't last long. He was like a helpless little boy. Antonio didn't seem anything like Zane, but then again, Antonio was not my fiancé. He could still remain somewhat detached.

I thought about Camela, Gabriel, their mother, Amelia, and father, Victor. I would not set Antonio up to lose me, too.

"I've waited this long," he said. "Take all the time you need."

LIKE RIPPLES across an ocean, the north field surged with rows of tiny blue agave starts. The fire had been a blessing and after the soil had been plowed and turned over, the earth was made only richer. In a few years, the new crop would yield a sweet, smoky flavor. On the south side, workers, young men and women, picked up the piñas and loaded them into the backs of trucks before heading back to the distillery where others waited to unload the agave heads and put them in the oven.

As the days went by, content just working side-by-side with Antonio, I still kept my secret. But because it felt so easy and so natural, because he was so gentle and kind, it was also difficult. While trying to protect his feelings, I'd been lying to him. Once again, I still played God. I couldn't help it. I wanted to spare him the pain of possibly losing someone else.

Later, inside the distillery, after checking the vats, I walked over to watch the workers as they unloaded the agave heads into the ovens. In the mulcher, the harvested piñas had already been roasting for forty-eight hours. I reached in and grabbed a handful of the roasted agave and then headed back toward Antonio's office. I knocked before entering and then handed him a piece.

"Thank you," he said, bringing it to his lips.

I was already chewing on the maguey. So delicious, it brought back memories, making me chuckle.

"What's so funny?" Antonio asked.

"I was remembering Gabriel and the way we'd sneak in there all the time and run away with hands full of this—" I paused to look at an expressionless Antonio. "Is it okay to talk about him?"

"I'd love to share my memories with someone," he replied, and I could see the warmth in his eyes.

I reached out and touched his arm. "You know, I can picture Victor now. He was the one that would chase us off and—"

"We can talk about Gabriel, but please don't mention the other person's name to me."

"That's a deal, partner," I said, extending my hand to shake his.

IN THE MORNING, I helped the girls with the labeling. My hands were busy, but my mind spun faster than the speed of sound. I would be hearing soon from Dr. Gonzalez the news about whether I was a good candidate for treatment or not. And what if I wasn't? I'd have to go home and start chemo. I'd finally have to say goodbye, maybe forever.

"Okay, it's time for a break," I announced, dusting my hands before heading off to Antonio's office. The time had come to have the conversation. I'd finally mustered up enough courage to tell him.

I stepped in as he shut down his computer. "Shall we call it a day?" he asked, surprising me.

"But I was just coming in to talk. I need to tell you something."

Antonio stood and came around his desk. "Can it wait?" he said, taking my hand to lead me out of his office. "Come with me out into the field before the sun sets. You can tell me on the way."

"But I think—"

He led me away in an awfully big hurry. "I want to make sure this crop is brought in on time. Some of the workers seem to be slacking off. It's always good for the jefe to show his face every once in a while."

"You mean *her* face," I said with a laugh, suddenly feeling a little uncomfortable at coming across too bossy. "They don't need micromanaging. Are you sure?" I asked as a worker brought him his horse. I climbed up behind him onto his horse.

"Now, what was it you wanted to tell me?"

This wasn't how I'd planned it, but I was running out of time. "I'm going back to the city to meet up with Lily tomorrow." I felt his back muscles tense up.

"Is she okay?"

"Yes, she's fine. I just—well. This is just so hard."

"You're not coming back?" He pulled the reins and twisted around in his saddle.

"I hope so. It's just that I've been sick—real sick—cancer sick. But I'm better. As a matter of fact, I'm doing so well—" He sat rigid. I gently pushed my face into his back as if I could breathe in some courage. "I'm beginning to wonder if there's been some sort of mistake. I think it's this place and all of the agave I chew on, and the Tequila," I said, giggling nervously on the outside, but on the inside, I was mush. "I'm seeing a doctor in Guadalajara to get my test results."

I sat scared and shaking now. Mounted on the back of a horse to give Antonio this news was certainly awkward, but it also prevented me from falling apart.

Antonio slid off the animal and looked up at me, his face suddenly drawn. I could see the sun setting in his eyes. Oh, how I hated letting him down.

"Why didn't you tell me?"

"You know I'm a strong woman. I didn't want you to see me as weak. Plus, our relationship has been, more often than not, contentious. I just barely learned you even liked me romantically."

He reached up to help me off the horse.

"Maya, you are a strong woman, but I also see that scared little girl inside that's so afraid of being hurt. Though it hurts that you kept this from me, I understand why."

I couldn't hold in the tears which quickly turned into sobs as he took me into his arms.

"I'm going with you to your appointment," he insisted.

"No, that's not necessary. Lily wants to come with me. I'll stay with her for a couple of days. Have some mother/daughter time," I said, rubbing his arm. I swiped my tears. "Besides, there's also a conference on campus where legislators are meeting with small producers. They're going to discuss a proposal to be included as part of the same protected regions as the big Tequila companies."

Antonio narrowed his eyes at me.

"Right now, the little guys, like *Los Olvidados* who have been distilling agave spirits for generations are not included in the protected regions," I said. "Our existence is being threatened. And—"

"¿Estás loca? Just like you to try and kill—" he paused, catching his *faux pas*, "—two birds with one stone. "When is that meeting?"

"Monday afternoon."

He pulled a little book out of his pocket with a pen attached to it. He then flipped to a page and drew a diagonal line across the page. "I'm taking a day off."

I smiled. "Good for you. But really, it's not necessary."

"If you won't let me go with you for support, then I'm sure you won't mind if I drive into the city to pick you up so that we can attend the meeting together, partner."

I smiled. "Good," I said. "Now let's get back on this beast and go check on those slackers."

AT TWILIGHT, we entered the field, and the last rays of sunlight pierced through the clouds, distorting our shadows. I panicked when I saw all of the chopped leaves and agave hearts abandoned on the ground, like unearthed bones and skulls in a graveyard.

"Where is everyone?" I asked Antonio, the alarm sounding in my voice.

Had the workers been scared off? Why had they abandoned their work?

"I don't know," he said, looking back and forth.

"Is there some kind of mutiny taking place?"

I'd even started to implement breaks, one in the morning and one in the afternoon. Had they been worked too hard, lately? I wondered. Had I not listened enough to their concerns? But it was harvest time, after all; it sort of had to be all-hands-on-deck.

Riding a little further into the field, the sun finally dipped behind the mountain range, splashing an array of reds, pinks and oranges across the sky. And then like the changing of guards, a huge moon stepped up to go on duty.

We traveled for a bit until I could see a cluster of lights.

"What's going on out there?" I asked, straining to make sense of what I saw.

We got closer and I could make out hundreds of little lights strung from trees beneath a mesh canopy. And then I heard whispering and giggling and the strum of a guitar. Suddenly people emerged from underneath the tent.

"Surprise!" they shouted, scaring the living daylight out of me.

Suddenly, someone in a giant sombrero stepped forward and removed the hat.

"Happy birthday, Mom!"

My breath caught in the back of my throat when I saw my daughter. Unable to say anything, I crossed my arms over my chest until at last I found my voice. "Lily! You almost gave me a heart attack!"

"You're not gonna die on my watch," Lily said, reaching out to take my hand. The mariachi's started to play *Feliz Cumpleaños* and the crowd joined in.

In shock, I looked around at all of the familiar faces. I noticed on the tables an assortment of empty Tequila bottles used as vases for the flowers and balloons.

As the crowd sang, "Happy birthday, to you, Maya!" I hoped I'd have many more.

"Do you like the plethora of piñatas?" Lily said, pointing to all of the stuffed papier-mâché candy-filled containers hanging from the nearby trees. "I couldn't decide on the donkey, Wonder Woman, the Lucha Libre fighter or Big Bird."

"I do like the Wonder Woman.".

"I was thinking of you."

"And the donkey?"

"You can be stubborn, sometimes," Lily said, and laughed.

People from town were present.

"Jefe!" Don Pio said, "Happy Birthday. I'm so glad we can celebrate with you."

"Me, too," I replied, thinking what a gift to have life for one more day.

"I can't believe you got through to Antonio," Don Pio said. "He even seems relieved to have you step in."

"Even if I'm a mujer?"

"He uses that as a term of endearment," my uncle said. "You're no longer that little girl."

I'd certainly acted like a child. I felt horrible. I'd just given Antonio the news, but now I needed to tell Don Pio. *How am I going to tell him?* I looked around. *I can't let these people down.*

"Happy birthday, mujer," Antonio said, stepping in and handing me a glass.

I could see the sorrow in his face and just wanted to reach out and comfort him for all the pain I'd caused; I wanted to kiss him as if that would make things all better, but I hesitated when I saw all of the women coming toward me.

"Happy Birthday, hermana," Teresa said, and I reached out to kiss her baby on the cheek.

Sister? I pulled away from the baby to stare at Teresa with a smile mirroring my own. *Is she just saying that?*

Soon Antonio was outnumbered by mujeres who were coming forward now with their children. And then I recognized the tall woman who'd come running out of Antonio's burning house the other night.

"Happy birthday, Maya," she said, and then turned to Antonio. "We are ready to work!" She laughed. "Mañana después de la fiesta."

"Well, I am not babysitting," Antonio said, hands-on-hip.

"After she risked her life going in to save your things from the fire, are you kidding?" I said.

Antonio gave a small smile, hugging the woman, and then Teresa placed the baby in his arms.

"Don't worry, Antonio," Lily said. "I'm setting up a daycare out here."

Antonio narrowed his eyes at her. "Que?"

"Soon this place will be running strong," Ofelia said, surprising me.

"Ofelia, you're here!" I said, so glad to see her, and reached out to hug her. "And you, too, Sylvia!" Sylvia's children, Mateo, Patricia and Cristina were also present as was Sylvia's husband. Leonardo also stood amongst the family members.

"And so am I." I recognized my older cousin's voice and turning to see her, moved me to tears.

"Angela, but you never come out here."

"I'm a woman, I can change my mind," she said.

Everyone laughed out loud.

"Besides, this is the only place where I don't feel so much pain," Angela added.

"Right? Hay algo mágico aquí."

I turned to Lily who held Leonardo's hand. "And what did you mean when you said you were setting up a daycare?"

"Don't worry, Mom. It's not what you think."

I took a breath. I wasn't quite ready to be a grandmother.

"I got an internship at the University for the agave research they're doing. Ofelia helped me get in."

"I only put in a good word," Ofelia said. "You did the work."

I brought my hand to my heart. "Wow, Lily! I didn't know you were doing that."

"Well, Mom, I'm a big girl capable of making my own decisions."

"Why yes. Yes, you are."

"After visiting the medical center with you and then talking to your doctor, I was fascinated by the research they're doing with agave. So, it looks like I'll be hanging out here a lot more."

"I couldn't be more ecstatic or proud," I said, hoping I'd have more time to hang out, too. More time to be a grandmother, some day.

Sylvia then carried out a cake from her bakery with enough candles on it to set off a fire alarm. And then the mariachis struck up the birthday song and everyone sang along:

Estas son las mañanitas, que cantaba el rey David,
Hoy por ser día de tu santo, te las cantamos a ti,
Despierta, mi bien Maya, despierta, mira que ya amaneció,
Ya los pajaritos cantan, la luna ya se metió.

This is the morning song that King David sang
Because today is your saint's day. We're singing it for you
Wake up, my dear Maya, wake up, look it is already dawn
The birds are already singing, and the moon has set . . . .

How lovely is the morning in which I come to greet you
We all came with joy and pleasure to congratulate you
The day you were born all the flowers were born
With jasmines and flowers we come to greet you
Because today is your saint's day, we come to sing to you.

Tears streamed down my face. I hadn't heard this song since I was a little girl and now the words were so powerful.

. . . I would like to be a Saint John
I would like to be a Saint Peter
To sing to you with the music of heaven
Of the stars in the sky
I have to lower two for you
One with which to greet you
And the other to wish you goodbye

I noticed Antonio wiping the tears from his eyes.

STANDING JUST outside the canopy, I held the reflection of the moon in my glass as I raised it to my lips. I set it down on a nearby table and then looked up. The stars seemed so close I could almost reach out and touch them, as if their light were emanating into the middle of my being. I wandered off into the field. Hovering just above agave tops, I thought I saw the silhouettes of my ancestors appearing like the wisps of smoke left after the candles had been snuffed. And then in the midst of more shadowy figures, Gabriel appeared.

"Happy birthday, Maya."

"Gabriel!" I shouted.

He stood tall in front of a verdant agave plant; two doves perched on the tip. A soft hand slipped into mine.

Lily had walked up. "Do you see them?" I asked, squeezing her hand while staring straight ahead. "Him?"

"Not yet," she said, hugging me now. "I'm going to head back to the guests. You can join the living when you're ready."

I laughed. "I'm ready. Just a few more minutes."

In the middle of the field, I stood like a small light-filled atom connected to the whole universe, and then Gabriel winked at me before vanishing into a fog of crystals.

I watched as one by one my ancestors ascended to the heavens as stars. *Nunca más serán los olvidados.* Never again will you be forgotten. I raised my arm to wave. "Goodbye. Until we meet again." Sensing the one that was my father, I blew a kiss. "Adiós, Papá." And then one more star twinkled brighter than them all. "Adiós, my angel boy. Thank you for looking after your sister."

WHEN I RETURNED to the party, I was surprised to hear Lily telling the same story Papá had told me when I was a girl.

"—and St. Peter asked that Domingo remove his hat before passing over," Lily said.

"In the distance, he thought he could hear the church bells. They gonged for the last time as he crossed over. And the pueblo's Tequila sales spiked slightly that week, for it was not a good idea to drink the water," she said, and everyone laughed.

But when I noticed Antonio, my heart leaped out to him. Behind the smile, I could see his pain. I should never have told him. He picked up his guitar and as if to hide his feelings, he started to strum a livelier tune. Abruptly, he stopped, and I followed his gaze to see a new guest approaching. I turned to see Don Pio giving Antonio a look of warning as he stepped over to stand in front of him, as if blocking him. And then, Don Pio slowly made his way over to greet the new guest.

Bruno stepped forward, removed his black hat, and handed me a giftwrapped package. He then turned to hand Don Pio a bottle labeled *Agave Azul de Hidalgo*. Don Pio wrapped his arms around his son.

"I think it might even taste better in the new bottle," Don Pio said, reaching over to gather some glasses off the table.

Bruno laughed. "Papá, it's all the same agave."

"And we're all the same blood," Don Pio added, clearly elated to have his son back.

Bruno took the bottle, reached for a glass and poured one for his father who waited as Bruno poured one for Antonio.

Fuming, Antonio stood, rigid as a smokestack, refusing to toast.

"We are all the same blood," Bruno said again, appearing to be sincere. "You heard Papá."

Antonio pivoted to walk away. I grabbed his hand to stop him before he got too far. "Antonio, can't you find it in your heart to forgive Bruno?" I asked, placing my other hand on his arm to get a better hold.

"Why should I?"

"It wouldn't necessarily be for Bruno, but for you and for the man who raised you. For Don Pio," I said, peering into Antonio's angry, wet eyes.

"I won't forgive Bruno, but I will make peace for Don Pio's sake."

He turned slowly and then walked back. Reluctantly, he picked up the glass Bruno had poured for him.

Bruno smiled as he poured a glass for me, too, and said, "Antonio always gets the pretty ones."

I couldn't help but blush.

"To a long and prosperous future," he added.

I clicked my glass. "Salud." I took a sip. "Umm. Nice silky finish."

Lily walked up and introduced herself. "Soy Lily."

"Mucho gusto. Soy Bruno."

"Oh yes, another cousin," Lily said, turning to me and whispering. "Remember, we're not the monarchy," she said, elbowing me gently in the ribs.

I cut a glance at her. "You don't even need to worry."

"I won't," Lily replied with a smile. "Are you happy, Mom?"

Tears welling again, I wrapped my arms around my girl. "There are no words."

THE MARIACHIS and the guests were in full swing when in the distance, I noticed the headlights from an approaching vehicle kicking up red dust. The car stopped and then someone stepped out.

As he got closer, I recognized the new guest. Victor Montoya walked up, holding an unwrapped box.

"Señor Montoya! What are you doing here?"

"¡Feliz cumpleaños, Maya!" Victor said. "Joaquin always said you were a good attorney, but that you'd make a better farmer."

I looked at him curiously as Antonio stepped closer.

"What are you doing here?" he asked Victor.

"*La sangre atrae*. It is time."

Sensing he might bolt again, I grabbed Antonio's hand as Victor approached him with arms open. Antonio stepped back, but I held firm.

"Hijo, can you please forgive me?" Victor asked. "I tried to—"

Antonio huffed, his lips pinched tight. He pulled away and I chased after him, catching up to him finally in the middle of the field. "Antonio," I whispered, breathless. "Can't you just let it go? I know it's not easy. I'm sure he did the best he could."

"How? By abandoning me and my brother, by starting a new family—"

I couldn't argue that. "I'm sorry."

He turned to face me, and the straight line of his mouth eased, the furrows on his forehead smoothing over like tumbled granite.

"If you can forgive, then I can try," he said.

In the short time I'd been in Mexico, I'd learned so much about the past, so much about forgiveness and letting go. "I know it hurts and will take some time. I know it's not easy, but we'll be better off in the long run."

"I'll do it for you, for your birthday, Maya," he murmured.

"Thank you, but please do it for yourself, Antonio."

"Bueno," he said. "I'll try."

I reached up to kiss him and together we walked back to the party. He slowly opened his arms to embrace his father.

AND WITH THAT small gesture of open arms, a true gift, I was shrouded in a sense of peace—both of us open and willing to forgive those who'd wounded us. By forgiving the demons of my past, I'd reconnected with my roots, and embraced a family and lineage that was somewhat forgotten after my mother, Rudy and I departed the farm. Antonio cemented a willingness to genuinely forgive Victor and Bruno someday, for himself, thereby releasing himself from the shackles of anger and resentment, the hurt that caused him to be alienated and misunderstood.

Chapter Thirty-Six

One More Present

LATER, AFTER ALL THE GUESTS HAD LEFT, LILY AND I returned to our room where I opened some of my gifts.

Lily stepped in front of me. "I have something to show you, Mom." She pulled up her sleeve. I burst out crying. Freshly tattooed on her wrist, inside a small heart, were the words *Amo a Mamá*.

"Jeez, Mom, I've never seen you cry as much as you do now."

"Oh my God. Sweetie, I don't know what to say. Thank you. I'm so happy you didn't tattoo that on your chest like the cabana boy—your angel."

"Or up here," she said laughing and tapping her forehead. "Yeah, even though I do love you, I knew you wouldn't love that so much."

We hugged. "You are the best gift ever, Lily."

"One more thing," she said, pulling away to pick up the box Victor had brought with him.

"It's not a birthday present," Lily said. "That's why it's not wrapped."

I looked at her curiously.

"I phoned Grandma just to see how she was doing and to invite her to the celebration."

"Did you tell her anything about me?"

"You mean about your cancer?" Lily shook her head. "She told me she wanted to send Grandpa's ashes back to where he belonged—home," Lily said. "And that she'd promised—"

"Whatever." I was about to add something snarky, but all at once realized I felt nothing. I tried to imagine how hard it might have been for

Mamá to return to a place where she'd felt so much guilt and shame. My mother didn't have a calling and perhaps she never would. And I would have to accept that.

"She sent the urn along with Victor," Lily said, tapping on the box.

Mamá had stayed in contact with Victor? I wondered, staring out the window. Of course, that would also explain his knowing so much about me. But just when I thought I'd found all the answers, there were even more questions about my mother and Victor for another day.

THE MOON WAS still bright enough to light the way as we headed back into the field. I carried the urn and Lily carried her grandfather's old hat as we got to the edge of the little stream where I'd spent time as a child—the place where I'd fished and drawn pictures with Papá, where I'd chased butterflies with Gabriel. Those were the memories I'd keep in my pocket, even though the others were no longer painful. Lily and I laid out some candles in little jars, one for as many good reminiscences as we could recall.

But this wasn't just a memorial to my father; this was a celebration of my life and a return to a childhood where I would now have choices, where I could decide how to live my life, even if it only lasted a short while. I wouldn't tell Lily about what her grandfather had done. There were just some things best left alone. That I was a better person today was all my daughter needed to know.

"Mom, when you're ready, I'd like to talk about my father. Maybe, you can tell me about the time he took me fishing?"

Afraid I might miss this opportunity to finally talk about the pachyderm that had lived in the room for so many years, I looked at her. "Of course, sweetie," I said and took a deep breath. I couldn't wait to share with Lily about all of the good qualities her daddy had. "You were only two. I don't know what he was thinking—he couldn't wait until you were a little older. He wanted to teach you how to ride a bike, how to ski."

In the moonlight, I could see the tears like little rivers gliding down Lily's cheeks. I reached out to hug her. "I'm so sorry, baby. I wish it could have turned out differently for your sake."

"It wasn't your fault, Mom. I can't even imagine." Lily said, wiping her face. "Es lo que es."

"Yes, it's what it is."

"Mom, I'm really scared. What if—"

"Sweetie, let's just have some faith."

"Faith? In what? I didn't grow up in the church."

"Well, how about this giant garden, for starters," I said, sweeping my arm out wide. "A garden is an evidence of faith. The field is still alive because our ancestors have taken care of and nurtured these plants, and the plants are what also nourished them. Let's have faith in the agave—that there really is something about it that can help us."

"I suppose that's something," Lily said.

Just as we stood ready to scatter my father's ashes, a gust of wind blew the hat out of Lily's hand. We watched as it skidded across the way, landing on a candle and catching fire before sailing off across the field. Had this sombrero, and the shadow it cast, finally come to the end of the cycle for the Hidalgo family? Perhaps it was kismet that the hat blew away as we prepared to say goodbye to Papá.

"You know, I'm sort of disappointed to learn that I'm not related to Pancho Villa," Lily said, eyes following the burning sombrero.

"Not as far as I know," I added, opening the urn, spilling out the powdery contents, scattering quickly as if joyous to be set free at last. I couldn't tell whether they were the embers from the charred hat or the fireflies like points of light now carrying the ashes across the rich, crimson valley, beyond the mountains and up into the starry, starry night.

Chapter Thirty-Seven

Fingers Crossed

THE NEXT AFTERNOON, WE SAT IN THE SCHOOL cafeteria at the University.

"How did Don Pio take the news?" Lily asked, and then took a sip of orange Fanta through a straw.

"I couldn't tell him. I'm just going to wait until after we see the doctor."

Lily set down her drink and reached for her fork. As she speared a piece of lettuce, she started laughing.

"What?" I asked.

"It's just hysterical," she said, raising the piece of lettuce. "All this time and you thought you were cousins."

Since the last trip to see her, I'd opened up to Lily about everything, including the fact that Gabriel was a ghost—at least of my own imagination—and that Antonio wasn't as awful as I'd always thought. "Amazing what you grow up believing, who you end up trusting, or not."

Lily picked up her utensils and cut into her enchiladas, changing the subject. "So, the deposition is set for next month and then trial after that."

"How are you feeling about that?"

"I'm so ready to move on with my life and get this over with. I'll need to go back to L.A."

"Get me the exact dates and I'll arrange to be with you."

Her knife clinked onto the table. "No way, Mom. We're not going to jeopardize your health by letting you leave the farm."

"You're assuming that I don't need to go back north for chemo." I blew into my soup-filled spoon. "I like your optimism."

"You're not."

"And you're not facing that man alone."

"I can handle myself," she said, picking her knife back up and stabbing the air. "I'm a strong woman. Remember, you raised me."

"You raised yourself."

"And I'm a real chingona fighter."

I cracked up. "Chingona, huh?"

"Not as bad ass as you punching Mr. Parker in the face."

I sobered, peering at her, wondering how she knew.

"I've read some of the preliminary declarations." She smiled, finished chewing and then licked her lips. "Maybe I'll have Grandma tag along for some support."

"Are you kidding?"

"Yes." Lily laughed. "Do you think she knows anything?"

"Well, I certainly didn't tell her," I said.

"What if she saw something on the news?"

"Again, she hasn't brought anything up. I haven't talked to her for a while. I raised my fork. "She knows nothing about my illness, right?" I said, cutting off the cheese stretching like elastic from my relleno.

"Right. But Mom, why not? Why haven't you told her?"

"She never could handle the stress," I replied, thinking about all the times I'd kept things to myself, only to protect my mother. To protect my father, Elliot, my daughter and even Zane. It was clear to me now how holding things in had been too heavy a burden for me. At some point, people do break. And fart.

"Hey Mom, speaking of news, when were you going to tell me that Zane got married."

I finished chewing and then swallowed. "I didn't think you'd be interested. You never cared for him."

Lily shook her head slightly and took another bite.

I remembered the recent call where Zane had told me to think about it. But there'd been nothing to think about and by the time he called me back, he'd already gotten married.

"Congratulations. Be happy," I'd told him.

There'd been a long silence on the other end. "Maya, are you sure?"

I was like a little boat that had drifted away, slowly and yet unstoppable. "Absolutely."

"You'd really like her," he'd said, sounding a bit deflated. "She's a lot like you."

I'd laughed out loud. "You mean she's kindhearted, compassionate, giving?" I said, and then realized he might have meant she was angry, self-righteous, and arrogant. "You'd better hope she's nothing like me," I added with a chuckle.

Zane laughed again. "Maya, I'm really sorry about everything. Can you forgive me?"

"I already have," I said, knowing now I wasn't doing it so much for him but for myself. I could no longer hold on to the anger. It wasn't good for my health. "And now I need to ask you a favor."

"Sure, anything."

"Will you please forgive me?"

I heard Zane clear his throat. "For what? Maya, you sound different. Like you've changed."

"Yes, I hope so," I answered. And, indeed, I'd felt the change. It hadn't happened overnight. It was like that song by the Eagles, *Peaceful Easy Feeling* that happened one moment at a time. *I've got that peaceful easy feeling . . . I'm already standing on the ground.*

Lily dabbed her lips with a napkin. "I'm sorry he let you down," she said. "There was just something a little off about him. I'm sorry."

"That was a gut feeling," I said, smiling. "Remember to always listen to your gut."

"I just always thought you deserved better."

"Some people just aren't meant to be in a relationship," I said.

"Yeah, I hear you," Lily said. "I think I'm better off alone."

"Oh, Lily, you're still young. You don't know what you're saying."

"Yeah well, I have goals."

I laughed.

"I've been talking a lot to Ofelia about school and my career. She's not in a relationship."

"I'm sure she'd like one. You know it's slim pickings in Sagrada Familia," I said.

"Unless you marry your cousin," Lily added with a chuckle.

"Maybe she'll meet someone at the University."

Lily shrugged her shoulders. "Having a relationship isn't a big deal. Besides, I'm not looking for a Prince Charming to save me."

"You know, having goals is good, and having a relationship is good, too. And you can have both. Especially, when you find a partner who supports you; someone who doesn't compete with you; someone who's always got your back. You want to be with someone who brings out the best in you."

Lily rolled her eyes. "No one will want me if my eyes get stuck in my head, right?"

I smiled, thinking about Zane, always competing—always fighting. He called it passion. If that was passion, I could let it go. I'd gotten to the place where I didn't want to argue anymore.

"What about Antonio?" Lily asked. "I mean, since he's not a cousin."

"Yeah, that's all still a little weird, but it's wonderful. He's a good person." I gazed off.

"And so?"

"As a matter of fact, he wanted to come to my appointment with me."

Lily leaned in. "You'd actually get him to leave the farm? Wow! He must really like you."

"He was just being nice. I told him not to."

THE NEXT MORNING, I pulled my hair back into a bun and put on my linen business suit, the little angel pin Lily had mailed to me still on the lapel. Lily, with her blonde hair loose, wore a pink, midriff-baring velour sweat suit, exposing a shiny jewel pierced through her navel. And as Lily hurried ahead, I noticed the bottom of the tattooed wings peeking out of her top. I smiled, thinking adoringly, *my little angel.*

When we got closer to the entrance, I noticed a tall man hanging out next to the statue of the old Spanish Friar Alcalde. Standing almost as tall as the sculpture, the man wore a white shirt and wrangler jeans. His head was covered with a white sombrero, but I could tell who he was just by the way his shoulders hunched slightly.

I slowed, Lily taking note of who caused my reaction and then I hurried over to give him a big hug. "Antonio! What are you doing here?"

"I told you I was going with you."

He actually showed up for me.

Lily smiled and winked at me before coming to my side and whispering, "This is what I meant, Mom, about you deserving better. This is the better that you deserve."

I smiled at her words, realizing she was right.

INSIDE DR. GONZALEZ'S cubicle, my eyes went directly to a crucifix on the wall. I hadn't noticed it before, or maybe because it was such a prevalent fixture everywhere I went now, I'd taken it for granted. *Like I'd taken God for granted. I'm sorry Lord, please be with me now.* I stopped breathing when Dr. Gonzalez walked in.

He extended his hand to Lily and me and then when it came to Antonio, Antonio introduced himself.

"I'm Antonio, Maya's friend."

We all took a seat.

"First of all, good news," the doctor said, holding up his two thumbs.

"What? I'm not going to die?" I asked, half-joking, fully hoping, and shaking uncontrollably now.

Dr. Gonzalez laughed. "No, Maya you're not. We're all going to die eventually, but for now, there's no sign of any cancer."

Lily and I burst into tears, jumping out of our seats to hug each other. Antonio got up, too, and wrapped his arms around both of us.

"We've compared the lab work from what Dr. Vaisman sent down and—well, quite frankly, it's unbelievable. Your white count is in the normal range. This all looks quite promising. The tumors are gone."

Am I hearing right? I pulled out of the group hug. "The tumors are gone?"

Dr. Gonzalez smiled and nodded.

"Oh, thank you, God," I shouted, and Antonio caught me before I collapsed to the floor. I sucked in a huge breath and let out a jagged sigh. He helped me to my seat. "Well, I've been taking the medication you gave me," I replied, my heart pounding.

Lily handed me a tissue.

"Yes, but understand," Dr. Gonzalez said. "These are the older lab results

259

from before you started the new treatment. I'm also looking at the x-rays and couldn't detect any new lesions. The walls are clean."

I struggled to comprehend what was being said and then I blew my nose. "So, did I ever have cancer in the first place?"

"Something changed from the time you left Los Angeles to the time you came down to Sagrada Familia," Dr. Gonzalez added.

"Well, I'm not working so hard, I guess. Less stress, plus I'm eating better. I've continued to take my other medication and—I've been drinking a lot more Tequila," I said, breaking out into a hysterical belly laugh. "I've also sort of become addicted to chewing on the roasted agave. Oh, and of course I'm still taking that agave sugar pill."

Dr. Gonzalez looked at me curiously. "Whatever you've been doing, just keep it up and I'd like to see you next week to make sure things are still under control."

"It's like some sort of miracle, right?" I asked, dabbing my eyes. Antonio reached over to squeeze my arm.

"We'll see," the doctor said. "I wouldn't quit praying."

With that, I looked up to the cross hanging on the wall. "Oh, thank you, God," I whispered, blessing myself, making the sign of the cross.

I turned to see Lily and Antonio both doing the same and before I might wake up from this fantastic dream, I said, "*Vámanos!* Let's get out of here!"

Antonio helped me up and we said goodbye to Dr. Gonzalez.

INSIDE ANTONIO'S truck, I noticed the flowers on the front seat.

"For me?" I asked as Lily scooted to the middle.

"Yes," Antonio said, a bit apologetically. "I didn't really know the protocol for when to give flowers. I mean what if it had been bad news? Would that have added insult to injury?"

"In that case, you could have said they were for me," Lily said, holding the bouquet now. "After all, I got an 'A' on my Yoga final."

"Can this day get any better?" I said with a laugh. "Hey, I'm starving. Let's celebrate and get something to eat before we drop Lily off at school.

My treat." I leaned forward and looked over at Antonio. "And then we'll still have time to attend that meeting."

Antonio turned toward me, "Maya, no more business for now. First, we'll celebrate and get something into your stomach, and then we'll just take our time getting home to the hacienda."

"Home," I whispered, liking the sweet taste and sound of that.

Acknowledgments

Like a color by number work of art, this story practically wrote itself-- well outside the lines--but not without the blood, sweat and tears of mi familia and fieldworkers dating centuries back before Pancho Villa traversed the agave fields.

I must acknowledge and thank so many and I apologize in advance should I miss anyone. But first, I am forever grateful to my daughters, Joy and Alexandra, my masterpieces who continue to teach me so much about life, who encouraged me to heed the call to return to Mexico when all seemed hopeless. While I may not have inherited the family Tequila business, I did reconnect with mi familia from Jesus Maria, Jalisco and came away with new relationships and a story for a sweeter mañana.

Thank you to my parents, Delfina and Chuck, to the Cordovas, Angelina, Laura, Sylvia, Cristina Alvaro, Everardo, Arnulfo, and so many others who took time to show me the ropes (made from agave, of course). To Jose and Catalina for all the taste testing. To Carla Bates for sharing her artist skills.

To the Warrior Girl, whose blog I followed at #laughingatcrohns.wordpress, you've made me laugh, cry and root for you. For the young man with Crohns in treatment at UCLA Medical Center, thank you for educating me. Thank you to Guillermo Toriz, PhD, assistant professor at the University of Guadalajara, for sharing with me a bit about your agave research. May it be that more can be done for the treatment of ulcerative colitis, irritable bowel syndrome, cancer, Crohn's and other colon diseases.

To all of my instructors and writing friends: to Lori Gambino and Melissa Stoppiello who were there from the beginning; to my amigas at Womxn's Write Inn, Liz González, Mary Camarillo, Mary Anne Perez,

Stephanie Barbé Hamer; to Caroline Leavitt who was "gobsmacked" by my story and showed me where to prune the ending; to Sheri Williams for her patience and kindness; to the keen eye of Kiana Yarde and to TouchPoint Press, mil gracias a todos!

To my husband, Jeff Gunn, where do I begin? Our story is still unfolding, the colors more vivid from one scene to the next. Te amo.

CPSIA information can be obtained
at www.ICGtesting.com
Printed in the USA
LVHW090541310822
727200LV00005B/552